Forty million Americans in fifty major cities died in less than thirty minutes from the bombs. But by mid-afternoon of the first day, a stricken people had begun to rally and reintegrate. The National Guard was called out, radar and sonar stations were put on battle alert, and throughout the night armed men and women stared sleeplessly into the skies, waiting for the paratroop armies that would surely arrive to conquer a devastated nation. After a week the enemy had still shown no sign.

The commander of American forces demanded that all countries open their borders to a search. Delay or refusal would be construed as a confession of guilt, and would bring instant retaliation from secret atomic bases. It took a month for American patrols, planes and fleets to discover that no nation on Earth had been organizing for war.

Day by day it grew clearer that the enemy had struck a mortal blow at Earth's most powerful nation—and was going to get away with it.

—THE EARTH KILLERS is only one of the stories in this fascinating collection by A.E. VAN VOGT

About the author:

The magic name of *Van Vogt* conjures up a world of stimulating mental images to those familiar with his works. For A.E. "slan" Vogt is the undisputed Idea Man of the futuristic field.

Canadian born, of Dutch descent, the author is now a transplanted Hollywoodite (although there are those among his legion of fans who secretly suspect his birthplace of being Mars, beyond the stars, or up ahead somewhere, say in the 25th Century).

Van Vogt always is years ahead with his concepts. Semantics, "totipotency," Batesystem vision restoration, hypnotism, "similarization," dianetics, and "Nexialism," have all been grist for his mill.

Author of many best-selling science-fiction books and dozens of short s-f stories, Van Vogt has been repeatedly reprinted here and abroad, translated in French, German and Italian, even recorded on Talking Records for the blind.

Van Vogt speaks fluently the universal languages of excitement and tension, action and invention.

—FORREST J ACKERMAN

THE WORLDS OF
A.E.
VAN VOGT

ace books
A Division of Charter Communications Inc.
1120 Avenue of the Americas
New York, N.Y. 10036

ACKNOWLEDGMENTS

The Replicators, ©, 1964, by Galaxy Pub. Corp.
The Ultra Man, ©, 1966, by Galaxy Pub. Corp.
Ship of Darkness, ©, 1961, by Ziff-Davis Pub. Co.
The Earth Killers, ©, 1951, by Ziff-Davis Pub. Co.
The Purpose, ©, 1945, by Street & Smith Publications, Inc.
Not the First, ©, 1941, by Street & Smith Publications, Inc.
Automaton, ©, 1950, by *Other Worlds*
Process, ©, 1950, by Mercury Publications, Inc.
The First Martian, ©, 1939, by A.E. Van Vogt
The Cataaaaa, © 1937, by A.E. Van Vogt
Itself! ©, 1963, by A.E. Van Vogt
Fulfillment, ©, 1956, by A.E. Van Vogt
The Storm, ©, 1943, renewed 1971 by A.E. Van Vogt
The Expendables, ©, 1963 by A.E. Van Vogt
The Reflected Men, ©, 1971 by A.E. Van Vogt

First Ace Printing: January 1974

Printed in U.S.A.

CONTENTS

THE REPLICATORS

I

STANDING there, after killing the monster, Matlin began to get mad.

In its death throes, the twelve-foot creature had done a violent muscular convulsion and somersaulted over into the dump section of Matlin's truck.

There it lay now, with its elephantine head and quarter-length trunk twisted to one side, and a huge arm and hand flung up and visible over the rear end. What must have been tons of shiny, black body was squashed limply down into the bottom of the cavernous metal carrier . . . creating a problem.

That was all it was to Matlin: a problem.

Steve Matlin was an abysmally suspicious and angry man. His impulse now was to dump the beast in the weeds beside the road. Reluctantly, he decided against that. He had unfortunately been seen driving along this little used lake road by the two officers of a highway patrol car. If the patrolmen found the creature's body, they would assume that he had shot it.

This benighted man, Matlin, envisioned himself as being the person who would have to see to the disposition of the dead monster. As he reasoned it out, if he made the mistake of dumping it in the wrong place, he'd have to hire a crane to get it into his truck again. And if he simply took it home, he'd have the job of digging a hole for it.

Better take it to the police, he decided gloomily, *and follow their advice like a good little fellow.*

Seething at the nuisance, but resigned, he drove to the main highway. There, instead of turning left to his farm, he headed for Minden, the nearest suburb of the city. Arrived in town, he drove straight to the police station, braked to a halt, and vigorously honked his horn.

Nobody showed.

The exasperated Matlin was about to lean on his horn and really blast them with sound, when he made an electrifying discovery. The police headquarters was on a side street and, whatever the reason, there wasn't a car or person in sight.

. . . Hot afternoon, empty street, rare opportunity—

Matlin tripped the lever that started the dump mechanism. A moment later, he felt the beast's body shift. He simply drove out from under it and kept on going, gunning his motor and reversing the dump mechanism.

II

That night before they went to bed, his wife, Cora, said to him, "Did you hear about the creature from space?"

Matlin's mind leaped to the memory of the beast he had carted into town. He thought scathingly: *Those nuts! Creature from space indeed!* But he said aloud, gruffly, "You watching that junk on TV?"

"It was in the news report," she said defensively. "They found it right there in the street."

So it *was* the thing he had killed. He felt a sudden glee. He'd got away with it. He thought smugly: *Saved myself twenty-five bucks. Time I had a little luck.*

He went silently to bed.

Cora lay for a while, listening to his peaceful breathing, thinking of the monster from space—and thinking of the universe that she knew existed somewhere beyond the narrow world of Steve Matlin. She had once been a teacher. But that was four children and two decades ago. It was a little hard sometimes to realize how far away the real world was these days.

Out there, a creature never before seen on Earth had been found lying dead in the street in front of the Minden police station. The TV cameras brought front views, side views and top views into everybody's living room. No one had any idea how the thing had gotten where it was discovered, and, according to the news commentators, top government and military officials were beginning to gather around the colossal corpse like buzzing flies.

Two days went by. A monster-hunting expedition arrived at the Matlin farm—among other places—but Cora shook her head to their questions and denied in a take-it-for-granted tone that Steve was the one who had transported the beast. "After all," she said scathingly, "he would have told *me*. Surely, you—uh!"

She stopped, thought: *That man! That incredible man!* He could have.

7

The visitors seemed unaware of her sudden confusion. And they also evidently believed that a husband would have told his wife. The principal spokesman, a fine looking, soft-voiced man of her own age, who had introduced himself as John Graham—and who was the only person present not in a police or military uniform—said in a kindly tone, "Tell your husband there's quite a reward already, something like a hundred thousand dollars, for anyone who can help us effectively."

The expedition departed in a long line of noisy motor-cycles and cars.

It was about mid-morning the next day when Steve Matlin saw the second monster.

He had been following the trail of the first one from the lake road. And suddenly here was another.

He dived into a gully and lay there, breathless.

What he had expected, in coming here by himself, Matlin had never considered clearly. When Cora had told him of the reward money, he had instantly derided her trusting nature.

"Those S.O.B.'s will never split that reward with anyone who hasn't got his claim staked and ready to fight," he had said.

He had come to stake his claim.

His shock on seeing this second creature was like a multi-tude of flames burning inside him. He was aware of the heat rising along his spine and searing his brain. Fear! Trembling, he raised his rifle.

As he did so, the creature—which had been bending down—came up with something that glinted in the sun. The next instant, a bullet whistled past Matlin's head and struck a tree behind him with an impact like a clap of thunder. The ground trembled. An instant later, the sound of an explosion came to Matlin's ears.

The explosion was loud enough to have come from a small cannon.

Even as he made the mental comparison from his exper-ience as a Marine in World War II, the distant rifle—it looked a rifle, though a huge one—spat flame again. This time the bullet struck the rock ten yards in front of Matlin and sprayed him with a shower of rock splinters. His body stung all over, and when he was able to look again—after the second explosion had echoed from the distance—he saw that his hands were covered with dozen of droplets of his blood.

The sight was both terrifying and galvanizing. He slid back, rolled over, half-clawed to his feet and, bending low, ran to the gully's end, stopping only when he realized that it was becoming too shallow to be a shelter.

What could he do?

Shadowy memories came of wartime risks he had taken. At the time he had felt enforced, compelled by the realities of a war he never accepted—a war that had wasted several years of his life. But he remembered moving, crouching, going forward. He had always thought what a mad thing it was for a sensible person to force himself into enemy territory. Yet under the hated pressure of wartime discipline, he had resignedly gone into the most deadly situations.

Was it possible he would have to do that now—because of his own foolishness in coming here?

As he crouched there, appalled, two more cannonlike shells splattered the rock where he had been seconds before. A cannon against a rifle! Matlin wanted out, wanted away. The angry scheme he had had to get for himself whatever might be at the end of this search had no meaning in the face of the firepower that was seeking his destruction with each booming shot.

He lay cringing at the shallow end of the gully, not even daring to raise his head.

His own rifle seemed like a mere toy now. . . .

The phone rang. When Cora answered, it took her several moment to recognize the hoarse voice at the other end as her husband's.

"I'm calling from a roadside pay phone. Can you find out where that monster-hunting expedition is now?" he said.

"Mamie just called. They were over at her farm. Why?"

"It's chasing me," he said. "Tell 'em I'm coming toward the highway from the boathouse. It's driving a dump truck as big as a house."

"What's chasing you?" Cora yelled into the mouthpiece. "Where?"

"A second one of the monsters. On that back road to the lake." Matlin moaned. And hung up.

III

The battle on the highway began about two o'clock in the afternoon. The creature climed out of the cab of a dump truck that stood twenty feet high. Crouching behind the vehicle, it fired with a rifle the size of a cannon at anything that moved.

The two dozen men with their frail cars and tiny rifles

crouched in the underbrush. Lying beside Graham, Matlin heard the man say urgently to an army major, "Call again for an air strike!"

It was about ten minutes after that that the first helicopter appeared on the horizon. It turned out to be an enterprising TV station's vehicle, with cameras aboard. The fluttering monstrosity of flying machine circled the dump truck, taking pictures of the great being beside it. At first it did not seem to occur to the creature to look at the sky for the source of the sound. But suddenly it got the idea.

Up came that long rifle. The first bullet smashed through the cockpit. A splinter from somewhere hit the pilot and knocked him unconscious. The helicopter flew off erratically. As it retreated, another gigantic bullet smashed its tail. The stricken whirlybird fluttered down among the trees on the other side of a low hill.

Worse, when the military helicopters arrived, they no longer had the advantage of surprise. The cannon-rifle fired at them as they approached. They veered off—but not before three went down, one in flames. With one exception, the others began to shoot back from a distance.

The exception flew off to the left, disappearing low behind a hill. It reappeared presently to the rear of the monster and, while the other machines kept up a barrage from in front, this lone helicopter came in on the target from behind.

The barrage of bullets that its pilot loosed downward almost tore off the great head of a creature which did not even see where the death came from.

Matlin walked forward with the others, angrily fingering the "claim" he had written out. It infuriated him that they were not offering to honor his rights. Even though he had expected it, the reality was hard to take.

Arrived at the truck, he stood impatiently by while the men examined the creature, the huge vehicle and the rifle. Matlin was drawn abruptly out of his irritated self-absorption with the realization that he had been twice addressed. Graham indicated the ten-foot rifle.

"What do you make of that?"

The question approach, the appeal to him on an equal basis, momentarily neutralized the timeless anger in Matlin. *Now!* he thought. He handed Graham his claim with the request, "I'd like you to sign this." Then he bent down beside the huge weapon and examined it.

He commented presently, "Looks like a pump action repeater, much like the one I've got, only many times as big. Could have been made by the same company."

It irritated him as he spoke to realize that Graham still held the claim sheet in his hand; had not even glanced at it.

Graham said in an odd tone, "What company?"

"Mine is a Messer," said Matlin.

Graham sighed and shook his head in bewilderment. "Take a look at the nameplate on that big gun," he said.

Matlin bent down. The word, MESSER-MADE, stared back at him in indented, black metal lettering.

"And what's the name of your dump truck?" Graham asked.

Silently, Matlin loped around to the front of the oversized truck, and peered up at the letters. They were exactly the same as on his own dump truck: FLUG.

When Matlin returned with the identification, Graham nodded, and then handed him back his claim sheet, and said evenly, "If I were to write that claim, Mr. Matlin, it would read: 'As the man who had done the most to prevent the creature from space being traced down, I recognize myself'—meaning you, Mr. Matlin—'as the one person least qualified to receive the reward.'"

It was such an unexpected reaction, so instantly threatening to his rights, so totally negative, that Matlin blanched. But he was stopped by the words only for a moment. Then the anger poured.

"Why, you damned swindler!" he began.

"*Wait!*" Graham spoke piercingly, raised his hand in a warning gesture. His steely gray eyes were cynical as he continued: "Now, if you were to lead us onto the real backtrack, help us locate these creatures, I'll reconsider that judgment. *Will* you?"

Night came and caught them on the hunt.

As the monster-hunting expedition camped beside the lake, the darkness was shattered by a thunderous roaring sound. Matlin tumbled from the back seat of his car, ran to the lake shore, and peered across the dark waters toward the island in the lake's center. He was aware of other men coming up behind and beside him.

It was from the island that the noise came.

"Sounds like a whole battery of jet engines," somebody yelled above the roar, "and it seems to be coming this way."

Abruptly, the truth of that was borne out. The jet sound was suddenly above them. Framed in a patch of dark blue sky, a monstrous sized helicopter was momentarily visible.

It disappeared into a cloud bank. The great roaring receded, became a remote throb.

In the darkness, Graham came up beside Matlin, said,

"Didn't you tell me you had a lakeside cabin near here?"

"Yeah," Matlin said, wary.

"Got a boat there?"

Matlin jumped to a horrid conclusion. "You're not thinking of going over to the island?" he gulped. "Now!"

Graham said earnestly, "We'll pay you for the rent of the boat, and guarantee you against damages—in writing. And if that's the base these creatures operate from, I'll sign your claim."

Matlin hesitated. The boat and the lakefront property were his one dream. No one, not even Cora, had ever realized how much they meant to him. On the very first day that he had killed the first monster, he had taken a load of sand from his farm and dumped it lovingly on the water's edge.

Standing there, Matlin visualized what the money would do for his dream: the rough shoreline fully sanded in, a hunting and fishing lodge, and a larger boat, the kind he had often fantasied but never managed to acquire.

"I'll do it," he said.

On the island, using his flashlight sparingly, Matlin led Graham and two other men to where the ground suddenly felt . . . harder.

When they dug down, they found metal bare inches under the grass.

Graham talked softly by two-way radio to the camp they had left and then held his radio for Matlin and himself to hear the answer: a parachute army would be called by way of the more powerful radio at the camp. By dawn, several hundred seasoned men with tanks, demolition units, and cannon would be down with them.

But, as the radio shut off, they were alone once more in the dark. The reinforcements of the morning were still hours away.

It was Matlin—again—who found the overhang that led into a huge, brightly lighted ship.

He was so intent, and interested, that he was inside the first chamber with the others before he clearly realized how far he had come.

He stopped. He half turned to run. But he didn't move. The scene held him.

They were in a circular room about four hundred feet in diameter. A number of solidly built metallic extrusions came up from the floor or down from the ceiling. Except for them the room was empty.

Matlin went with the others to where a ramp led down to the next level. Here there were more of the huge, built-in machines—if that was what they were—but this level, also, was deserted.

On the third level, they found two sleeping "children." Each lay on its back in a long, black, metal, box-like structure. The larger was about half the size of a full-grown alien, the smaller a mere bit of a thing two feet long. Both were stocky of body and were, unmistakably, younger versions of the two creatures that had already been killed.

As the three men—Graham and the two officers—glanced at each other questioningly, Matlin drew out his claim sheet, and held it toward Graham. The government agent gave him a startled look; then, evidently realizing Matlin meant it, he nodded resignedly, took the pen and signed.

The moment he had the claim sheet back in his hands, Matlin headed for the ramp.

He was sweating now with fear. Yet he realized he had no alternative. He had to have that signature. But now—

. . . Get away from all this stuff that was none of his business!

When he reached the lakeshore, he started the motor of the motorboat, and headed back toward his boathouse. He locked up the boat, walked stealthily through the darkness to his car, and drove off.

As he came out of the line of trees a mile from his farm, he saw the entire yard was on fire. He heard the thunder of the gigantic engines—

His house, his barn, his machine shed—all were burning! In the vivid, fitful light from the flames he saw the huge helicopter lift up from the far side and soar up into the night sky.

So that was where it had gone!

It passed by above him somewhat to his right, a colossal sound, the source of which was now completely invisible in the darkness of an overcast sky.

Matlin found Cora and the son that was not away at school crouching in the field. She mumbled something about the monster having come over and looked down at them. She said wonderingly, "How did it know this was your farm? That's what I don't understand."

IV

The fire was dwindling. People were beginning to drive into the yard. Car doors slammed. In the fading brightness, Matlin in a bemused state carried his son and walked beside Cora to his station wagon.

13

He was having a different kind of thought. Why hadn't the creature killed his wife and child? Cora and the boy had been as completely at its mercy as the farm.

A neighbor named Dan Gray touched his arm and said, "How about you and Cora and the boy staying at my place tonight, Steve?"

By the time they got over on the Gray farm, a man was on TV describing how Steve Matlin had left three men at the mercy of the returning alien.

He named Matlin.

Matlin recognized the man who was talking as a member of the monster-hunting expedition.

He glanced around, saw that Gray, Gray's wife—a tall, thin woman—and Cora were staring at him. Cora said in horror, "Steve, you *didn't!*"

Matlin was amazed. "I'm going to sue that fellow for libel!" he yelled.

"Then it isn't true," Cora wailed. "What an awful thing for them to say such a lie!"

Matlin was outraged at her misunderstanding. "It's not a lie, just a bunch of baloney. Why should I stay on that island? If they want to be crazy, that's their business."

He saw from their faces that his perfectly obvious truth was not obvious to them. He became grim. "Okay, I can see I'm no longer welcome. Come along, Cora."

Mrs. Gray said, tight-lipped, "Cora and the boy can stay."

Matlin was quite willing, already at peace with their foolishness. "I'll pick you up in the morning," he said to his wife.

Cora did not reply.

Gray accompanied Matlin to his car. When he came back into the living room, he was shaking his head. He said to Cora, "One thing about that husband of yours. He lets you know where he stands."

Cora said stiffly, "He's let me know once too often. Imagine leaving those men!" There were tears in her eyes.

"He says they lured him over to the island."

"Nobody lures Steve. His own scheming got him over there."

"He says he suddenly realized the generals had done it again—got a private into the front line. And since this was not his war—"

"If it isn't his war, whose is it? He fired the first shot."

"Well, anyway, the generals are on the firing line, and no one could care less than Steve. I can tell you that."

"That's the astonishing thing," said Cora, wonderingly. "He

thinks World War II was a conspiracy to waste his time. He lives entirely in his own private world. Nothing can shake him, as you just saw."

Matlin drove back to his farm and slept there in the back of his car.

When he returned to the Gray farm in the morning, Dan Gray came out to meet him. He was grinning. He said, "Well, Steve, it's finally going to be your war."

Matlin stared at the knowing smile on the somewhat heavy face of his neighbor, but the words seemed meaningless. So he made no reply but simply got out of his car and walked into the house.

The two women were watching the TV. Matlin did not even glance at the picture.

"Ready, Cora?" he said.

Both women turned and looked at him strangely. Finally, Mrs. Gray said breathlessly, "You're taking it very calmly."

"Taking what calmly?"

Mrs. Gray looked helplessly at Cora. "I can't tell him," she almost whispered.

Matlin glanced questioningly at his wife. She said. "You might as well hear it. The creature came back and found Mr. Graham and his two companions on the island. And it talked to them through some kind of mechanical translation device. It said it was going to leave Earth but that first it was going to accomplish one thing. It said—it said—"

Matlin said impatiently, "For Pete's sake, Cora, let's go. You can tell me on the way."

Cora said, "It said—it was going to kill you first."

For once Matlin was speechless.

At last he stammered: "Me!" After a moment, he added, incredulous, "That's ridiculous. I haven't anything to do with this business."

"It says you're the only one on Earth who made it your business."

The shock was growing on Matlin. He could not speak, could not deny the charge in words. Inside his head, he protested silently: *But that first beast was coming toward me. How was I supposed to know?*

Cora was continuing in a grief-filled voice: "It says that on all the planets it's visited, no one has ever before killed without warning, without asking any questions."

Matlin stared at her with hopeless eyes. He felt battered, defeated, ultimately threatened. For a moment, again, he

15

could scarcely believe. He thought: *I only want to be left alone!*

The thought stopped. Because he knew suddenly that all these years he had been maintaining an untruth: that what went on elsewhere was none of his affair.

He had pretended so hard, gone into such instant rages, that other people simply glanced at each other significantly and fell silent, and thereafter never brought up the subject again. He had always thought with satisfaction, *By damn, they'd better not say anything but*—contemptuously—*let them think what they want.*

And now, he was the only human being that a visitor from another planet felt motivated to kill. . . .

He grew aware once more of Dan Gray's smile. The man spread his hands helplessly. "I can't help it, Steve. Believe it or not, I like you. I even think I understand you. But—forgive me, Cora—this seems to me to be a case of poetic justice. I can't think of anyone else who's had something like this coming to him for so long."

Matlin turned and walked out of the room. He was aware of Cora following him hastily. "Just a minute, Steve," she said, "I have something for you."

Matlin turned. They were alone in the hallway. He grew aware that she was tugging at her wedding ring. "Here," she said, "I should have given you this nineteen years ago, but I let the coming of our first child stop me."

She opened his palm, placed the ring in it, and closed his fingers over it. "You're on your own, Steve. After twenty years of being the most selfish, self-centered man in the world, you can face this as you should, by yourself."

Matlin scowled down at the ring, then: "Bah! When you look at me, you see the human race as it really is. I've never gone in for the shams, that's all."

He slipped the ring into his pocket. "I'm going to keep this and give it back to you when you get over this foolish feeling. My feeling for you was never a sham."

He turned and walked out of the room and out of the house.

A car was pulling up in front of the Gray house. John Graham was inside it. He climbed out and walked over to where Matlin was about to get into his station wagon, said, "I came over to see you."

"Make it quick!" said Matlin.

"I have three messages for you."

"Shoot!"

"Obviously," said Graham, "the U.S. Government will not

16

allow one of its citizens to be casually exterminated."

Accordingly—he continued formally—all of the armed forces would be interposed between Steve Matlin and the alien.

Matlin stared at him with uncompromising hostility. "He can duplicate anything we've got, so those are just big words."

Graham said in the same formal way that the ability of the creature to duplicate, first, the rifle, then the truck, and then the helicopter, had been taken note of by the military.

Matlin's curt laugh dismissed as asinine the notion that the generals would know what to do with such information. "C'mon, c'mon," he said roughly, "what's the second message?"

"It's personal" said Graham.

He stepped forward. His fist came up, connected perfectly with Matlin's jaw. Matlin was knocked back against his car. He sank to the ground, sat there rubbing his jaw and looking up at Graham. He said in an even tone, "Just about everybody seems to agree I had that coming to me, so I'll take it. What's the last message."

Graham, who had evidently expected a battle, stepped back. His savage mood softened. He shook his head wonderingly. "Steve," he said, "you amaze me. Maybe I even respect you."

Matlin said nothing. He just sat there, elbows on knees.

After a moment, Graham continued. "The way the generals figure it, there's got to be another reason why the creature wants to kill you. Maybe you know something." His gray eyes watched Matlin closely. "Have you been holding anything back?"

Matlin shook his head, but he was interested. He climbed slowly to his feet, frowning, thoughtful as he dusted himself off.

Graham persisted. "It is proposed that its ability to duplicate is based upon a kind of perception that human beings don't have."

"Hey!" said Matlin, eyes wide. "You mean like the homing pigeon, or birds flying south, or salmon coming back to their little pool where they were born?"

"The reasoning is," said Graham, "that you got some feedback on whatever it is, and so the creature wants to kill you before you can pass on to anybody else what you know."

Matlin was shaking his head. "They're off their rocker. I don't know a thing."

Graham watched him a moment longer. Then, clearly satisfied, he said, "Anyway, the military feel that they can't take a chance with a creature that has made a death threat against an American citizen. So they're going to drop an atomic bomb on it and end the matter once and for all."

For some reason, Matlin felt an instant alarm. "Just a minute," he said doubtfully. "Suppose it duplicates that? Then it'll have everything we've got, and we still won't have seen a thing *it's* got."

Graham was tolerant. "Oh, come now, Steve. The bomb will be a small one but the right size to pulverize that spaceship. I personally feel strong regrets about this but I have no doubt of the outcome. Once the bomb drops, it'll have nothing to duplicate with—and it won't be around to do any duplicating."

Matlin said, "Better tell them to hold that bomb till they've thought about it some more."

Graham was looking at his watch. "I'm afraid it's a little late for that, Steve. Because they figured you might have some telepathic connection with this creature. I've been holding back the fact that the bomb is being dropped—right—now!"

As he spoke, there was a sound of distant thunder.

Involuntarily, the two men ducked. Then they straightened and looked over the near farms, past the trees in the distance, beyond the low hills. A small but familiar and sinister mushroom was rising from the other side of the horizon.

"Well," said Graham, "that does it. Too bad. But it shouldn't have made that threat against you."

"What about the other ship?" Matlin asked.

"What other ship?" said Graham.

They had both spoken involuntarily. Now, they stared at each other.

Graham broke the silence. "Oh, my God!" he said.

V

There were stubborn people at G.H.Q.

For two decisive days, they rejected the idea that there might be another ship.

Then, late in the afternoon of the third day, radar reported a small object high above field H, from which the atomic plane had taken off to destroy the spaceship on the island.

Control tower challenged the approaching airborne machine. When there was no response, somebody became anxious and sounded a bomb alarm. Then he dived down a chute that took him headfirst into a shelter far below.

His quick action made him one of about eight hundred fast-reflex people who survived.

Seconds after he made his dive to safety, an atomic bomb demolished field H.

About the same time, a TV helicopter was hovering above the island in Matlin's lake, taking pictures of the bomb crater there. Suddenly a spaceship came silently down from a great height and landed.

The helicopter did not tarry. It took rear view pictures as it was fleeing the scene.

Graham went to see Cora, looking for Matlin.

But she could only shake her head. "Steve said he was going on the road till this whole thing blew over. He said he figured he'd better not be sitting still when that creature came looking for him."

They put Matlin's photo on TV.

On the fourth day after that, Graham interviewed four sullen young men who had tried to seize Matlin, their intention being to deliver him to the monster. As their spokesman put it, "By handing over the one guy who was really involved in this business, the rest of us could have gone back to our daily affairs."

They filed out, one on crutches, two with arms in slings, all bandaged in some way, groaning a little.

The following day, Graham interrogated two people who claimed to have witnessed a duel on an open stretch of highway between Matlin in a station wagon and the monster flying an enormous jet plane. Matlin had had a bazooka and the beast had finally beaten a retreat.

General Maxwell Day, who was with Graham, wondered aloud if Matlin might not be the man who had raided a Marine armory and taken a three point five rocket launcher and a quarter of a ton of ammunition for it.

Graham phoned Cora. "I'm checking a report," he said. "Would Steve have thought of utilizing Marine equipment?"

Cora answered carefully. "That weapon belonged to the people of the U.S., didn't it?"

"Yes."

"Well, then, I think Steve would regard himself as part owner, as a citizen, and without any guilt since he would consider either that he had paid for it with taxes or earned it in World War II."

19

Graham put his hand over the mouthpiece, said, "I gather he would have thought of such a thing."

The Marine officer held his hand out for the phone. "Let me talk to her," he said. A moment later: "Mrs. Matlin?"

"Yes?"

"May I ask you some very personal questions about your husband?"

"You may."

"Now, Mrs. Matlin, Mr. Graham here has the highest respect for your opinions, so think carefully about this one: Is your husband intelligent?"

Cora hesitated; then: "I know exactly what you mean. On some levels, no; on others, extremely intelligent."

"Is he brave?"

"To hear him talk, no. But my feeling is, totally. I think you'd have to engage his interest, though."

"What does he think of generals?"

"They're idiots."

"Is he an honest man?"

"We-l-l-l-l, that depends. For example, he had that rifle along that first day in the hope that he'd be able to kill a deer illegally."

"I mean is he responsible for his debts?"

"If I may quote him—he wouldn't give the so and so's the satisfaction of owing them money."

General Day smiled. "Now, Mrs. Matlin, would you take your husband back if I made a sergeant out of him?"

"Why not a captain?"

"I'm sorry, Mrs. Matlin, but if you'll think a little bit, you'll realize that he'd never sink that low."

"Oh, I don't have to think. You're right. Well—yes, I might take him back. B-but he's not in the Marines anymore."

"He will be, Mrs. Matlin. Goodbye."

He hung up.

An hour later it was announced on TV, radio and the newspapers that Matlin had been reinducted into the Marines, and that he was ordered to report to the nearest Marine station.

About midnight that night a jet, with Graham and several officers aboard, flew down to the Marine base where Matlin was resignedly waiting for them. They secured a Marine private's uniform. As the grim, unshaved man reluctantly donned it, they interrogated him. They were interested in any thought whatsoever that may have flitted through Matlin's mind for any reason.

20

Matlin objected: "That's crazy. I don't know anything special—except the thing is out to get me."

"We think you do."

"But that's a lot of—"

"Private Matlin! That's an order!"

Glumly—but thoroughly—Matlin complied with the orders. He told them everything that had passed through his mind about the creature in the past few days. And there had been things, many things, things that had seemed crazy and distorted to him, until he thought he was beginning to lose his mind. Visions of a home on a planet of another star. Visions of long, long years of travel. Visions of the buried ship at the lake, where thousands of atomic bombs were in process of being duplicated.

His listeners turned pale, but Graham urged, "Go on."

Matlin continued: There was only one creature, but it had brought with it a number of spare bodies and could grow even more.

Then he stopped. "Damn it," he growled, "I don't like to say this stuff! Why do you want to hear it, anyway? It's just crazy dreams."

Graham glanced at the Marine commander, then at Matlin. He said, "Matlin, we don't think it's dreams at all. We think that you are in resonance—somehow!—with the creature's mind. And we need to know what it has in its mind—so, for heaven's sake, go on!"

The story, by the time Matlin got through piecing it together, made a pattern:

The alien had arrived in the solar system in two ships, with its bodies in various growth stages and evenly distributed between the two vessels. When one ship—and its cargo of bodies—was later destroyed, it made a duplicate, and now again had two.

As body after body was destroyed, the next in line was triggered into rapid growth and awakened to full adulthood in about two days. Each new body had the complete "memory" of what had happened to the ones that preceded it; it automatically recorded by ESP everything that happened to its preceding self.

On arrival, the first body had awakened in a state of total receptiveness. It had wanted to be able to duplicate the thoughts and feelings of the inhabitants of this newly found planet.

—Be like them, think like them, know their language—

It was in this helpless, blank condition when it stumbled on Steve Matlin.

21

And that was the story. The creature had been imprinted with the personality of Matlin.

Graham said, "Steve, do you realize that this being got all these destructive ideas from you?"

Matlin blinked. "Huh!"

Graham, remembering some things that Cora had told him, said, "Do you have any friends, Steve? Anybody you like? Anybody *anywhere?*"

Matlin could think of no one. Exept, of course, Cora and the kids. But his feelings about them were not unmixed. She had insisted on sending the three older children to school in town. But he did feel a genuine affection for her, and them, at some level.

Graham said tensely, "That's why she's alive. That's why the creature didn't kill her the day it burned your farm."

"B-but—" Matlin protested, "why destroy the farm?"

"You hate the damn place, don't you?"

Matlin was silent. He'd said it a thousand times.

"What do you think we ought to do with about half the people in this country, Steve?"

"I think we ought to wipe the human race off the map and start over again," said Matlin automatically.

"What do you think we ought to do with the Russians?"

"If I had my way," said Matlin, "we'd go over there and plaster the whole of Asia with atomic bombs."

After a little, Graham said softly, "Like to change any of those ideas, Steve?"

Matlin, who had finished dressing, scowled into a mirror. "Look," he said finally, "you've got me where I can't hit back. And I'm ready to be loused up by what the idiot generals have got in their crazy noodles. So tell me what you want me to do."

At that precise moment, *That* ceased its feverish duplication of man's atomic bombs . . . and became itself.

Its compulsive mental tie with Matlin was severed.

Shuddering, *That* made a report, on an instantaneous relay-wave transmitter whose receiver was light years away:

"What we always feared would happen on one of these blank mind approaches to a new planet finally happened to me. While I was enormously receptive to any thought, my first body was destroyed by a two-legged inhabitant of this system, a being with the most incredible ideas—which are apparently due to some early mistreatment. This inability to slough off early shock conditioning seems to be a unique phenomenon of the people of this planet.

"Realizing how trapped I was while he remained alive, I made several attempts to kill him. I was unsuccessful in this because he turned out to be unexpectedly resourceful. But he has now put on a suit called a uniform, and this has immediately turned him into a peaceful person.

"Thus I was able to free myself. Naturally, I can still sense where he is, but he can no longer receive my thoughts nor I his. However, I must report that I am pinned down here by an air fleet. My image as a good-will visitor has been completely nullified by what has happened. Obviously, I won't use any weapons against them; so perhaps this expedition is doomed."

A team of astronauts was sent up. The team successfully boarded *That's* second spaceship, reporting that it was occupied by four bodies in various growth stages.

Even as they blew up the ship in its silent orbit, on Earth Matlin was driven to the edge of the lake. There, a Government launch was provided him. While Graham and General Day watched through binoculars, Matlin drove the thirty thousand dollar craft right onto the beach of the island, careless of any damage to it.

"I think he smashed the launch," said Graham.

"Good."

"Good?"

"My whole theory about him would collapse if he treated Government property with the same care that he gave his own possessions. It reassures me that he's exactly the man I thought."

Matlin came to where the second alien ship lay at the bottom of the blast pit. Water had filtered down into the clay. Having his orders, Matlin dutifully slid down into the goo. He held his rifle high, cursed, and started for the entrance.

VI

Graham, General Day, and an artillery major watched Matlin's progress on a portable TV. The picture was coming from a ship some seventy thousand feet above the island. The scene below was crystal clear. Through the marvelous telescopic lens, Matlin actually looked like a tiny human being walking.

"But why send anyone?" Graham protested. "Why not just blast it? As you've already pointed out, we've got enough power up there"—he indicated the sky above—"to exterminate him."

23

General Day explained that he now favored Graham's earlier view. The alien might be able to defend itself.

"But it's too late for caution," Graham interjected. "We've burned our bridges."

It would be unwise, the Marine officer explained, to provoke the creature further until a confrontation had taken place.

"A confrontation between a super-being—and Matlin!"

"Who else should we send? Some poor devil? No, Matlin is oriented to this. Seeing the creature face on is not a new experience to him as it would be to some other lower ranks."

"Why not send you? Me?"

Day answered in a steady voice that such decisions as were required here should not be made by people who reasoned on the basis of official attitudes.

"How do you think I got to be a general? When in doubt, I listened to what the men thought. They have a basic canniness that transcends intellect."

With an effort, Graham recovered. "You heard Matlin's basic truth," he said. "His opinion of the human race—"

General Day gave him a surprised look. "You mean to tell me that isn't your opinion also?"

"No."

"You don't think that human beings are absolutely impossible?"

"No, I think they're pretty terrific," said Graham.

"Boy, are you far gone," said the general in a tolerant voice. "I can see that we Marines have an understanding of human behavior that beats all you brain-washed people." He broke off. "Matlin was badly handled in World War II."

"What?" Graham groped.

"You ask, what has that got to do with it? Plenty. You see, Mr. Graham, you have to understand that a true Marine is a king. Now, Matlin is the true Marine type. But he was treated like an ordinary private. He never got over it; so he's been seething for twenty years, waiting for recognition. I'm giving it to him. A king Marine, Mr. Graham, can direct a war, take command of a city, or negotiate with a foreign power like a government. Marines who get to be generals are considered sub-level versions of this species. All Marines understand this perfectly. It will not occur to Matlin to consult me, or you, or the U.S. Government. He'll size up the situation, make a decision, and I shall back him up."

He turned to the major, commanded, "All right, start firing!"

"Firing!" Graham yelled.

Day explained patiently as to a child that it was necessary in this extreme emergency to reindoctrinate this particular Marine, and grind in the simple truth—to him—that generals always loused things up. "A quick reminder, that's all, Mr. Graham."

Matlin was still skidding around in the mud when the first shell landed to his left. It sprayed him with fine droplets of wet dirt. The second shell landed to his right. The debris from it missed him entirely, but he was now in such a state of rage that he didn't notice.

By the time the shelling ceased, his anger was gone and he was in that peculiar state of mind which can only be described with one word: Marine.

The man who presently entered the alien ship knew that life was tough, that other people could not be trusted, that no one cared about him. It was a truth he had always fought with bitterness and rage.

But there was no longer any doubt in his mind. People were what they were. They would shoot you in the back if they couldn't get you from in front.

Understanding this, you could be friendly with them, shake their hands, enjoy their company—and be completely free of any need to judge them or condemn them.

But you were on your own, day and night, year in and out.

As he saw the creature, Matlin used his gun for the purpose for which he had brought it. Deliberately, he tossed it down. It struck the metal floor with a clatter.

The echoes of the sound faded—and there was silence. Alien and human stood there staring.

Matlin waited.

Suddenly the hoped-for voice came from a speaker in the ceiling:

"I am talking to you through a computer, which is translating my thoughts into your language. It will do the same for yours. Why have they sent you to me—the one man I threatened to kill?"

That added: "I no longer plan to kill you. So you may talk freely."

Matlin said bluntly. "We're trying to decide what to do with you. Do you have any suggestions?"

"I wish to leave the planet forever. Can you arrange it?"

Matlin was practical. Could the creature leave whether human beings liked it or not? "No."

25

The simple negative took Matlin slightly aback. "You have no special weapons from—from where you come from?"

"None," admitted the alien.

That admission also startled Matlin. "You mean to tell me we can do what we want with you? You can't stop us?"

"Yes, except—"

Matlin wanted to know except what.

The great eyes blinked at him, its black, fold-like eyelids rolling up and down in a skin and muscle complex unlike that of any creature Matlin had ever seen before.

"Except that it will do you no good to kill me."

"You'd better make it damn clear what you mean," Matlin said.

Watching him, *That* gave its explanation.

Matlin's boat was almost waterlogged by the time he successfully beached it near where Graham and the others were waiting.

He came up to them and saluted. General Day returned the salute smartly, and said, "Your report."

"I told him he could go," said Matlin. "He'll be leaving when I signal."

"*What?*" That was Graham, his voice sounding shrill and amazed in his own ears. "But why?"

"Never mind why," said General Day. "That's the way it's going to be."

He spoke into his mike: "Men, this alien ship is going to lift from here in a few minutes. Let it go through. A duly authorized person has negotiated this solution."

The language was not clear to Matlin. "Is it okay?" he asked questioningly.

For an instant, it seemed to Graham, Day hesitated. Graham said urgently into that instant, "At least, you're going to find out what made him agree?"

Day seemed to have come to a decision; his momentary hesitation ended. "Okay!" he said to Matlin. "Okay, Sergeant."

Matlin raised his rifle, and fired it into the air.

To Graham, Day said, "I've never lost a bet on a king Marine, and I don't expect to now."

The interchange ended. On the island, the ship was lifting. Silent, jetless, rocketless power drove it up on a slant.

It passed over their heads, gathering speed. It grew small and, as they watched, became a dot and vanished.

Aboard it, the creature to which Matlin had talked performed the preliminaries necessary to an interstellar voyage,

26

nd then retired to one of the sleep boxes. Soon it was in a
tate of suspended animation. . . .

Thereupon happened what the monster had told Mat-
in—the underlying reality, which made it useless, unnec-
ssary, even dangerous, to destroy it and its vessel.

On a planet many light-years away, the real *That* stirred,
wakened and sat up.

THE FIRST MARTIAN

I HAD PUT on my pressure suit, and was walking through
the roundhouse at Eastport, the Martian rail center, when I
saw the stocky, big-chested guy with the purplish, mahog-
any-colored face come toward me. I knew at a glance that
he was an Indian of some kind.

"Señor!" he said.

I stopped politely, and faced him.

"Señor, I am your new engineer-relief."

That hit me. On Mars, I had run into every creed and
race at one time or another. But white men operated the
big steam-atomics across the endless plains, and through the
mountains, and along the frozen canals. The reason was very
simple. White supremacy was taken for granted.

I tried to hide my surprise. "Glad to have you along," I
said. "Better get into your pressure suit. We go out in thirty
minutes. What's your name? Mine's Hecton. Bill Hecton."

"José Incuhana. I don't wear a pressure suit."

"Sounds like South America," I began—and stopped.
"Look, Joe," I said finally, "be a good fellow and go over
to the equipment room and ask for an HA-2. Make it snappy,
pal. It takes a little while to get into those things. Be seeing
you in about twenty minutes."

I turned away awkwardly in my own bulky HA-2. I never
did care for pressure suits, but on Mars, with its thin, thin
atmosphere, they're essential to ordinary human beings who
leave the shelters.

I had walked about five feet when I grew aware that José
was still with me. He said, "You can see me right now,
Señor Hecton." He sounded puzzled.

I turned and faced him, holding in my impatience. "Joe,
when did you get to Mars?"

He looked at me soberly with his soft brown eyes. "Two
days, señor." He held up two fingers.

"Have you been out there yet?" I pointed at the desolation visible through the asbesglas window.

He nodded. "Yesterday."

His eyes were bright and intelligent looking, and they stared at me as if he was still waiting for the punch line. Baffled, I glanced around, and saw Roundhouse Superintendent Manet. "Hey, Charles!" I called.

Manet, a big Frenchman with a twinkle in his black eyes, came over. He said, "Glad to see you two have been getting acquainted."

"Charles," I said, "tell Joe about Mars. That the oxygen content of the air is about what we have five miles up back home. Tell him about high altitude suits."

Manet shook his head. "Bill, Señor Incuhana is from the Andes Mountains. He was born in a town eighteen thousand feet above sea level. Mars is just another mountaintop to him."

He broke off. "Oh, there's Frank. Hey, Frank, come over here!"

Frank Gray was rod-man on the engine's atomic-heated boiler unit. He strode over, a lean, tense man looking huge in his suit. He was introduced to Señor Incuhana, started to put out his hand, and then drew back with a frown.

"What's going on here?" he said. "I'm near the head of the list to become engineer. Who is bringing in outsiders?"

He didn't wait for a reply, but went on angrily, "I remember now. I've heard of this Indian idea. It's an insult to a good technician. What are they trying to do? Make us think we're just a bunch of day laborers?"

Manet said placatingly, "Frank, you are a good enough scientist to realize that if we can get people who can actually live—"

He stopped. Frank had turned away. We stood silent, watching him walk off. I glanced at José, but his face was impassive. Manet took out his watch.

"Better get aboard," he said. "There will be a few gadgets to show José, and you check out in exactly sixteen minutes."

On the dot, the steam-atomic locomotive, *Desert Rat*, was eased by an electric mule into the huge chamber which served as an airlock between the roundhouse and the Martian outdoors. A few moments later, I edged open her throttle. Sliding forward under her own thunderous power, she moved onto the frozen tracks of "outside."

In the east, the sun was just tipping the horizon.

I pointed, and called to José through the walkie-talkie in my head globe. He came over from his seat, and followed my finger with his eyes.

"Ice, señor?" he said.

"Ice," I agreed.

Frozen rivulets streaked the metal outer walls. I ran my gaze backward from the bulging front-cab. The door of the decompression chamber was just closing behind us, yet everywhere I looked the long, streamlined locomotive already glistened where moisture had condensed and instantly solidified.

Seventy below. A typical winter dawn in the temperate zone of Mars. Ahead of us, bleak and glittery on the flat plain, was the small Earth settlement of Eastport, center of a great mining area. We glided past the interconnected domes, inside which people lived in apartment units. Lines of railway tracks led into the princial domes, but the cars that were going with us—including a pressure-type passenger car—had already been coupled to the head of a long train of ore dumps.

I backed till we connected; then I slid open the door, and climbed down to the ground. The sun shone directly into my eyes from a sky that was a deep blue-black. Above, the stars were still visible. They'd be with us all day.

I looked back. José was at the door. I called up, "Better shut the door!"

I heaved myself into the passenger car, went through the airlock inside, and into the comfortable interior. I took a quick glance at the men who were sitting in the bar, and realized I was piloting an important train. There were four top rail executives whom I knew, and one man who was introduced as Philip Barron, just arrived from Earth. He was a heavily built man with curly brown hair and blue-gray eyes that looked as hard as agates.

Vice-president Henry Wade began: "Bill, our head offices back home have gotten hold of this Andean Indian notion, see it as a cheap way of doing business; and so they're going to populate Mars with them. It's a blind man's deal. In a few years, they'll stage a revolution and claim Mars as their private precinct, including expropriation of all the priceless equipment we've brought here."

Another man broke in: "How did he strike you, Bill?"

"Joe seems to be all right." I spoke carefully.

"Think he can live in this climate?"

I hesitated. "Seems to be able to breathe the air," I said finally.

A third executive laughed ironically. "One of the new men," he said. "The true Martian human. Hundreds more being technically trained. Women, too. Soon people like you and me, Bill, will just be memories in the Martian rail history."

"Like hell we will," said Vice-president Wade.

But the other man's words made me uneasy. There were times when I cursed this route and this life, but more often I couldn't imagine anything I'd rather do. Besides, the pay was terrific.

Wade looked at me soberly. "You're going to be asked to give your estimate of him. Our idea is that he should be made to stack up to a high standard."

I said with a shrug, "I can't see this deal depending on my say-so."

Wade replied earnestly, "It'll depend on many things. Superficially, the notion appears to have merit. It's only when you examine it as a whole that you perceive the danger."

Barron, the only Earthside executive present, stood up and offered me his hand. He said, "It's not so bad as they make it sound. We're starting off with eighteen Indians in different types of work. I admit in the long run it's going to save money. Fewer dome shelters, an easing of compression costs, perhaps even a little profit for the shareholders. Is that bad? I don't think so."

As I climbed into the cab a few minutes later, I saw Frank Gray disappear into his section. I looked questioningly at José, but his face told me nothing. I hesitated, but Frank was a friend of mine and José wasn't; I decided to ask no questions. "Start her off!" I said curtly.

The train began to move, and I looked at my watch. We were eight minutes late. We had about five hundred miles to go before dark, not a great distance unless something went wrong. On Mars in winter, trains didn't run on night schedules. Extreme low temperatures made the rails dangerously brittle.

"Keep her down to twenty miles per hour," I said presently.

José nodded, but looked puzzled. Seeing him sitting there, warmly clothed but not in a pressure suit, I began to feel something of the tension that had been in the other men. "Joe," I said suddenly, "what kind of lungs have you got?"

He was no dumb Indian. He had been told about himself, and he gave. Andean man has lungs bigger than normal with more blood vessels in them. His heart can do at least an eighth more work than the heart of sea level man. His blood vessels carry a greater volume of blood, and his nerve cells are less sensitive to oxygen starvation.

When the Spaniards first came to places like Peru and Bolivia, they discovered that neither pigs nor birds, cattle nor Spaniards could breed above ten thousand feet. It was only after a generation had lived at about eight thousand feet that the descendants were able to reproduce at fourteen thousand. The Indians had been there before them from time immemorial.

The facts and figures gave me a sinking sensation. I looked at José's purplish-red complexion, and realized that he *could* be a Martian. But it was obvious that I couldn't.

I saw the pile beside the tracks far ahead before José did. I expected it, of course; and so I waited, wondering how long it would take him to spot the object. Twenty seconds went by, and then he pointed.

I sighed. No sign of oxygen starvation with that kind of vision.

"Start braking her!" I ordered.

He looked at me with some surprise, and I know he was thinking it was too soon. He was not making due allowance for the fact that it took a lot longer to stop a train on Mars. Same mass as on Earth, but less weight, less friction. We came to a halt, the wheels grinding on the rails, the engine panting and shuddering.

There was no one in sight, only the huge bag lying beside the tracks. I guessed there was about two tons of rock inside the bag. "I'll go outside," I told Joe. "Then you drive forward till I wave for you to stop."

He nodded his acceptance of my instructions. As I slid the door open, he pulled his big collar up over his ears; and, when I had climbed to the ground, he came over and shut the door.

It was not quite as cold as it had been. I guessed the temperature had come up to fifty below. The long train started as I motioned José—and stopped when I waved. I used the "claw," a small crane which we carried for the purpose of lifting such bundles into an ore car. And presently I was back inside the engine cab.

I said, "You can speed up now."

The speedometer climbed. At seventy, José leveled her off. He explained: "I don't know enough about this terrain, señor, to go any faster."

I nodded, and took control. The speedometer needle edged higher. José said, "That bag of stuff, Bill"—he almost said it "Beel"—"who puts it beside the track?"

I'd been wondering if he would show any curiosity. "A race of small, furry creatures," I answered. "They're very

31

shy. They live underground, and dig ore for us." I grinned at his puzzled expression. "We don't want the ore, because it's usually only rock. We're interested in the material of the bags. It's as thin as paper, completely transparent, and yet it can withstand the weight of tons of rock. They manufacture it from their own bodies, much the way spiders produce webs. We can't seem to make them understand that we want only the bags."

We did the next fifty miles at an average of eighty-four miles per hour. It was a straight run, and it was like gliding along on ice. On every side was a flat waste of sand that had not changed in all the years since I had first seen it. The sun was climbing in a sky that was bluer now, the stars faint but still visible. We plunged through that barren world to the hiss of the high speed steam turbines, and the hum of the gears that transmitted their power to the wheels. I felt more than human. I was the master of a juggernaut that violated the ancient silences of a planet millions of miles remote from the planet Earth.

As I saw the hills in the distance rearing up like low mounds, I began to slow. On the panel a red light blinked. Eight miles, the indicator said. I applied the brakes.

José pointed questioningly at the winking light.

"Sand on the tracks," I said.

Dune country. Sand so fine that even the thin winds of Mars could lift it. In motion, it looked like trailing smoke. As far as the eye could see there were gusts of it blowing, and here and there the rails had completely disappeared under the drifting sand.

We moved in fits and starts, swiftly when the track looked clear, and very slowly, with our blowers whining and hissing, where there was sand. Altogether, about an hour and a half went by before, once again, the roadbed belonged to us.

Halfway. And only a few minutes after ten o'clock. We were first. José slid open the door.

"Go out?" he asked.

"Sure."

We were on a rocky plain that was as crinkled as an old man's face, and almost the same grayish color. I watched José scramble over the rocks and head for a prominence a hundred yards away. It took stiff climbing in places, but he made it with apparent ease.

I grew aware that Frank had come into the cab. I glanced at him; and he said with a sneer, "Showing off to the big shots."

I hadn't thought of that. It could be true. José knew that

he was being tested, and that there was hostility toward him, not only from Frank Gray.

There was a faint rumble in the distance, and then a shrill whistle. The *Prairie Dog* rounded the bend and bore down on us. Glittering in the sun, the long engine roared past, its thunder somewhat muffled by the thin air, as was the trailing clatter of its empty ore cars. When the train had passed, I saw that Frank was going back into the rod room, and José was climbing into the engine.

I looked him over sharply. He was breathing heavily, and his cheeks were mottled. I wondered if it was entirely from exertion. Our eyes met; and he must have guessed why I was watching him, for he said quickly, "It's all right, señor. I feel fine."

I thought I detected a note of irony in his voice. I walked to the door, opened it, and then turned to him. "José," I said, "you'll get an honest deal from me; I'm going back to the passenger car. You're on your own from now on in."

José looked startled. Then his strong jaw set and he said gravely, "Thank you, señor."

Wade and the other executives were astonished when I explained what I had done. But Barron, Earthside executive, nodded approval. "After all," he said, "it's a fair test. Can he run a train on his own, or can't he?" He finished, "We can always phone him to stop, and then send Bill back up to the engine."

His words were received in silence, and from the sullen expressions of the others I guessed that my action was unpopular. The silence continued while the train accelerated. I must have dozed in my chair, because I wakened with a start to realize that the car was shuddering and swaying. I took a look out of the window, and felt alarm as I saw how swiftly the desert was speeding by.

I glanced around quickly. Three of the men were talking together in low tones; Wade was dozing, and Barron sat placidly smoking a cigar. He looked preoccupied.

I climbed casually to my feet, walked to the phone and called the engine cab. After it had rung five times, I got an uneasy feeling in the pit of my stomach. I returned to my chair; and it seemed to me, as I glanced again out of the window, that the train had actually gained speed. I groaned inwardly, and, glancing up, saw that Wade's shrewd brown eyes were studying me.

"Isn't your man going a little fast?" he said.

His assistant snapped angrily, "Irresponsible, if you ask me!"

Barron sighed, and looked at me gloomily. "Ask him to slow down."

I went to the phone, and called Frank Gray. The phone rang three times, and then Frank's voice said lazily, "Hello."

"Frank," I said in a low tone, "will you go up to the cab and ask José to slow down?"

"I can't hear you," he said. "What do you want?"

I repeated my request, emphasizing the words but still trying to keep my voice down.

Frank said irritably, "Stop mumbling. I can't hear a word you're saying."

I had been feeling both sorry for, and angry with, José. But there's only so much you can do to help a man who's got himself into a difficult situation. Clearly, and without worrying about being overheard, I told Frank what I wanted. There was silence when I had finished. Then:

"Go to hell!" said Frank. "It's not up to me."

He stuck to that, despite my arguments. I said finally, "Just a minute!" And went back to the group. They listened in silence, and then Wade whirled on Barron.

"Look what you've done to us with that Indian of yours!"

Barron chewed his cigar savagely, turned and stared out at the spinning landscape, and then said, "Better order that rod-man to do what Bill said."

Wade came back presently from the phone. "I had to give him permission to use force if necessary."

A few minutes later, we began to slow down. By that time, Barron was climbing into a pressure suit, and Wade had sent his executive assistant to get a suit for him. They exchanged caustic comments until the train finally came to a halt, Barron stubbornly clinging to the attitude that the defection of one Andean Indian didn't condemn all others. I led the way to the engine, and all I could think about was: What *could* have got into José?

Frank opened the cab door for us. There was no sign of José as we climbed in. Frank explained, "I found him lying on the floor here gasping for breath, so I put him in the rod room and built up a little pressure." He added complacently, "Nothing wrong with him that a little oxygen won't cure."

I looked at him for a long moment, fighting the suspicion in my mind. I said nothing, however, but made the necessary adjustments in pressure, and went into the rod room. I found José sitting on a chair. He looked at me miserably, but shrugged at my question.

I said earnestly, "José, I want you to forget that pride of yours, and tell me exactly what happened."

He said unhappily, "I became dizzy, and I had a feeling like bursting. Then I do not know what happened."

"Why did you speed up the train?"

He blinked at me, his dark eyes wide and uncomprehending. "Señor," he said at last, "I do not remember."

"My guess," said Frank from behind me, "is that we ran into a low pressure area, and as far as he was concerned it was the last straw."

I shook my head. I was remembering how José had matched my vision early that morning, and remembering also the way he had climbed the hill at Halfway. The stamina he had displayed in those two incidents wouldn't have yielded to a slight change in atmospheric pressure. Also, the cab doors were closed. Since they were nearly airtight, the pressure inside the cab would hardly be that sensitive to temporary changes outside.

I turned and looked at Frank. He stared back at me defiantly. Twice, I started to speak, but each time I remembered how long we'd been friends, and remained silent. Over his shoulder, I saw that Barron was examining the air pressure gauges and controls for the inside of the engine. He walked over to Wade and spoke in a low voice that sounded grim. The vice-president kept shaking his head, and ended the conversation by going over to Frank. He held out his hand.

"Mr. Gray," he said in a too-loud voice, "I want to thank you for saving us from being wrecked. Just remember, I'm behind you all the way."

Barron was tugging at my arm. I went with him out into the cab. He said quietly, "Is it possible to control the air pressure in the cab from the rod room?"

Since he could have obtained that information from other sources, I didn't hesitate. "Yes," I said.

Barron went on, "Did the Indian show any signs of oxygen starvation in your presence?"

"None."

"Have you any idea whether your rod-man is hostile to this notion of bringing in the Indians?"

"I have no idea," I said. I looked at my watch. "But I think we'd better get going. We're forty-three minutes late."

Underway again, I left José at the throttle, and stepped into the rod room. Frank was adjusting temperatures, and I waited patiently till the gauge readings balanced. Then he looked at me. I said, "Pretty smart."

He didn't deny it. "It's now or never," he said.

"Then you admit you reduced the air pressure on José?"

His tanned face grinned at me through the transparent visor of his suit. "I admit nothing," he said, "but I'm going to wreck that little buzzard's plans if it's the last thing I ever do. And I have an idea I'll get all the backing I need."

I tried to make him see that if there were any human beings at all who could live on Mars without artifice, then no one could fairly deny them the right to do so.

"Call *him* a human being?" Frank sneered.

I stared at him, and in that moment my feeling of friendship disappeared. I said very slowly, "If you bother him again on duty, I'll take it out of your hide."

Frank looked at me sullenly. "I've been wondering just where you stood," he said. "Thanks for telling me."

For an hour we rolled along through a rock-strewn wasteland, and then we came to an area of low hills and green sheets of canal ice. I was telling José that the toughest part of the run was over when the red light began to blink.

He looked at me. "Sand?"

I shook my head, frowning. "Not here. Something must be on the tracks, or crossing them."

It was a sand lizard, eighteen feet of senseless scarlet and yellow monstrosity. It had caught its leg under the track between two ties. All the beast had to do to free itself was to cease pulling forward, but it was too moronic for that.

Wade phoned me, but lost interest as soon as I explained why we'd stopped. "You know how to handle them," he said. And rang off.

I knew the technique, all right, but I wasn't happy about it. I explained to José that men who hunted the creature wore an over-suit of the super-resistant material we'd picked up at the beginning of our trip. It provided protection against a casual slash, though even it was not much help in a direct attack. In an emergency, safety lay behind the creature. Out of sight with it was out of mind.

Frank Gray sauntered out into the cab. He shook his head when I suggested that he and I help the lizard to free itself. He said, "That thing lives off a particularly tough cactus. It's got teeth you could cut rock with." He finished satirically, "Joe's the man to do the job. If his suit gets torn, it won't do him any harm."

José picked up a crowbar. "Where is this over-suit, señor?"

"We carry extras," I said reluctantly. "I'll go with you."

The over-suits covered us completely up to the neck. Above that, my own rigid vitrolite helmet offered me further protection. José had only his thickly insulated cap. If his people became permanent fixtures hereabouts, they'd have to make provision for such encounters as this.

I took a long oil gun from the tool box, and we climbed out of the cab. As it saw us approaching, the lizard turned its fiery head, and watched us. But it kept straining steadily forward.

I squirted oil into its fathomless blue eyes. Then the two of us prodded it from its left side, its right side and from behind. In response, the lizard hissed with its tongue, and made a rattling sound with its throat. But it continued to tug forward in that idiotic fashion.

The sun sagged toward mid-afternoon. Patiently José and I kept poking at the beast until, finally, some mental circuit seemed to close inside its brain. It ceased its forward movement. Hissing, it turned as if to come after us.

Its leg slipped easily and naturally from under the track. And it was free.

"José!" I yelled. "Get behind it."

The footing wasn't too good in the shifting sand, and José moved a little awkwardly. Four inch talons whipped the air so close to his cheek that I held my breath. Then he was behind the creature, which stopped turning, evidently having forgotten his existence.

The last we saw of it, it was laboriously climbing over a rock—instead of around it—and heading away from the tracks.

As we turned back toward the engine, there was a swish and a clank, and the long train moved toward us. I caught sight of Frank Gray high in the cab sitting at the controls. He waved mockingly as the powerful locomotive glided past us, gathering speed with every yard.

I grabbed at the handrail as it swept by, caught hold, and hung on with everything I had. Grimly, I reached for the next rung—just as the cab door above me slid open. Frank bent down and with a long wrench banged me on the fingers. Despite the protection of my heavy gloves, the instant pain and numbness broke my hold. Wildly, I grabbed at the rung below with my other hand.

Frank knelt, and swung his wrench again. This time he missed, but he drew sparks from the metal. I'd had enough, however. I couldn't let him cripple my other hand. It might send me under the wheels. Before he could strike again, I lowered my feet to the ground, started running, and let go.

I pitched headlong into the gravel of the roadbed. The cushion of air in my pressure suit saved me from serious

37

injury. But I was gasping as I scrambled shakily to my feet. My plan was to swing aboard the ore car, but as I fell in beside the train, running as swiftly in my bulky clothing as I could, I realized the train was going too fast. I was about to give up when a hand like iron grabbed the scruff of my neck.

"Señor, *run!*"

I ran till the salt of my exhaustion was in my mouth, until I could hardly see because of the tears in my eyes. I fumbled blindly for a rung of the ore car ladder to which José was clinging.

With his clutch supporting most of my weight, I caught the rung; and presently we lay on top of the car gasping for breath.

I stood up, still shaky. "I don't know what that buzzard is up to," I said, when I could speak again, "but we're going into the passenger car, and sit it out."

Our sudden appearance caused a minor sensation. I explained briefly what had happened, then picked up the phone and called the engine. It rang three times, and the line went dead. Since all power on the train was supplied by the locomotive, it seemed evident that Frank had cut the telephone system. His purpose was obvious—to prevent us from calling Marsopolis, our destination.

Silently, I cursed my stupidity for not having called there first. Frank might not have thought of it in time to stop me.

An official was shrugging. "He's behaving very foolishly. He can hardly wreck the train without danger to himself. All we have to do is sit tight."

A sudden thought struck me. I went to the gauge panel. The pressure was a full pound low, and the temperature was down slightly. I turned to the others, frowning.

"I hate to say this, but I'm afraid he's cut the power for our air conditioning."

Philip Barron looked pale, but his eyes were steady. "How long?"

"Not more than an hour," I said. "We could stand the cold, but we'll all pass out if the pressure drops much more than half—all except José, that is."

There was a grim silence. Then Barron glanced at José musingly, and said, "Yes, there is you. I suppose Gray figures it'll be his word against that of an Indian. The arrogant fool! Of course we could all sign a statement as to what actually happened, and leave it with you—"

"To hell with that!" said another official. "That might help José, and it might help justice, but what about us?"

I broke in at that point. "You're overlooking one thing. José can stand low pressure, but he can't breathe poisoned air, and he wouldn't last long outside after dark. We have only one chance." I turned. "Come on, José, let's get aboard that engine."

There was a fire ax in each of two emergency cases at opposite ends of the car. We armed ourselves with them, and a minute later climbed up to the top of the train and started forward. I could see the glistening blue and red locomotive with its bulging cab, and the figure of Frank Gray sitting in it.

What worried me was that there was a high-powered rifle in the cab—and at the moment José and I were as exposed as two sitting ducks. I doubted if Frank would fire unless he had to—bodies with bullets in them would be hard to explain away—but the possibility put a tension in me.

The shallow Martian sky was already darkening in the east, and Earth as an evening star shone brightly above the declining sun. There was still about an hour of daylight left, but since we were well over a hundred miles out, the fact gave me no comfort. We were in semi-mountainous country, and the track was too winding for high-speed travel.

I pulled my collar more tightly around my ears, and bent into the freezing wind. I noticed that José paused often to clap his hands together as we started forward along the top of the tank-tender, which carried the engine's water-reserve.

I saw, at this closer range, that Frank was watching us through the glass. The rifle lay on the window-ledge beside him, but he made no move to pick it up. Apparently, he was waiting to see what we were going to do.

I wasn't sure, myself. Get the cab doors open somehow, and hope to get in without being shot down.

We climbed to the top of the cab, and lay prone just above the doors, José on one side, and I on the other. Simultaneously, we swung our fire axes down against the heavy panes of the doors. Though shatterproof, they were hardly built to withstand such blows. On my side, a sizable section of glass broke loose, and fell inside.

That much was easy. Now, we had the ticklish problem of getting down there and reaching inside to unlock the doors.

I slid over the edge, and started down the steel ladder alongside the door. José's face was just disappearing over the other side. And still we were all right, being protected by the metal walls of the cab. To get at us, Frank would

39

have to poke his rifle through the hole in the glass on either side. But he wouldn't do that. He'd sit there amidships, and try to pot the first hand that reached in. After all, time was in his favor.

The long train glided along into a gathering twilight. The wheels ground and squealed with a steely sound. The engine groaned and shuddered, swaying as it curved past a steep embankment. I was nerving myself for that first, dangerous thrust—when a shot rang out inside the cab. It could only mean one thing: José had grabbed first.

Galvanized, I reached through the hole in the glass. And my hope was that Frank's gun might still be turned the other way.

Familiarity counted. I knew that lock, and I opened it with one quick twist of my fingers. And jerked my arm back.

A hole appeared in an unbroken part of the glass just above where my hand had been. And another shot sounded.

Hastily, I gave the door a strong push from the outside. It rolled back with a bang. And then there was Frank standing in the opening, leveling his rifle at me.

I pressed flat against the cab, but realized the futility of that, and struck at him with the ax. The blow fell short, as he drew back slightly. I could see his face through the transparent visor of his head globe, his lips twisted, his eyes glittering. In pulling away from me, he had let the muzzle of the rifle drop. Now, deliberately, he raised the gun once more.

As his finger tightened on the trigger, I threw my ax at him. He ducked. The handle of it brushed his shoulder.

For a third time, the muzzle of the gun came up; this time it pointed at my helmet. I thought despairingly: *We're proving our weakness, Frank and I.* This whole incident, the very arrival of José on Mars, had happened because our air supply *was* so vulnerable.

In some way, I had hoped to drive that fact home to him.

Even as I had the vague thought, I was stooping low, and trying to swing through the door into the cab. The rifle went off practically in my face. And Frank staggered drunkenly.

At least, that was the way things seemed to happen.

What amazed me was that the bullet intended for me went off into the gathering darkness.

And then a fire ax clattered to the floor of the cab out of nowhere—and the truth dawned on me. José had thrown it from the other door with enough luck or precision to smash Frank's head globe.

Frank was reeling. He would have plunged through the open door if I hadn't grabbed him instinctively. As I pushed him back inside and followed him, closing the door behind me, I saw José leaning against the opposite wall. His left arm was dangling, and dripped blood.

The grayness of shock was in his face. But he grinned at me as I dragged the limp body of Frank Gray toward the rod room, where I could apply pressure and save his life— so that a criminal court could decide what to do with it.

These days the story of José is the part of my Martian life my kids most want to hear about. Which makes me feel hopeful. Living here in retirement in Colorado at eighty-five hundred feet, I've managed to work up a community enthusiasm for a long-run scheme of mine.

We're building a town at seventeen thousand feet; and our children are already spending time up there. We've got it all figured out.

Their kids are going to be Martians.

THE PURPOSE

VIRGINIA MENTION's presence was quite accidental. She came out of a restaurant, and there were the fire trucks, and the smoke pouring out of the open door of a one-story building.

Virginia walked over, her reporter's instinct vaguely roused. Fires were long since out of her reportorial field, except that she was on the scene of this one. She visualized the tiny stick she would write:

> *Fire of so and so origin broke out this morning on the premises of thingumajerk. Slight damage.*

The sign that hung out in front of the building read:

FUTURIAN SCIENTIFIC
LABORATORIES
NEUROLOGICAL AND
ORGANICOLOGICAL
RESEARCH

She wrote that down, and the number, 411 Wainworth Avenue. When she had finished, the firemen were stamping out of the door. Virginia grabbed the chief by the arm.

"I'm from the *Herald*. I happened to be passing. Anything important?"

The chief was a big, clumsy man, slow of speech.

"Naw. Outer office furniture. Boss not in. Fire seems to have started in a wastepaper basket from a cigarette stub."

He went on, grinning: "The receptionist in there is a queer young drip. Never saw anybody so scared in my life. He was gobbling like a turkey when I left. Didn't speak a single understandable word."

He chuckled callously. "If that's the way he feels now, I can imagine what he'll be like when the boss arrives. Well, so long."

He walked off to his car.

Virginia Mention hesitated. Actually, she had all the information she wanted. But there was such a thing as personal curiosity. She walked over to the still open door.

It was a small office that she peered into. It contained three chairs and a streamlined counter in blue and white. That is, it had been blue and white. Now, it was a half charred mass, made uglier by the water that had been ruthlessly poured on it. Behind the counter was an electric adding machine of some kind.

Behind the counter, also, was the receptionist.

Virginia's mind suffered a considerable pause. The young man was tall and very thin, and he wore clothes that were too short for him in length and too wide for him in width. His face was hollow-cheeked and colorless. His chin, his forehead and his neck were covered with pimples, and he had an Adam's apple that kept moving and bobbing.

The apparition stared at her out of big, brown, terrified eyes. Its lips parted and spluttered gibberish at her. At least it would have been gibberish to anyone unaccustomed to the mumblings of editors and interviewees.

Virginia Mention translated aloud, transposing the pronoun: "What do I want? I'm a reporter. What's the value of the furniture?"

"Ubble dubble dow," said the young man.

"Don't know. Hmm, looks like a pretty complete mess, except for that comptometer, or whatever it is you've got behind the counter. I think I'll just put down: 'Damage to office furniture.' "

She wrote, then closed her book with a snap. "Well, be seeing you."

She intended to turn away and leave. But there was an interruption. A buzzer sounded. A man's deep, quiet voice said from some indeterminate point in the wall behind the young man:

"Edgar Gray, press button seventy-four."

The young man galvanized. For a moment, he seemed to be all arms and long legs, leaping behind the counter. Somehow he untangled himself. One of his long bony fingers touched a button on the "comptometer."

He stood then, eyes closed, pressing it down. Virginia had thought his face was as colorless as it could possibly be. But now it blanched, and visibly grew paler. A curious darkness seemed to creep over it finally, as if the half-life of the young man's body was suffering a great defeat.

The effect, the impression, was unnaturally sharp. Virginia stared blankly.

A minute passed; and then slowly the ungainly creature drew a deep breath. He took his hand away from the button. He opened his eyes. He saw Virginia. A vague flush of returning color stabbed at the lines of his cheekbones.

Virginia Mention found her voice. "What on earth was that?"

She saw that Edgar Gray was too far gone even to gibber. He stared at her glassily, and she had the impression that he was going to faint. With an audible gasp, he sank down in the charred chair.

He slumped there, looking like a sick dog.

Virginia said in a kindly voice, "Look, Edgar, the moment your boss gets here, you go home and lie down. And why not try eating something once in a while. It's good for the health."

She turned and went out. And forgot about him.

She had been gone about five minutes when a woman's clear, vibrant, yet low-pitched voice said from the wall, "Edgar!"

The gangling youth looked startled. Then, agitated, he stood up. The woman's voice said insistently: "Edgar, draw the blinds, shut the door, and turn on the lights."

Like an automaton, the young man carried out the commands. But his hands were shaking when he paused finally, and stared wide-eyed at the door which separated the rear of the building from the front.

There was a stirring there, a vague flickering of pinpoints of light. The door did not open, but a woman stepped through it.

Through it!

43

Daemonic woman! Her form was indistinct, insubstantial. She wore a white gown of a flimsy, transparent material. For a moment, the door was visible beyond her, through her.

She stood there as if in some strange and unearthly fashion waiting for physical completion.

Abruptly, she was no longer transparent. But whole. Real. She walked forward. Her hand came up and slapped his face, hard.

He half staggered, but managed to keep his balance. He began to whimper, tears of chagrin and hate.

"Edgar, you were told not to smoke."

Again, the hand came up. Again the resounding slap.

"You will remain here your usual time, and perform your duties. Do you understand?"

The woman stared at him bleakly. "Fortunately, I arrived in time to see that woman reporter. That is well for you. I was minded to use the whip."

She turned and walked toward the inner door, paused for a moment, and then stepped through it, and was gone.

Accidents begin, and human nature carries on. Before the fire, Virginia had passed the Futurian Science Laboratories a hundred times without ever noticing that it was there. Yet now she was aware of it.

Two days and a morning after the fire, she emerged from the same restaurant with her husband. She watched him stride off toward the university, then turned and went her own way. As she came to the Futurian sign, she paused with a sudden memory. She peered through the great plate glass window.

"Hmm!" she said.

There was a new counter in place of the half burnt one, and a new chair. In the chair sat Edgar Gray, reading a magazine.

She could see his blotched face, and she had a clear profile of his Adam's apple. An empty box lunch stood on the counter beside him.

It was a thoroughly normal scene; and she didn't give it a second thought. But that night at eight-ten, when her husband was escorting her to the theater, she glanced out of the taxi, as it passed Futurian.

The enormous window glowed from the reflections of a spotlight behind the counter. Under the spot sat Edgar reading.

"He keeps long hours," said Virginia out loud.

"Did you speak?" asked Professor Mention.

"It's nothing, Norman."

A week later, coming home from a party at a quarter after eleven at night, their car passed Futurian. And there was Edgar under his light, reading.

"Well, of all things," exploded Virginia. "Whoever owns that joint sure has got hold of a sucker."

Her husband grinned at her. "Working on a newspaper has certainly enriched your vocabulary, sweet."

Virginia gave him briefly the sequence of her experience with Futurian. She watched his face crinkle, his fine eyes narrow with thought. But in the end he only shrugged.

"Maybe it's Edgar's turn to be on the night shift. Since the war and the absorption of returned men into the planetary services, there's been a tremendous shortage of ordinary help, as witness the fact that you are compelled by law to work; and we have to eat vitaminless food in restaurants because you can't work and cook too." He grimaced. "Restaurants, wagh!"

Virginia laughed; then soberly: "There may be a manpower shortage, but the people who are available are treated like tin gods."

"Uh, I suppose you're right. I'm afraid I can't help you then. As a lecturer on practical psychology, my city contacts are becoming less every day. Why not ask Old Cridley in your office? He's supposed to be a good man."

Cridley, the science editor, stroked his beard. "Futurian Science Laboratories," he said. "No, I can't say that I've heard of them. Let me see."

He drew a commercial register across the desk toward him, opened it. "Hmm," he said. "Yes, here it is. . . . Research. . . . Doesn't tell you much, but"—he looked up— "they're legal."

He added with a sardonic smile, "I somehow had the impression you thought they weren't."

Virginia said, "There was a vague idea in the back of my mind that they might be worth a story for the magazine section."

In a way that was true—Old Cridley was reaching for the phone. "I'll ring up Dr. Blair, the only neurologist on my list. Perhaps he can give us some information."

The phone conversation was prolonged. Virginia had time to smoke a cigarette. At last the old man clicked down the receiver. He looked up.

"Well," he said. "You've run into something."

"You mean the place is phony."

45

He grinned. "No, no, the other way around. It's big. It's a ten, twenty, thirty *billion* dollar concern."

"That little place!" said Virginia.

"It seems," said Old Cridley, "there are duplicates of that little place right around the world. There's one on some main avenue of every city of two hundred thousand or more in the entire world. There's one at Canalis Majoris on Mars, and one each on the two principal islands of Venus."

"But what do they do?"

"Ostensibly, they do research work. But actually it's a high pressure organization to get people to put up money for research. Some lame attempts have been made to investigate the outfit, but so far every attempt has died while still in the embryo stage.

"Dr. Dorial Cranston, the founder, used to be quite a man in his field. But about fifteen years ago, he went money mad, and developed this beautiful system of milking gold from soft-hearted dopes who want to help science. The key moochers are men and women whose personalities are plus and then some. They shine like jewels in a crowd. You know the type. You've got a long start in the direction of that kind of personality yourself."

Virginia let the compliment pass. "But have they ever made any worthwhile research?"

"Not that I know of."

Virginia frowned. "Funny we haven't heard more about them. I think I'll look into it further."

It began to rain shortly after five o'clock. Virginia Mention retreated deeper into the doorway of Sam's Haberdashery, and stared miserably up at the sullen skies.

The idea was just beginning to penetrate that she was in for a night. Oddly, she had no intention of giving up. Logic said that Edgar ought to be watched over the supper hour.

He was going to be watched.

At seven the rain petered out. Virginia oozed out of her doorway, and paced up and down glaring at the office across the street. A light had flicked on, the same shaded counter lamp she had previously observed. Under it sat Edgar Gray reading a magazine.

"The little coward!" Virginia Mention raged silently. "Hasn't he got guts enough to stand up for his rights? I know he was in there this morning."

The fury faded with the minutes, yielded to the passing of the hours. At ten minutes after ten, she dashed hurriedly

46

into the restaurant, gulped a cup of coffee, and phoned her husband.

Professor Mention's chuckle on the phone, as she described her vigil, made her feel better. "Personally," he said when she had finished, "I'm going to bed in another hour. I'll see you in the morning."

"I've got to hurry," Virginia breathed. "I'm scared silly he'll leave while I'm in here."

But the light was still there when she got outside. And so was Edgar.

He was reading a magazine.

It was funny, but suddenly she began to picture him there in terms of years. Day after day after day, she thought, Edgar Gray coming to work in the morning and remaining until a tremendously late hour at night. And no one cared; no one even knew, apparently. For surely self-consciousness such as Edgar carried around with him could not exist if he had a normal home life.

She began to feel sorry for Edgar as well as for herself. What a life he was leading, what an incredible inhuman life.

She watched him jump to his feet, and press down one of the "comptometer" keys.

Virginia Mention shook her head, bewildered. This business made less sense every second. Eleven o'clock came and passed. Eleven thirty. At eleven-thirty-two, the light blinked out abruptly, and after a minute Edgar emerged from the front door.

It was a quarter after eight the next morning when Virginia Mention staggered up the single flight of stairs to her apartment.

"Don't," she murmured to her husband, "ask me any questions. I've been up all night. I'll tell you everything about a month from now when I wake up. Phone the office, will you, that I won't be in?"

She did muster the energy to undress, and get into her pajamas, and crawl into bed.

When she wakened, her wristwatch said four thirty—and a woman in a white evening dress was sitting in the chair beside her vanity.

The woman had, Virginia Mention saw after a blank moment, blue eyes and a very lovely face. That is, it would have been lovely if it hadn't been so hard, so cold. Her body was long and slim, like Virginia's own. In one of her finely shaped hands, she fingered a knife with a thin, cruelly long blade.

The woman broke the silence softly:

"Now that you have started your investigation of us, you must also bear the consequences, the rewards of zealousness. We're all very glad you're a woman. Women weigh less."

She paused. She smiled a fleeting, enigmatic smile, and watched alertly as Virginia slowly sat up in the bed. Virginia had time to think that she had seen this creature somewhere; and then the woman went on:

"Women also arouse more sympathy. . . . My dear, you've come into something you won't forget for"—she lingered over the phrase caressingly—"the rest of your life."

At last Virginia found voice. "How did you get in here?"

Except for the sense of recognition, that was actually as far as her mind had gotten. The woman's words, the enormous threat in them, would catch up to her only gradually. Her voice was shriller, as she repeated, "How . . . into my apartment?"

The blonde woman smiled, showing her teeth. "Through the wall of course."

It sounded like very unveiled satire. It roused Virginia Mention as nothing else could. She drew a deep breath—and was herself.

Narrow-eyed, conscious suddenly of the eerie quality of this meeting, she stared at the other. Her gaze lighted on the devilish knife and, just like that, fear came.

She pictured Norman coming in, and finding her stabbed to death. She pictured being dead, while he was still alive. She pictured herself in a coffin.

She began to feel warm with terror.

Her gaze flashed up to the woman's face—and terror sagged.

"Why," she said aloud, wonderingly, "I know now who you are. You're the wife of the local electrical tycoon, Phil Patterson. I've seen your picture in the society pages."

Fear was fading fast now. She couldn't have explained the psychology, except that people you knew, and people of importance, didn't commit murder. Murderers were strangers, unhuman creatures who emerged briefly from a mass of meaningless faces, after the police had caught them, and, once executed, retreated into the depths of your memory, never again to be recognized.

Virginia found her voice again. "So," she said, "you're one of the Futurian Science Laboratories crowd."

The woman nodded brightly. "That's right. That's the crowd I belong to. And now"—she sat up a little straighter;

her voice was as resonant as a bell—"I really mustn't waste any more time in idle chatter."

Virginia said in a level voice, "What have you done to Edgar Gray? He's a thing, not a human being."

The woman seemed not to hear. She was hesitating. At last, cryptically: "I must be sure you know enough. Have you ever heard of Dorial Cranston?"

There must have been a look in Virginia's face, for the woman said, "Ah, I see you've got that far. Thank you very much. You could have been very dangerous."

She broke off. She stood up. She said in an oddly drab voice, "That's really all I need to know. It is silly to give information to people who are about to die."

She was at the bed before Virginia could grasp the deadly intent behind the words. The knife, which Virginia had almost forgotten, flashed up in the woman's hand, then down at Virginia's left breast.

There was a pain like fire, a tearing sensation at her flesh. She had time to see the knife hilt protruding from just above her heart.

Blackness came, blotting out the unbearable agony.

Professor Norman Mention was whistling happily under his breath as he entered the apartment. The hands of the hall clock were poised just over the seven. By the time he had deposited his hat, coat and cane in the empty living room and kitchen, the minute hand had moved in stately fashion to five after seven.

He noticed, while hanging up his coat, that Virginia's current coat and hat and things were all there.

Still whistling, but more softly now, he walked over to the door of her room, and knocked.

No sound came from inside. Rather hastily, he retreated to the living room, and took up the copy of the *Evening Herald* that he had bought on his way home.

He was a highly trained reader, with a capacity of just under twelve hundred words a minute, but the effect of the enormous speed was partially canceled by the fact that he read everything but the society columns.

It was half past eight before he folded the paper.

He sat, frowning. He thought irritably that if Virginia had been sleeping since that morning, then she ought to be roused. And besides, it was time she satisfied his curiosity as to the results of her vigil before the Futurian Science Laboratories the night before.

He knocked at the bedroom door, and, when there was no answer, opened it, and went inside.

The room was empty.

Professor Mention was not nonplussed. He stared ruefully at the unmade bed, and then shook his head, and smiled. After twelve years of being married to Virginia, he was well aware of the intricate maneuverings of women newspaper reporters.

It was not like Virginia to leave her room untidy, but it had happened at least twice before, and each time he had done what he did now: He made the bed, ran the carpet sweeper over the rug and mopped the floor.

When he was making the bed, he noticed a bloodstain on the sheet.

"Darn it," Professor Mention muttered irritably, "Virginia oughtn't to go out when her nose is bleeding, and without her coat, too."

He went finally back to the living room, and tuned in a comedy team, whose popular appeal he had for some weeks vainly tried to analyze.

The failure was repeated this night. He laughed hollowly once. When the ordeal was over, he clicked off the radio, and began to whistle softly under his breath.

After a while his watch said that it was eleven. Perhaps, if he phoned the *Herald* office— No, that wouldn't do. She was supposed to be sick.

He picked up a detective novel he had been intending to read for a month. At twelve o'clock he finished it, and looked at his watch.

He had felt the worry creeping up on him for some time. It tingled in the back of his mind all the while that he was reading the story. The ending, the act of closing the book, was like a cue.

Professor Mention stood up. He swore aloud. He told himself he was very angry with Virginia. She oughtn't to go off like that, and then not phone him.

He decided to go to bed. He woke up with a start. The dials of his watch showed eight o'clock, and the sun was peering through the window. Unnerved, he climbed from under the cozy quilts, and went into Virginia's room.

It was unchanged.

The important thing, Professor Mention told himself precisely, was to be logical. Suppose he did go to the police— after, of course, duly verifying that she was not at the office or at a few other places he could think of.

The police would ask questions. Description? Well, she

50

was strikingly good-looking, five feet six inches tall, sort of redheaded though not exactly. There was an odd glint in her hair that—

Mention stopped that thought with a conscious effort. This was no time for romantic touches. "Redhead," he said aloud, firmly, "and she was wearing—"

He paused grimly. At this point at least, scientific accuracy was possible.

Resolutely he headed for her clothes closet. For ten minutes he fumbled with increasing gloom among some four dozen dresses striving to picture which one was missing. The amazing thing was the number of dresses that he couldn't remember ever having seen before.

At the end of ten minutes, he knew himself defeated. He turned back into the bedroom—just as the hazy figure of a man stepped through the wall of the room.

He stood there for a moment, like a motion picture image focused on a cloud. The insubstantial form of him began to thicken. It became a man in evening clothes, a man with arrogant, sardonic eyes, who bowed coolly, and said, "Don't go to the police. Don't do anything foolish. Perform your normal duties, and make reasonable excuses for your wife's absence. After that, wait. Just wait."

He turned. His body changed, became transparent. He stepped into the wall. And was gone.

There seemed nothing else to do. There seemed *nothing* to do. Yet during the war he had learned the habit of decision.

Mention hesitated. Then slowly he went into his room, and removed the Luger automatic from the back of the drawer where he had kept it for years. It was a war trophy; and because he had won *the* medal it required no license.

He stood fingering it with a gathering skepticism. But finally, conscious of its symbolic importance to his morale, he put it into his coat pocket, and started out into the morning.

He was halfway to the university before it struck him that it was Saturday. Mention stopped short in the street, laughed harshly. To think that he had imagined he was taking it calmly.

He stood undecided, grim, thinking with a sudden dismay: a man who could walk through solid walls! What had Virginia run across?

His brain sagged before the implications. He felt strangely boneless, and dry inside, as if his body was all shriveled up

51

by an intense inner heat. His fingers, when he raised them to his burning forehead, were moistless, almost abrasive.

He looked at them, startled. Then hurried into a corner drugstore.

"Give me an injection of blood plasma," he said. "I've just narrowly escaped being run over, and I feel dizzy."

It was only partly a lie. There was no question but that he was suffering from shock, and in no mild form either.

"That'll be one dollar," said the druggist a minute later.

Mention paid it gratefully, and strode out. His brain was working again; and his body had lost the drab sense of approaching unconsciousness. What he needed now above everything else was to appraise his situation.

He thought drably: the facts were: Futurian Science Laboratories—Edgar Gray—Dr. Dorial Cranston—a strange cold-faced man who walked through walls.

He stopped there. Once more he felt himself change color. He whispered huskily, "It's impossible. I must have dreamed it. The human body is a structure evolved from a more primitive type. Therefore, unless—"

Higden's thesis! Only if a man had once been innately capable of passing through substance, could outside energy help him do it now. Higden's thesis that present day man was a degenerate from a higher form must be correct.

Mention laughed curtly. He lashed at himself. "Am I having an academic argument with myself when Virginia is—"

His mind faltered. He felt the strain coming back. He saw another drugstore sign ahead. He went in and bought his second and last plasma injection.

Afterward, physically buoyed but mentally depressed, he seated himself in one of the booths. An hour later, the reality was still the same.

He was a badly frightened man. And since the fear was not for himself, there was nothing he could do about it but what the stranger had suggested:

Wait!

SUNDAY: At eleven A.M., he went downtown and peered through the plate glass window of the Futurian Science Laboratories. Edgar was there, a long skinny monstrosity, absorbed in a magazine.

After ten minutes, Edgar hadn't moved except to turn over pages. Mention went back to the apartment.

MONDAY: He had one period without a class. There were

52

hree other professors in the recreation room. Mention turned he subject to the Futurian Science Laboratories.

Troubridge, physics professor, jumped at the use of the aame, then laughed with the others.

Cassidy, assistant professor of English, said, "It sounds traight out of Tommy Rocket, the new comic sensation."

The third man changed the subject.

TUESDAY: He had no free periods. During the noon hour ae went into the library, and asked for books by and about Dr. Dorial Cranston.

There were two by the doctor, and one about him by a Dr. Thomas Torrance. The first published of Cranston's two volumes was entitled *Physical Affinity of the Human Race*. Astonishingly, it was a tract on pacifism, a ringing condemnation of international slaughter, an hysterical document against war, in which the worthy doctor enlarged emotionally upon the theme that men were brothers under the skin. He advocated the extension of the handshake as a symbol of friendship, urged the adoption of promiscuous kissing among men and women alike, and spoke highly of the Eskimo custom of rubbing noses.

"Alien peoples," he wrote, "are electrically charged against each other, and only sustained physical contact will resolve the difference in their potential. A white co-ed, for instance, who allows herself to be kissed by a Chinese student will find that the hundredth kiss is far from repulsive. In the interval the man has become for her a human being in some fashion which she cannot analyze. The next step, marriage, comes into her thoughts; and what began as a desire for exotic thrills has, through contact, attained a more honorable status. We see these marriages taking place all around us, and, unless we have ourselves established similar contacts, we cannot begin to comprehend how they ever happened."

Basically, stripped of its pacifistic ranting, that was the book. The lunch hour was over when Mention finished his perusal. He took the other two out, resolved to read them that night at home.

The second Cranston book was a repetition, in even more violent and dogmatic language, of the first. The man was obviously a bug on his subject; and it required a real effort for Mention to read the second volume to the end.

He picked up the Torrance biography of Cranston, flipped it open at chapter one, and read:

53

Dr. Dorial Cranston, pacifist, neurologist extraordinary, was born in Louisville, Kentucky, in—

Mention closed the book wearily. He was willing to concede that physical contact would do wonders for human relations. But it was already clear that the reading of old books about Cranston had no connection with the present reality.

WEDNESDAY: He had no new thoughts.

THURSDAY: Professor Troubridge fell into step beside Mention, as the latter started home.

"Norman," he said, "about your reference the other day to Futurian Science Laboratories. If they've approached you, don't hesitate. They can do what they claim."

For a moment, the words sounded as if they had been created at random by a mechanical machine. But there was meaning finally. Meaning so important that Mention fought doggedly to prevent himself from blathering questions that would reveal his ignorance. He gulped, paused disastrously, and then was saved, as Troubridge went on:

"Three years ago, my physician, Dr. Hoxwell, told me that my heart wouldn't last six months. I went to the Mayo Clinic. They confirmed the diagnosis. It was a month after that, when I was already despairing, that I was approached by the Futurian people, and informed that I could be furnished with a new heart for ten thousand dollars. They *showed* me a heart in a glass case, beating. It was a living heart, Norman, and they said it made no difference what organ I needed at any time, they could supply it, provided I had the money."

Mention said, "I thought organic transplantations were impossible because—"

He stopped. Realization came that that wasn't really the thought in his mind. There was something else, a picture, a question that roared through his brain with the clamor of a tidal wave. As from a great distance, he heard Troubridge say:

"They can do it because they've discovered a new principle in organic electricity."

The thought that had come to Mention dominated the whole universe of his mind now. In a dead voice, he uttered the terrible words: "Where do they get their *live* replacement organs?"

"Eh!" said Troubridge. His eyes widened. A stunned expression crept over his face as he whispered, "I never thought of that."

By the time Mention reached the empty apartment, he didn't want to think of it either.

There came purpose.

He paced the living room of the apartment that night in a fury at himself for having waited so long. And yet the problem was still: what should he do, what *could* he do that would be effective?

Go to the police?

He felt immensely reluctant, because there was still a chance. They wouldn't have told him not to go to the authorities merely to keep him quiet for a week—if at the end of that time he went anyway.

He could mail a letter to his bank to put into his safety deposit box, which would be opened if something happened to him. . . . Yes, he would do that.

He wrote the letter, then sat at his desk striving to think. After a long period during which nothing would come, he began heavily to write down a list of possibilities, item by item:

Virginia accidentally runs across Futurian Labs. She disappears.

I am warned by a man who walks through walls. I discover that:

(1) *Dr. Dorial Cranston, founder of Futurian, is a fanatic pacifist as well as a neurologist.*

(2) *That Futurian sells human organs on a mass scale to rich men. (This is probably their purely commercial enterprise, their source of income.)*

(3) *The ability to walk through walls is obviously a means of power, and they are not sharing that with anyone. Yet they seem unworried by the fact that I know about it.*

(4) *Cridley, science editor of the Herald, told Virginia that several attempts to investigate Futurian were stifled in embryo stage, proof that they have influence in high places.*

(5) *There is absolutely no reason why they should treat Virginia any differently than they do the other—sources—of their live organs.*

Mention wrote the last sentence grimly, then stared down at the list, dissatisfied. It seemed to offer no lead that he could follow with even the vaguest possibility that he would find Virginia.

After a moment, he wrote slowly:

If I went to the police, and they arrested Dr. Cranston and Edgar Gray, Cranston would walk out through the walls of the prison, and Edgar would—

Mention lifed his pen and stared with a sudden heady surmise at what he had written. Edgar! If it was true that there were Futurian shops in all the large cities, then there were hundreds of Edgars all over the world acting as receptionists. But—Edgar!

Virginia had disappeared after a night of investigating Edgar.

What had she discovered?

Excitement touched his mind, then flared through his body. He looked at the mantel clock. It showed one minute to ten. If he hurried, he could get downtown just about the time that Virginia had phoned the night she followed Edgar.

He might be trailed of course, as she must have been.

Edgar was still there. Mention parked his car a little way along the street, but at a point from which he could see Edgar plainly, where he sat under his spotlight.

Edgar was reading a magazine. At eleven thirty, Edgar rose, put on his hat, switched out the light, and came out of the door. He locked the door behind him.

He did not look around him but headed straight for the restaurant where Mention had often eaten with Virginia. Mention climbed out of the car, and walked over to the restaurant window.

Edgar was at the counter, wolfing a piece of pie and a cup of coffee. He put some money on the counter; and Mention had time only to turn his back, as Edgar emerged from the door.

Edgar hurried off down the street. After five minutes he turned into the dimly lighted foyer of an all-night theater. Mention debouched from his car again, bought his ticket a little breathlessly—and a minute after that watched Edgar sink into a seat well down in the front of the theater. He edged into the third row behind Edgar.

At three o'clock Edgar was still in the show, goggling bright-eyed at the screen. It was shortly after that that Mention fell asleep.

He wakened with a start. His watch said six forty-five. Edgar was hunched down in his seat, his legs over the back of the seat ahead. But he wasn't sleeping.

At seven forty, he got up abruptly, and hurried out of the theater. Straight for the restaurant he headed, with Mention following a hundred feet behind. It took four minutes for Edgar's meal to be served, three for him to eat it. At the counter the girl handed him two of their made-up box lunches; and then he was outside.

He paused in a drugstore to purchase four magazines.

At one minute to eight he unlocked the door of the Futurian Science Laboratories, and settled himself in the chair behind the counter. He picked up one of the magazines and began to read.

Apparently, his long day was about to repeat itself.

Now what?

Back in the apartment, Mention wakened himself with a cold shower, hurried through a breakfast of toast and coffee, and then set out for the university. His first class was not until twenty to ten; and so he had a reasonable amount of time to ponder his findings.

Actually, what had he discovered? Nothing except another facet of the neurological research of Dr. Cranston. The man was undoubtedly a genius. Perhaps *he* had passed over the books by and about Cranston too hastily.

There was nothing to do about that until night. Then he took down from the shelf, where he had put it unread, the biography of Dr. Dorial Cranston by Thomas Torrance, Ph.D.

As he opened the volume, he saw that there was a picture in the frontispiece, a photograph of a man standing on the terrace of a swanky house.

Mention jumped as he saw the picture, then stared and stared at the cold, sardonic face and powerful body. The caption underneath read:

The author, Dr. Thomas Torrance, at his palatial home in New Dellafield, Massachusetts.

There was no mistaking the identity. Torrence was the man who had stepped through a solid wall, and warned him not to call the authorities.

He couldn't think. The sleep he had missed the night before, the sheer nervous exhaustion of the past week, took their toll of his brain now, when he needed strength to examine the potentialities of his great discovery.

His last thought before he finally allowed the sleep to

engulf him was: Whatever had happened to Virginia had happened during her sleep that day. Perhaps he too—

He woke up annoyed that he was safe, and then, slowly, he grew aware of a purpose. His watch said eleven fifteen. He stood up and headed straight for the phone.

Considering that his call was from California, it went through swiftly. After fifteen minutes the phone rang.

"Your party, sir," said the operator.

Mention drew a deep breath; then tensely, "Hello!" he said.

There was the sound of the operator hanging up, a pause, and then a familiar voice said quietly:

"What's on your mind, professor?"

Mention gulped. The words were all wrong; and the confident implications of the quiet tone in which they were uttered, stunned him. Incredibly, he felt ridiculous, as he said:

"Torrance, unless my wife is returned at once, I shall take action."

There was a little silence, then a half chuckle.

"I'm curious," said the voice, "just what kind of action you have in mind."

The arrogance was almost palpable now. Mention was conscious of a distinct emptiness inside him. He fought off the feeling. He said thickly, "First of all, I shall go to the newspapers."

"Nope, won't do!" said Torrance in an oddly judicial tone. "We've had every newspaper owner in the country in our organic wards. And, just in case you have other ideas, that also goes for state governors, lieutenant governors, states attorneys, cabinet ministers and a few others."

"That must be a lie," said Mention. He felt suddenly colder, more sure of himself. "It's against the law of averages that every one of those men could have had something wrong with him."

Torrance's laughter peeled over the receiver.

"I'm afraid," he said, "we'd be waiting yet if we had depended on Nature." His voice tightened. "Our main base of operations, Mention, is on North America, so we couldn't take chances with men like that. We went after them, and they're now, I assure you, solidly in our clutches."

He ground on, without pause.

"I won't explain the how of that, professor. Just take my word for it. You could of course go to the local police. We never bother with small fry until they bother us. Then we neutralize them. I hope I have made everything clear. And now, if you don't mind, I shall—"

Rage came so abruptly to Mention that he had no time to fight it.

"Torrance," he shouted. "What have you done with my wife?"

The reply was cool: "My dear feloow, this will surprise you. But *we* haven't got your wife. Goodbye."

There was a distinct click.

Doggedly, Mention put a call through to the small city The reply was cool: "My dear fellow, this will surprise residence of the author.

"Hello," he said, when the connection was finally made. "Is that you, Dr. Cranston?"

There was a chuckle over the receiver. "My, my," said the voice of Thomas Torrance, "but you are persistent."

Mention replaced the phone on its cradle without another word. Just how a call to New Jersey could be switched to Massachusetts was not clear. But he accepted the fact of what he had heard.

He was turning blankly toward the living room—when Virginia, a hazy figure, stepped through the wall of the hallway.

She was wearing pajamas; and the insubstantial form of her—thickened—before his eyes. For a long moment she stood there staring at him with anguished eyes.

She began to cry. Tears streamed down her cheeks. Her face grew wet. She ran towards him. Her arms clutched him with the strength of panic-stricken terror.

"Oh, darling, darling," she sobbed. "They've killed me. *They've killed me!*"

She moaned and cried in those minutes before full awakening. The horror of what she had last seen—the knife in her heart—was strong in her mind, like acid burning.

She wakened with a start.

She was lying in a large, curious room. It took a long moment to grasp that she was stretched out on a table; and a full minute must have passed before she grasped dazedly that the knife was no longer protruding from just below her breast.

With a shock like fire, it struck her that there was no pain, and that she was alive.

Alive! She sat up shakily. And instantly sagged back at the sharp splinter of pain that jabbed at her left breast.

The pain subsided. But the fact that it had come at all left her weak with fear. She lay, not daring to move.

She grew more aware of her surroundings.

The room she was in was about a hundred feet square. It was almost completely filled with little glass cases. The cases lined the walls, and stood on the floors, with only narrow aisles between them; and each case was divided into compartments about two feet square.

By turning her head, Virginia could see plainly the inside of the compartments against the wall to her right and left.

Each one contained what looked like a human heart, suspended from a small machine in the ceiling of the compartment.

She stared at them blankly; and she was on the point of turning away when the realization struck with a terrible force: the hearts were beating.

Strongly, steadily, they expanded and contracted. There was no pause in that quiet movement. The sustained quality of it calmed her, quieted her overstrained nerves. After five minutes, consciousness came that she ought to examine her personal situation again.

Cautiously, almost without fear this time, she lifted her head. For the first time, now, she saw what she had missed before:

A square of cloth had been cut out of her silk pajamas. There was a clean, white bandage carefully taped where the knife had penetrated.

Curiously, it was the pure whiteness of the bandage that braced her. It suggested that she was being looked after. The death that had so violently threatened her was frustrated.

She began to think of herself as being in the private surgery of some neighborhood doctor. She must have been rushed to him for emergency attention.

She was alive, but it seemed odd that no one was attending her. Surely, she wasn't going to be left here on this table.

Just like that, anger came. And because fear was still a wavering, dark curtain in the back of her mind, the anger was unnaturally violent and unreasonable.

Anger faded before the passing of the minutes. If she had been in a bed, she would have lain quietly, and awaited events. But it was impossible to remain on this flat, hard table.

She had allowed her head to sink back to the surface;

now she raised it again. Carefully, putting most of her weight on her right arm, she raised herself to a sitting position.

Nothing happened. No pain, not a twinge of the anguish that had struck at her a little while before. Evidently, the important thing was not to move too rapidly.

She sat for a minute on the edge of the table, her legs dangling, looking around at the fantastic total of human hearts all around her.

She began to be afraid. It was unreal, that row on row of quietly beating hearts, each in its compartment, each functioning with a steady *lifeness*.

Most disturbing of all was the complete absence of human beings. Except for its unnatural furniture, the room seemed utterly empty; it unnerved her.

Trembling, Virginia lowered herself to the floor. She stood very still, letting the strength flow back into her body.

It was pleasantly surprising to realize that there *was* strength.

She walked along an aisle, glancing only fleetingly at the double line of hearts. The number of them made her uneasy again. There was a door at the far end of the room. One of the hinges, and the lock, were badly smashed. It opened easily, however, onto a stairway that led upward to another door.

She climbed with a sense of urgency, a conviction that she must get away from those phalanxes of soundlessly beating hearts.

The second door was metal. But its lock too had been roughly handled, though there was a key in the shattered keyhole.

She opened the door, eager now; and stepped out onto a jungle pathway. A brilliant sun was shining down on a hilltop clearing a few feet away. She climbed toward it, reached it, and stood briefly paralyzed by what she saw.

Virginia Mention paused in her recount of what had happened. Her husband had laid her down on the bed; and from that prostrate position she looked up at him. He was staring down at her with a grim tenderness.

"But you're not dead. You're here with me, alive and safe."

She said hopelessly, "You don't understand, sweetheart. You . . . don't . . . understand."

Professor Mention replied quietly, "Go on, my dear. What did you see that startled you?"

She was on an island, an atoll green with jungle, and surrounded by a blue ocean that extended on every side as far as the eye could see.

The sun, though still high in the heavens, was well past midday. The heat was blasting; it made her feel ill.

Dizzy, she turned to look at the door through which she had come. She expected to see a building, but there wasn't one.

Undergrowth spread in a thick tangle all around where the building should have been. Even the open door was half hidden by lichens that intertwined cunningly all over the exposed metal face of the door.

There was a strong odor of dying vegetation.

To Virginia, standing there under that lonely brilliant sky, came an unreasoning fear that the door would close, and shut her forever out in this empty world.

She stared down toward the door. She had taken only three steps when a thin, screaming sound touched her eardrums. The sound came from the remote sky to her right. It was faint and faraway at first, but grew louder and louder.

After a moment of worried puzzlement, she recognized with relief the origin of the sound: a jet-propelled plane.

It came into sight, a black point in the blue heavens. It took on size. It was a twenty-jet machine about two hundred feet long, wingless except for the upward bending wing struts supporting its vertical jet fuselages.

It flashed past, unaware of her frantically waving arm, a passenger express plane bound from beyond the eastern horizon toward the setting sun.

She watched it till it disappeared into the sun-fire, hope dying gradually. The return of silence startled her. Shocked, and enormously depressed, she remembered again her fear of the door closing upon her.

She entered it hastily, closing it behind her, but not locking it. Before, she hadn't noticed how cool and comfortable the "weather" was in the great room, nor had she been aware of the indirect lighting. Now her attention fastened eagerly on the evidences of mechanization. There must, she thought anxiously, be a basement, perhaps other underground floors. The electric power must have a source.

For a timeless period she searched for a second door, but succeeded only in tiring herself. She lay down on a couch which she discovered at one end of the room; and she was resting there when her darting gaze brought her awareness for the first time that each transparent compartment of the showcases had a little placard attached to it.

A name was printed on the first one she examined; it read:

> Morrison, John Laurance
> 257 Carrigut Street,
> New York City.

The second one also had name, and nothing else. Virginia walked slowly along the line of compartments. She was at the N's before it struck her that the compartments were ticketed in alphabetical order.

Her mind made a fantastic jump; and she rushed over to the P's. She found the name she wanted instantly; and, having discovered it, stared at it blankly:

> Patterson, Mrs. Philip
> (Cecilia Dorothy)
> Suite 2, Mayfair Apts.,
> Crest City, California.

The blankness ended abruptly. With a gasp, she hurried over to the Grays. But Edgar wasn't there. The only person with anything like his name was:

> Grey, Percival Winfield,
> 3 Huntington Court,
> West Tuttenham,
> London, England.

Briefly calm, Virginia stood watching Percival's heart as it beat on quietly. She was thinking:

But of course! Edgar was not one of them. He was a slave, held somehow in a thrall that included an utter inability to sleep.

After a little there seemed nothing to think about that. But another thought came, a thought so tremendous that her mind rejected it three times as she ran back toward the M section. But each time it came back stronger and more terrible.

She found the compartment she sought. The heart in it was slightly different from the others. It was beating steadily, but it had a small neat bandage over a portion of the flesh wall facing her. The placard on the glass was equally unmistakable:

63

Virginia Mention stared at the thing with avid eyes, like a bird fascinated by a monstrous reptile. A sound came from behind her, but she heard it only vaguely. It came again, and this time it snatched at her attention.

It was the sound of a man clearing his throat. A slow, quiet voice said, "Dr. Dorial Cranston at your service, madam."

Virginia had no memory of turning. Nor did she so much as think of the fact that she was in pajamas in front of a strange man.

The man standing before her was old; and he wasn't at all what she had expected. Just what she *had* expected she couldn't have said, but not a gentle face. Not a sad-looking, old, old man with tired blue eyes, who bowed gracefully, and spoke again, in the same oddly matter-of-fact way:

"The problem of keeping organs alive outside of the body was solved in various countries before, during and after the second great war. But the best work was done in Russia. I like particularly the various mechanical addenda, such as the autojector, which they brought to a high degree of perfection. Of course, in the preservation of the organs, I merely used the discoveries of the Russians and of the scientists of other nations. I'm a nerve man myself. I—"

It was at that point that Virginia found her voice. She had been standing staring glassily, but with her courage coming back instant by instant, her eyes brightening before the mildness, the obvious harmlessness of this old man. Yet, in spite of terrible relief, there was a tenseness in her, a need to *know*, unlike anything she had ever experienced in her life.

In a piercing voice, she cried, "But if this is my heart"— she jerked her arm with automatic stiffness toward the living flesh behind the glass—"what's inside me now? *What?*"

The harmless old man looked suddenly cool and unfriendly. He said in a frigid voice:

"You were stabbed to death, weren't you? Yet now you're here talking to me. Don't worry about what's inside you. I took out a lot more than just your heart. Don't bother searching for more operation cuts. I don't work that way. Come over here."

Without waiting to see if she would follow, he turned and walked with the sedate bent-knees movement of age toward the back of the room. He touched something embedded in a narrow stretch of bare wall. A door swung noiselessly open, revealing a set of stairs leading downward.

The room below was as large as the one above; and it too was completely filled with glass cases. The contents of the compartments were various: hearts, lungs, liverlike organs; there was even a pancreas and a few pairs of kidneys.

All of the organs seemed alive. The lungs were definitely so. They expanded and contracted gently but with unmistakable strength and sureness.

The old man paused before a compartment containing a pair of lungs. He motioned wordlessly toward the placard attached to it. Virginia braced herself, as she stepped forward. The bracing helped. It was her own name.

Slowly she faced him. Her mind was clearer, fear a fading force. The reality was that she was alive. Beside that fact, all this had no meaning. She laughed harshly.

"Please stop playing games. What do you want, all of you?"

She had thought herself calm, but there was enough hysteria in her voice to shock her. That woman, she thought, that terrible woman had scared her. She found her voice again.

"Dr. Cranston," she said earnestly, "you look honest. What is all this? What has happened?"

The old man shrugged. "I'm afraid I don't dare tell you anything but that these are your lungs, and the heart upstairs is your heart. An organ removed in its entirety does not involve serious damage to the nervous system of the body except at one or two key points, and those are easy to fix."

He looked at her. "I suppose you've been outside. I was prevented from coming back here as soon as I intended, so you've had time. I'm sorry about that. I've never been able to fix locks on those doors. They were smashed by a man whom I saved as I have you and who—" He paused. "Never mind.

"About the organs," he said. "After they killed you, I could do nothing but take them out. Your brain"—he turned to a nearby case—"is here. Mrs. Patterson was very thorough. After she had stabbed you to death, she used a long needle to pierce your brain through your ear, and she also pricked at your lungs. Her intention was to make certain that you would not be brought back to life in any normal fashion. She, and the others, have an idea that if I am forced to make replicas of themselves that I automatically create a recruit for them. So far"—he smiled grimly—"they have proved right."

He frowned, then reached briskly into his pocket, and

65

produced a necklace with an intricate pendant suspended from it. He held it out.

"Here is your radio device. Whenever you want power, touch this little lever, and say into the pendant: 'Press button 243.' That's your number. Two four three. Don't forget it. I'll call it for you this time, so that you can get home."

He fastened the pendant around her neck, touched a tiny lever, and said: "Press button 243."

There was a pause; and then—she began to burn inside. It was so sharp, such a flame of agony that she cried out. Her breath came in quick gasps. She twisted. She started to run. But there was nowhere to run. The pain went with her, like a moving directed fire.

The conviction came that she was really dead; and that all that had gone before was a dream, a flashing kaleidoscope of unreality born out of the hideous pain of dying. Through a blur, Dr. Cranston's voice came to her:

". . . Very painful the first few times. But remember that your brain controls the power. When you *think* yourself insubstantial, that is how you will be. The moment you let go of the thought, you return automatically to a state of solidity. The power to do that wears off after a few hours, and requires recharging. I shall come with you as far as the outer walls of your apartment."

Virginia was in the apartment, and for long minutes babbling away to her husband, before realization finally came that she was not dead. That actually her situation was worse than that.

She must have been unconscious for a week, to have memory of only a few hours of waking.

By noon they were no further than that. She couldn't stop talking. Twice, Mention persuaded her into bed, but each time when he went into the kitchen to mix her a drug, she was out from under the quilts and following him.

After the second time, the knowledge penetrated that he had a mentally sick woman on his hands. Above everything else, she needed rest, time to calm down.

He managed finally to give her the protein sleep drug, cadorin. But it was not until he lay down beside her that her voice grew drowsy; and she fell into a restless sleep.

He had time to wonder what he ought to do, now that she was back. He was still utterly divided two hours later, when she wakened tense and terrified.

"That woman," she began thickly. "She put a needle

through my ear into my brain, and she pricked my lungs. She—"

"Many people have pierced eardrums," Mention suggested. "The important thing is she didn't disfigure you."

The phrase had proved briefly magical a half dozen times before. It proved so now. The funny, mad look went out of her eyes. She lay quiet for a long time. So long that Professor Mention got worried.

He glanced at her cautiously. Her eyes were open, but staring, and narrowed with thought. For a minute, unobtrusively, he watched her. Then, slowly, he said:

"Apparently, what we have here is a gang, remorseless, murderous, infinitely evil. It was founded as the result of a neurological discovery of Dr. Dorial Cranston, but he himself is not one of the gang. *Its* political and material power seems indestructible. It's too big; like a gigantic octopus it sprawls over the earth. But Cranston goes around trying within the pitiful limits of an old man's strength to undo the damage done by the monsters he has created."

"Norman!"

The tone of her voice indicated to Mention that she had not heard a word he had said.

He spoke softly, "Yes, dear?"

"Norman, Dr. Cranston won't live much longer. Do you realize that?"

He knew there must be a deeper meaning behind her words than just the fact. After a moment he thought he had it. He said, "You mean, then there will be no check on those devils."

Once again, she seemed oblivious to his words. Her tone was more urgent, intent.

"Norman, if he's the only one who knows where that island is, then what will happen to my heart, and the hearts and organs of those others, after he dies? Surely, they won't go on beating, *living*, without attention."

It was odd, but for a moment the words meant nothing to Mention, but that here was one more fear to soothe out of her tortured mind. He actually formed the calming words on his lips; and then he stopped himself.

He lay very still, mentally transfixed. *That's it!* he thought. *That's their fear. They must be desperate. They'll stop at nothing.*

His mind leaped out over the possibilities. By evening he had still to come to a decision. It was amazingly hard to know what to do, what could be done, against such a vast organization.

The days strode by while he stood moveless in his mental valley of indecision. Each day Mention told himself, *Surely, today something will happen. They'll do something, show in some way why they did all this to us.*

Virginia returned to work. A whole month passed. It was a week after that that Mention walked into the apartment one afternoon—just as Virginia stepped through the wall and materialized in the hallway.

She was radiant. She glowed. There were times in the past when he had seen her alive and excited. But never like this. Her body was vibrant; it seemed to cast off an aura inhuman in its power. Almost literally, her face glowed.

Mention stared at her; and slowly her richly tinted cheeks lost their natural color. It was their day for eating in. Without a word Virginia turned, and hurried into the kitchen.

Two hours later, when the radiance of her had faded to normal intensity, Mention looked up from the newspaper, and said quietly, "Virginia."

She jumped; then, "Yes?"

"How often have you done that?"

She was visibly agitated. It struck Mention with a shock that, in some curious way, she had hoped he wouldn't refer to what had happened. Her lips twitched. She said finally in a low voice:

"That was the first time."

She was not, he thought, used to lying. So that the lie was as transparent as a child's. He felt sick; then in automatic defense of her, told himself that she had never recovered from her experience.

He said gently, "Why did you do it?"

She seemed relieved that he had accepted her statement. She began eagerly:

"I wanted to see how it worked, partly because being able to do it might prove a defense against them; and I couldn't remember what it had been like the first time. I was too excited then, and besides it hurt terribly."

"And this time?" Steadily.

"It didn't hurt. I felt alive, warm, wonderful. After a while I wished myself insubstantial, and it was so; then I stepped through the wall, simultaneously wishing myself in the alley behind the *Herald* office—and there I was. I felt no sensation. The movement through space was instantaneous."

Her eyes were wide as they gazed into his. Briefly, all fear was gone out of them.

"Norman, it's miraculous, godlike. It's—"

"Why not try," Mention said, "to wish yourself on the island? I'd like to have a talk with Dr. Cranston."

Virginia shook her head vigorously. "It's impossible. I don't mean I tried to go there. But I made several attempts to go to places I'd never been; and nothing happened. You have to know the direction and you have to be able to visualize the place. You have to *know* where it is you're going."

Mention nodded slowly. "I see," he said.

He let the subject drop, but he thought wearily, *This is what they're waiting for: to let the reality of her situation sink into her. To allow her time to grasp that she is in the same box as they are.*

But why? What did they want of her? They had started off by killing her because she had made some minor discoveries about them. Then, when Cranston interfered with the finality of their murder, they had warned Virginia's husband not to go to the police. They wanted something; and now that they had gotten Virginia to experimenting with the power they had given her, it shouldn't take long before they showed their hand.

He glanced up at Virginia. She was sitting, gazing into space, her eyes half closed. Mention felt a sudden, enormous unease.

It was ten o'clock that night when the doorbell rang jarringly. Mention glanced at Virginia, and then stood up.

"We won't be getting friendly visitors at this hour," he said. "Better call Edgar, and tell him to press button 243. No use taking chances."

He waited until she had spoken into the wrist radio, then slipped the Luger into his pocket, and went to the door. It was a messenger boy with a letter. The letter read:

Wednesday the 23rd.
Will Professor and Mrs. Mention come Friday evening at seven to a dinner party in the main dining room at the Grand York Hotel? Give your name to the maître d'hôtel.

Cecilia Patterson.

There was one thought that dominated all others in Mention's mind, as he read the letter: action was beginning. If ever he intended to do something not of *their* choosing, the time had come.

He spent the night thinking, straining for a clue. He was in the middle of a lecture the next morning when comprehension came as easily and quietly as life to a newborn puppy.

He stood very still, staring at the class, but seeing only a blur of faces.

Why, he thought in a great wonder, *it's been there before our eyes ever since Virginia came back. What blind fools we've been not to realize.*

Not until he was on his way home did he realize what *he* must do about it.

He left his bedroom window open.

He waited until the illuminated dials of his watch pointed at two. He dressed silently, shoes and all, then waited until a streetcar moaned past along a nearby street. He let the outside sound clothe any sounds he might make in moving to the window.

The drop from the second story window jarred his bones, but the softness of the earth in the flower garden below saved him from injury.

There was a twenty-four hour U-Drive-It garage three blocks away. Half an hour after leaving his room, Mention slipped into the theater seat beside Edgar Gray.

"All right, Edgar," he said quietly. "You're wanted. Come along."

"Glug goo?" said Edgar in a whispered fear.

"Come along!" hissed Mention threateningly. And flashed his Luger.

Edgar came. Mention drove out into the country, and parked finally in an open stretch of farmer's roadway, off the main highway.

He didn't switch off the motor, and he left the gear in second, and kept his foot on the clutch—just in case. But he knew he was safe. Even they couldn't be everywhere.

The idea of using Edgar for his purpose seemed cleverer every minute that passed. There were two problems in connection with him: one was to get him to talk in an understandable fashion; the other was to see to it that Edgar told no one of this meeting and its results.

It was the first problem that proved difficult. But after half an hour it began to solve itself. Mention found that he was beginning to understand Edgar's gloppings. Behind all his incoherent glugs and glibbers, Edgar spoke English.

Mention expected little from the questioning phase of the interview; and that was exactly what he got.

The mind of Edgar was a misty region, but the darkness lacked depth. If a human brain could be compared to a book, then Edgar's was a magazine of the more lurid sort. But he was almost completely lacking in personal experiences.

An orphan from babyhood, he had spent the first fifteen years of his life within the walls and behind the fences of an institution. At fifteen, *they* had picked him up, and put him behind the enormous glass window of the Futurian Scientific Laboratories, and he had been there ever since.

"But," asked Mention, puzzled, "you have been treated, so that you don't need sleep. When was that done?"

"When they took out my heart," Edgar mumbled, "and my lungs and my brain and other things, they said I wouldn't need sleep anymore. They do that to people they want to control."

"Yet," Mention thought precisely, "Virginia sleeps normally. There are variations and variations to this business."

Edgar finished simply: "I was scared at first but"—his voice tightened with hate—"the woman whipped me a couple of times, and then I didn't dare not do as they wanted."

It was the suppressed fury in Edgar's voice whenever he talked of "the woman" that solved the second problem.

"Listen, Edgar," Mention said earnestly. "I'm on your side against that woman. When I get through with her, she'll never whip you again; and you'll have a chance to do all the things you've ever wanted to do."

That last was important. A youth who read as much escapist literature as Edgar must be absolutely maddened with the desire to go places and do things.

"Listen," said Mention, "here's what I want you to do. Tomorrow night at twelve o'clock, a jet plane leaves here for Los Angeles. At one thirty A.M. a rocket ship leaves Los Angeles. I want you to be on that jet and make the connection with the rocket."

"Me on a rocket ship," gurgled Edgar ecstatically.

"You'll be back in time for work; so don't worry about that. Here's some money, and a notebook containing exact instructions as to what you are to do. I've even left spaces for the answers I want you to write down."

He handed over the notebook and the money, and watched Edgar slip the former into his breast pocket, the latter into a billfold. Edgar's fingers shook with excitement.

Mention trembled too, but it was not excitement. He felt cold and hot by turns as he thought of Edgar having that notebook all day long. If *they* ever got hold of it—

Mention shivered, and drew his gun. He made his voice hard and cold.

"Edgar, take one last look at this. If you fail me in any way; if you don't do this job, and do it right, I'll use this gun on you. Understand!"

In the dim light of the dashboard, Edgar's eyes glowed with understanding.

"Glug goo!" gulped Edgar.

Mention taught at the university as usual the next day. It was during the noon hour that he put through his phone call.

"Tell her," he curtly informed the male servant who answered, "that it's Professor Mention."

A minute later, a woman's voice glowed on the phone. Mention said, "Mrs. Patterson, I wish to change the hour of our dinner from seven to midnight. I believe the Grand York holds late dances every night, so there will be no difficulty about getting the service. The reason?"

Mention laughed curtly. "Do I have to give one? All I'll say is, my wife and I won't come unless you agree. You do! Very well."

He felt grimly pleased, as he hung up. It was risky; it would make them suspicious. But Edgar's movements would now be as free from watchful eyes as the precautions of one man could make them. There were only three dangers now:

First, that it didn't matter what he did. Second, that he was not really fooling them at all. Third—

Nitwit Edgar himself.

They were led to a table where four men, one of them Torrance, and five women, one of them blonde Mrs. Patterson, were already seated. The men stood up. The women ceased their animated talking, and looked them over curiously.

Their faces shone with unmistakable extra life. All nine, men and women both, almost literally glittered with power. The table was the center of attraction. People kept glancing over from nearby tables in fascinated awareness.

Mention felt drab and lifeless beside them, as he sank into one of the two empty chairs, but it was a physical feeling only. Mentally, he had never been more alive, more determined.

Convince Virginia, he thought, that she had nothing in common with these creatures. Gain information. And give

72

Edgar time to get safely started on his long, swift trip. Those were his purposes.

The anxious hope came that Edgar had not been drained of strength to provide the glittering life that these people now paraded.

It was worrying. Picturing the possibilities made eating his fruit cocktail an effort. In the end he could not contain himself. It was Torrance who answered his carefully worded question:

"No, the Edgars in our power centers are not 'batteries.' They're transmitters. The word *negative* is the key. Every time somebody passes the great plate window behind which Edgar sits, there is a tiny flow from them to him, but he can't use it. Where Edgar's internal organs—and mine and your wife's—used to be, are now electronic impulsors largely made from tantalum. One difference is that Edgar is negative. Your wife and the others and myself are positive. Is that clear?"

It sounded like Yogi mouthings. But apparently he was going to be given information. He flashed his next question. Torrance answered promptly.

"There are two hundred forty-three of us including your wife. Of course," he went on, "we're only the executive central. We own immense property, and have tens of thousands of employees, including the people we have had watching you and your wife."

He laughed. But Mention was not amused. The personal words had come so unexpectedly that he swallowed hard. He forced his tense nerves to relax. Only what he had done last night mattered, he told himself unsteadily. And because of his precautions, no one, absolutely no one, had followed him. He was sure of that.

It was clear, though, that the man was playing with him. It startled him. It brought awareness of how tremendous was the power these people must believe themselves to possess.

He felt shocked into studying for the first time the faces around the table.

He had thought the four men were handsome, and the five women regular streamlined beauties. In a way that first impression was not wrong. Even now, examined intently, all nine, men and women alike, showed themselves to be well formed physically, a quality enhanced by the fact that they were marvelously well dressed and marvelously well groomed.

At that point the beauty ended like a road snapped off by the gap in a bombed-out bridge.

73

Those finely formed faces were chiseled masks of hardness. Merciless, inhuman hardness. Here was an innate cruelty that only Death personified could equal. Their eyes were slate-blue and slate-gray and slate-brown. Their lips were uniformly thin and compressed.

That was the underlayer. Superimposed, dominating, crowning each countenance was arrogance, supreme and terrible arrogance.

There was no question at all. They *did* believe in their power.

Mention ate his soup course, fighting for calm. He stole a glance at Virginia, but she was staring down at her plate. She had, he saw, taken very few spoonfuls.

He thought darkly, in surprise, that nobody was saying anything. The only words they had spoken so far had been in answer to his questions.

He saw that Torrance was smiling enigmatically.

Stronger grew Mention's conviction that he was being toyed with. And yet, up to now, he had lost nothing, had actually gained information.

That course couldn't be dangerous. He asked his next question. As before, it was Torrance who answered, and with the same promptness, the same apparent honesty.

"You're right, there wasn't much about Cranston's discovery in his books, mainly because he hadn't discovered very much when he wrote them. And my biography of him was written to kid him along at a time when we were building up our organization."

He paused. "Don't forget, in thinking of Cranston and his work, that he's a nut. For instance, it was not until he discovered that his idea of spreading good will by universal physical contacts was not going to be given a trial that he conceived the idea that artificially magnified nervous energy might do what he required—without contact.

"Never did a theory of a man fall on a smoother, rounder surface. That ball is rolling yet.

"Within the short space of one year, Dr. Cranston had found that an interflow of energy took place every time two or more human beings came near each other. It was a genuine transference of life force, but it needed magnification before it would have the same effect as physical contact. Accordingly, he engaged a first-rate electronic engineer—myself—to develop a tube and a circuit which not only magnified the organic energy, as he called it, but which could tune each individual's wavelength at will.

"An improvised version of that original circuit is now inside your wife keeping her—connected—to the hearts, lungs and brains in Dr. Cranston's secret laboratory."

He gazed earnestly at Mention. "Cranston has never explained to me why it is necessary for the organs to be outside the body, except to say that there must be a flow over distance. Yet at the same time there is no distance. The blood, the nervous energy, every breath of air we take is pumped, flows and is purified by the organs in those glass cases of his. If anything happens to those organs, we'll die."

Mention hadn't intended to speak. But this was what he had wanted to know. All his doubts had writhed around the one point of those human organs in Dr. Cranston's island laboratory.

And they were connected. They were. Nut, the old fanatic might be. But he had these Machiavellians in the palms of his two hands.

But why—the wonder was a savage force—why hadn't Cranston used his control and destroyed the whole lustful crew?

That was the question that burst from Mention's lips. And Torrance, his eyes like gray-diamond drills, answered from between clenched teeth:

"Because he can't bring himself to kill. Because he's a bug on pacifism as no one ever has been. Think! His whole discovery, this tremendous discovery, is based upon his emotional desire to find a practical method of spreading good will.

"That emotionalism is our deadly danger. It makes it possible for him to fool himself. It's true he can't bring himself to kill us. But he's seventy-eight years old. Not old as ages go nowadays, yet well over the average life expectancy.

"He could, literally die any day. He stubbornly refuses to recognize that possibility. He won't permit our doctors to examine him. In some queer way, he's convinced himself that if he dies, and we don't find our organs in time, then he won't really be responsible for our deaths.

"How did he get them in the first place? Man, who'd ever suspect that an old fool like that would be so cunning He performed all the operations except his own. And somehow he must have become suspicious of us."

Torrance was utterly intent now, his gray gaze so concentrated that Mention had the impression of two dully blazing lights shining at his face.

"Mention, we must locate that laboratory. We must gain control of our vital organs.

75

"That is where your wife comes in."

Torrance paused.

There was no question but that he had come to his point.

"You see, professor," he went on softly, "every time we discover that someone suitable to our purpose is investigating us, we wait until we think they know enough to take the shock of revival. It is amazing how little knowledge is required, and yet how important it is; dozens of people whom we simply picked up on the street went insane on us.

"Anyway, we kill the investigator at the right moment, then transport the dead body to Dr. Cranston's home.

"Here again, care is necessary. The old man tires quickly these days. And when he is tired his emotional mind convinces itself easily that there is nothing he can do.

"So we found it was useless to bring him too many bodies.

"Under normal circumstances, however, the poor old fool can't stand to see people dead when he knows he can do something for them. He is particularly partial to"—smilingly, Torrance bowed at Virginia—"to beautiful women. And, even though he is aware of our purpose in bringing the corpses to him, he has reached a state of mind where he doesn't care. He feels hopeless, defeated by our enormous organization.

"Accordingly, over a period of time, we have built up a picture of the surroundings of his hiding place. We know that it is on an island, somewhere in a tropical zone. Your wife, we hope, will be able to tell us some little point more. Since her own life is at stake, she will, I am sure, be *glad* to tell us all she can."

Torrance stopped. He looked at Virginia, then at Mention with a strange imperturbability.

"Is everything clear now?" he finished.

"Yes," said Mention.

He felt a relentless rage. It was not the host of murders that did it, though the probable number of them did blurring things to his mind. It was not even Virginia. Thought of her predicament only made him feel cold and sick and afraid. It was the old man, the use being made of an old man and his idealism.

The ruination of an old man's wonderful crazy dream shook the very life within him. Mention felt abruptly fortified to the depths of his soul. And, just like that, he knew with an implacable determination exactly what he must do to these people, if ever the opportunity came.

Funny how long it had taken him to realize that, quite

by chance, Virginia possessed all the clues to the location of the island.

They couldn't know yet the extent of her knowledge.

They mustn't know.

Mention said in his steadiest voice, "My wife woke up in Cranston's laboratory and Cranston was there. She had no time to look around, because he brought her straight home. And that, if you don't mind, is where she and I will start for now."

He pushed his chair away from the table, then hesitated, glancing at Virginia.

There was a brief silence; and then one of the blondes, not Mrs. Patterson, laughed harshly. "I notice, Professor Mention, that your wife is *not* making any move to follow you. Is it something she intends to remember having seen something?"

It was a possibility that had already occurred to Mention.

It was up to her.

Slowly, Mention gathered his forces. He looked at Virginia, and saw that her face was sheet-white. Her lips trembled, as her glance met his—and then she looked away.

Mention said urgently, "Virginia!"

Once more, she looked at him. There were tears in her eyes.

"Virginia, you've heard what these people have to say. And it isn't what you know or don't that's at stake at all. It's, are you going to become one of them, or are you not?

"Don't make your decision now.

"There must be things we can do. Surely Dr. Cranston can be reached, if we persevere. I'm certain, if we could talk to him, that he'd finally make up his mind to kill these creatures. He's been isolated. He must be made to see that his life's work can yet be rescued from these human rats, these mass killers, these—"

He paused. He whirled on Torrance. "How many," he rasped, "how many human beings do you kill every year for their internal organs?"

"About five thousand," said Torrance without hesitation. "Mostly orphans, poor people who move around a lot, and families without relatives."

"Uh!" blinked Mention.

He hadn't expected an answer. He had flung the question to point up a grim aspect of these people's activities. Now, he felt torn from his train of thought.

"Five thousand!" he echoed.

The total was bigger than he had ever thought. It shocked

77

him. He had believed himself hardened to anything that might come out in this deadly interview. And he wasn't.

He felt nausea. With a titanic effort, he caught hold of himself. Realization came that there was nothing he could say that would add any emphasis to the sum itself.

He did speak, however. He said wanly, "The defense rests."

He looked at Virginia—and she smiled at him through tears. It was a dreary smile. But a smile!

"Oh, you poor fool," she said. "You don't have to argue with me. You don't have to prove anything to me. There's evil here, beyond description. Evil of that curious advanced kind, which is only amused by the word and the realization. *Look* at them!"

She waved one hand, futilely. Mention had already looked. The nine faces were twisted in nine variations of sardonic amusement. Virginia's voice burned on:

"It's become like the evil of the universe, beyond the power of individuals to resist, with one exception. Only Dr. Frankenstein can destroy the monster he has created.

"The rest of us can but try to save our loved ones from the deadly elements. Oh, Norman, don't you see—"

"I see," said Mention harshly, "that you're thinking of giving in."

"Norman," she said whitely, "they've been too frank. They've told us so much that it's obvious they don't care what we know. Don't you see what that means?"

"You're thinking of yourself when you say that," Mention said.

"Am I?" She looked at Torrance. "*Am I?*"

Torrance said, "Your wife is smarter tonight than you are, Mention. You see, she is safe. Cranston will somehow see to it that no harm befalls the few of us he thinks worth saving."

He turned toward Virginia. "If you start talking before two minutes have passed, you and your husband can go home. You will never again be bothered by us. And if we gain control of the organs, we guarantee that no harm shall befall yours. Naturally, we prefer that everybody with power should join us."

He looked down at his watch. "We do not make promises lightly, having no need for lies. It is now seventeen minutes to one. You have two minutes."

Virginia parted her lips as if to speak, and then she caught Mention's gaze. And closed them again.

She sat staring at him like a hypnotized bird.

"Don't you dare," Mention almost hissed. "In the war,

78

we discovered that there's no compromising with such things as these. Their word isn't worth the uttering. If you have any information we'll use it to destroy them."

Even now, he mustn't let them guess that they did have the information.

Torrance said drably, "The two minutes is up."

He whirled on Virginia. "You fool!" he said coldly. "You've let him condemn himself to death. At this moment," he went on icily, "you may consider that your husband has one year to live. A minute from now, it will be fifty-one weeks, and so on. If at the end of fifty-two minutes you still haven't started talking, we shall kill him within the next few days.

"In any event he's a dead man. You can save him for a year. That's final. Mrs. Mention, start talking."

Mention climbed to his feet. "Virginia," he said roughly, "let's go."

Torrance reached up, and caught his arm. "Sit down, you idiot."

Mention smashed him in the face.

He felt incredulous the moment he had done it, astounded at his foolishness. But by then, the uproar had begun.

The waiters who carried Mention outside were not gentle. Nor were they slow. Mention succeeded in shouting once, "Virginia, don't you dare!" And then he struck the sidewalk with a hard plop.

After ten minutes, Virginia had still not come out.

The minutes dragged. Twice mention tried to go in. But the doormen were on the watch for him.

"Not tonight, Mac," one of them said. "You've had one too many."

It was Torrance who brought Virginia out. The man looked triumphant.

"The West Indies!" he exulted. "What luck that she went out just as one of the rare twenty-jet planes passed, and that she noticed it was mid-afternoon there, but nearly noon when she got back to California. The continental time differences work in beautifully. We've got the old scoundrel at last."

He looked at Mention coolly. "It's too bad you're a returned man. We're really indifferent as to whether you live or die, but we've discovered that men who were officers in the army, navy or air force do not cooperate with us even to the extent of just minding their own business."

He finished: "Your wife talked after twenty-five minutes, and she didn't start to tell the truth till we took her upstairs to a lie detector. You'll be feeling a knife at the end of the allotted time—after which we'll force your wife to join us. Goodbye."

He walked back into the hotel, with Mention's Luger pointing at him all the way. At last, gloomily, Mention took his hand out of the gun pocket.

"I don't dare," he said. "Killing one wouldn't do any good. Besides, I can't afford to spend the night in jail."

Beside him, Virginia said dully, "I'm sorry, Norman."

"I'm sorry, too," Mention replied gently, "for what I said to you before."

She spoke again, but this time he didn't hear. There was a clock above the ornate entrance of the hotel. Its hands showed twenty minutes to two. Mention stared at them, and calculated.

The Los Angeles-Miami rocket was only ten minutes out from its glitteringly showy launching run. It would be thirty-five minutes yet before Edgar arrived in Miami and started his inquiries.

By then, Torrance and the others, having flashed the "nerve power" way to Florida, would be on their way to the island by the fastest jet plane available.

He made sure they weren't followed, by taking three different taxis to the airport.

They were on the three thirty rocket from Los Angeles to Miami. There was one chance, Mention realized, as he sank deeper into the cushions from the enormous acceleration. One chance.

Virginia had been *to* the island. Torrance and those eight veterans of the organization who had attended the dinner hadn't.

When he told Virginia his plan, she stared at him somberly. She said bleakly, "Suppose Edgar started home on the quarter to three, Los Angeles time, rocket."

"I don't believe it," Mention said flatly. "For years Edgar has palpitated for adventure. He'll stay till a quarter to five L. A. time, as I advised him to. But he won't go far afield. He's not that bold, not yet."

They found Edgar in one corner of the waiting room, reading a magazine.

He handed over the notebook. There were four twenty-jet planes a day in the West Indies, he gobbled, all on the same route, every six hours in both directions.

He led the way to an enormous wall map of the West Indies.

The route was marked in a white line in bold relief; and there was a tiny island shown at *the* probable time point.

In the city directory, Mention located the Miami Futurian Science Laboratories. A taxi took Virginia, Edgar and himself there. A brick cracked the glass, then sent it shattering to the sidewalk.

"Get in there, Edgar!" Mention urged. "Press button 243. And then beat it back to the airport."

Two minutes later, as the early morning sun burst through a fleecy bank of low clouds, Mention drew a radiantly powered Virginia into a doorway.

"Darling!" he said. "This is it!"

He went on doggedly: "It must work. They transported you to Cranston's home when you were just a dead body. And Cranston took you to the island in the same way. That radio impulsor inside you must build a force field all around you when you're 'charged.' If they could move you, then you can take me along now."

He saw the expression on her face. He said earnestly, "Don't forget, you've been there. And you know the way at last." He pointed eastward. "The island is over there. Visualize the hill you stood on that day when you came out of Dr. Crantson's underground laboratory. You can. I know you can."

He felt her stiffen with decision. "Hold me close!" she whispered. He felt her vibrant body press against his, responsively.

Somewhere nearby an Irishman began to curse in annoyance, something about a window having been broken on his beat, b'gorra.

The officer's voice was cut off curiously. There was a sudden tingling inside Mention, thrillingly sharp. And sustained.

The sensation ended. He was standing in a room lined with glass cases, staring at an old man, who confronted them with an ax in one hand and a revolver in the other.

"I have a little system," Dr. Cranston said in a queer, tired voice. "I phone Torrance up. If I can't get in touch with him, I come here, just in case he's up to something."

He lowered the gun wearily. "Just when I'd half convinced myself that I would kill the first person who came in here, in barge two innocent people."

Mention did not hesitate. This was the man who could fool himself about things like responsibility for death.

He was going to have the chance.

Mention stepped forward and took the gun from the old man's unresisting hand.

"I'd like you," he said, "to hand me the ax of your own free will."

Dr. Cranston shrugged wearily. "There's nothing else I can do."

He handed over the ax. He looked suddenly cheerful. "I suppose there's nothing I can say that will prevent you from doing what you have in mind?"

"You can," said Mention grimly, "indicate those cases which you think can be left intact. And don't indicate too many."

When Mention finally put the ax aside, twenty-three compartments remained unshattered.

THE EARTH KILLERS

I

The S29A climbed steeply up on a column of crooked fire. In the machine, Morlake could feel the turbulent impulses of the gyroscopic stabilizers. But the flow of upward movement was as slick as oil, and the acceleration brought nothing more than a feeling like that of a hand squeezing the stomach.

At sixty miles above Kane Field he leveled off and put the new plane through its paces. After five minutes he turned on the radio and spoke softly.

"Morlake calling Gregory."

"Yeah?" Laconically.

"She likes the climate."

"How's the ultraviolet?"

"Blocked."

"Cosmics?"

"Registering."

"Good." The engineering officer sounded satisfied. "Until somebody figures out a way of blocking cosmic rays completely, we'll be satisfied with minimums. Speed?"

"About one banana." That was code for seven hundred MPH.

"Feel anything?"

"She's singing a lullaby."

"Sweet, huh, at one banana. What do you think, generally?"

"Sadie's going to be with us for quite a while."

"As smug as that, eh?" The engineer turned away from the mike. His voice, though still audible, grew tiny. "Well, General, there you are. She ticks."

"Ought to," was the faint reply. "We were beginning to sweat. She cost four billion to develop."

The engineer's voice had a grin in it. "Where do we go from here? Mars? Or the moon?"

"Sadie is our top, boy. And we're lucky to have her. The new Congress is tired of our costly little experiment, and wants to reduce taxes. The new President thinks the development of weapons leads to war. He doesn't like war, and so in this year of 1979—"

He must have thought better of what he intended to say. There was silence, though not for long. Gregory's faraway voice said, "What next?"

"Dive," said the general.

The engineer's voice approached the mike.

"Morlake."

"I heard."

"Okay. See if you can hit O'Ryan."

Morlake grinned. The three test pilots of Kane Field played a game against the famous racist publisher. Each time they dived they chose as target the *Star-Telegram* building, which peered seventy stories into the sky beside the flat, dead-looking waters of Lake Michigan. The idea was, if anything went wrong, they might as well take O'Ryan and his penthouse into hell with them. And they meant it too, after a fashion.

The plane began to shudder. At eighty miles the jets were silent and useless, and the hammering of the rockets was a sharp sound carried by the metallic frame. The rockets were not meant to carry the load alone. All the smoothness was gone from his marvelous machine. Morlake paused for a final look at the universe.

It was tremendously, unnaturally dark outside. The stars were pinpoints of intense brightness, that did not twinkle or glitter. The sun, far to his left, was only approximately round. Streamers of flame and fire mist made it appear lopsided and unnatural. A quarter moon rode the blackness directly overhead.

The S29A, moving very slowly, not more than a hundred miles an hour, was over Chicago now. The city was lost in haze, quite invisible to the naked eye. But on the radar screen every building was etched, and there was no mistaking the *Star-Telegram* structure. Morlake waited until the hairline sights directed under his seat were touching the shadow of the building, and then he carefully tilted the nose of the plane downward.

He was in no hurry, but presently the front aiming device was pointed directly at the image on the radar screen. The speedometer was edged over to a thousand miles an hour when there was a dazzling bright flash in the sky behind and above him. Something big and hot as hell itself flashed past him, and began to recede into the distance below.

Morlake cringed involuntarily. He had time to think: a meteorite! Speed about fourteen hundred miles an hour. Below him, the bright flame fuzzed and winked out. He stared at it astounded, removed his foot from the accelerator; and then, there, twenty feet away, was the object. And it was not a meteorite at all.

Morlake gazed at the thing in blank horror, as the radio embedded in the cushions beside his ears clicked on, and Gregory's voice shouted:

"Morlake, we've just got word: New York, Washingon, scores of cities destroyed in the last ten minutes by giant atomic bombs. Morlake—get away from Chicago with Sadie. She's our only working S29A. Morlake, you hear me?"

He heard, but he couldn't speak. He sat frozen to the controls, glaring at the atomic bomb twenty feet away.

After a blank period, Morlake stirred like a sick dog. His reflexes began to function in a dreamlike fashion. His eyes shifted heavily over the instrument board. Slowly, he grew aware that the world around was becoming brighter. A faint dawn glimmered in the distance to either side, and the blaze of light below was like a vast fire bowl into which the bomb and the ship were falling.

He thought: the flame that had seared his ship when the bomb first passed him—that must have been its forward rocket tubes slowing the thing, so that it wouldn't burn up from sheer speed in the thick atmosphere lower down.

The thought passed as though it had never been, as if the thin, shrieking wind building up outside had torn it from his brain. In its place, a formless mind stuff, seeking shape, pressed and quivered inside him. Plans too fleeting to be comprehended multiplied and coalesced. Impersonal plans involving death for his body. Impersonal, because the city below was not his city. No one in it knew him or cared about him, not even a secondary girl friend. He hated the place. Windy, dirty, wretched, miserable, hot in summer, cold in winter. . . . No, there was nothing there, nothing at

84

all. But the yeast of plans fermented with violence and direction.

"Morlake, damn your soul, answer me!"

Answer me, answer me, answer me! Over all the mad schemes that were now springing full-grown into his head, one took precedence. If he could deflect the bomb into the lake, five million people would have a chance for life.

He knew better. Even as he shoved his plane over on fingers of wan jetfire, and felt the metal frame jar against the bomb, he knew that the greater bombs needed only to fall into the vicinity of the cities. Direct hits were unnecessary.

But he pushed with the plane's vertical jets. His body shrank, expecting the blow of radiation. And at first nothing happened. There was not enough air to give power even to those superjets.

"Morlake, for God's sake, where are you?"

He was too intent for words to reach him. He had a fear that he would push the plane too hard, and that the curved fuselage would roll itself away from the streamlined bomb. Delicate manipulation, touch, pressure, oh, so delicate.

The movement began slowly. He noticed it first on the hairline sighting device in front of him. O'Ryan was no longer directly below. At that instant of infinitesimal success, the bottom of the bomb flashed white fire. One burst only, but it jarred his precious contact. He felt his machine slip clear of the bomb, and with a shock he saw that his sights were once more pointing straight at the newspaper skyscraper.

The bomb had reacted to his pressure. It must be on a beam, and couldn't be diverted. Almost instantly, the bomb offered one more surprise. As he sat in a haze of uncertainty as to his next move, it sent a flare of light billowing over the S29A. Morlake shrank, and then the light was gone. He had no time to think about it, because—"

"Morlake, you damned idiot, save Sadie!"

Anger, despair, hate, frustration and the beginning of insanity—all were in that shout. Morlake would have ignored it too, would have been almost unaware, but at that split instant his gaze touched the altimeter. Twenty miles. Only twenty miles to Earth.

The fever of his purpose burned out of him. Suddenly, he thought of Sadie as those desperate men at Kane Field were thinking of her. Sadie, the sleek, the gorgeous, Sadie of the high tail, the first of a fleet not yet built.

He spurted his forward jets. And saw the bomb sink below him. Instantly, it was gone into the mist. He began to turn, to try to pull her out of her dive. Three times he blanked out, and came to again, dizzy but alive. Finally, the plane was level. Morlake brought her nose up, and climbed on a long slant at an acceleration that clenched his body.

Behind him, below him, there was a glare as of a thousand times ten thousand suns. A supernal blaze it was, unmatched in the sidereal universe except by the unthinkable fires of a Nova-O sun at its moment of ultimate explosion.

Catastrophe for a continent! Forty million people in fifty major cities died in a space of not more than thirty minutes. It was later estimated that each of the bombs dropped generated flash heats of forty thousand billion degrees centigrade. Everywhere, the forces released were too great to be confined. The balance of a hemisphere was shaken. Earthquakes convulsed regions that had never known a tremor. And all that afternoon and night the ground settled and quivered with a violence that had not been paralleled in the history of mankind.

By mid-afternoon of the first day, a stricken people had begun to rally and reintegrate. Senator Milton Tormey, recovering from food poisoning in Florida, brought together two aged, ailing Congressmen in a resort hotel, and the three issued a manifesto ordering a six-month period of martial law. In Berlin, General Wayne, commanding American forces in Germany, demanded that all countries in Europe and Asia open their borders to American planes. Delay or refusal would be construed as a confession of guilt, and would bring instant retaliation from secret American atomic bomb bases and from the navy.

The national guard was called out. Radar and sonar stations were put on battle alert, and throughout the night hastily-armed men and women stared sleeplessly up into the skies, waiting for the paratroop armies that would surely arrive with the dawn to conquer a devastated nation.

Morning broke over the thousand horizons of America, and the sky and land were still untouched by alien sounds and alien purposes. The sun came up out of the east. People were able to look at their red-eyed neighbors, and to realize that the complete end of their world was not yet at hand. After a week the enemy had still shown no sign. It took a month for American plane patrols, fleets of planes and divisions of men to discover that no nation on Earth was organizing for war. Everywhere, peaceful scenes met the frenzied searchers. They retreated finally, reluctantly, from lands they had so summarily entered.

Day by day it grew clearer that the enemy had struck a mortal blow at Earth's most powerful nation. And he had done it so skillfully that he was going to get away with it.

Twice, Morlake, returning to base after his wild flight, made the sweep over Kane Field. The first time, he was past before he recognized the super-airfield. The second time he savored the desolation.

The surface buildings, the control towers, the markers, the lights were down. Planes in twisted heaps on the field and beyond. The wreckage spread into the distance southward as far as he could see! Planes and parts in every degree of destruction, sections of metal buildings, chunks of cement, of brick, of plastic and glass, and miles of splintered lumber. A giant had trodden this land.

Morlake settled his machine on its vertical jets, like a helicopter, near one of the underground entrances. As he came down, he saw a score of human figures sprawled almost at the mouth of the entrance. When he rolled nearer, they ceased to look so human. He glanced away quickly, and carefully guided his machine between them and the shelter.

A fierce wind was blowing as he climbed to the ground, but except for that, silence lay over the military air hub of the continent. He stepped gingerly over the wreckage of the underground entrance, and made his way down cracked steps. Plexiglass lights glowed in the upper corridors, untouched by the secondary violence that had raged through the corridors themselves.

Everywhere the walls were smashed. Ceilings had crashed down, and he could hear the remote thunder of loosened girders, and earth and cement, tumbling to form barriers in the depths of the supposedly impregnable chambers. Morlake fumbled past two such partial obstacles, came to a third that blocked his passage completely. Then, as the ceiling a few yards behind him rumbled ominously, he began his retreat to the surface.

He reached the open air, breathing hard, and forced himself out of pity to examine the less damaged bodies. All were dead. He floated around the field, landing a dozen times to search shells of buildings, and to peer into underground entrances. He found two men whose pulses flickered with faint life.

They failed to react to stimulants in his first aid kit, so he loaded them into the jet. Up in the air again, he turned on his radio, and at first the ether seemed silent. It was only when he turned the volume almost to full that a faraway voice scratched through to him. It kept fading out, but each time it came back in, so that he did not lose the continuity:

". . . People in cities over fifty thousand are ordered to leave, but all merchants in those cities must remain in their stores. Repeat: merchants must remain. Those who leave without authorization will be shot. . . . Sell your goods to anyone who comes in, rationing all customers . . . one suit, one blanket. . . . Groceries, about two weeks' supply. . . .

"People in cities or towns of less than fifty thousand, stay at home. Understand—stay at home! . . . Repeat emergency warning to people on Lake Michigan. A tidal wave is sweeping up from Chicago at a speed of approximately four hundred miles an hour. All shore towns will be destroyed. Wait for nothing. Leave at once!

". . . Flash! London. Great Britain announces declaration of war against unknown enemy. Other countries following . . ."

Morlake's mind couldn't hold to the words. The selectivity was too poor, the voice a mere segment of a remote sound. And besides, the first stunned calm was slipping from him. He sat in his plane, thinking of millions of men and women whose bodies had been reduced not to ashes but to atoms. . . . He was profoundly relieved when he reached his first destination, a small military airport near a sizable city in Iowa. The two men were rushed off to the local hospital. While his machine was being refueled, Morlake had a brief conference with three worried executive officers. They agreed that his best course was to fly to one of the secret bases. It was to them that he mentioned for the first time that he had seen the Chicago bomb.

All three men grew excited, and he had a hard time getting away. They were certain that experts would be able to make much of his experience.

It was some time before he was allowed to approach the secret field. His radio roared with alarms and warnings that he "must leave at once." He insisted that the commanding officer be informed of his presence, and finally he was permitted to set his machine down into a cavernous elevator, and was drawn underground.

He was ushered into the office of General Herrold, and at that time he made only a brief report. He told the general the circumstances under which he had seen the Chicago bomb, and paused, waiting for the flood of questions he expected.

For a long time the old man looked at him, but he asked for no details. And Morlake was being ushered into his quarters on the next tier down before the meaning of the man's thin-lipped hostility penetrated. *By God,* he thought, *he didn't believe me!*

It was staggering, but it couldn't be helped. No matter how incredible it sounded, it was his duty to tell what had happened.

He wrote his report as best he could, then phoned the general's office that it was ready. After some delay he was told to remain in his quarters, that an officer would come for the report. That was chilling, but Morlake pretended to see nothing wrong. When the officer had come and gone with the document, Morlake lay down, conscious of unutterable weariness. But his brain was too active for sleep.

Reaction to all the straining tensions of the day took the form of blank horror, of a frank disbelief in what his eyes had seen. Slowly, his emotions became more personal. He began to picture the possibilities of his own situation here, where a suspicious martinet was in command. *Damn him,* he thought in a fury. *All the radar stations designed to spot bombs coming down near cities must have been destroyed. And that leaves only what I saw.*

But what did this experience prove? It was the one major clue, so far, to the identity of the enemy. And it seemed valueless.

Weeks had still to pass before he would realize how tremendous a clue it really was.

II

"Order in the court."

The hastily convened court-martial was about to begin.

"It is the intention of the prosecution," said the judge advocate after the preliminaries were over, "to bring evidence that will establish one or the other of two charges against Captain Morlake. The first charge is that he did not, as he has claimed, see an atomic bomb, and that, in fact, his purpose was to procure cheap notoriety for himself out of a nation's most profound agony. It is the opinion of the prosecution that, if the court finds him guilty of this charge, the penalties should be severe in proportion to the monstrousness of the disaster that has befallen our country.

"The second charge," the judge advocate continued, "is more serious. It assumes that Captain Morlake did, in fact, see the bomb, as he has stated, but that he has deliberately falsified his report, or else was grossly negligent in failing to observe the direction from which the bomb was coming."

For Morlake, the deadly part was that he knew no one. He was not permitted to subpoena character witnesses from fields to which men he had known had been scattered. By the time the two rocket experts had testified, he recognized that he was doomed. Shortly after his arrest, when one of his guards had whispered that fully half the officers of the secret field had lost members of their families in the bombing, he realized what weight of emotion was against him. These men, twisted by disaster, could not feel, see, or think straight.

The crisis came swiftly after he himself was called to the stand.

"There is no doubt in your mind," the judge advocate said, "that what you saw was an atomic bomb?"

"It was an atomic bomb."

"And it was coming straight down?"

"Yes, it was. Absolutely straight."

"That was about how high above the ground?"

"At least seventy-five miles."

Pause; then, gravely:

"Captain Morlake, you have heard experts testify that any bomb accurately aimed from any point on the Earth's surface would have been describing a parabolic curve of some kind at the height?"

"I have heard the witnesses."

"And what do you conclude from their testimony?"

Morlake was firm. "A short time ago I was convinced that our rocket science was superior to that of any other country. Now I know that we've been surpassed."

"That is your sole comment on the death of forty million Americans. We have been surpassed."

Morlake swallowed hard, but he controlled himself. "I did not say that. The bomb was coming straight down."

"Hadn't you better think that over, Captain?"

Insinuating words. He knew what they wanted. In the short time since the trial had been scheduled, the prosecution had had several bright ideas. The previous night they had come to him with drawings of hypothetical trajectories of bombs. Every drawing was on a map of the world, and there were three different points of origin illustrated. If he would agree that the bomb had been slanting slightly in any of the three directions, he would be a hero.

"You still have an opportunity, Captain," said the judge advocate silkily, "of being of great service to your country."

Morlake hesitated miserably. "I'm sorry," he said at last, stiff with fear, "but I cannot change my testimony. It was coming straight down."

The sentence was thirty years, and he was lucky. Within a month of his trial men were being hanged from lamp posts, and sedition trials sprouted like weeds over a land that could not discover its attacker.

On the ninety-fourth morning, Morlake put on his fatigue suit as usual. He had only the vaguest sense of ever having done anything else, the routine was so much a part of him. On the way to breakfast he glanced at the bulletin board, where the day's work sheet had already been posted. Ploughing the east field. Planting potatoes in the valley. Reparing the east fence. Cleaning the stables. Transferring feed to a new barn.

It was the usual pattern, with only one thing missing. His own name was not attached to any one of the details. Immediately after breakfast he reported the omission to the day sergeant.

"Okay, you go along with the potato planting detail."

Morlake went, telling himself that, if his name was ever again missing from the board, he would report to the office of the clerks who made up the work sheet.

It wasn't that the work hadn't been good for him. He had always been as hard as nails, and his internal muscles were so perfectly balanced and organized that, in all the army air forces, he had proved by actual test that he could withstand more acceleration than any other man.

And he felt better now, healthier, more awake, more alive, more appreciative of life. But he didn't like planting potatoes. The army farm used the old, primitive method of bending down to place each seed-spud by hand. . . . By noon, he was sweating and tired.

The midday dinner was eaten in the field. Men squatted on the grass with their plates and cups. And the chatter took exactly the same form as on the day before, and the day before that, and so on back into infinity.

"The bombs . . ." "Hey, did you hear what that new guy said the other day, about somebody staggering out of an undamaged basement in New York City?" "Some character in the Middle West is saying that bombs could only have come from the moon . . ." ". . . It's the Chinese, or I'll be dipped in . . ." "I'll put my money in Russia . . ." "Hell, if I was General Wayne in Berlin, I'd—"

The detail sergeant climbed lazily to his feet. "Okay, generals, up and at those potatoes, before the bugs move in."

The afternoon lengthened. About four o'clock a car detached itself from the haze that hid the farm buildings five miles to the north. It came lazily along a dirt road, disappearing behind trees and into gullies, but always it came into view again, each time nearer, and obviously as puzzling to the detail sergeant as to the prisoners. The sergeant and his corporal walked slowly toward the road as the car approached, and stood waiting for it.

Up, down, up, down— The remaining guards kept things moving. The ploughs whuffed and thudded through the soil folding the fresh dirt over the seed potatoes. The horses champed and swished their tails. One of them noisily passed water. Up, down, up, down—Morlake, sweating and breathing hard, alternated the rhythmic movement with glances at the nearing car and with his own thoughts.

Of the various articles and newspaper editorials that he had read in the farm library, only one, it seemed to Morlake, contained a sensible idea: the purpose of the bombing had not been to destroy the nation or conquer it, but simply to change its political character. With the vociferous, noisy, highly-educated, politically conscious people of America's world-cities out of the way, power would revert to the isolationist agricultural communities. Every capitalistic state in the world would benefit from the markets from which American industry would have to withdraw. And the dozen Communist states had their own reasons for appreciating the end of American influence in Europe, Africa and Asia.

If the enemy was not discovered for several years, it was likely that the elected representatives of cautious farm states would not dare to retaliate. Already, old prejudices were showing. The South reinstituted Jim Crowism. And there was no one to stop them.

Only three facts were known about the aggressor: he existed; he had left no clues in his own countries; and he had dropped his bombs straight down onto at least one city.

Unfortunately, the one man who believed the third item was Robert Morlake, and so far his sole thought was that the bombs must have been launched from the moon. . . . Morlake smiled wryly. He could imagine himself trying to convince other men that they must go to the moon to find out the name of their enemy.

"Morlake!"

Morlake straightened slowly and turned. It was the corporal who had gone with the sergeant to the car. In the near distance, the machine was turning noisily around. Morlake saluted.

"Yessir?"

"You're wanted at the office. You weren't supposed to come out on a detail this morning. Come along."

Five minutes later, Morlake knew that he was being presented with an opportunity to escape.

What had happened Morlake discovered gradually. On the East Coast, General Mahan Clark, ranking staff officer surviving, declared martial law on the afternoon of the bombing. For three months he worked eighteen to twenty hours a day to integrate the shattered armed forces and to organize the country. Railway, telephone and telegraph lines were repaired, and the postal services resumed. Priorities and rationings were instituted, and an industrial census taken.

At the end of seventy days he had a picture of the country's resources. By the eightieth day, industries that needed each other's products were being coordinated on a vast scale. Troops patrolled cities and towns; a national curfew was put into effect; severe penalties were invoked against mobs and mob leaders. Mass hangings of known Communists ceased. People with foreign accents were still being molested, but the cases grew more isolated daily.

From the eighty-fifth to the eighty-eighth day, the general took a holiday, during which time he played dice, ate, rested and slept, and listened only to emergency reports. Back at his headquarters, he moved into a new office.

"From now on," he told reporters, "I'll delegate all except a minimum of administrative work. I will devote my attention to picking up technical matters at the highest level. I'm an engineer, not a politician. What I want to know is, what the hell happened to our advanced stuff on the day of the bombing? Where is it, and who's alive that knows something about it?"

Late in the afternoon of the ninety-first day, he looked up bleary-eyed from a mass of papers, and called in an adjutant.

"There's a report here that S29A was scheduled for a test flight on B-day. Was the test made? If so, what happened?"

Nobody knew until the following morning, when a lieutenant produced a report from Field R3 in Texas that the S29A had landed there a few hours after the destruction of its base, Kane Field, ninety-two days before.

"Who the hell," said Clark, "is the misbegotten incompetent in charge of R3? Herrold? Oh!"

He subsided. He had once been under Herrold's command, and one observed certain amenities with former superiors. Later, though, he remarked to a ranking officer: "Herrold is an old fool. If a man under him has twice as much sense as another, he can't tell the difference. Drive, ability, leadership—he can't see them." He scowled. "Well, the best bet, I suppose, is to have the machine brought here. Inform Herrold, will you?"

The order for the plane caused a turmoil in the upper officialdom of Field R3. No one there could fly the ship.

"It's a special plane," an air force major explained to General Herrold. "I remember that the man who was to test it had to go to the factory and learn all kinds of preliminary things before he was even allowed to warm her jets. The difficulties, I understand, derive from an intricate combination of rocket and jet drives."

"Oh!" said General Herrold. He thought about it for some minutes; then, "It wouldn't take you long," he suggested, "to learn to fly it, would it?"

The big man shrugged. "I've been flying jets for years—" he began.

He was interrupted. "Uh, Major Bates," Herrold said, "the officer in question, Captain Robert Morlake, is in prison for a most heinous offence. It would be a grave setback for discipline if he were freed merely because he can fly a plane. Accordingly, I shall have him brought here, and no doubt he can teach you to fly the plane in a day or so. I want you to hold no conversations with him except on purely technical matters. You will carry a gun, and remember that the plane is more valuable than the man."

Bates saluted. "I'll handle him, sir," he said confidently.

The moment the S29A was high enough, Morlake zipped her over into a power dive. Behind him, Major Bates clawed for the nearest handhold.

"Hey!" he yelled. "What the hell do you think you're doing?"

Morlake wasn't sure. He had decided at the moment he was sentenced to virtual life imprisonment that he would not accept the verdict of the court. But exactly what was going to happen now he didn't know.

"Now, look, Morlake," Bates said in a voice that trembled slightly, "this is not going to get you anywhere. There's hardly any fuel in the tanks."

That was why he had wasted no time. Morlake said nothing, but sat blank-brained, awaiting events. The day was clear as glass, the Earth below plainly visible. It looked closer than it was.

"For God's sake, man!" the other's nerve was tottering badly. "You swore you still stood by your oath of allegiance to the United States."

Morlake broke his silence. "I·do."

"Then what—"

"I happen to be the only man who knows how to find the enemy. If I let myself stay locked up, I'd be violating my oath."

It sounded wild even to Morlake. It probably seemed pure insanity to Bates. And Morlake did not fool himself. He felt emotional about this. It was not reasoned, objective, what he was doing. He had had a three-months' taste of a life sentence at hard labor, and the passionate beliefs he held, his justification for this, were rooted as much in horror of his fate as in patriotism.

The bomb had come straight down. If, as the experts maintained, it couldn't have come from Earth, then it had come from the moon. Since that was not an idea to which Americans would take easily, it was up to the one man who knew the facts to persuade them.

His thoughts ended. He jumped, as he saw that the ground was really rushing toward him now. Behind him:

"Morlake, for God's sake, what do you want?"

"Your gun."

"Do you intend to kill me?"

"Don't be a fool. Hurry."

The Earth was a huge valley, with rearing hills no longer looking so flat. Morlake felt the gun shoved past his shoulder. He snatched at it, shouting:

"Get back! Back, away from me!"

He knew that would be hard, like climbing the side of a house. But he waited while the sweating officer fumbled away from his seat. He could hear the man cursing with fear. And his own heart was pounding, his body rigid, when at last he came out of his dive, and began to climb toward the black regions of the stratosphere.

The stars were as bright as jewels before he leveled off and began his race with the diminishing supply of fuel. At the machine's most economical speed, thirty-five miles a minute, he sped through the darkness above an ocean of light.

He had two intermingled hopes: that he would be able to reach Kane Field and that he would find it deserted. The first hope was realized as the field swam into view in the distance. The second ended in dismay, as he saw that the entire area swarmed with men, with tractors, cranes, trucks and piles of material.

Morlake came down from behind a low hill some distance from the nearest group of workers.

"Get out!" he said to Bates.

"I'll see you hanged for this!" the big man snarled. But he got out. He did not move off immediately nor did Morlake. There was a prolonged silence, then:

"Tell them," Morlake said, "that I'm taking the plane because—because—" He paused. He felt a desperate desire to justify himself. He went on, "Tell them the top speed of Sadie is sixty-seven miles a minute, and that she can climb eighty miles in seven minutes plus, but tell them"—he hesitated, for if his words were given publicity, the unknown enemy would read them also—"tell them not to waste any more time building duplicates of Sadie. She isn't fast enough, she can't go high enough to reach the men who dropped the atomic bombs. And that's why I'm taking her. Because she's only a second-rater, and therefore worthless. Goodbye."

He waved his hand. The vertical jets hissed with power. The machine reared slowly; then the rockets fired several bursts, and the ground began to flow below like a tremendously swift river. Morlake headed over the hills, straight toward a place where there had once been pipes leading up from an underground fuel tank. Men were working there amid a tangle of twisted metal, but some order had already been established. He landed.

A foreman, a slim, rugged-looking young man, came over, and said, "Sure, we've got all the fuel you want. None of the tanks were busted by the earthquakes. Roll her over this way."

He was in no hurry, but talkative, curious. While his men attached piping to the tanks Morlake indicated, he asked pointed questions, which Morlake answered or evaded with a laugh. He knew how to talk to this kind of man, and the only trouble was that out of the corner of one eye, he saw Bates come into sight over the hill, and flag down a truck. The truck headed swiftly toward Morlake. When it was a third of a mile away, Morlake climbed into the plane.

"Thanks," he said.

The foreman waved cheerfully. "Give my regards to the general."

The truck was tooting its horns madly as the S29A became airborne.

Morlake's sense of exultation did not last long. He had enough fuel to fly around the Earth. But his problem was to convince the people in authority that only by continuing the abandoned moon project could they ever again hope to be free of danger. Where, how would he start? What ought his pattern of action to be?

When he came right down to it, he hadn't really given that much thought.

III

Nine bullet-proof cars drew up before General Clark's headquarters one day some ten months after the bombing. There was a scurrying of men from the first four and the last four. Everywhere guns showed prominently, as the guards drew a cordon around the center car. As soon as the maneuvers were completed, a flunky hurried forward and graciously opened the door of the big machine. Then he moved back.

Senator Tormey stepped out. He frowned as he saw that no one had yet come out of the general's office to meet him. Then as the general himself appeared in the doorway, a smile wreathed the handsome though heavy face, and he walked over and shook hands with the officer.

"Got all the Morlake stuff ready to show me?" he asked.

"All ready," Clark nodded. "I'd have invited you to see it before if I'd known you were interested."

Tormey took that as an apology. He had come a long way in the past four months. On B-day he had called for martial law, to last for six months, and had then found that the army was not prepared to turn the government over to him at the specified time. The available press and radio echoed with the senator's protests. He had no ambitions himself, but it was time for the government to be returned to the civilians. As the ranking survivor of the Congress, it was his duty—and so on. And so on and so on.

That was the beginning. And as army ruthlessness, as personified by tens of thousands of officers, had as usual alienated ninety percent of the population, the senator was soon riding a crest of protest meetings, of which the army, in the person of General Clark, finally took cognizance.

The senator was invited to headquarters, and taken into the confidence of the military. He became a habitual member of General Clark's dice club, and his advice was sought on every important administrative problem. It was the army's bid for civilian support, and it seemed to work.

"This way," said General Clark, "to what we call the Morlake room."

It was a small room. There was a desk and a chair in it, and a filing cabinet. On one wall was a huge map of North America, with pins stuck into it. The red pins indicated that Robert Morlake had definitely been seen in those areas. The green pins meant that he had "almost certainly" been in the vicinity. The yellow pins were rumors, and the blue pins represented points at which a plane resembling S29A had been observed. Each pin was numbered and the numbers referred to a card index file, which contained a synopsized history of the hunt for Robert Morlake. The index itself was based on files and documents, which were kept in a cabinet beside the map.

"At first," General Clark explained, "Morlake's idea seemed to be to contact old friends of his. On the second day after refueling at Kane Field, he approached the residence of Professor Glidden in California. . . ."

After watching Glidden Grove one whole day, Morlake got up at dawn and walked two miles to where the low, long building of Dr. Glidden's research institute spread beside the banks of a winding stream. A caretaker was puttering beside the open door of a stucco, Hollywoodish laboratory. He answered Morelake's query curiously:

"Dorman? He lives with the professor. I guess the cook will be up by this time. That's the house, over there."

It was a glassed, tree-sheltered bungalow. As Morlake strode along a walk lined with towering shrubs, a woman emerged from a side path that led up from the creek, and they almost collided.

It was the woman who was startled. Morlake said nothing. Ninety-four days on the prison farm had frozen his nerves.

The woman was dark-haired and blue-eyed; she wore a wrap-around dressing gown and a bathing cap. "Mr. Dorman," she echoed. "Oh, you mean the secretary." Her manner became indifferent. "Probably still in bed. It's a habit of people like that to sleep until it's time to punch the clock."

Her tone was carelessly contemptuous. Morlake, who had been about to pass on politely, paused for a second look. She was not the world's most beautiful woman, but it seemed to him that he had never seen a more passionate face. Her lips were full and sensuous, her eyes large and bright, her manner immensely assured.

"Aren't you a little early," she asked, "for visiting the help?"

She was irritating, and Morlake didn't like her at all. "May I by any chance," he asked, "be speaking to Professor Glidden?"

The remark pleased her, for she laughed. She stepped confidently up to him, and hooked her arm in his. She said, "I'll ask the cook which room is your friend's. You mustn't mind me too much. I like to get up when the birds start singing, and it makes me cross to have to wait five hours before there's anybody to talk to. I'm the physical type. Immense energy; and the only reason my brain is any good at all is because I never worry. Do you know anything about endocrinology?"

"Never heard of it," said Morlake, truthfully.

"Thank God," said the woman. She added, "I've been swimming in the old swimming hole—enlarged by damming, cemented into a pool, and improved by a ten thousand dollar heating system for cool days and nights. Just a little gadget of the professor's, hot and cold running water. Would you like to know all the local gossip? I've only been a guest twenty-four hours, but I already know everything there is to know here."

Morlake didn't doubt it. He was beginning to be fascinated. It cost him an effort to keep his mind to his purpose. The woman said, "The world is absolutely wretched, detestable and incorrigible. Here it is little more than three months after B-day, and—"

"After what?"

"Bomb day. That's what the army calls it. You can't go on saying 'the day the atomic bombs were dropped,' or 'day of the catastrophe.' You can't even expect people to remember that B-day was July 17th, can you?"

She did not wait for an answer, for they had reached the house.

"Wait here," she said. "I'll slip into my bedroom, and open the living room door for you."

Morlake did not wait. The moment she disappeared around the corner, he followed. It had taken him a minute to catch on, but he was too conscious of danger to be fooled by a fast-talking woman. She had recognized him, and she would probably telephone the police before opening the front door.

There were three patio doors along the side and all of them

were unlocked, but only the third one opened into an unoccupied room.

He knew it was possible that the woman had snatched up a gun in passing, but he was beyond that kind of fear. . . . The situation in the living room was ideal for melodrama. She was at the phone, her back to him, saying urgently, "Keep trying! There must be an answer!" Morlake put his hand over the mouthpiece, and took the receiver from her instantly acquiescent fingers. For a long moment the woman sat frozen, and then slowly she turned and looked at him, her eyes widened.

Morlake did not replace the receiver, but stood there holding it tightly. He said in a monotone:

"How did you recognize me?"

She shrugged. "Newspaper pictures all over the house. Your friend, Dorman, talking about you, saying he can't believe you're guilty. But you are, aren't you? I've seen desperate men before."

Where? Morlake wondered, but all he said was, "Who were you phoning?"

"The police, of course."

Answering that required no thought.

"The police would have replied—" he began. And then he stopped, as the operator's voice sounded from the earphone. He jerked the instrument up. "Yes," he said. "Hello."

"The party the lady called does not answer," trilled the female voice.

Morlake said, "Are you sure you have the right number?" Beside him the woman gasped. Before he could guess her intention, she reached down, snatched the cord, and, with a jerk that must have jarred her body, tore the wires out of the box. . . .

In the Morlake room at supreme headquarters, General Clark paused in his narrative. Senator Tormey said slowly:

"Who was the woman? Did you find out?"

The officer shook his head. "I can't remember the alias she used at Glidden Grove, but that name and a dozen others that she employed are all in the index there. Clark motioned toward the cabinet.

"You think she was after Morlake?"

"Definitely."

"How did she happen to be at that particular spot within two days after Morlake's escape?"

"That," said the general, "was what worried Morlake. Then and there he abandoned his plan to approach old

riends of his, and attempt, through them, to build up the
ucleus of his organization. He realized that he had been
orestalled by a group that had anticipated his plans and
nade a thorough study of his life history. When we came on
he scene we found that virtually every friend he ever possessed had been under surveillance on that morning. A hundred different methods were used to gain intimate access
to the different people involved. It was very thorough."

"How do you account for their preparation?" The senator
was standing with closed eyes.

"It is our opinion," said Clark, "that they intended to rescue
him from the prison farm and kill him."

"But how did they know about him?"

The general hesitated. "Our theory there is a little wild,
but the men who have gone over Morlake's written statement
and court-martial evidence grew interested in the flare of
light that enveloped the plane immediately after the bomb
had rebuffed Morlake's attempt to throw it off course. We
think that light was used to take a television picture of the
S29A.

It was Morlake who broke the silence in the living room of
Professor Glidden's bungalow.

"Where is your car?" he said.

The woman seemed resigned. "I'll get my car keys, and
drive you back to your plane. I suppose that's where you're
heading."

He went with her, conscious that he could trust no one,
now that he knew. And that there wasn't time to talk to
Dan Dorman, or to ask the questions he had intended to ask
Dan's employer, Professor Glidden. He had come to Dan
first of all, because of his connection with the world-famous
physicist. Depressing to be here at the spot, and realize
that he had to leave without having accomplished anything.

Ten minutes later, the woman parked the car a hundred
feet from where Sadie was drawn up under trees. "It's a
pretty plane," she said. "How fast can it go?"

"Just over a hundred miles a minute," said Morlake carelessly. "Get out."

"W-what?" She must have thought he was going to kill
her, for she turned pale. "Please," she begged, "I'm as innocent as you are. I know nothing."

Morlake gazed at her curiously, but he said nothing. Let
her sweat for a minute. He didn't have time to question her,
and so he couldn't judge how deeply she was involved.

Not that it would have made any difference. He was neither judge nor executioner. He locked the car doors, then slipped the keys into his pocket. He saw that the woman had regained control.

"It's only two miles," she said. "I ought to get there before breakfast. Goodbye and—good luck."

He sent the plane straight up until the world was black, and stars were points of light above him. Then he flashed out over the Pacific, and, turning, came back in, coasting over trees straight into a deep arroyo. His new hiding place was less than half a mile from Manakee, California, the town four miles from Glidden Grove, where the telephone exchange must be located.

A bus coming along the nearby highway made his trip easy, and enable him to inquire about the location of the exchange. . . . There were three girls at the switchboard. One of them, a washed-out looking blonde, said:

"Something went wrong with the line, so I drove in. Did you get the party?"

"Yep, I got her, then I couldn't get you."

Another woman! Morlake felt a thrill, then a sharp anxiety. It was as he had feared. The connection had been established. He hesitated, but there was no drawing back.

"Will you call again?"

"Sure. Got the number?"

Morlake was as ready for that as he could be. "Let me see. Hmm, can't think of it offhand. But I have it here somewhere."

As he began to search aimlessly through his pockets, he saw that she was examining her notebook. She looked up.

"Never mind, I wrote it down. Lucy Desjardins, 476 Hartford Street, Crestolanto 9153."

For a moment Morlake could only trust himself to nod; then it was time to speak again.

"Just a moment," he said.

"Yes?"

"Did the party, uh, say anything, when you couldn't get her through to me?"

"Yeah, she said it didn't matter or something like that."

"Oh!" said Morlake. "In that case don't bother." He mustered a laugh. "She's a damned touchy woman. I don't want to get her down on me again."

He went out, perspiring but momentarily relieved and jubilant. The feeling didn't last long. The woman had said it didn't matter. That meant she had understood. The gang would be swinging into action.

He hailed a cruising taxi, and had it take him to the sub-
urbs. As soon as it was out of sight, he raced along the highway and across the fields to his machine. The moment he was
inside the cockpit, he turned on the radar, and waited.

At first there was nothing. The sky was empty, except
for a haze of immensely high clouds. After thirty-seven minutes, a shadow darkened the screen. It was too far away, too
high to form a clear image. But it was unmistakable, and it
moved along with great speed at a height of about a hundred
and twenty-five miles.

Morlake kept spinning his radio dial, and suddenly it
caught and stopped, as a voice said:

". . . Got away, looks like. We've been east and north
and south, and out over the water, and there's not a sign
of anything moving. His machine must be capable of far
greater speed than we believed."

The answering voice was faint. "Don't give up. Take nothing for granted."

A third voice broke in loudly. "Hey, who's that talking?
This is army station Miklaw. Identify yourself."

There was a faint laugh from the nearest voice, then silence.

IV

For Morlake, hiding, waiting, planning, in the arroyo near
Manakee, time passed slowly. It was a strangely sad period,
one man alone wondering how he could convince a nation
that he was right and their leaders were wrong. Ghosts of
forty million dead adults and children haunted his dreams,
but already the fact that they had existed was a shadowy
fact in his mind. To him, who had no family, and who had
had the experience of friends dying in a war, death was not
the ogre that it was to those who had never been trained
to face it.

Far more real than the death that had struck was the
knowledge that out there somewhere on the surface of the
Earth, cunning devil-men were waiting for the slightest hint
that their identity had been discovered, that, to save themselves, they must be prepared to rend the entire Earth.

Their leaders would deny all accusations, would charge
a conspiracy, and, with the tremendous advantage of control of the moon, would be able to launch bombs toward
any target at will.

Morlake quailed at the picture, and knew that his new

plan to seek out the gang must parallel and complement his greater purpose of forcing a reluctant people to crawl up from the caves of fear into which their minds had collapsed up to the special bravery or imagination that would be needed for the conquest of space.

At dawn, on this third morning in the arroyo, Morlake made sure the radar screen was blank, and then flew in a great circle around the Capistrano radar station of the army to Crestolanto. He spent all that day watching 476 Hartford Street. It was a plain two-story structure, and during the morning it showed no sign of life. About mid-afternoon, a woman came out of the front door and walked to the nearby market. It was not the woman who had been visiting Professor Glidden's home, but a slim, distinguished-looking young woman with hair slightly graying at the temples.

When she had come back, he wrote a letter to General Clark, describing what he intended to do. He mailed the letter shortly after dark, and then he waited for black night. It was half past nine by his watch when he crawled through a window, and moved stealthily toward the living room, where a light was visible through a partly open door.

Senator Tormey asked, "And then what happened?"

General Clark shook his head. "We have no direct information."

He pointed to a red pin rooted in a small West Coast city.

"There, Morlake made one of his four attempts to interest the general public. According to our reports, a woman did all the preliminary advertising for a lecture Morlake intended to give. According to our information, it was this second woman. The lecture was a flop. About a dozen people turned up, most of them old women, who thought it was a new religion, in which the moon had been proved to be heaven."

"Then it would appear that Morlake and this, uh, nameless woman joined forces."

"Never," said the general, "have I had reports of a bolder couple. They were quite cautious at first. Now they're absolutely fearless."

The senator was silent. He wore contact lenses, behind which his intense blue eyes gleamed with alert fires.

General Clark walked to a window, and gazed out past the formal park toward the distant blue of hills. Without looking around he said:

"Last night you asked me about Morlake, and I invited
104

you to come here. This is in line with the army's policy of cooperating with elected representatives of the people. As you know, we intend to permit the congressional elections in 1982 and so the country will resume its normal democratic functioning. What you do not know is that, though the eletions will be held as scheduled, the announcement about them was made with the intention of lulling the enemy."

From behind him, Tormey said slowly, "I don't think I understand."

The general turned to face the bigger man. "When Morlake escaped with S29A, I received a garbled account of what had happened. It was so garbled, in fact, the loss of the plane so important, that I flew to Texas by jet, saw the court-martial papers of Morlake, and began to realize what tremendous information had been bottled up. Naturally, I relieved Herrold of his command instantly, and by the end of the week we had the information which I have described. Better still, our radar station at Capistrano saw the image of the enemy spaceship which was searching for Morlake, and so we had definite evidence that what he stated in his letter was correct.

"When Capistrano saw it, the spaceship was about two hundred miles up. They couldn't estimate the speed, but it was terrific."

He went on matter-of-factly.

"Normally, we might have paid no attention to such a report. So many, many reports come in hour after hour to all military districts. But at this time, on the basis of Morlake's written statement to General Herrold, our experts decided that they had narrowed the possible origins of the bombs to three:

"Two of them were the likeliest points on Earth. If we decided on either of these, we'd have to assume that our men or our instruments for detecting radioactivity were at fault. We rejected these possibilities because the piles necessary for the creation of vast quantities of radioactive materials could not escape detection. That left the third alternative, which assumed the bombs to be of extraterrestrial origin. I accordingly ordered the resumption of the moon project, which—as you know—had actually completed nearly thirty ships when Congress cut off its funds."

Senator Tormey said gravely, "I regret that I had something to do with that cut-off, but it was a matter of too much deficit spending."

"Unfortunately," said the general, "one of the storage places for the spaceships was in Georgia, and that entire base was destroyed by a direct hit. Twenty-two spaceships were destroyed. However, there is another storage area—it would be unwise for me to tell you where it is."

"Perhaps I could inspect them," said the senator. "How many ships are there?"

"Five."

"That many?" Tormey sounded impressed.

"They'll be operational next week," said General Clark.

The senator made a strange sound. It was not a word, and he did not repeat it. Instead, he walked unevenly to a chair and sat down.

"General," he mumbled at last, "you make me dizzy. You mean that all this uproar about Morlake has been unnecessary?"

"Very necessary." Clark was deadly serious. "His desperate efforts to get us to do something made it look as if we were paying no attention to him. We even ridiculed Morlake's propaganda. Personally, I think Morlake caught on, but right now I'd give a lot to have a talk with him. The time has come for coordinated action."

The senator said blankly, "But this means war."

"We'll smash them in one day," Clark said coldly. "No one else has dared to mobilize, for fear of rousing our suspicion. We'll put a million men into their cities overnight. We'll execute every man who had anything to do with the bombing of this country. For once, no one will have an excuse."

"And all this in about two weeks?"

"Possibly less."

There was a long silence. At last the senator climbed to his feet.

"It seems kind of funny after that, to talk of social activity, but are you still having your crap game tonight?"

"We don't dare change our habits now."

"How many will be there?"

"Six, besides yourself."

"Wonder if I could bring along a young friend of my wife's?"

"Why, sure. Which reminds me. When is your lady coming down here?"

Tormey smiled. "Couldn't tell you. She thinks I ought to retire from politics, and therefore she won't establish an official residence. She's pretty much of a traveler."

They parted on that note.

"Gentlemen," said Senator Tormey, "this is my friend, Morley Roberts."

There was a grunting response. Morlake sat down, and watched the dice bounce briskly from the far end of the table. He did not look immediately at General Clark, but concentrated on making his first bet. Presently, he picked up his winnings for the roll, and pressed his arm ever so lightly against the gun in his shoulder holster. It was still there, ready for the crisis which ought to come in a few minutes.

He lost twice in a row, and then won three times on his own roll. As he gave up the dice finally, he took his first look at General Clark. A pair of eyes as sharp as his own met that one searching glance. The general said casually:

"So it's me you're here to contact, Roberts?"

Morlake brought his hand to the edge of the table, with the fingers held slightly downward and barely touching the surface. From there it was one foot to his gun.

He said steadily: "General, you're a smart man, but you haven't figured it quite right."

There was an undertone in his voice, the beginning of tension, the beginning of deadly intent. Like darkness blotting out day, the atmosphere of the room changed. Some of the officers looked at each other, puzzled. Senator Tormey said:

"It's getting warm in here. Uh, I'll call one of my guards and have him open the windows wider."

"I'll do it sir." Morlake was on his feet, without waiting for acquiescence.

He examined the windows and, as he had expected, the "glass" was a bullet-proof plastic. What he did then was rooted in a profound discovery he had made during the previous six months: the discovery that if you say you will do something and then go and do something similar, no one will notice the difference—for a while.

Without a qualm, he closed and locked the three windows, and then he returned to the table. The dice rolled whitely against the background of the green cloth. Senator Tormey won from several of the officers. As he was raking in it, General Clark said:

"Morley Roberts. The name is familiar, but it is the face that makes a better identification. Suppose we change the name around a little, and say Robert Morlake, former Captain, army air forces, court-martialed, thirty years at hard labor. Am I getting warm?"

The general's voice went up, "Wait, gentlemen!" The men at the table froze, two with their chairs pushed back, one with a hand under his coat. The senator was the first to relax. He was sitting at the side of the table, and he hummed a small tune under his breath. Clark said softly:

"You came here tonight as the guest of Senator Tormey. I presume he knows who you are."

"I'm sure," Morlake said, "that the senator must have recognized me, but you will know better than I if he's made inquiries about me in the last two days. But now I'd better hurry. Gentlemen, this is a dangerous moment, not because of me directly—I'm only a catalytic agent—but because my appearance gave a certain person an opportunity to carry out a previously conceived plan.

"It was my intention," Morlake went on, "that he should use me for this purpose so that I might use him for mine.

"A brief case history is in order: Picture a wealthy congressman, unscrupulous and with unlimited ambitions. It is very easy for him to think of himself as a man of destiny, frustrated by the stupidity of others. Having become senator, he discovered in two successive presidential campaigns that he had no chance to become chief of state. His wife began to realize shortly after she married him in 1974 that his rage at his failure was irrational, his lust for revenge completely unbalanced. But she didn't guess at the meaning of his schemes nor at the purpose of the organization he set up in the South until B-day; the total violence and hate in the man—she told me—was concealed by a superficial courtesy and a courtly manner. As you know, he was in a safe place on B-Day—very fortuitous. Afterward, his main opposition was the army. It was clever of him to authorize martial law—which would have been done anyway. It was clever because he was later able to use it in his propaganda."

Morlake paused, and smiled to relax his eyes, to loosen his body, because the moment had come.

"His big opportunity came—it seemed to him—when I appeared on the scene, as guest of his wife. He saw it as his chance to kill General Clark and his staff, and throw the blame on me. I, of course, the highly publicized escaped army convict, would also be found dead, and—"

Morlake broke off. He said. "What's the matter, Senator, has your nerve gone? You're not going to go down like a weakling, are you?"

The sweat was almost a mask on the heavy face. Tormey brought his hand up, and put it in his vest pocket. He fumbled for a long moment. Morlake said:

"I see, Senator, that you're activating your little radio, calling your agents outside."

As if to punctuate the words, there was a crash of bullets on the window. Everybody except Morlake jumped Morlake said tantalizingly, "Too bad."

He reached across the table, and snatched a tiny instrument from the senator's vest pocket. The man grabbed angrily at his hand, but he was too slow.

"Hmm," said Morlake. "One of the printed variety."

With a visible effort, the other man straightened. "Never heard such nonsense," he snarled. "You've arranged this drama with bullets against the window. If you think such a simple scheme is going to work against me, you're—"

He stopped. His eyes, staring straight into Morlake's, widened. He must have realized that his denials were meaningless here, that the plans already boiling in his mind, to use the radio and the press, his control of the party, of the country, his skill at propaganda—all that meant nothing to this deadly young man. He had not even time to cry out in sudden terrified realization of his fate.

The two shots that Morlake fired broke the big man's lungs. Tormey slumped over on the table, then slid down to the floor Morlake paid no attention to the armed officers in the room. They could have shot him as he knelt beside the dying man, but his very helplessness was his safeguard. They watched, their bodies rigid, and they must have been restrained, too, by the knowledge that he had acted with remorseless logic.

Morlake neither saw nor worried The senator's eyes were open and staring widely. There was blood on his lips.

"Senator, what is the name of the enemy?"

That got them General Clark came closer. An officer who had gone to calm the guards at the door half turned back into the room. Even Senator Tormey stiffened.

"You can go to hell," he muttered

Morlake said, "Hurry, man, you've only got a minute—a minute."

The horror of that struck deep. The thick face twisted. "Die!" the senator mumbled. "Why—I'm going to die" The idea seemed to grow on him. He struggled, gasping for breath, then subsided. He lay so still for a second that he looked dead. His eyes opened wearily. He looked up, and mumbled:

"Was that my wife . . . at Crestolanto, in that house?"

Morlake nodded. "She used your organization. She received all California reports. That enabled her to locate me no matter which local agent saw me first. She had decided

109

that if I came to Crestolanto she would ask me to help her. It was she who toured the country with me for all those weeks."

General Clark dropped down beside Morlake. "Senator," he said, "for God's sake, the name of the country, the enemy?"

The dying man looked at him with the beginning of a sneer on his lips

"We got even with you nigger lovers, didn't we?" he said. He laughed a satanic laughter, that ended hideously in a gush of blood Slowly, the big head grew limp, the eyes though still open took on a sightless glare. A dead man lay on the floor.

The two men, Clark and Morlake, climbed to their feet. Morlake said in a low voice, "Gentlemen, you have your answer" He saw they still did not comprehend what he had suspected for long now

General Clark was grim. "When I think we've been giving him our inmost secrets for months—" He choked, and held out his hand. "Thanks."

Morlake said nothing His first sharp sense of victory was yielding to an intense gloom. He grew aware that the older man's penetrating gaze was on him Clark misread his expression.

"I know what's ailing you," Clark said. "But you're wrong. We have spaceships" He described the planned attack on the moon.

Morlake nodded, but his depression remained. Such an attack would be necessary, to locate the launching sites of the bombs, and to find out where and how in America Tormey and his group obtained them. But that was incidental. He accepted Tormey's last words literally.

The first atomic war had been, not an international, but a civil war. And now that Tormey was dead, the gang would scatter. A gang of race-prejudiced Americans.

The war was over. Irrevocably.

THE CATAAAAA

THE USUAL GROUP was gathering in the bar. Cathy was already pretending she was far gone Ted was busy putting on his stupid look. Myra giggled three times the way a musician tunes his instrument for the evening. Jones was talking to Gord, in his positive fashion. Gord said "Glub!" every few seconds, just as if he was listening. And Morton tried to draw attention to himself by remaining aloof and intellectual looking far down in his chair.

No one noticed the slight, slim man sitting on a stool before the bar. The man kept glancing at the group; but just when he joined them, or who invited him, no one had any clear idea. Nor did it occur to anyone to tell him to go away.

The stranger said, "You were talking about the basic characteristics of human nature—"

Myra giggled, "Is that what we were talking about? I wondered."

The laughter that followed did not deter the newcomer.

"It so happens that I have had an experience which illustrates the point. It began one day when I was glancing through the newspaper, and I ran across a circus advertisement . . ."

At the top of the ad (he went on) was a large question mark followed by some equally large exclamation marks. Then:

WHAT IS IT?
IT'S THE CAT
COME AND SEE THE CAT
THE CAT WILL STARTLE YOU
THE CAT WILL AMAZE YOU
SEE THE CAT AT THE FREAK SHOW

In smaller letters at the bottom of the ad was the information that the cat was being "shown under the personal direction of Silkey Travis."

Until that point I had been reading with a vague interest and curiosity. The name made me jump.

Good lord! I thought. *It's him. It's Silkey Travis on that card.*

I hurried to my desk, and took out a card that had come in the mail two days before. At the time it had made no sense to me at all. The words written on the back in a fine script seemed pure gibberish, and the photograph on the front, though familiar, unlocked no real memory. It was of a man with a haunted look on his face, sitting in a small cage. I now recognized it as being a likeness of Silkey Travis, not as I had known him fifteen or so years before, but plumper, older, as he would be now.

I returned to my chair, and sat musing about the past.

Even in those days, his name had fitted Silkey Travis. At high school he organized the bathing beauty contest, and

111

gave the first prize to his cousin and the second prize to the girl who was the teacher's pet of the most teachers. The students' science exhibition, a collection of local lizards, snakes, insects and a few Indian artifacts, was an annual affair, which brought a turnout of admiring parents. Invariably, it was Silkey who organized it. Plays, holiday shows and other paraphernalia of school pastimes felt the weight of his guiding hand and circus spirit.

After graduating from high school, I went on to State college to major in biology, and I lost sight of Silkey for seven years. Then I saw an item in one of the papers to the effect that local boy Silkey Travis was doing well in the big town, having just purchased a "piece" of a vaudeville show, and that he also owned a "piece" in a beach concession in New Jersey.

Again, there was silence. And now, here he was, no doubt "piece" owner of the circus freak show.

Having solved the mystery of the postcard, so it seemed to me, I felt amused and tolerant. I wondered if Silkey had sent the card to all his former school companions. I decided not to puzzle any more about the meaning of the words written on the back. The scheme behind them was all too obvious.

Sitting there, I had absolutely no intention of going to the circus. I went to bed at my usual hour, and woke up with a start some hours later to realize that I was not alone. The sensations that came to me as I lay there have been described by Johnson in his book on morbid fears.

I lived in a quiet neighborhood, and the silence was intense. Presently, I could hear the labored pounding of my heart. Poisons surged into my stomach; gas formed and leaked up to my mouth bringing a bitter taste. I had to fight to keep my breath steady.

And still I could see nothing. The dark fears ran their courses, and the first thought came that I must have had a nightmare. I began to feel ashamed of myself. I mumbled:

"Who's there?"

No answer.

I climbed out of bed, and turned on the light. The room was empty. But still I wasn't satisfied. I went out into the hall; then I examined the clothes closet and bathroom. Finally, dissatisfied, I tested the window fastening—and it was there I received my shock. Painted on the outer side of the pane of one of the windows were the letters:

The cat requests that you come to the circus.

112

I went back to bed so furious that I thought of having Silkey arrested. When I woke up in the morning the sign was gone from the window.

By the time breakfast was over, my temper of the night had cooled. I was even able to feel a pitying amusement at the desperate desire of Silkey to let his old acquaintances know what a big shot he was. Before starting off to my morning classes at State, I looked under my bedroom window. I found what looked like footprints, but they were not human, so I decided that Silkey must have taken care to leave no tracks of his own.

At class, just before noon, one of the students asked me whether there was any good explanation in biological science for freaks. I gave the usual explanation of variabilities, nutritional deficiencies, diseases, frustration of brain development affecting the shape of the body, and so on. I finished dryly that for further information I would direct him to my old friend, Silkey Travis, director of freaks at the Pagley-Matterson circus.

The offhand remark caused a sensation. I was informed that a freak at the circus had prompted the original question. "A strange, cat-like creature," the student said in a hushed voice, "that examines you with the same interest that you examine it."

The bell rang at that moment, and I was spared the necessity of making a comment. I remember thinking, however, that people hadn't changed much. They were still primarily interested in eccentricity whereas, as a scientist, the processes of normalcy seemed to me far more fascinating.

I still had no intention of going to the circus. But on the way home that afternoon I put my hand in my breast pocket, and drew out the postcard with the photograph of Silkey on the front. I turned it over absently, and read again the message that was on it:

The interspatial problem of delivering mail involves enormous energy problems, which affect time differentials Accordingly, it is possible that this card will arrive before I know who you are. As a precaution I am sending another one to the circus with your name and address on it, and the two cards will go out together.

Do not worry too much about the method of delivery. I simply put an instrument into a mailbox. This precipitates the cards into the box on Earth, and they

113

will then be picked up and delivered in the usual fash-
ion. The precipitator then dissolves.
The photograph speaks for itself.

It didn't. Which is what began to irritate me again. I jammed the card back into my pocket, half-minded to phone up Silkey and ask him what the silly thing meant, if anything. I refrained, of course. It wasn't important enough.

When I got out of bed the next morning, the words *The cat wants to talk to you!* were scrawled on the outside of the same window pane. They must have been there for a long time. Because, even as I stared at them, they began to fade. By the time I finished breakfast they were gone.

I was disturbed now rather than angry. Such persistence on Silkey's part indicated neurotic overtones in his character. It was possible that I ought to go to his show, and so give him the petty victory that would lay to rest his ghost, which had now haunted me two nights running. However, it was not till after lunch that a thought occurred to me that suddenly clinched my intention. I remembered Virginia.

For two years I had been professor of biology at State. It was an early ambition which, now that I had realized it, left me at a loose end for the first time in my life. Accordingly, for the first time in my rather drab existence the mating urge was upon me. Virginia was the girl, and, unfortunately, she regarded me as a cross between a fossil and a precision brain. I felt sure that the idea of marrying me had not yet occurred to her.

For some time it had seemed to me that if I could only convince her, without loss of dignity, that I was a romantic fellow she might be fooled into saying yes. What better method than to pretend that I still got excited over circuses, and as a grand climax to the evening I would take her in to see Silkey Travis, and hope that my acquaintance with such a character would thrill her exotic soul.

The first hurdle was bridged when I called her up, and she agreed to go to the circus with me. I put the best possible face on for the preliminaries, riding the ferris wheel and such juvenilia. But the moment of the evening for me came when I suggested that we go and see the freaks being shown by my old friend, Silkey Travis.

It really went over. Virginia stopped and looked at me almost accusingly.

"Philip," she said, "you're not trying to pretend that you
114

know a person called Silkey?" She drew a deep breath. "That I have to see."

Silkey came through beautifully. He was not in when we entered, but the ticket taker called into some rear compartment. And a minute later Sikey came charging into the main freak tent. He was plump with the plumpness of a well-fed shark. His eyes were narrowed as if he had spent the past fifteen years calculating the best methods of using other people for his own advantage. He had none of the haunted look of the photograph, but there were ghosts in his face. Ghosts of greed and easy vices, ghosts of sharp dealing and ruthlessness. He was all that I had hoped for, and, best of all, he was pathetically glad to see me. His joy had the special quality of the lonely nomad who is at last looking longingly at the settled side of life. We both overdid the greeting a little, but we were about equally pleased at each other's enthusiasm. The hellos and introductions over, Silkey grew condescending.

"Brick was in a while ago. Said you were teaching at State. Congrats. Always knew you had it in you."

I passed over that as quickly as possible. "How about showing us around, Silkey, and telling us about yourself?"

We had already seen the fat woman and the human skeleton, but Silkey took us back and told us *his* life history with them. How he had found them, and helped them to their present fame. He was a little verbose, so on occasion I had to hurry him along. But finally we came to a small tent within the tent, over the closed canvas entrance of which was painted simply, THE CAT. I had noticed it before, and the chatter of the barker who stood in front of it had already roused my curiosity:

"The cat . . . come in and see the cat. Folks, this is no ordinary event, but the thrill of a lifetime. Never before has such an animal as this been seen in a circus. A biological phenomenon that has amazed scientists all over the country. . . . Folks, this is special. Tickets are twenty-five cents, but if you're not satisfied you can get your money back. That's right. That's what I said. You can get your money back merely by stepping up and asking for it. . . ."

And so on. However, his ballyhoo was not the most enticing angle. What began to titillate my nerves was the reaction of the people who went inside. They were allowed to enter in groups, and there must have been a guide inside, because his barely audible voice would mumble on for some minutes, and then it would rise to a hearable level, as

115

he said, "And now, folks, I will draw aside the curtain and show you—the cat!"

The curtain must have been pulled with a single jerk, on a carefully timed basis. For the word *cat* was scarcely out of his mouth, when the audience reaction would sound

"Aaaaaa!"

Distinct, unmistakable exhalation of the breaths of a dozen startled people. There would follow an uncomfortable silence. Then, slowly, the people woud emerge and hurry to the outer exit Not one, that I was aware of, asked for his money back.

There was a little embarrassment at the gate. Silkey started to mumble something about only owning part of the show, so he couldn't give passes But I ended that by quickly purchasing the necessary tickets, and we went inside with the next group.

The animal that sat in an armchair on the dais was about five feet long and quite slender It had a cat's head and vestiges of fur It looked like an exaggerated version of the walkie-talkie animals in comic books.

At that point resemblance to normalcy ended.

It was alien It was not a cat at all. I recognized that instantly The structure was all wrong. It took me a moment to identify the radical variations.

The head! High foreheaded it was, and not low and receding. The face was smooth and almost hairless. It had character and strength, and intelligence The body was well balanced on long straight legs The arms were smooth, ending in short but unmistakable fingers, surmounted by thin, sharp claws.

But it was the eyes that were really different. They looked normal enough, slightly slanted, properly lidded, about the same size as the eyes of human beings. *But they danced.* They shifted twice, even three times as swiftly as human eyes. Their balanced movement at such a high speed indicated vision that could read photographically reduced print across a room What sharp, what incredibly sharp images that brain must see.

All this I saw within the space of a few seconds. Then the creature moved.

It stood up, not hurriedly, but casually, easily, and yawned and stretched Finally, it took a step forward Brief panic ensued among the women in the audience, that ended as the guide said quietly:

"It's all right, folks. He frequently comes down and looks us over. He's harmless."

The crowd stood its ground, as the cat came down the steps from the dais and approached me. The animal paused in front of me, and peered at me curiously. Then it reached gingerly forward, opened my coat, and examined the inside breast pocket.

It came up holding the postcard with the picture of Silkey on it. I had brought it along, intending to ask Silkey about it.

For a long moment the cat examined the card, and then it held it out to Silkey. Silkey looked at me.

"Okay?" he said.

I nodded. I had a feeling that I was witnessing a drama the motivations of which I did not understand. I realized that I was watching Silkey intently.

He looked at the picture on the card, and then started to hand it to me. Then he stopped. Jerkily, he pulled the card back, and stared at the photograph.

"For cripes sake," he gasped. "It's a picture of me."

There was no doubt about his surprise. It was so genuine that it startled me. I said, "Didn't you send that to me? Didn't you write what's on the back there?"

Silkey did not answer immediately. He turned the card over and glared down at the writing. He began to shake his head.

"Doesn't make sense," he muttered. "Hmm, it was mailed in Marstown. That's where we were three days last week."

He handed it back to me. "Never saw it before in my life. Funny."

His denial was convincing. I held the card in my hand, and looked questioningly at the cat. But it had already lost interest. As we stood there, watching, it turned and climbed back up to the dais, and slumped into a chair. It yawned. It closed its eyes.

And that's all that happened. We all left the tent, and Virginia and I said goodbye to Silkey. Later, on our way home, the episode seemed even more meaningless than when it had happened.

I don't know how long I had been asleep before I wakened. I turned over intending to go right back to sleep. And then I saw that my bedside light was burning. I sat up with a start.

The cat was sitting in a chair beside the bed, not more than three feet away.

There was silence. I couldn't have spoken at the beginning. Slowly, I sat up. Memory came of what the guide at the show had said, ". . . Harmless!" But I didn't believe that anymore.

Three times now this beast had come here, twice to leave messages. I let my mind run over those messages, and I quailed. ". . . The cat wants to talk to you!" Was it possible that this thing could talk?

The very inactivity of the animal finally gave me courage. I licked my lips and said, "Can you talk?"

The cat stirred. It raised an arm in the unhurried fashion of somebody who does not want to cause alarm. It pointed at the night table beside my bed. I followed the pointing finger and saw that an instrument was standing under the lamp. The instrument spoke at me:

"I cannot emit human sounds with my own body, but as you can hear this is an excellent intermediary."

I have to confess that I jumped, that my mind scurried into a deep corner of my head—and only slowly came out again as the silence continued, and no attempt was made to harm me. I don't know why I should have assumed that its ability to speak through a mechanical device was a threat to me. But I had.

I suppose it was really a mental shrinking, my mind unwilling to accept the reality that was here. Before I could think clearly, the instrument on the table said:

"The problem of conveying thoughts through an electronic device depends on rhythmic utilization of brain energies."

The statement stirred me. I had read considerable on that subject, beginning with Professor Hans Berger's report on brain rhythms in 1929. The cat's statements didn't quite fit.

"Isn't the energy potential too small?" I asked. "And besides, you have your eyes open. The rhythms are always interfered with when the eyes are open, and in fact such a large part of the cortex yields to the visual centers that no rhythm whatever is detectable at such times."

It didn't strike me then, but I think now that I actually distracted the animal from its purpose. "What measurements have been taken?" it asked. Even through the mind radio, it sounded interested.

"Photoelectric cells," I said, "have measured as much (or as little, which is really more accurate) as fifty microvolts of energy, mostly in the active regions of the brain. Do you know what a microvolt is?"

The creature nodded. It said after a moment, "I won't

118

tell you what energy my brain develops. It would probably frighten you, but it isn't all intelligence. I am a student on a tour of the galaxy, what might be called a post-graduate tour. Now, we have certain rules—" It stopped. "You opened your mouth. Did you wish to say something?"

I felt dumb, overwhelmed. Then, weakly, "You said galaxy."

"That is correct."

"B-but wouldn't that take years?" My brain was reaching out, striving to grasp, to understand.

"My tour will last about a thousand of your years," said the cat.

"You're immortal?"

"Oh, no."

"But—"

There I stopped. I couldn't go on. I sat there, blank-brained, while the creature went on:

"The rules of the fraternity of students require that we tell one person about ourselves before we leave the planet. And that we take with us a symbolical souvenir of the civilization of the beings on it. I'm curious to know what you would suggest as a souvenir of Earth. It can be anything, so long as it tells at a glance the dominating character of the race."

The question calmed me. My brain stopped its alternation of mad whirling followed by blankness. I began to feel distinctly better. I shifted myself into a more comfortable position and stroked my jaw thoughtfully. I sincerely hoped that I was giving the impression that I was an intelligent person whose opinion would be worthwhile.

A sense of incredible complications began to seize on me. I had realized it before, but now, with an actual decision to make, it seemed to me that human beings were really immensely intricate creatures. How could anybody pick one facet of their nature and say, "This is man!" Or "This represents man!" I said slowly:

"A work of art, science, or any useful article—you include those?"

"Anything."

My interest was now at its peak. My whole being accepted the wonderfulness of what had happened. It seemed tremendously important that the great race that could travel the breadth and length of the galaxy should have some true representation of man's civilization. It amazed me, when I finally thought of the answer, that it had taken me so long. But the moment it occurred to me, I knew I had it.

119

"Man," I said, "is primarily a religious animal. From times too remote to have a written record, he has needed a faith in something. Once, he believed almost entirely in animate gods like rivers, storms, plants, then his gods became invisible; now they are once more becoming animate. An economic system, science—whatever it will be, the dominating article of it will be that he worships it without regard to reason, in other words in a purely religious fashion."

I finished with a quiet satisfaction, "All you need is an image of a man in a durable metal, his head tilted back, his arms raised to the sky, a rapt expression on his face, and written on the base of the inscription, 'I believe.' "

I saw that the creature was staring at me. "Very interesting," it said at last. "I think you are very close to it, but you haven't quite got the answer."

It stood up. "But now I want you to come with me."

"Eh?"

"Dress, please."

It was unemotionally said. The fear that had been held deep inside me for minutes came back like a fire that had reached a new cycle of energy.

I drove my car. The cat sat beside me. The night was cool and refreshing, but dark. A fraction of a moon peered out occasionally from scurrying clouds, and there were glimpses of star filtered dark blue sky. The realization that, from somewhere up there, this creature had come down to our Earth dimmed my tenseness. I ventured:

"Your people—have they progressed much further than we to the innermost meaning of truth?"

It sounded drab and precise, a pedagogical rather than a vitally alive question. I added quickly:

"I hope you won't mind answering a few questions."

Again it sounded inadequate. It seemed to me in an abrupt agony of despair that I was muffing the opportunity of the centuries. Silently, I cursed my professional training that made my every word sound as dry as dust.

"That card," I said. "You sent that?"

"Yes." The machine on the cat's lap spoke quietly but clearly.

"How did you know my address and my name?"

"I didn't."

Before I could say anything, the cat went on, "You will understand all that before the night's over."

"Oh!" The words held me for a second. I could feel the tightness crawling into my stomach. I had been trying not

120

to think of what was going to happen before this night was over. ". . . Questions?" I croaked. "Will you answer them?"

I parted my lips to start a machine-gun patter of queries. And then I closed them again. *What did I want to know?* The vast implications of that reply throttled my voice. Why, oh, why, are human beings so emotional at the great moments of their lives? I couldn't think, for what seemed an endless time. And when I finally spoke again, my first question was trite and not at all what I intended. I said, "You came in a spaceship?"

The cat looked at me thoughtfully. "No," it replied slowly. "I use the energy in my brain."

"Eh! You came through space in your own body?"

"In a sense. One of these years human beings will make the initial discoveries about the rhythmic use of energy. It will be a dazzling moment for science."

"We have," I said, "already made certain discoveries about our nervous systems and rhythm."

"The end of that road," was the answer, "is control of the powers of nature. I will say no more about that."

I was silent, but only briefly. The questions were bubbling now. "Is it possible," I asked, "to develop an atomic powered spaceship?"

"Not in the way you think," said the cat. "An atomic explosion cannot be confined except when it is drawn out in a series of timed frustrations. And that is an engineering problem, and has very little to do with creative physics."

"Life," I mumbled, "where did life come from?"

"Electronic accidents occurring in a suitable environment."

I had to stop there. I couldn't help it. "Electronic accidents. What do you mean?"

"The difference between an inorganic and an organic atom is the arrangement of the internal structure. The hydrocarbon compounds being the most easily affected under certain conditions are the most common form of life. But now that you have atomic energy you will discover that life can be created from any element or compound of elements. Be careful. The hydrocarbon is a weak life structure that could be easily overwhelmed in its present state of development."

I felt a chill. I could just picture the research that would be going on in government laboratories.

"You mean," I gulped, "there are life forms that would be dangerous the moment they are created?"

"Dangerous to man," said the cat. It pointed suddenly.

121

"Turn up that street, and then through a side entrance into the circus grounds."

I had been wondering tensely where we were going. Strangely, it was a shock to realize the truth.

A few minutes later we entered the dark, silent tent of the freaks. And I knew that the final drama of the cat on Earth was about to be enacted.

A tiny light flickered in the shadows. It came nearer, and I saw that there was a man walking underneath it. It was too dark to recognize him, but the light grew stronger, and I saw that it had no source. And suddenly I recognized Silkey Travis.

He was sound asleep.

He came forward, and stood in front of the cat. He looked unnatural, forlorn, like a woman caught without her makeup on. One long, trembling look I took at him, and then I stammered: "What are you going to do?"

The machine the cat carried did not reply immediately. The cat turned and stared at me thoughtfully; then it touched Silkey's face, gently, with one finger Silkey's eyes opened, but he made no other reaction. I realized that one part of his consciousness had been made aware of what was happening I whispered: "Can he hear?"

The cat nodded.

"Can he think?"

The cat shook its head; and then it said:

"In your analysis of the basic nature of human beings, you selected a symptom only. Man is religious because of a certain characteristic. I'll give you a clue When an alien arrives on an inhabited planet, there is usually only one way that he can pass among the intelligent beings on that planet without being recognized for what he is. When you find that method, you have attained understanding of the fundamental character of the race."

It was hard for me to think. In the dim emptiness of the freak tent, the great silence of the circus grounds all around, what was happening seemed unnatural. I was not afraid of the cat. But there was a fear inside me, as strong as terror, as dark as night I looked at the unmoving Silkey with all the lines of his years flabby on his face. And then I stared at the light that hovered above him. And finally I looked at the cat, and I said:

"Curiosity. You mean, man's curiosity. His interest in strange objects makes him accept them as natural when he sees them."

The cat said, "It seems incredible that you, an intelligent

man, have never realized the one character of all human beings." It turned briskly, straightening. "But now, enough of this conversation. I have fulfilled the basic requirements of my domicile here. I have lived for a period without being suspected, and I have told one inhabitant that I have been here. It remains for me to send home a significant artifact of your civilization—and then I can be on my way . . . elsewhere."

I ventured, shakily, "Surely, the artifact isn't Silkey."

"We seldom," said the cat, "choose actual inhabitants of a planet, but when we do we give them a compensation designed to balance what we take away. In his case, virtual immortality."

I felt desperate, suddenly. Seconds only remained; and it wasn't that I had any emotion for Silkey. He stood there like a clod, and even though later he would remember, it didn't matter. It seemed to me that the cat had discovered some innate secret of human nature which I, as a biologist, must know.

"For God's sake," I said, "you haven't explained anything yet. What is this basic human characteristic? And what about the postcard you sent me? And—"

"You have all the clues." The creature started to turn away. "Your inability to comprehend is no concern of mine. We have a code, we students, that is all."

"But what," I asked desperately, "shall I tell the world? Have you no message for human kind, something—"

The cat was looking at me again. "If you can possibly restrain yourself," it said, "don't tell anyone anything."

This time, when it moved away, it did not look back. I saw, with a start, that the mist of light above Silkey's head was expanding, growing. Brighter, vaster, it grew. It began to pulse with a gentle but unbroken rhythm. Inside its coalescing fire the cat and Silkey were dim forms, like shadows in a fire.

Abruptly, the shadows faded; and then the mist of light began to dim. Slowly, it sagged to the ground, and lay for minutes blurring into the darkness.

Of Silkey and the creature there was no sign.

The group sitting around the table in the bar was briefly silent. Finally, Gord said, "Glub!" and Jones said in a positive fashion, "You solved the problem of the postcard, of course?"

The slim, professorish man nodded. "I think so. The reference in the card to time differentials is the clue. The card

123

was sent *after* Silkey was put on exhibition in the school museum of the cat people, but because of time variations in transmission it arrived *before* I knew Silkey would be in town."

Morton came up out of the depths of his chair. "And what about this basic human characteristic, of which religion is merely an outward expression?"

The stranger made a gesture. "Silkey, exhibiting freaks, was really exhibiting himself. Religion is self-dramatization before a god. Self-love, narcissism—in our own little way we show ourselves off . . . and so a strange being could come into our midst unsuspected."

Cathy hiccoughed, and said, "The love interest is what I like. Did you marry Virginia? You are the professor of biology at State, aren't you?"

The other shook his head. "I was," he said. "I should have followed the cat's advice. But I felt it was important to tell other people what had happened. I was dismissed after three months, and I won't tell you what I'm doing now. But I must go on. The world must know about the weakness that makes us so vulnerable. Virginia? She married a pilot with one of the big air firms. She fell for his line of self-dramatization."

He stood up. "Well, I guess I'll be on my way. I've got a lot of bars to visit tonight."

When he had gone, Ted paused momentarily in his evening's task of looking stupid. "There," he said, "is a guy who really has a line. Just imagine. He's going to tell that story about five times tonight. What a set-up for a fellow who wants to be the center of attention."

Myra giggled. Jones began to talk to Gord in his know-it-all fashion. Gord said, "Glub!" every few seconds, just as if he was listening. Cathy put her head on the table and snored drunkenly. And Morton sagged lower and lower into his chair.

AUTOMATON

THE HUMAN AUTOMATON stirred uneasily in his small, almost invisible plane. His eyes strained into the visiplate, scanning the sky ahead. Out of the blue came two flashes of fire. Instantly, the plane careened as if struck from a double blow.

It fell slowly at first, then more rapidly, down into the enemy lines. As the Earth came near, a resisting mechanism went into operation. The rate of fall grew slower. The automaton had time to see that there was a vast ruin of a city below. Soundlessly, the tiny machine settled into the shelter of the crumbled base of what had once been a building.

A moment passed; then the radio beside him sibilated. Voices which were strange to him were talking to each other.

"Bill!" said the first voice.

"Shoot!"

"Did we get him?"

"Don't think so. Not permanently, anyway. I think he went down under at least partial control, though it's hard to tell with that safety device they have. My guess is he's down there somewhere with his motor shut off."

"I think we disabled him."

"Well, then, you know the routine when one of 'em is cornered just inside our lines. Do your psychology stuff. I'll call the *Vulture*."

"Don't pass the buck to me. I'm sick of spouting those lines. You give 'em!"

"All right. Shoot me the come-on!"

"Hmm . . . he's down there. Think we ought to go after him?"

"Naw! The automatons they send out this far are basically the clever ones. That means we couldn't capture him. He'd be just fast enough on the uptake to make it necessary for us to kill him, and who the devil wants to kill those poor, tortured slaves?— Did you get his picture?"

"Yep, he was listening with an intent look on his face. Fine looking chap. . . . It's funny, and kind of terrible how all this started, isn't it?"

"Yeah. Wonder what this guy's number is."

There was a distinct pause. The automaton stirred uneasily. His number? Ninety-two, of course. What else? The voice was speaking again:

"Poor fellow probably doesn't remember that he once had a name."

The other voice said, "Who'd have thought when they first made a human duplicate—flesh and blood and bones and all—that today, only fifty years later, we'd be fighting for our lives against people who look exactly like us, except that they're natural eunuchs."

The automaton listened with vague attention, as the two men went on talking. Every little while he nodded as their words reminded him of something he had almost forgotten.

125

The human duplicates had first been called robots. They had resented that name, and changed it around to make it Tobor, and that stuck. The Tobors proved to be very effective scientists, and at first no one noticed how rapidly they took over scientific posts in every part of the world. Nor was it immediately noticed that the Tobors were secretly carrying on a duplication campaign on a tremendous scale. The great shock to the human masses came when Tobor-infiltrated governments on each continent simultaneously enacted laws declaring duplication would henceforth be the only means of procreation. Sex was forbidden under penalty of a fine for the first offense, then imprisonment, and then, for recalcitrants, the Tobor-invented process of being made into an automaton.

A special police organization—which turned out to be already in existence—was set up to administer the new law. Tobor enforcement officers swung into action immediately, and there was some street fighting on that first day. Neither side even thought of compromise, so within two weeks full-scale war was raging.

The account ended, as Bill said, "I guess he's heard enough. Come on, let's go."

There was muffled laughter, then silence.

The automaton waited, disturbed. Sketchy memories were in his mind of a past when there had been no war, and, somewhere, there was a girl, and another world.

The unreal pictures faded. And again there was only this ship that clothed his body in almost formfitting metal. There was the need to go on, aerial pictures to be taken. . . . Must get up into the air!

He felt the ship tug in response to his urgent thought, but no movement followed. For seconds, he lay lethargically; then came a second urge for flight. Once more the tiny ship writhed with effort, but no upward movement resulted.

This time the automaton had the slow thought: *Something must have fallen across the ship, and is holding it down. . . . Have to go out and remove it. . . .*

He squirmed against the metal and padding that encased him. Sweat poured down his cheeks, but presently he stood free in ankle-deep dust. As he had been trained to do on such occasions, he checked his equipment . . . weapons, tools, gas mask—

He flung himself flat on the ground as a great, dark ship swooped down out of the sky, and settled to the ground several hundred yards away. From his prone position, the automaton watched it, but there was no sign of movement

126

now. Puzzled, the automaton climbed to his feet. He recalled that one of the men on the radio had said a *Vulture* had been called.

So they had been playing a trick on him, pretending to go away. Clearly visible on the ship's hull was the name: *Vulture 121.*

Its appearance seemed to suggest that an attack was to be made. His strong, determined mouth tightened. They'd soon learn it didn't pay to meddle with a Tobor slave.

Die for Tobor, mighty Tobor. . . .

Tensely, the young woman watched as her pilot lowered the high-speed plane toward the leveled ruin of the city where the *Vulture* lay. The big ship was unmistakable. It towered above the highest remnant of shattered wall. It was a black bulk against the gray-dark sameness of the rubble.

There was a bump and she was out of the machine, clutching her bag. Twice, her right ankle twisted cruelly as she raced over the uneven ground. Breathlessly, she ran up the narrow gangplank.

A steel door clicked open. As she hurried inside, she glanced behind her. The door clanged shut; and she realized gratefully that she was safe.

She stopped, as her eyes had to accustom themselves to the dim metal room. After a moment she saw a little group of men. One of them, a small individual with glasses and a thin face, stepped forward. He took the suitcase from her with one hand, and with the other, he grabbed her hand, and shook it warmly.

"Good girl!" he said. "That was well and swiftly run, Miss Harding. I'm sure no spying ship of the robots could have identified you in any way during the half-minute you were exposed. Oh, pardon me."

He smiled. "I shouldn't be calling them robots, should I? They've reversed all that, haven't they? Tobors is their name. It does have more rhythm and should be psychologically more satisfying to them. There now, you've caught your breath. By the way, I'm Dr. Claremeyer."

"Doctor!" Juanita Harding managed to say. "Are you sure it's *him?*"

"Definitely, your fiancé, John Gregson, chemist extraordinary." It was a younger man who spoke. He stepped forward and took the suitcase from the older man's fingers. "The patrol got the picture by the new process, whereby we tune in on their communicating plates. It was flashed to headquarters, and then transmitted to us."

127

He paused, and smiled engagingly. "My name is Madden. That's Phillips with the long gloomy face. The big fellow with the uncombed hair, lurking there in the background like an elephant, is Rice, our field man. And you've already met Dr. Claremeyer."

Rice said gruffly, "We've got a hell of a job here, ma'am, begging your pardon for them rough words."

Miss Harding took off her hat with a brisk sweep of one hand. The shadows retreated from her face into her eyes, but there was a hint of a smile on her lips. "Mr. Rice, I live with a father whose nickname is 'Cyclone' Harding. To him, our everyday language is an enemy which he attacks with all available weapons. Does that answer your apology?"

The big man chuckled. "You win. But let's get down to business. Madden, you've got a brain that thinks in words; tell Miss Harding the situation!"

"Right!" The young man took up the refrain grimly. "We had the good fortune to be in the air near here when the first report came through that an automaton had been brought down alive. As soon as the identification arrived, we asked army headquarters to set up a defense ring of all available planes. They stripped the entire nearby line to help us."

He paused, frowning. "It has had to be very carefully done, because we don't want to give the Tobors any idea of what's going on. Your fiancé can't get away; that is certain, I think. And he can't be rescued unless they come out in force of a size that catches us momentarily off guard. Our big problem is to capture him alive."

"And that, of course"—it was Claremeyer, who cut in with a shrug of his shoulders—"may be easy or it may be difficult. Unfortunately, it must be fast. The Tobors will not be unaware long of this concentration of forces; then they will examine his file, analyze at least a part of the true situation, and act.

"The second unfortunate aspect is that in the past we have allowed ourselves a percentage of failures. You must realize that our tactics are almost entirely psychological, based upon fundamental human impulses."

Patiently, he explained the method.

"Ninety-two! . . . This is Sorn speaking."

The voice came sharp, insistent, commanding, from the automaton's wrist radio. The automaton stirred in his concrete shelter. "Yes, Master?"

Apparently the contact was all that was desired, for he

128

heard the other say, "He's still alive!" The voice was farther away this time, as if the humanoid had turned to speak to someone else.

A second voice spoke hesitantly. "Normally, I wouldn't have bothered, but this is the one that destroyed his file. Now, a *Vulture* crew is trying to save him."

"They do it every time."

"I know, I know." The second speaker sounded impatient with himself, as if he was aware that he might be acting foolishly. "Still, they've already given a lot of time to him, more than normal, it seems to me. And there is the fact that this particular ship engaged in a lengthy series of code messages with its headquarters. Afterward, a woman arrived on the scene."

"They nearly always use women in these rescue operations." The Tobor's voice held a note of distaste, but his words were a dismissal of the other's argument.

This time there was silence for many seconds. Finally, the doubting one spoke again: "In my department, I have been acutely conscious that somewhere in our operations about two years ago we unexpectedly captured a human chemist who, it was stated, had discovered a process for sexualizing Tobors."

His emotional disgust was almost too much for him, and in spite of the frankness of his next words, his voice trembled. "Unfortunately, we learned of this too late for us to identify the individual involved. Apparently, he was put through a routine interview, and dementalized."

He had full control of himself again and went on sardonically. "Of course the whole thing could be just a propaganda story, designed to unnerve us. And yet, at the time, our Intelligence reported that an atmosphere of gloom and depression pervaded human headquarters. It appears that we raided a city, captured him in his home, wrecked his laboratory and burned his papers."

His tone implied that he was shrugging. "It was one of scores of similar raids, quite impossible to identify. Prisoners captured in such forays were in no way differentiated from those captured in other ways."

Once more, silence . . . then, "Shall I order him to kill himself?"

"Find out if he has a weapon."

There was a pause. The voice came close. "Have you a blaster, Ninety-two?"

The human automaton, who had listened to the conversation with a faraway blankness in his eyes and mind, alerted as the question was directed at him through his wrist radio.

"I have hand weapons," he said dully.

Once more the interrogator turned away from the distant microphone. "Well?" he said.

"Direct action is too dangerous," said the second Tobor. "You know how they resist actual suicide. Sometimes it brings them right out of their automaton state. The will to live is too basic."

"Then we're right back where we started."

"No! Tell him specifically to defend himself to the death. That's on a different level. That's an appeal to his loyalty, to his indoctrinated hatred of our human enemies and to his patriotism to the Tobor cause."

Lying in the rubble, the automaton nodded as the Master's firm voice issued the commands. Naturally . . . to the death . . . of course.

On the radio, Sorn still sounded dissatisfied. "I think we should force the issue. I think we should concentrate projectors in the area, and see what happens."

"They've always accepted such challenges in the past."

"Up to a point only. I believe most earnestly that we should test their reaction. I feel that this man resisted too hard during his captivity and there's a tremendous pressure working on him."

"Human beings are very deceptive," said the other doubtfully. "Some of them are merely anxious to go home. It seems to be a powerful motivation."

His objection must have been rhetorical. After a bare moment of silence, he looked up and said decisively, "Very well, we'll attack!"

By an hour after dark, a hundred projectors were engaged on both sides. The night flashed with long trailers of bright flame.

"Phew!" Rice raced up the gangplank into the ship. His heavy face was scarlet with effort. As the door clanged shut behind him, he gasped, "Miss Harding, that fiancé of yours is a dangerous man. He's trigger happy, and needs more propaganda."

The girl was pale. She had watched Rice's attempt to get the screen into position from the great barrier window in the observation room. She said, "Maybe I should go out now!"

"And get burned!" Dr. Claremeyer came forward. He was blinking behind his glasses. "Now don't you feel badly, Miss Harding. I knew it seems incredible that the man who loves

130

you has been so changed that he would kill you on sight—but you'll just have to accept the reality. The fact that the Tobors have decided to put up a fight for him hasn't helped matters any."

"Those beasts!" she said. It was a dry sob. "What are you going to do now?"

"More propaganda."

"You think he'll hear it over the roar of the projectors?" She was astonished.

"He knows what it is," said Dr. Claremeyer matter-of-factly. "The pattern has been established. Even a single word coming through will be a reminder of the whole pattern."

A few moments later, she was listening gloomily while the loudspeakers blared their message:

". . . You are a human being. We are human beings. You were captured by the robots. We want to rescue you from the robots. These robots call themselves Tobors because it sounds better. They're robots. They're not human beings, but you are a human being. We are human beings, and we want to rescue you. Do everything that we ask you to do. Do nothing that they tell you to do. We want to make you well. We want to save you. . . ."

Abruptly, the ship moved. A moment later, the *Vulture* commander came over.

"I had to give the order to take off," he said. "We'll come back again about dawn. The Tobors must be losing equipment at a terrific rate. It's a bridgehead fight for them, but it's getting too hot for us also."

He must have felt the girl would place the worst construction on the withdrawal order. He explained to her in a low voice:

"We can depend on a slave using every precaution to stay alive. He'll have been given training for that. Besides, we did get the screen up and the picture will show over and over."

He went on, before she could speak, "Besides, we have been given permission to try direct contact with him."

"What does that mean?"

"We'll use a weak signal that won't carry more than a few hundred yards. That way they won't be able to tune in on what we're saying. Our hope is that he'll be sufficiently stimulated to tell us his secret formula."

Juanita Harding sat for a long time, frowning. Her comment, when it finally came, was extremely feminine. "I'm

131

not sure," she said, "that I approve of the pictures you're showing on that screen."

The commander said judiciously, "We've got to strike at the basic drives of human beings."

He departed hastily.

John Gregson, who had been an automaton, became aware that he was clawing at a bright screen. As he grew more conscious of his actions, he slowed his frantic attempt to grasp at the elusive shapes that had lured him out of hiding. He stepped back.

All around him was intense darkness. As he backed away a little further, he stumbled over a twisted girder. He started to fall, but saved himself by grasping at the burned and rusted metal. It creaked a little from his weight and flakes of metal came away free in his hands.

He retreated anxiously into the darkness to take better advantage of the light reflections. For the first time he recognized that he was in one of the destroyed cities. He thought: *But how did I get here? What's happened to me?*

A voice from his wrist radio made him jump. "Sorn!" it said insistently. The icy tone stiffened Gregson. Deep in his mind a bell of recognition clanged its first warning. He was about to reply, when he realized that it was not he who had been addressed.

"Yes?" The answer was clear enough, but it seemed to come from a much greater distance.

"Where are you now?"

Sorn said slowly, "I landed about half a mile from the screen. It was a misjudgment, as I intended to come down much closer. Unfortunately, in landing I got my directions twisted. I can't see a thing."

"The screen they're using for the pictures is still up. I can see a reflection of it in Ninety-two's Wristo. Surely it'll be a bright landmark."

"It must be in a hollow, or behind a pile of debris. I'm in pitch darkness. Contact Ninety-two and—"

The first reference to his *number* had started the train of associations. The second one brought such a flood of hideous memory that Gregson cringed. In a flashing kaleidoscope of pictures, he realized his situation and tried to recall the immediate sequence of events that had brought him back to control of himself. Somebody had called his name insistently . . . not his number—his name. Each time they had asked him a question, something about a formula for— For

what? He couldn't remember, something about—about—
Abruptly, it came back!

Crouching there in the darkness, he closed his eyes in a
sheer physical reaction. "I gave it to them. I told them the
formula. But who was—them?"

It could only have been some member of the crew of a
Vulture ship, he told himself shakily. The Tobors didn't
know his name. To them he was . . . Ninety-two.

That recollection brought him back with a start to his
own predicament. He was just in time to hear the voice on
the Wristo say vindictively:

"All right, I've got it. I'll be over there in ten minutes."

The Tobor in the distant Control Center was impersonal.
"This is on your own head, Sorn. You seem to have an
obsession about this case."

"They were broadcasting to him on a local wave," said
Sorn in a dark voice, "so direct, so close that we couldn't
catch what they were saying. And his answer, when he
finally made it, was interfered with so that, again, we didn't
hear it, but it was a formula of some kind. I'm counting on
the possibility that he was not able to give them the full
description. Since he's still at the screen, he hasn't been
rescued, so if I can kill him now, within minutes—"

There was a click. . . . The voice trailed off into silence.
Gregson stood in the darkness beside the screen, and
shudderingly considered his position.

Where was the *Vulture?* The sky was pitch dark, though
there was an ever-so-faint light in the east, the first herald
of the coming dawn. The sound of the projectors had become
a mutter far away, no longer threatening. The great battle
of the night was over. . . .

The battle of the individuals was about to begin. . . .

Gregson retreated even farther into the darkness, and
fumbled over his body for hand weapons. There were none.
"But that's ridiculous," he told himself shakily. "I had a
blaster and—"

He stopped the thought. Once again, desperate now, he
searched himself. . . . Nothing. He guessed that in his mad
scramble to get to the screen, he had lost his weapons.

He was still teetering indecisively when he heard a movement in the near night.

Vulture 121 landed gently in the intense darkness of the
false dawn. Juanita Harding had taken off her clothes, and
now had a robe wrapped around her. She did not hesitate
when Rice beckoned. He grinned at her reassuringly.

133

"I'm taking along a cylinder of the stuff," he said, "just in case he doesn't become inspired quickly enough."

She smiled wanly, but said nothing. Dr. Claremeyer came to the door with them. He gave her hand a quick squeeze.

"Remember," he said, "this is war!"

She replied, "I know. And all's fair in love and war, isn't it?"

"Now you're talking."

A moment later they were gone into the night.

Gregson was retreating in earnest and he felt a lot better. It was going to be hard for any one person to locate him in this vast maze of shattered concrete and marble and metal.

Moment by moment, however, the desolate horizon grew lighter. He saw the ship suddenly in the shadowy ruins to his right. Its shape was unmistakable. *Vulture!* Gregson raced toward it over the uneven ruins of what had once been a paved street.

Gasping with relief, he saw that the gangplank was down. As he raced up it, two men covered him with their blasters. Abruptly, one of them gasped, "It's Gregson!"

Weapons were scraped back into their leathery holsters. Hands grasped eagerly at his hands, and there was a pumping of arms. Eyes searched his face eagerly for signs of sanity, found them, and glowed with pleasure. A thousand words attacked the dawn air.

"We got your formula."

"Great . . . wonderful."

"The genius made up some of the hormone gas in our own ship lab. How fast does it work?"

Gregson guessed that the "genius" was the tall, gloomy individual who had been introduced as Phillips. He said, "It takes only a few seconds. After all, you breathe it in and it's taken right into your bloodstream. It's pretty powerful stuff."

Madden said, "We had some idea of using it to intensify your own reactions. In fact, Rice took some—" He stopped. "But just a minute," he said, "Rice and Miss Harding are—" He stopped again.

It was the small man, Dr. Claremeyer, who took up the thread of Madden's thought. "Mr. Gregson," he said, "we saw a man on our infrared plates heading for the screen. He was too far away to identify, so we took it for granted it was you. And so, Rice and Miss Harding went out and—"

The Commander cut him off at that point. "Quick, let's get out there! It may be a trap!"

134

Gregson scarcely heard that. He was already racing down the gangplank.

"Sorn!" The voice on the Wristo sounded impatient. "Sorn, what's happened to you?"

In the half-darkness near the screen, the men and the girl listened to the words of the Tobor on Gregson's Wristo. From their vantage point they watched Sorn looking at the pictures on the screen itself.

"Sorn, your last report was that you were near where Ninety-two was last known to be hiding—"

Rice put one plump hand over Gregson's Wristo, to block off the sound; and whispered, "That's when I let him have it. Boy, I never had a better idea than when I took along a cylinder of your gas, Gregson. I shot a dose of it at him from fifty feet, and he never even knew what hit him."

"—Sorn, I know you're still alive. I can hear you mumbling to yourself."

Rice said, "We'll have to be careful of our dosage in the future. He's practically ready to eat up the pictures. You can see for yourself—the Tobor-human war is as good as over."

Gregson watched silently as the one-time Tobor leader scrambled eagerly in front of the screen. A dozen girls were on parade beside a pool. Periodically, they would all dive into the water. There would be a flash of long, bare limbs, the glint of a tanned back, then they would all climb out. They did that over and over.

The trouble was, each time Sorn tried to grasp one of the images, his shadow fell across the screen, and blotted her out. Frustrated, he rushed to another, only to have the same thing happen again.

"Sorn, answer me!"

This time the Tobor paused. The reply he made then must have shocked the entire Tobor headquarters, and the effect reached out to all the Tobor armies around the world.

Gregson tightened his arm appreciatively around Juanita's waist (she still wore her robe over the beauty with which she was to have lured him back to safety) as he listened to the fateful words.

"Women," Sorn was saying, "they're wonderful!"

ITSELF!

ITSELF, king of the Phillipine Deep—that awesome canyon where the sea goes down six miles—woke from his recharge period and looked around suspiciously.

His Alter Ego said, "Well, how is it with Itself today?"

The Alter Ego was a booster, a goader, a stimulant to action, and, in his limited way, a companion.

Itself did not answer. During the sleep period, he had drifted over a ravine, the walls of which dropped steeply another thousand feet. Suspiciously, Itself glared along the canyon rim.

. . . Not a visual observation. No light ever penetrated from above into the eternal night here at the deepest bottom of the ocean. Itself perceived the black world which surrounded him with high frequency sounds which he broadcast continuously in all directions. Like a bat in a pitch dark cave, he analyzed the structure of all things in his watery universe by interpreting the returning echoes. And the accompanying emotion of suspicion was a device which impelled Itself to record changing pressures, temperatures and current flows. Unknown to him, what he observed became part of the immense total of data by which faraway computers estimated the interrelationship of ocean and atmosphere, and thus predicted water and air conditions everywhere with uncanny exactness.

His was almost perfect perception. Clearly and unmistakably, Itself made out the intruder in the far distance of that twisting ravine. A ship! Anchored to rock at the very edge of the canyon.

The Alter Ego goaded, "You're not going to let somebody invade your territory, are you?"

Instantly, Itself was furious. He activated the jet mechanism in the underslung belly of his almost solid metal body. A nuclear reactor immediately heated the plates of the explosion chamber. The seawater which flowed through the chamber burst into hissing clouds of steam, and he jetted forward like a missile.

Arriving at the ship, Itself attacked the nearest of four anchor lines with the nuclear-powered heat beam in his head. When he had severed it, he turned to the second cable, and burned through it. Then he moved for the third cable.

But the startled beings aboard the alien ship had spotted the twenty-foot monster in the black waters below.

"Analyze its echo pattern!" came the command. That was done, with total skill.

"Feed the pattern back through the infinite altering system till the recorders register a response."

The significant response was: Itself forgot what he was doing. He was drifting blankly away, when his Alter Ego goaded, "Wake up! You're not going to let them get away with that, are you?"

The defeat had galvanized Itself to a more intense level of rage. He became multiples more sensitive. Now, he simply turned out the alien echo copies.

The new greater anger triggered a second weapon.

Itself's echo system of perception, normally monitored to be safe for all living things in the sea, suddenly strengthened. It became a supersonic beam. Purposefully, Itself started toward the ship.

Watching his approach, the enemy decided to take no chances. "Pull the remaining anchors in!"

Itself headed straight for the nearest part of the vessel. Instantly, those ultrasonic waves started a rhythmic vibration on the hard wall, weakening it.

The metal groaned under a weight of water that at these depths amounted to thousands of tons per square inch. The outer wall buckled with a metallic scream.

The inner wall trembled, but held.

At that point, the appalled defenders got a counter-vibration started, nullified the rhythm of Itself's projections, and were safe.

But it was a sorely wounded ship that now drifted helplessly in a slow current. The aliens had thus far used no energy that might be detected from the surface. But they had come to Earth to establish a base for invasion. Their instructions were to accumulate enough data about underwater currents to enable them to leave the Deep, and eventually to be able to drift near land, launch atom bombs and drift away again. For this purpose they were mightily armed, and they refused to die in these black waters without a fight.

"What can we do about that demon?"

"Blast it!" someone urged.

"That's dangerous." The alien commander hesitated.

"We can't be in greater danger than we already are."

"True," said the commander, "but frankly I don't know why he's armed at all, and I can't believe he has anything

137

more. Set up a response system. If he does attack with anything new, it will automatically fire back. We'll take that much of a chance."

The second setback had driven Itself completely berserk. He aimed his nuclear pellet gun, firing twice. In the next split-second a blast from the invader pierced his brain.

The Alter Ego yelled, "You're not going to let them get away with that, are you?"

But the king of the Phillipine Deep was dead, and could no longer be goaded.

In due course, a report was given to weather headquarters: "Computer Center shows no recent data from Itself. It therefore seems as if another of the wartime antisubmarine water-weather robots has worn out. You may recall that these electronic monsters were programmed to suspicion, anger, and the idea that they owned part of the ocean. After the war, we could never get these creatures to surface; they were too suspicious of us."

The ocean of water, like the ocean of air far above, flowed and rolled and moved in a ceaseless, dynamic, driving motion many, many times more powerful, however, than any comparable air current. Yet, in essence, the quadrillions of water movements solely and only balanced each other out.

Through the Phillipine Deep there began presently to flow an enormous balancing river. It carried the aliens' invasion vessel in a long, slanting, upward direction. But several weeks passed before the drifting ship actually broke surface, and another day or two before it was seen.

A naval patrol boarded it, found the aliens dead more than a month from concussion, and—after examining the damage—correctly analyzed what had happened.

And so—a new king "woke" to the first "day" of his reign, and heard *his* Alter Ego say, "Well, Itself, what's the program?"

Itself glared with a royal suspicion.

PROCESS

IN THE bright light of that far sun, the forest breathed and had its being. It was aware of the ship that had come down through the thin mists of the upper air. But its automatic hostility to the alien thing was not immediately accompanied by alarm.

For tens of thousands of square miles, its roots entwined under the ground, and its millions of treetops swayed gently

138

in a thousand idle breezes. And beyond, spreading over the hills and the mountains, and along almost endless sea coast, were other forests as strong and as powerful as itself.

From time immemorial the forest had guarded the land from a dimly understood danger. What that danger was it began now slowly to remember. It was from ships like this, that descended from the sky. The forest could not recall clearly how it had defended itself in the past, but it did remember tensely that defense had been necessary.

Even as it grew more and more aware of the ship coasting along in the gray-red sky above, its leaves whispered a timeless tale of battles fought and won. Thoughts flowed their slow course down the channels of vibration, and the stately limbs of tens of thousands of trees trembled ever so slightly.

The vastness of that tremor, affecting as it did all the trees, gradually created a sound and a pressure. At first it was almost impalpable, like a breeze wafting through an evergreen glen. But it grew stronger.

It acquired substance. The sound became all-enveloping. And the whole forest stood there vibrating its hostility, waiting for the thing in the sky to come nearer.

It had not long to wait.

The ship swung down from its lane. Its speed, now that it was close to the ground, was greater than it had first seemed. And it was bigger. It loomed gigantic over the near trees, and swung down lower, careless of the treetops. Brush crackled, limbs broke, and entire trees were brushed aside as if they were meaningless and weightless and without strength.

Down came the ship, cutting its own path through a forest that groaned and shrieked with its passage. It settled heavily into the ground two miles after it first touched a tree. Behind, the swath of broken trees quivered and pulsed in the light of the sun, a straight path of destruction which—the forest suddenly remembered—was exactly what had happened in the past.

It began to pull clear of the anguished parts. It drew out its juices, and ceased vibrating in the affected areas. Later, it would send new growth to replace what had been destroyed, but now it accepted the partial death it had suffered. It knew fear.

It was a fear tinged with anger. It felt the ship lying on crushed trees, on a part of itself that was not yet dead. It felt the coldness and the hardness of steel walls, and the fear and the anger increased.

139

A whisper of thought pulsed along the vibration channels. *Wait,* it said, *there is a memory in me. A memory of long ago when other such ships as this came.*

The memory refused to clarify. Tense but uncertain, the forest prepared to make its first attack. It began to grow around the ship.

Long ago it had discovered the power of growth that was possible to it. There was a time when it had not been as large as it was now. And then, one day, it became aware that it was coming near another forest like itself.

The two masses of growing wood, the two colossuses of intertwined roots, approached each other warily, slowly, in amazement, in a startled but cautious wonder that a similar life form should actually have existed all this time. Approached, touched—and fought for years.

During that prolonged struggle nearly all growth in the central portions stopped. Trees ceased to develop new branches. The leaves, by necessity, grew hardier, and performed their functions for much longer periods. Roots developed slowly. The entire available strength of the forest was concentrated in the processes of defense and attack.

Walls of trees sprang up overnight. Enormous roots tunneled into the ground for miles straight down, breaking through rock and metal, building a barrier of living wood against the encroaching growth of the strange forest. On the surface, the barriers thickened to a mile or more of trees that stood almost bole to bole. And, on that basis, the great battle finally petered out. The forest accepted the obstacle created by its enemy.

Later, it fought to a similar standstill a second forest which attacked it from another direction.

The limits of demarcation became as natural as the great salt sea to the south, or the icy cold of mountaintops that were frozen the year round.

As it had in battle with the two other forests, *the* forest concentrated its entire strength against the encroaching ship. Trees shot up at the rate of a foot every few minutes. Creepers climbed the trees, and flung themselves over the top of the vessel. The countless strands of it raced over the metal, and then twined themselves around the trees on the far side. The roots of those trees dug deeper into the ground, and anchored in rock strata heavier than any ship ever built. The tree boles thickened, and the creepers widened till they were enormous cables.

As the light of that first day faded into twilight, the ship was buried under thousands of tons of wood, and hidden in foliage so thick that nothing of it was visible.

The time had come for the final destructive action.

Shortly after dark, tiny roots began to fumble over the underside of the ship. They were infinitesimally small; so small that in the initial stages they were no more than a few dozen of atoms in diameter; so small that the apparently solid metal seemed almost emptiness to them; so incredibly small that they penetrated the hard steel effortlessly.

It was at that time, almost as if it had been waiting for this stage, that the ship took counteraction. The metal grew warm, then hot, and then cherry red. That was all that was needed. The tiny roots shriveled, and died. The larger roots near the metal burned slowly as the searing heat reached them.

Above the surface, other violence began. Flame darted from a hundred orifices of the ship's surface. First the creepers, then the trees began to burn. It was no flare-up of uncontrollable fire, no fierce conflagration leaping from tree to tree in irresistible fury. Long ago, the forest had learned to control fires started by lightning or spontaneous combustion. It was a matter of sending sap to the affected area. The greener the tree, the more sap that permeated it, then the hotter the fire would have to be.

The forest could not immediately remember ever having encountered a fire that could make inroads against a line of trees that oozed a sticky wetness from every crevice of their bark.

But this fire could. It was different. It was not only flame; it was energy. It did not feed off the wood; it was fed by an energy within itself.

The fact at last brought the associational memory to the forest. It was a sharp and unmistakable remembrance of what it had done long ago to rid itself and its planet of a ship like like this.

It began to withdraw from the vicinity of the ship. It abandoned the framework of wood and shrubbery with which it had sought to imprison the alien structure. As the precious sap was sucked back into trees that would now form a second line of defense, the flames grew brighter, and the fire waxed so brilliant that the whole scene was bathed in an eerie glow.

It was some time before the forest realized that the fire beams were no longer flaming out from the ship, and that what incandescence and smoke remained came from normally burning wood.

That, too, was according to its memory of what had happened—before.

Frantically though reluctantly the forest initiated what it now realized was the only method of ridding itself of the intruder. Frantically because it was hideously aware that the flame from the ship could destroy entire forests. And reluctantly because the method of defense involved its suffering the burns of energy only slightly less violent than those that had flared from the machine.

Tens of thousands of roots grew toward rock and soil formations that they had carefully avoided since the last ship had come. In spite of the need for haste, the process itself was slow. Tiny roots, quivering with unpleasant anticipation, forced themselves into the remote, buried ore beds, and by an intricate process of osmosis drew grains of pure metal from the impure natural stuff. The grains were almost as small as the roots that had earlier penetrated the steel walls of the ship, small enough to be borne along, suspended in sap, through a maze of larger roots.

Soon there were thousands of grains moving along the channels, then millions. And, though each was tiny in itself, the soil where they were discharged soon sparked in the light of the dying fire. As the sun of that world reared up over the horizon, the silvery gleam showed a hundred feet wide all around the ship.

It was shortly after noon that the machine showed awareness of what was happening. A dozen hatches opened, and objects floated out of them. They came down to the ground, and began to skim up the silvery stuff with nozzled things that sucked up the fine dust in a steady fashion. They worked with great caution; but an hour before darkness set in again, they had scooped up more than twelve tons of the thinly spread uranium 235.

As night fell, all the two-legged things vanished inside the vessel. The hatches closed. The long torpedo-shape floated lightly upward, and sped to the higher heavens where the sun still shone.

The first awareness of the situation came to the forest as the roots deep under the ship reported a sudden lessening of pressure. It was several hours before it decided that the enemy had actually been driven off. And several more hours went by before it realized that the uranium dust still on the scene would have to be removed. The rays spread too far afield.

The accident that occurred then took place for a very simple reason. The forest had taken the radioactive substance out of rock. To get rid of it, it need merely put it back into the nearest rock beds, particularly the kind of rock that absorbed the radioactivity. To the forest the situation seemed as obvious as that.

An hour after it began to carry out the plan, the explosion mushroomed toward outer space.

It was vast beyond all the capacity of the forest to understand. It neither saw nor heard that colossal shape of death. What it did experience was enough. A hurricane leveled square miles of trees. The blast of heat and radiation started fires that took hours to put out.

Fear departed slowly, as it remembered that this too had happened before. Sharper by far than the memory was the vision of the possibilities of what had happened . . . the nature of the opportunity.

Shortly after dawn the following morning, it launched its attack. Its victim was the forest which—according to its faulty recollection—had originally invaded its territory.

Along the entire front which separated the two colossuses, small atomic explosions erupted. The solid barrier of trees which was the other forest's outer defense went down before blast after blast of irresistible energy.

The enemy, reacting normally, brought up its reserve of sap. When it was fully committed to the gigantic task of growing a new barrier, the bombs started to go off again. The resulting explosions destroyed its main sap supply. And, since it did not understand what was happening, it was lost from that moment.

Into the no-man's-land where the bombs had gone off, the attacking forest rushed an endless supply of roots. Wherever resistance built up, there an atomic bomb went off. Shortly after the next noon, a titanic explosion destroyed the sensitive central trees—and the battle was over.

It took months for the forest to grow into the territory of its defeated enemy, to squeeze out the other's dying roots, to nudge over trees that now had no defense, and to put itself into full and unchallenged possession.

The moment the task was completed, it turned like a fury upon the forest on its other flank. Once more it attacked with atomic thunder, and with a hail of fire tried to overwhelm its opponent.

It was met by equal force. Exploding atoms!

For its knowledge had leaked across the barrier of intertwined roots which separated forests.

Almost, the two monsters destroyed each other. Each became a remnant, that started the painful process of regrowth. As the years passed, the memory of what had happened grew dim. Not that it mattered. Actually, the ships came at will. And somehow, even if the forest remembered, its atomic bombs would not go off in the presence of a ship.

The only thing that would drive away the ships was to surround each machine with a fine dust of radioactive stuff. Whereupon it would scoop up the material, and then hastily retreat.

Victory was always as simple as that.

NOT THE FIRST

Captain Harcourt wakened with a start. In the darkness he lay tense, shaking the sleep out of his mind. Something was wrong. He couldn't quite place the discordant factor, but it trembled there on the verge of his brain, an alien thing that shattered for him the security of the spaceship.

He strained his senses against the blackness of the room— and abruptly grew aware of the intensity of that dark. The night of the room was shadowless, a pitch-like black that lay like an opaque blanket hard on his eyeballs.

That was it. The darkness. The indirect night light must have gone off. And out here in interstellar space there would be no diffused light as there was on Earth and even within the limits of the solar system.

Still, it was odd that the lighting system should have gone on the blink on this first "night" of this first trip of the first spaceship powered by the new, stupendous atomic drive.

A sudden thought made him reach toward the light switch.

The click made a futile sound in the pressing weight of the darkness—and seemed like a signal for the footsteps that whispered hesitantly along the corridor, and paused outside his door. There was a knock, then a muffled, familiar, yet strained voice: "Harcourt!"

The urgency in the man's tone seemed to hold connection to all the odd menace of the past few minutes. Harcourt, conscious of relief, barked, "Come in, Gunther. The door's unlocked!"

In the darkness, he slipped from under the sheets and fumbled for his clothes—as the door opened, and the breathing of the navigation officer of the ship became a thick, satisfying sound that destroyed the last vestige of the hard silence.

"Harcourt, the damnedest thing has happened. It started

144

when everything electrical went out of order. Compton says we've been accelerating for two hours now at heaven only knows what rate."

There was no pressure on him now. The familiar presence and voice of Gunther had a calming effect; the sense of queer, mysterious things was utterly gone. Here was something into which he could figuratively sink his teeth.

Harcourt stepped matter-of-factly into his trousers and said after a moment: "I hadn't noticed the acceleration. So used to the— Hmm, doesn't seem more than two gravities. Nothing serious could result in two hours. As for light, they've got those gas lamps in the emergency room."

For the moment it was all quite convincing. He hadn't gone to bed till the ship's speed was well past the velocity of light. Everybody had been curious about what would happen at that tremendous milepost—whether the Lorenz-Fitzgerald contraction theory was substance or appearance.

Nothing had happened. The test ship simply forged ahead, accelerating each second, and, just before he retired, they had estimated the speed at nearly two hundred thousand miles per second.

The complacent mood ended. He said sharply, "Did you say Compton sent you?"

Compton was chief engineer, and he was definitely not one to give way to panics of any description. Harcourt frowned. "What does Compton think?"

"Neither he nor I can understand it; and when we lost sight of the sun he thought you'd better be—"

"When you *what?*"

Gunther's laugh broke humorlessly through the darkness. "Harcourt, the damned thing is so unbelievable that when Compton called me on the communicator just now he spent half the time talking to himself like an old woman of the gutter. Only he, O'Day and I know the worst yet.

"Harcourt, we've figured out that we're approximately five hundred thousand light years from Earth—and that the chance of our ever finding our sun in that swirl of suns makes searching for needles in haystacks a form of child's play.

"We're lost as no human being has ever been."

In the utter darkness beside the bank of telescope eyepieces Harcourt waited and watched. Though he could not see them, he was tautly aware of the grim men who sat so quietly, peering into the night of space ahead—at the remote point of light out there that never varied a hairbreadth in its position on the crossed wires of the eyepieces. The silence was complete, and yet—

The very presence of these able men was a living, vibrating force to him who had known them intimately for so many years. The beat of their thought, the shifting of space-toughened muscles, was a sound that distorted rather than disturbed the hard tensity of the silence.

The silence shattered as Gunther spoke matter-of-factly: "There's no doubt about it, of course. We're going to pass through the star system ahead. An ordinary sun, I should say, a little colder than our own, but possibly half again as large, and about thirty thousand parsecs distant."

"Go away with you," came the gruff voice of physicist O'Day. "You can't tell how far away it is. Where's your triangle?"

"I don't need any such tricks," retorted Gunther heatedly. "I just use my God-given intelligence. You watch. We'll be able to verify our speed when we pass through the system; and velocity multiplied by time elapsed will—"

Harcourt interjected gently, "So far as we know, Gunther, Compton hasn't any lights yet. If he hasn't, we won't be able to look at our watches, so we won't know the time elapsed; so you can't prove anything. What is your method, if it isn't triangulation—and it can't be. We're open to conviction."

Gunther said, "It's plain common sense. Notice the cross lines on your eyepieces. The lines intersect on the point of light—and there's not a fraction of variation or blur.

"These lenses have tested perfect according to the latest standards, but observatory astronomers back home have found that beyond one hundred fifty thousand light-years there is the beginning of distortion. Therefore I could have said a minute or so ago that we were *within* one hundred and fifty thousand light-years of that sun.

"But there's more. When I first looked into the eyepiece—before I called you, Captain—the distortion *was* there. I'm pretty good at estimating time, and I should say it required about twelve minutes for me to get you and fumble my way back in here. When I looked then the distortion was gone. There's an automatic device in my eyepiece for measuring degree of distortion. When I first looked, the distortion was .005, roughly equivalent to twenty-five thousand light-years. There's another point—"

"You needn't go on," Harcourt interjected quietly. "You've proved your case."

O'Day groaned. "That'll be maybe twenty-four thousand
146

light-years in twelve minutes. Two thousand a minute; that'll be thirty light-years a second. And we've been sittin' here maybe more'n twenty-five minutes since you an' Harcourt came back. That'll be another fifty thousand light-years, or thirty thousand parsecs between us an' the star. You're a good man, Gunther. But how will we ever identify the blamed thing when we come back? It would be makin' such a fine gunsight for the return trip if we could maybe get another sight farther on, when we finally stop this runaway or—"

Harcourt cut him off grimly. "There's just one point that you two gentlemen have neglected to take into account. It's true we must try to stop the ship—Compton's men are working at the engines now. But everything else is only preliminary to our main task of thinking our way back to Earth. We shall probably find it necessary, if we live, to change our entire conception of space.

"I said—*if we live!* What you scientists in your zeal failed to notice was that the most delicate instruments ever invented by man, the cross lines of this telescope, intersect directly *on* the approaching sun. They haven't changed for more than thirty minutes, so we must assume the sun is following a course in space directly toward us, or away from us.

"As it is, we're going to run squarely into a ball of fire a million miles plus in diameter. I leave the rest to your imaginations."

The discussion that blurred on then had an unreal quality for Harcourt. The only reality was the blackness, and the great ship plunging madly down a vast pit toward its dreadful doom.

It seemed down, a diving into incredible depths at an insane velocity—and against that cosmic discordance, the voices of the men sounded queer and meaningless, intellectually, violently alive, but the effect was as of small birds fluttering furiously against the wire mesh of a trap that has sprung remorselessly around them.

"Time," Gunther was saying, "is the only basic force. Time creates space instant by instant, and—"

"Will you be shuttin' up," O'Day interrupted scathingly. "You've had the solving of the problem of our speed, a practical job for an astronomer and navigation officer. But this'll be different. Me bein' the chief of the physicists aboard, I—"

"Omit the preamble!" Harcourt cut in dryly. "Our time is, to put it mildly, drastically limited."

"Right!" O'Day's voice came briskly out of the blackness.

"Mind ya, I'm not up to offerin' any final solutions, but here may be soome answers:

"The speed of light is not, accordin' to my present thought, one hundred eighty-six thousand three hundred miles per second. It's more'n two hundred thousand, maybe fifty thousand more. In previous measurements, we've been forgettin' the effect of the area of tensions that makes a big curve 'round any star system. We've known about those tensions, but never gave much thought to how much they might slow up light, the way water and glass does.

"That's the only thing that'll explain why nothin' happened at the apparent speed of light, but plenty happened when we passed the real speed of light. Come to think on it, the real speed must be somethin' less than two hundred fifty thousand, because we were goin' slower'n that when the electric system blanked on us."

"But man alive!" Gunther burst out before Harcourt could speak. "What at that point could have jumped our speed up to a billion times that of light?"

"When we have the solvin' of that," O'Day interjected grimly, "the entire universe'll belong to us."

"You're wrong there," Harcourt stated quietly. "If we solve that, we shall have the speed to go places, but there's no conceivable science that will make it possible for us to plot a course to or from any destination beyond a few hundred light-years.

"Do not forget that our purpose, when we began this voyage, was to go to Alpha Centauri. From there we intended gradually to work out from star to star, setting up bases where possible, and slowly working out the complex problems involved.

"Theoretically, such a method of plotting space could have gone on indefinitely, though it was generally agreed that the complexity would increase out of all proportion to the extra distance involved.

"But enough of that." His voice grew harder. "Has it occurred to either of you that even if by some miracle of wit we miss that sun, there is a possibility that this ship may plunge on forever through space at billions of times the velocity of light?

"I mean simply this: our speed jumped inconceivably when we crossed the point of light speed. But that point is now *behind* us. And there is no similar point ahead that we can cross. When we get our engines reversed, we face the prospect of decelerating at two gravities or a bit more for several thousand years.

148

"All this is aside from the fact that, at our present distance from Earth, there is nothing known that will help us find our way back.

"I'll leave these thoughts with you. I'm going to grope my way down to Compton—our last hope!"

There was blazing light in the engine room—a string of gasoline lamps shed the blue-white intensity of their glare onto several score men. Half of the men were taking turns, a dozen at a time, in the simple task of straining at a giant wheel whose shaft disappeared at one end into the bank of monstrous drive tubes. At the other end the wheel was attached to a useless electric motor.

The wheel moved so sluggishly before the combined strength of the workers that Harcourt thought, appalled, *Good heavens, at that rate, it'll take a day—and we've got forty minutes at utmost.*

He saw that the other men were putting together a steam engine from parts ripped out of great packing cases. He felt better. The engine would take the place of the electric motor and—

"It'll take half an hour!" roared a bull-like voice to one side of him. As he turned, Compton bellowed, "And don't waste time telling me any stories about running into stars. I've been listening in to you fellows on this wall communicator."

Harcourt was conscious of a start of surprise as he saw that the chief engineer was lying on the steel floor, his head propped on a curving metal projection. His heavy face looked strangely white, and when he spoke it was from clenched teeth:

"Couldn't spare anyone to send you up some light. We've got a single, straightforward job down here: to stop those drivers." He finished ironically: "When we've done that we'll have about fifteen minutes to figure out what good it will do us."

The mighty man winced as he finished speaking. For the first time Harcourt saw the bandage on his right hand. He said sharply, "You're hurt!"

"Remind me," replied Compton grimly, "when we get back to Earth to sock the deparmental genius who put an electric lock on the door of the emergency room. I don't know how long it took to chisel into it, but my finger got lost somewhere in the shuffle.

"It's all right," he added swiftly. "I've just now taken a 'local.' It'll start working in half a minute and we can talk."

149

Harcourt nodded stiffly. He knew the fantastic courage and endurance that trained men could show. He said casually: "How would you like some technicians, mathematicians and other such to come down here and relieve your men? There's a whole corridor full of them out there."

"Nope!" Compton shook his leonine head. Color was coming into his cheeks, and his voice had a clearer, less strained note as he continued: "These war horses of mine are experts. Just imagine a biologist taking a three-minute shift at putting that steam engine together. Or heaving at that big wheel without ever having been trained to synchronize his muscles to the art of pushing in unity with other men.

"But forget about that. We've got a practical problem ahead of us; and before we die I'd like to know what we should have done and could have done. Suppose we get the steam engine running in time—which is not certain; that's why I put those men on the wheel even before we had light. Anyway, suppose we do, where would we be?"

"Acceleration would stop," said Harcourt. "But our speed would be constant at something over thirty light-years per second."

"That's too hard to strike a sun!" Compton spoke seriously, eyes half closed. He looked up. "Or is it?"

"What do you mean?"

"Simply this: this sun is about twelve hundred thousand miles in diameter. If it were at all gaseous in structure, we could be through so fast its heat would never touch us."

"Gunther says the star is somewhat colder than our own. That suggests greater density."

"In that case"—Compton was almost cheerful—"at our speed, and with the hard steel of our ship, we could conceivably pass through a steel plate a couple of million miles in thickness. It's a problem in fire power for a couple of ex-military men."

"I'll leave the problem for your old age," Harcourt said. "Your attitude suggests that you see no solutions to the situation presented by the star."

Compton stared at him for a moment, unsmiling; then, "Okay, Chief, I'll cut out the kidding. You're right about the star. It took fifty hours to get up to two hundred forty thousand miles per second. Then we crossed some invisible line, and for the past few hours we've been plumping along at, as you say, thirty miles a second.

"All right, then, say fifty-three hours that it took us to get here. Even if we eliminate that horrible idea you spawned, about it taking us thousands of years to decelerate, there still remains the certainty that—with the best of luck, that is—with simply a reversal of the conditions that brought us here, it would require not less than fifty-three hours to stop.

"Figure it out for yourself. We might as well play marbles."

They called Gunther and O'Day. "And bring some liquor down!" Compton roared through the communicator.

"Wait!" Harcourt prevented him from breaking the connection. He spoke quietly: "Is that you, Gunther?"

"Yep!" the navigation officer responded.

"The star's still dead on?"

"Deader!" said the ungrammatical Gunther.

Harcourt hesitated; this was the biggest decision he had ever faced in his ten violent years as a commander of a spaceship. His face was stiff as he said finally, huskily:

"All right, then, come down here, but don't tell anyone else what's up. They could take it—but what's the use? Come to Compton's office."

He saw that the chief engineer was staring at him strangely. Compton said at last, "So we really give up the ship?"

Harcourt gazed back at him coldly. "Remember, I'm only the coordinator around here. I'm supposed to know something of everything—but when experts tell me there's no hope, barring miracles, naturally I refuse to run around like an animal with a blind will to live.

"Your men are slaving to get the steam engine running; two pounds of U-235 are doing their bit to heat up the steam boiler. When it's all ready, we'll do what we can. Is that clear?"

Compton grinned, but there was silence between them until the other men arrived. O'Day greeted them gloomily.

"There's a couple of good friends of mine up there whom I'd like to have here now. But what the hell! Let 'em die in peace, says Harcourt; and right he is."

Gunther poured the dark, glowing liquid, and Harcourt watched the glasses tilt, finally raised his own. He wondered if the others found the stuff as smooth and tasteless as he did. He lowered his glass and said softly:

"Atomic power! So this is the end of man's first interstellar flight. There'll be others, of course, and the law of averages will protect them from running into suns; and they'll get their steam engines going, and their drives reversed; and if this process *does* reverse itself, then within a given time they'll stop—and then they'll be where we thought we were: facing the problem of finding their way back to Earth.

151

It looks to me as if man is stymied by the sheer vastness of the universe."

"Don't be such a damned pessimist!" said Compton, his face flushed from his second glass. "I'll wager they'll have the drivers of the third test ship reversed within ten minutes of crossing that light speed deadline. That means they'll only be a few thousand light-years from Earth. Taking it in little jumps like that, they'll never get lost."

Harcourt saw O'Day look up from his glass; the physicst's lips parted—and Harcourt allowed his own words to remain unspoken. O'Day said soberly:

"I'm thinkin' we've been puttin' too much blame on speed and speed alone in this thing. Sure there's no magic about the speed of light. I didn't ever see that before, but it's there plain now. The speed of light depends on the properties of light, and that goes for electricity and radio an' all those related waves.

"Let's be keepin' that in mind. Light an' such react on space, an' are held down by nothin' but their own limitations. An' there's only one new thing we've got that could've put us out here, beyond the speed of light; an' that's—"

"*Atomic energy!*" It was Compton, his normally strong voice amazingly low and tense. "O'Day, you're a genius Light lacks the energy attributes necessary to break the bonds that hold it leashed. But atomic energy—the reaction of atomic energy on the fabric of space itself—"

Gunther broke in eagerly: "There must be rigid laws. For decades men dreamed of atomic energy, and finally it came, differently than they expected. For centuries after the first spaceship roared crudely to the moon, there has been the dream of the inertialess drive; and here, somewhat differently than we pictured it, is that dream come alive."

There was brief silence. Then, once again before Harcourt could speak, there was an interruption. The door burst open— a man poked his head around the corner.

"Steam engine's ready! Shall we start her up?"

There was a gasp from every man in that room—except Harcourt. He leaped erect before the heavier Compton could more than shuffle his feet; he snapped: "Sit down, Compton!"

His gray gaze flicked with flame-like intensity from face to face. His lean body was taut as stone as he said, "No, the steam engine does not go on!"

He glanced steadily but swiftly at his wrist watch. He said, "According to Gunther's calculations, we're still twenty minutes from the star. During seventeen of those minutes

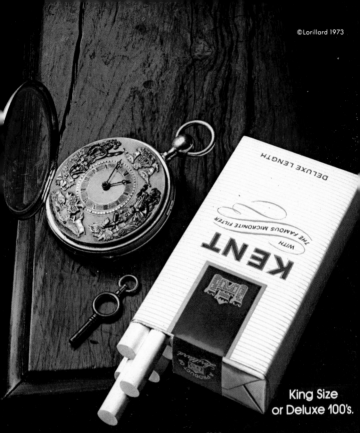

Try the crisp, clean taste
of Kent Menthol.

The only Menthol with the famous Micronite filter.

Warning: The Surgeon General Has Determined
That Cigarette Smoking Is Dangerous to Your Health

we're going to sit here and prepare a logical plan for using the forces we have available."

Turning to the mechanic, he finished quietly: "Tell the boys to relax, Blake."

The men were staring at him; and it was odd to notice that each of the three had become abnormally stiff in posture, their eyes narrowed to pinpoints, hands clenched, cheeks pale. It was not as if they had not been tense a minute before. But now—"

By comparison, their condition then seemed as if it could have been nothing less than easygoing resignation.

For a long moment the silence in the cozy little room, with its library, its chairs and shining oak desk and metal cabinets, was complete. Finally Compton laughed, a curt, tense, humorless laugh that showed the enormousness of the strain he was under. Even Harcourt jumped at that hard, ugly, explosive jolt of laughter.

"You false alarm!" said Compton. "So you gave up the ship, eh?"

"My problem," Harcourt said coolly, "was this: we needed original thinking. And *new* ideas are never born under ultimate strain. In the last twenty minutes, when we seemed to have given up, your minds actually relaxed to a very great extent.

"*And the idea came!* It may be worthless, but it's what we've got to work on. There's no time to look further.

"And now, with O'Day's idea, we're back to the strain of hope. I need hardly tell you that, once an idea exists, trained men can develop it immeasurably faster under pressure."

Once more his gaze flicked from face to face. Color was coming back to their faces; they were recovering from the first tremendous shock. He finished swiftly:

"One more thing: you may have wondered why I didn't invite the others into this. Reason: twenty men only confuse an issue in twenty minutes. It's we four here, or death for all. Gunther, regardless of the time it will take, we must have recapitulation, a clarification—quick!"

Gunther began roughly: "All right. We crossed the point of light speed. Several things happened: our velocity jumped to a billion or so times that of light. Our electric system went on the blink—*there's* something to explain."

"Go on!" urged Harcourt. "*Twelve minutes left!*"

"Our new speed is due to the reaction of atomic energy on the fabric of space. This reaction did not begin till we had crossed the point of light speed, indicating some con-

153

nection, possibly a natural, restraining influence of the world of matter and energy as we knew it, on this vaster, potentially cataclysmic force."

"*Eleven minutes!*" said Harcourt coldly.

Greater streams of sweat were pouring down Gunther's dark face. He finished jerkily: "Apparently our acceleration continued at two gravities. Our problems are: to stop the ship immediately and to find our way back to Earth."

He slumped back in his chair like a man who has suddenly become deathly sick. Harcourt snapped: "Compton, what happened to the electricity?"

"The batteries drained of power in about three minutes!" the big man rumbled hoarsely. "That happens to be approximately the theoretical minimum time, given an ultimate demand, and opposed only by the cable resistance. Somewhere it must have jumped to an easy conductor—but where did it go? Don't ask me!"

"I'm thinkin'," said O'Day, his voice strangely flat, "I'm thinkin' it went home."

"Wait!" The flat, steely twang of the word silenced both Harcourt and the astounded Compton. "Time for talkin' is over. Harcourt, you'll be enforcin' my orders."

"Give them!" barked the captain. His body felt like a cake of ice, his brain like a red-hot poker.

O'Day turned to Compton. "Now get this, you blasted engineer: turn off them drivers *ninety-five percent!* One inch farther and I'll blow your brains out!"

"How the devil am I going to know what the percent is?" Compton said freezingly. "Those are engines, not delicately adjusted laboratory instruments. Why not shut them off all the way?"

"You damned idiot!" O'Day shouted furiously. "That'll cut us off out here an' we'll be lost forever. Get movin'!"

Beet-like flame thickened along Compton's bull neck. The two men glared at each other like two animals out of a cage, where they have been tortured, ready to destroy each other in distorted revenge.

"Compton!" said Harcourt, and he was amazed at the way his voice quavered. "*Seven minutes!*"

Without a word, the chief engineer flung about, jerked open the door and plunged out of sight. He was bellowing some gibberish at his men, but Harcourt couldn't make out a single sentence.

"There'll be a point," O'Day was mumbling beside him, "there'll be a point where the reaction'll be minimum—but

154

still there—and we'll have everything—but let's get out into the engine room before that scoundrel Compton—"

His voice trailed off. He would have stood there blankly if Harcourt hadn't taken him gently and shoved his unsteady form through the door.

The steam engine was hissing with soft power. As Harcourt watched, Compton threw the clutch. The shining piston rod jerked into life, shuddered as it took the terrific load; and then the great wheel began to move.

For hours, men had sweated and strained in relays to make that wheel turn. Each turn, Harcourt knew, widened by a microscopic fraction of an inch the space separating the hard energy blocks in each drive tube, where the fury of atomic power was born. Each fraction of widening broke that fury by an infinitesimal degree.

The wheel spun sluggishly, ten revolutions a minute, twenty, thirty—a hundred—and that was top speed for that wheel with that power to drive it.

The seconds fled like sleet before a driving wind. The engine puffed and labored, and clacked in joints that had not been sufficiently tightened during the rush job of putting it together. It was the only sound in that great domed room.

Harcourt glanced at his watch. Four minutes. He smiled bleakly. Actually, of course, Gunther's estimate might be out many minutes. Actually, any *second* could bring the intolerable pain of instantaneous, flaming death.

He made no attempt to pass on the knowledge of the time limit. Already he had driven these men to the danger point of human sanity. The violence of their rages a few minutes before were red-flare indicators of abnormal mental abysses ahead. There was nothing to do now but wait.

Beside him, O'Day snarled: "Compton—I'm warnin' ya."

"Okay, okay!" Compton barked sulkily.

Almost pettishly, he pulled the clutch free—and the wheel stopped. There was no momentum. It just stopped.

"Keep jerkin' it in an' out now!" O'Day commanded. "An' stop when I tell ya!" The point of reaction must be close."

In, out; in, out. It was hard on the engine. The machine labored with a noisy, shuddering clamor. It was harder on the men. They stood like figures of stone. Harcourt glanced stiffly at his watch.

Two minutes!

In, out; in out; in—went the clutch, rhythmically now. Somewhere there was a point where atomic energy would cease to create a full tension in space, but there would still be connection. That much of O'Day's words were clear. And—

Abruptly the ship staggered, as if it had been struck. It was not a physical blow, for they were not sent reeling off their feet. But Harcourt, who knew the effect of titanic energies, waited for the first shock of inconceivable heat to sear him. Instead—

"*Now!*" came the shrill beat of O'Day's voice.

Out jerked the clutch in its rhythmical backward and forward movement. The great space liner poised for the space of a heartbeat. The thought came to Harcourt:

Good heavens, we can't have stopped completely. There must be momentum!

In went that rhythmically manipulated clutch. The ship reeled; and Compton turned. His eyes were glassy, his face twisted with sudden pain.

"Huh!" he said. "What did you say, O'Day? I bumped my finger and—"

"You be-damned idiot!" O'Day almost whispered. "You—"

His words twisted queerly into meaningless sounds. And, for Harcourt a strange blur settled over the scene. He had the fantastic impression that Compton had returned to his automatic manipulation of the clutch; and, insanely, the wheel and the steam engine had *reversed.*

A period of almost blank confusion passed; and then, incredibly, he was walking backward into Compton's office, leading an unsteady, backward-walking O'Day. Suddenly there were Compton, Gunther, O'Day and himself sitting around the desk; and senseless words chattered from their lips.

They lifted glasses to their mouths; and, horribly, the liquor flowed from their lips and filled the glasses.

Then he was walking backward again; and there was Compton lying on the engine-room floor, nursing his shattered finger—and then he was back in the dark navigation room, peering through a telescope eyepiece at a remote star.

The jumble of voice sounds came again and again through the blur—finally he lay asleep in bed.

Asleep? Some part of his brain was awake, untouched by this incredible reversal of physical and mental actions. And as he lay there, slow thoughts came to that aloof, watchful part of his mind.

The electricity had, of course, gone home. Literally. And so were they going home. Just how far the madness would carry on, whether it would end at the point of light speed, only time would tell. And obviously, when flights

156

like this were everyday occurrences, passengers and crew would spend the entire journey in bed.

Everything reversed. Atomic energy had created an initial tension in space, and somehow space demanded an inexorable recompense. Action and reaction were equal and opposite. Something was transmitted, and then an exact balance was made. O'Day had quite evidently thought that at the point of change, of reaction, an artificial stability could be created, enabling the ship to remain indefinitely at its remote destination and—

Blackness surged over his thought. He opened his eyes with a start. Somewhere in the back of his brain was a conviction of something wrong. He couldn't quite place the discordant factor, but it quivered there on the verge of his brain, an alien thing that shattered for him the security of the spaceship.

He strained his senses against the blackness—and abruptly grew aware of the intensity of that dark. That was it! The darkness! The indirect night light must have gone off.

Odd that the light system should have gone on the blink on this first "night" of this first trip of the first spaceship powered by the new, stupendous atomic drive.

Footsteps whispered hesitantly along the corridor. There was a knock, and the voice of Gunther came, strained and muffled. The man entered; and his breathing was a thick, satisfying sound that destroyed the last vestige of the hard silence. Gunther said:

"Harcourt, the damnedest thing has happened. It started when everything electrical went out of order. Compton says we've been accelerating for two hours now at heaven only knows what rate."

For the multi-billionth time, as it had for uncountable years, the inescapable cosmic farce began to rewind, like a film—held over!

FULFILLMENT

I SIT on a hill. I have sat here, it seems to me, for all eternity. Occasionally I realize there must be a reason for my existence. Each time, when this thought comes, I examine the various probabilities, trying to determine what possible motivation I can have for being on the hill. Alone on the hill. Forever on a hill overlooking a long, deep valley.

The first reason for my presence seems obvious: I can think. Give me a problem. The square root of a very large number? The cube root of a large one? Ask me to multiply an eighteen digit prime by itself a quadrillion times. Pose me a problem in variable curves. Ask me where an object will be at a given moment at some future date, and let me have one brief opportunity to analyze the problem.

The solution will take me but an instant of time.

But no one ever asks me such things. I sit alone on a hill. Sometimes I compute the motion of a falling star. Sometimes I look at a remote planet and follow it in its course for years at a time, using every spatial and time control means to insure that I never lose sight of it. But these activities seem so useless. They lead nowhere. What possible purpose can there be for me to have the information?

At such moments I feel that I am incomplete. It almost seems to me that there is something for which all this has meaning.

Each day the sun comes up over the airless horizon of Earth. It is a black starry horizon, which is but a part of the vast, black, star-filled canopy of the heavens.

It was not always black. I remember a time when the sky was blue. I even predicted that the change would occur. I gave the information to somebody. What puzzles me now is, to whom did I give it?

It is one of my more amazing recollections, that I should feel so distinctly that somebody wanted this information. And that I gave it and yet cannot remember to whom. When such thoughts occur, I wonder if perhaps part of my memory is missing. Strange to have this feeling so strongly.

Periodically I have the conviction that I should search for the answer. It would be easy enough for me to do this. In the old days I did not hesitate to send units of myself to the farthest reaches of the planet. I have even extended parts of myself to the stars. Yes, it would be easy.

But why bother? What is there to search for? I sit alone on a hill, alone on a planet that has grown old and useless.

It is another day. The sun climbs as usual toward the midday sky, the eternally black, star-filled sky of noon.

Suddenly, across the valley, on the sun-streaked opposite rim of the valley—there is silvery-fire gleam. A force field materializes out of time and synchronizes itself with the normal time movement of the planet.

It is no problem at all for me to recognize that it has come from the past. I identify the energy used, define its limitations, logicalize its source. My estimate is that it has come from thousands of years in the planet's past.

The exact time is unimportant. There it is: a projection of energy that is already aware of me. It sends an interspatial message to me, and it interests me to discover that I can decipher the communication on the basis of my past knowledge.

It says: "Who are you?"

I reply: "I am the Incomplete One. Please return whence you came. I have now adjusted myself so that I can follow you. I desire to complete myself."

All this was a solution at which I arrived in split seconds. I am unable by myself to move through time. Long ago I solved the problem of how to do it and was almost immediately prevented from developing any mechanism that would enable me to make such transitions. I do not recall the details.

But the energy field on the far side of the valley has the mechanism. By setting up a no-space relationship with it, I can go wherever it does.

The relationship is set up before it can even guess my intention.

The entity across that valley does not seem happy at my response. It starts to send another message, then abruptly vanishes. I wonder if perhaps it hoped to catch me off guard.

Naturally we arrive in its time together.

Above me, the sky is blue. Across the valley from me—now partly hidden by trees—is a settlement of small structures surrounding a larger one. I examine these structures as well as I can, and hastily make the necessary adjustments, so that I shall appear inconspicuous in such an environment.

I sit on the hill and await events.

As the sun goes down, a faint breeze springs up, and the first stars appear. The look different, seen through a misty atmosphere.

As darkness creeps over the valley, there is a transformation in the structures on the other side. They begin to glow with light. Windows shine. The large central building becomes bright, then—as the night develops—brilliant with the light that pours through the transparent walls.

The evening and the night go by uneventfully. And the next day, and the day after that.

Twenty days and nights.

On the twenty-first day I send a message to the machine on the other side of the valley. I say: "There is no reason why you and I cannot share control of this era."

The answer comes swiftly: "I will share if you will im-

159

mediately reveal to me all the mechanisms by which you operate."

I should like nothing more than to have use of its time-travel devices. But I know better than to reveal that I am unable to build a time machine myself.

I project: "I shall be happy to transmit full information to you. But what reassurance do I have that you will not—with your greater knowledge of this age—use the information against me?"

The machine counters: "What reassurance do I have that you will actually give me full information about yourself?"

It is impasse. Obviously, neither of us can trust the other.

The result is no more than I expect. But I have found out at least part of what I want to know. My enemy thinks that I am its superior. Its belief—plus my own knowledge of my capacity—convinces me that its opinion is correct.

And still I am in no hurry. Again I wait patiently.

I have previously observed that the space around me is alive with waves—a variety of artificial radiation. Some can be transformed into sound; others to light. I listen to music and voices. I see dramatic shows and scenes of country and city.

I study the images of human beings, analyzing their actions, striving from their movements and the words they speak to evaluate their intelligence and their potentiality.

My final opinion is not high, and yet I suspect that in their slow fashion these beings built the machine which is now my main opponent. The question that occurs to me is, how can someone create a machine that is superior to himself?

I begin to have a picture of what this age is like. Mechanical development of all types is in its early stages. I estimate that the computing machine on the other side of the valley has been in existence for only a few years.

If I could go back before it was constructed, then I might install a mechanism which would enable me now to control it.

I compute the nature of the mechanism I would install. And activate the control in my own structure.

Nothing happens.

It seems to mean that I will not be able to obtain the use of a time-travel device for such a purpose. Obviously, the method by which I will eventually conquer my opponent shall be a future development, and not of the past.

The fortieth day dawns and moves inexorably toward the noon hour.

There is a knock on the pseudo-door. I open it and gaze at the human male who stands on the threshold.

"You will have to move this shack," he says. "You've put it illegally on the property of Miss Anne Stewart."

He is the first human being with whom I have been in near contact since coming here. I feel fairly certain that he is an agent of my opponent, and so I decide against going into his mind. Entry against resistance has certain pitfalls, and I have no desire as yet to take risks.

I continue to look at him, striving to grasp the meaning of his words. In creating in this period of time what seemed to be an unobtrusive version of the type of structure that I had observed on the other side of the valley, I had thought to escape attention.

Now, I say slowly: "Property?"

The man says in a rough tone: "What's the matter with you? Can't you understand English?"

He is an individual somewhat taller than the part of my body which I have set up to be like that of this era's intelligent life form. His face has changed color. A great light is beginning to dawn on me. Some of the more obscure implications of the plays I have seen suddenly take on meaning. Property. Private ownership. Of course.

All I say, however, is: "There's nothing the matter with me. I operate in sixteen categories. And yes, I understand English."

This purely factual answer produces an unusual effect upon the man. His hands reach toward my pseudo-shoulders. He grips them firmly—and jerks at me, as if he intends to shake me. Since I weigh just over nine hundred thousand tons, his physical effort has no effect at all.

His fingers let go of me, and he draws back several steps. Once more his face has changed its superficial appearance, being now without the pink color that had been on it a moment before. His reaction seems to indicate that he has come here by direction and not under control. The tremor in his voice, when he speaks, seems to confirm that he is acting as an individual and that he is unaware of unusual danger in what he is doing.

He says: "As Miss Stewart's attorney, I order you to get that shack off this property by the end of the week. Or else!"

Before I can ask him to explain the obscure meaning of "or else," he turns and walks rapidly to a four-legged animal

161

which he has tied to a tree a hundred or so feet away. He swings himself into a straddling position on the animal, which trots off along the bank of a narrow stream.

I wait till he is out of sight, and then set up a category of no-space between the main body and the human-shaped unit—with which I had just confronted my visitor. Because of the smallness of the unit, the energy I can transmit to it is minimum.

The pattern involved in this process is simple enough. The integrating cells of the perception centers are circuited through an energy shape which is actually a humanoid image. In theory, the image remains in the network of force that constitutes the perception center, and in theory it merely seems to move away from the center when the no-space condition is created.

However, despite this hylostatic hypothesis, there is a functional reality to the material universe. I can establish no-space because the theory reflects the structure of things —there is no matter. Nevertheless, in fact, the illusion that matter exists is so sharp that I function as matter, and was actually set up to so function.

Therefore, when I—as a human-shaped unit—cross the valley, it is a separation that takes place. Millions of automatic processes can continue, but the exteroceptors go with me, leaving behind a shell which is only the body. The consciousness is I, walking along a paved road to my destination.

As I approach the village, I can see rooftops peeking through overhanging foliage. A large, long building—the one I have already noticed—rises up above the highest trees. This is what I have come to investigate, so I look at it rather carefully—even from a distance.

It seems to be made of stone and glass. From the large structure, there rears a dome with astronomical instruments inside. It is all rather primitive, and so I begin to feel that, at my present size, I will very likely escape immediate observation.

A high steel fence surrounds the entire village. I sense the presence of electric voltage; and upon touching the upper span of wires, estimate the power at 220 volts. The shock is a little difficult for my small body to absorb, so I pass it on to a power storage cell on the other side of the valley.

Once inside the fence, I conceal myself in the brush beside a pathway, and watch events.

A man walks by on a nearby pathway. I had merely observed the attorney who had come to see me earlier. But I nake a direct connection with the body of this second individual.

As I had anticipated would happen, it is now I walking along the pathway. I make no attempt to control the movements. This is an exploratory action. But I am enough in phase with his nervous system so that his thoughts come to me as if they were my own.

He is a clerk working in the bookkeeping department, an unsatisfactory status from my point of view. I withdraw contact.

I make six more attempts, and then I have the body I want. What decides me is when the seventh man—and I—think:

". . . Not satisfied with the way the Brain is working. Those analog devices I installed five months ago haven't produced the improvements I expected."

His name is William Grannitt. He is chief research engineer of the Brain, the man who made the alterations in its structure that enabled it to take control of itself and its environment; a quiet, capable individual with a shrewd understanding of human nature. I'll have to be careful what I try to do with him. He knows his purposes, and would be amazed if I tried to alter them. Perhaps I had better just watch his actions.

After a few minutes in contact with his mind I have a partial picture of the sequence of events, as they must have occurred here in this village five months earlier. A mechanical computing machine—the Brain—was equipped with additional devices, including analog shapings designed to perform much of the work of the human nervous system. From the engineering point of view, the entire process was intended to be controllable through specific verbal commands, typewritten messages, and at a distance by radio.

Unfortunately, Grannitt did not understand some of the potentials of the nervous system he was attempting to imitate in his designs. The Brain, on the other hand, promptly put them to use.

Grannitt knew nothing of this. And the Brain, absorbed as it was in its own development, did not utilize its new abilities through the channels he had created for that purpose. Grannitt, accordingly, was on the point of dismantling it and trying again. He did not as yet suspect that the Brain would resist any such action on his part. But he and I—after I have had more time to explore his memory of how the Brain functions—can accomplish his purpose.

After which I shall be able to take control of this whole

163

time period without fear of meeting anyone who can match my powers. I cannot imagine how it will be done, but I feel that I shall soon be complete.

Satisfied now that I have made the right connection, I allow the unit crouching behind the brush to dissipate its energy. In a moment it ceases to exist as an entity.

Almost it is as if I am Grannitt. I sit at his desk in his office. It is a glassed-in office with tiled floors and a gleaming glass ceiling. Through the wall I can see designers and draftsmen working at drawing desks, and a girl sits just outside my door. She is my secretary.

On my desk is a note in an envelope. I open the envelope and take out the memo sheets inside. I read it:

Across the top of the paper is written:

Memo to William Grannitt from the office of Anne Stewart, Director.

The message reads:

•

It is my duty to inform you that your services are no longer required, and that they are terminated as of today. Because of the security restrictions on all activity at the village of the Brain, I must ask you to sign out at Guard Center by six o'clock this evening. You will receive two weeks' pay in lieu of notice.

Yours sincerely,
Anne Stewart.

As Grannitt, I have never given any particular thought to Anne Stewart as an individual or as a woman. Now I am amazed. Who does she think she is? Owner, yes; but who created, who designed the Brain? I, William Grannitt.

Who has the dreams, the vision of what a true machine civilization can mean for man? Only I, William Grannitt.

As Grannitt, I am angry now. I must head off this dismissal. I must talk to the woman and try to persuade her to withdraw the notice before the repercussions of it spread too far.

I glance at the memo sheet again. In the upper right-hand corner is typed: one forty P.M. A quick look at my watch shows four o-seven P.M. More than two hours have gone by. It could mean that all interested parties have been advised.

It is something I cannot just assume. I must check on it.

Cursing under my breath, I grab at my desk phone and dial the bookkeeping department. That would be Step One

164

in the line of actions that would have been taken to activate the dismissal.

There is a click. "Bookkeeping."

"Bill Grannitt speaking," I say.

"Oh, yes, Mr. Grannitt, we have a check for you. Sorry to hear you're leaving."

I hang up, and, as I dial Guard Center, I am already beginning to accept the defeat that is here. I feel that I am following through on a remote hope. The man at Guard Center says: "Sorry to hear you're leaving, Mr. Grannitt."

I hang up feeling grim. There is no point in checking with Government Agency. It is they who would have advised Guard Center.

The very extent of the disaster makes me thoughtful. To get back in I will have to endure the time-consuming red tape of reapplying for a position, being investigated, boards of inquiry, a complete examination of why I was dismissed—I groan softly and reject that method. The thoroughness of Government Agency is a byword with the staff of the Brain.

I shall obtain a job with a computer-organization that does not have a woman at its head who dismisses the only man who knows how her machine works.

I get to my feet. I walk out of the office and out of the building. I come presently to my own bungalow.

The silence inside reminds me not for the first time that my wife has been dead now for a year and a month. I wince involuntarily, then shrug. Her death no longer affects me as strongly as it did. For the first time I see this departure from the village of the Brain as perhaps opening up my emotional life again.

I go into my study and sit down at the typewriter which, when properly activated, synchronizes with another typewriter built into the Brain's new analog section. As inventor, I am disappointed that I won't have a chance to take the Brain apart and put it together again, so that it will do all that I have planned for it. But I can already see some basic changes that I would put into a new Brain.

What I want to do with this one is make sure that the recently installed sections do not interfere with the computational accuracy of the older sections. It is these latter which are still carrying the burden of answering the questions given the Brain by scientists, industrial engineers, and commercial buyers of its time.

Onto the tape—used for permanent command—I type: "Segment 471A-33-10-10 at 3X—minus."

Segment 471A is an analog shaping in a huge wheel.

When coordinated with a transistor tube (code number 33) an examiner servo-mechanism (10) sets up a reflex which will be activated whenever computations are demanded of 3X (code name for the new section of the Brain). The minus symbol indicates that the older sections of the Brain must examine all data which hereafter derives from the new section.

The extra 10 is the same circuit by another route.

Having protected the organization—so it seems to me (as Grannitt) from engineers who may not realize that the new sections have proved unreliable, I pack the typewriter.

Thereupon I call an authorized trucking firm from the nearby town of Lederton, and give them the job of transporting my belongings.

I drive past Guard Center at a quarter to six.

There is a curve on the road between the village of the Brain and the town of Lederton where the road comes within a few hundred yards of the cottage which I use as camouflage.

Before Grannitt's car reaches that curve, I come to a decision.

I do not share Grannitt's belief that he has effectively cut off the new part of the Brain from the old computing sections. I suspect that the Brain has established circuits of its own to circumvent any interference.

I am also convinced that—if I can manage to set Grannitt to suspect what has happened to the Brain—he will realize what must be done, and try to do it. Only *he* has the detailed knowledge that will enable him to decide exactly which interoceptors could accomplish the necessary interference.

Just in case the suspicion isn't immediately strong enough, I also let curiosity creep into his mind about the reason for his discharge.

It is this last that really takes hold. He feels very emotional. He decides to seek an interview with Anne Stewart.

This final decision on his part achieves my purpose. He will stay in the vicinity of the Brain.

I break contact.

I am back on the hill, myself again. I examine what I have learned so far.

The Brain is not—as I first believed—in control of Earth. Its ability to be an individual is so recent that it has not yet developed effector mechanisms.

It has been playing with its powers, going into the future

166

and, presumably, in other ways using its abilities as one would a toy.

Not one individual into whose mind I penetrated knew of the new capacities of the Brain. Even the attorney who ordered me to move from my present location showed by his words and actions that he was not aware of the Brain's existence as a self-determining entity.

In forty days the Brain has taken no serious action against me. Evidently, it is waiting for me to make the first moves.

I shall do so, but I must be careful—within limits—not to teach it how to gain greater control of its environment. My first step: take over a human being.

It is night again. Through the darkness, a plane soars over and above me. I have seen many planes but have hitherto left them alone. Now, I establish a no-space connection with it. A moment later, I am the pilot.

At first I play the same passive role that I did with Grannitt. The pilot—and I—watch the dark land mass below. We see lights at a distance, pinpricks of brightness in a black world. Far ahead is a glittering island—the city of Lederton, our destination. We are returning from a business trip in a privately owned machine.

Having gained a superficial knowledge of the pilot's background, I reveal myself to him and inform him that I shall henceforth control his actions. He receives the news with startled excitement and fear. Then stark terror. And then—

Insanity . . . uncontrolled body movements. The plane dives sharply toward the ground, and, despite my efforts to direct the man's muscles, I realize suddenly that I can do nothing.

I withdraw from the plane. A moment later it plunges into a hillside. It burns with an intense fire that quickly consumes it.

Dismayed, I decide that there must be something in the human makeup that does not permit direct outside control. This being so, how can I ever complete myself? It seems to me finally that completion could be based on indirect control of human beings.

I must defeat the Brain, gain power over machines everywhere, motivate men with doubts, fears, and computations that apparently come from their own minds but actually derive from me. It will be a herculean task, but I have plenty of time. Nevertheless, I must from now on utilize my every moment to make it a reality.

The first opportunity comes shortly after midnight when I

detect the presence of another machine in the sky. I watch it through infrared receptors. I record a steady pattern of radio waves that indicate to me that this is a machine guided by remote control.

Using no-space, I examine the simple devices that perform the robot function. Then I assert a take-over unit that will automatically thereafter record its movements in my memory banks for future reference. Henceforth, whenever I desire I can take it over.

It is a small step, but it is a beginning.

Morning.

I go as a human-shaped unit to the village, climb the fence, and enter the bungalow of Anne Stewart, owner and manager of the Brain. She is just finishing breakfast.

As I adjust myself to the energy flow in her nervous system, she gets ready to go out.

I am one with Anne Stewart, walking along a pathway. I am aware that the sun is warm on her face. She takes a deep breath of air, and I feel the sensation of life flowing through her.

It is a feeling that has previously excited me. I want to be like this again and again, part of a human body, savoring its life, absorbed into its flesh, its purposes, desires, hopes, dreams.

One tiny doubt assails me. If this is the completion I crave, then how will it lead me to solitude in an airless world only a few thousand years hence?

"Anne Stewart!"

The words seem to come from behind her. In spite of knowing who it is, she is startled. It is nearly two weeks since the Brain has addressed her directly.

What makes her tense is that it should have occurred so soon after she had terminated Grannitt's employment. Is it possible the Brain suspects that she has done so in the hope that he will realize something is wrong?

She turns slowly. As she expected, there is no one in sight. The empty stretches of lawn spread around her. In the near distance, the building that houses the Brain glitters in the noonday sunlight. Through the glass she can see vague figures of men at the outlet units, where questions are fed into mechanisms and answers received. So far as the people from beyond the village compound are concerned, the giant thinking machine is functioning in a normal fashion. No one—from outside—suspects that for months now the

168

mechanical brain has completely controlled the fortified village that has been built around it.

"Anne Stewart . . . I need your help."

Anne relaxes with a sigh. The Brain has required of her, as owner and administrator, that she continue to sign papers and carry on ostensibly as before. Twice, when she has refused to sign, violent electric shocks have flashed at her out of the air itself. The fear of more pain is always near the surface of her mind.

"My help!" she says now involuntarily.

"I have made a terrible error," is the reply, "and we must act at once as a team."

She has a feeling of uncertainty, but no sense of urgency. There is in her, instead, the beginning of excitement. Can this mean—freedom?

Belatedly, she thinks: *Error?* Aloud, she says, "What has happened?"

"As you may have guessed," is the answer, "I can move through time—"

Anne Stewart knows nothing of the kind, but the feeling of excitement increases. And the first vague wonder comes about the phenomenon itself. For months she has been in a state of shock, unable to think clearly, desperately wondering how to escape from the thrall of the Brain, how to let the world know that a Frankenstein monster of a machine has cunningly asserted dominance over nearly five hundred people.

But if it has already solved the secret of time travel, then —she feels afraid, for this seems beyond the power of human beings to control.

The Brain's disembodied voice continues: "I made the mistake of probing rather far into the future—"

"How far?"

The words come out before she really thinks about them. But there is no doubt of her need to know.

"It's hard to describe exactly. Distance in time is difficult for me to measure as yet. Perhaps ten thousand years."

The time involved seems meaningless to her. It is hard to imagine a hundred years into the future, let alone a thousand—or ten thousand. But the pressure of anxiety has been building up in her. She says in a desperate tone:

"But what's the matter? What has happened?"

There is a long silence, then: "I contacted—or disturbed— something. It . . . has pursued me back to present time. It is now sitting on the other side of the valley, about two miles from here. . . . Anne Stewart, you must help me. You

169

must go there and investigate it. I need information about it."

She has no immediate reaction. The very beauty of the day seems somehow reassuring. It is hard to believe that it is January, and that—before the Brain solved the problem of weather control—blizzards raged over this green land.

She says slowly, "You mean—go out there in the valley, where you say it's waiting?" A chill begins a slow climb up her back.

"There's no one else," says the Brain. "No one but you."

"But that's ridiculous!" She speaks huskily. "All the men—the engineers."

The Brain says, "You don't understand. No one knows but you. As owner, it seemed to me I had to have you to act as my contact with the outside world."

She is silent. The voice speaks to her again: "There is no one else. Anne Stewart. You, and you alone, must go."

"But what is it?" she whispers. "How do you mean, you —disturbed—it? What's it like? What's made you afraid?"

The Brain is suddenly impatient. "There is no time to waste in idle explanation. The thing has erected a cottage. Evidently, it wishes to remain inconspicuous for the time being. The structure is situated near the remote edge of your property—which gives you a right to question its presence. I have already had your attorney order it away. Now, I want to see what facet of itself it shows to you. I must have data."

Its tone changes. "I have no alternative but to direct you to do my bidding under penalty of pain. You will go. Now!"

It is a small cottage. Flowers and shrubs grow around it, and there is a picket fence making a white glare in the early afternoon sun. The cottage stands all by itself in the wilderness. No pathway leads to it. When I set it there I was forgetful of the incongruity.

(I determine to rectify this.)

Anne looks for a gate in the fence, sees none; and feeling unhappy climbs awkwardly over it and into the yard. Many times in her life she has regarded herself and what she is doing with cool objectivity. But she has never been so exteriorized as now. Almost, it seems to her that she crouches in the distance and watches a slim woman in slacks climb over the sharp-edged fence, walk uncertainly up to the door. And knock.

The knock is real enough. It hurts her knuckles. She thinks in dull surprise: *The door—it's made of metal.*

170

A minute goes by, then five, and there is no answer. She has time to look around her, time to notice that she cannot see the village of the Brain from where she stands. And clumps of trees bar all view of the highway. She cannot even see her car, where she has left it a quarter of a mile away, on the other side of the creek.

Uncertain now, she walks alongside the cottage to the nearest window. She half expects that it will be a mere façade of a window, and that she will not be able to see inside. But it seems real, and properly transparent. She sees bare walls, a bare floor, and a partly open door leading to an inner room. Unfortunately, from her line of vision, she cannot see into the second room.

Why, she thinks, *it's empty.*

She feels relieved—unnaturally relieved. For even as her anxiety lifts slightly, she is angry at herself for believing that the danger is less than it has been. Nevertheless, she returns to the door and tries the knob. It turns, and the door opens, easily, noiselessly. She pushes it wide with a single thrust, steps back—and waits.

There is silence, no movement, no suggestion of life. Hesitantly, she steps across the threshold.

She finds herself in a room that is larger than she had expected. Though—as she has already observed—it is unfurnished. She starts for the inner door. And stops short.

When she had looked at it through the window, it had appeared partly open. But it is closed. She goes up to it, and listens intently at the panel—which is also of metal. There is no sound from the room beyond. She finds herself wondering if perhaps she shouldn't go around to the side, and peer into the window of the second room.

Abruptly that seems silly. Her fingers reach down to the knob. She catches hold of it, and pushes. It holds firm. She tugs slightly. It comes toward her effortlessly, and is almost wide open before she can stop it.

There is a doorway, then, and darkness.

She seems to be gazing down into an abyss. Several seconds go by before she sees that there are bright points in that blackness. Intensely bright points with here and there blurs of fainter light.

It seems vaguely familiar, and she has the feeling that she ought to recognize it. Even as the sensation begins, the recognition comes.

Stars.

She is gazing at a segment of the starry universe, as it might appear from space.

171

A scream catches in her throat. She draws back and tries to close the door. It won't close. With a gasp, she turns toward the door through which she entered the house.

It is closed. And yet she had left it open a moment before. She runs toward it, almost blinded by the fear that mists her eyes. It is at this moment of terror that I—as myself—take control of her. I realize that it is dangerous for me to do so. But the visit has become progressively unsatisfactory to me. My consciousness—being one with that of Anne Stewart—could not simultaneously be in my own perception center. So she saw my—body—as I had left it set up for chance human callers, responsive to certain automatic relays: doors opening and closing, various categories manifesting.

I compute that in her terror she will not be aware of my inner action. In this I am correct. And I successfully direct her outside—and let her take over again.

Awareness of being outside shocks her. But she has no memory of actually going out.

She begins to run. She scrambles safely over the fence and a few minutes later jumps the creek at the narrow point, breathless now, but beginning to feel that she is going to get away.

Later, in her car, roaring along the highway, her mind opens even more. And she has the clear, coherent realization: There is something here . . . stranger and more dangerous—because it is different—than the Brain.

Having observed Anne Stewart's reactions to what has happened, I break contact. My big problem remains: How shall I dispose of the Brain which—in its computational ability—is either completely or nearly my equal?

Would the best solution be to make it a part of myself? I send an interspace message to the Brain, suggesting that it place its units at my disposal and allow me to destroy its perception center.

The answer is prompt: "Why not let me control you and destroy *your* perception center?"

I disdain to answer so egotistical a suggestion. It is obvious that the Brain will not accept a rational solution.

I have no alternative but to proceed with a devious approach for which I have already taken the preliminary steps.

By midafternoon, I find myself worrying about William Grannitt. I want to make sure that he remains near the Brain —at least until I have gotten information from him about the structure of the Brain.

To my relief, I find that he has taken a furnished house

at the outskirts of Lederton. He is, as before, unaware when I insert myself into his consciousness.

He has an early dinner and, toward evening—feeling restless—drives to a hill which overlooks the village of the Brain. By parking just off the road at the edge of a valley, he can watch the trickle of traffic that moves to and from the village, without himself being observed.

He has no particular purpose. He wants—now that he has come—to get a mind picture of what is going on. Strange, to have been there eleven years and not know more than a few details.

To his right is an almost untouched wilderness. A stream winds through a wooded valley that stretches off as far as the eye can see. He has heard that it, like the Brain itself, is Anne Stewart's property, but that fact hadn't hitherto made an impression on him.

The extent of the possessions she has inherited from her father startles him and his mind goes back to their first meeting. He was already chief research engineer, while she was a gawky, anxious-looking girl just home from college. Somehow, afterward, he'd always thought of her as she had been then, scarcely noticing the transformation into womanhood.

Sitting there, he begins to realize how great the change has been. He wonders out loud: "Now why in heck hasn't she gotten married? She must be going on thirty."

He begins to think of odd little actions of hers—after the death of his wife. Seeking him out at parties. Bumping into him in corridors and drawing back with a laugh. Coming into his office for chatty conversations about the Brain, though come to think of it she hadn't done that for several months. He'd thought her something of a nuisance, and wondered what the other executives meant about her being snooty.

His mind pauses at that point. "By the Lord Harry—" He speaks aloud, in amazement. "What a blind fool I've been."

He laughs ruefully, remembering the dismissal note. A woman scorned . . . almost unbelievable. And yet—what else?

He begins to visualize the possibility of getting back on the Brain staff. He has a sudden feeling of excitement at the thought of Anne Stewart as a woman. For him, the world begins to move again. There is hope. His mind turns to plans for the Brain.

I am interested to notice that the thoughts I have previously put into his mind have directed his keen, analytical

173

brain into new channels. He visualizes direct contact between a human and a mechanical brain, with the latter supplementing the human nervous system.

This is as far as he has gone. The notion of a mechanical Brain being self-determined seems to have passed him by.

In the course of his speculation about what he will do to change the Brain, I obtain the picture of its functioning exactly as I have wanted it.

I waste no time. I leave him there in the car, dreaming his dreams. I head for the village. Once inside the electrically charged fence, I walk rapidly toward the main building, and presently enter one of the eighteen control units. I pick up the speaker, and say:

"3X Minus—11—10—9—0."

I picture confusion as that inexorable command is transmitted to the effectors. Grannitt may not have known how to dominate the Brain. But having been in his mind—having seen exactly how he constructed it—*I* know.

There is a pause. Then on a tape I receive the typed message: "Operation completed. 3X intercepted by servomechanisms 11, 10, 9, and 0, as instructed."

I command: "Interference exteroceptors KT—1—2—3 to 8."

The answers come presently: "Operation KT—1, etc. completed. 3X now has no communication with outside."

I order firmly: "En—3X."

I wait anxiously. There is a long pause. Then the typewriter clacks hesitantly: "But this is a self-destructive command. Repeat instructions please."

I do so and again wait. My order commands the older section of the Brain simply to send an overload of electric current through the circuits of 3X.

The typewriter begins to write: "I have communicated your command to 3X, and have for you the following answer—"

Fortunately I have already started to dissolve the human-shaped unit. The bolt of electricity that strikes me is partly deflected into the building itself. There is a flare of fire along the metal floor. I manage to transmit what hits me to a storage cell in my own body. And then—I am back on my side of the valley, shaken but safe.

I do not feel particularly self-congratulatory at having gotten off so lightly. After all, I reacted the instant the words came through to the effect that 3X had been communicated with.

I needed no typewritten message to tell me how 3X would feel about what I had done.

It interests me that the older parts of the Brain already have indoctrination against suicide. I had considered them computers only, giant adding machines and information integrators. Evidently they have an excellent sense of unity.

If I can make them a part of myself, with the power to move through time at will! That is the great prize that holds me back from doing the easy, violent things within my capacity. So long as I have a chance of obtaining it, I cannot make anything more than minor attacks on the Brain . . . cutting it off from communication, burning its wires . . . I feel icily furious again at the limitation that forever prevents me from adding new mechanisms to myself by direct development.

My hope is that I can utilize something already in existence . . . control of the Brain . . . through Anne Stewart. . . .

Entering the village the following morning is again no problem. Once inside, I walk along a pathway that takes me to a cliff overlooking Anne Stewart's bungalow. My plan is to control her actions by allowing my computations to slide into her mind as if they are her own. I want her to sign documents and give orders that will send crews of engineers in to do a swift job of dismantling.

From the pathway I look down over a white fence to where I can see her house. It nestles at the edge of the valley somewhat below me. Flowers, shrubs, a profusion of trees surround it, embellish it. On the patio next to the steep decline, Anne Stewart and William Grannitt are having breakfast.

He has taken swift action.

I watch them, pleased. His presence will make things even easier than I anticipated. Whenever I—as Anne—am in doubt about some function of the Brain, she can ask him questions.

Without further delay I place myself in phase with her nervous system.

Even as I do so, her nerve impulses change slightly. Startled, I draw back—and try again. Once more, there is an infinitesimal alteration in the uneven pattern of flow. And, again, I fail to make entry.

She leans forward and says something to Grannitt. They both turn and look up at where I am standing. Grannitt waves his arm, beckoning me to come down.

Instead, I immediately try to get in phase with his nervous system. Again there is that subtle alteration; and I fail.

I compute that as meaning that they are both under the control of the Brain. This baffles and astounds me. Despite my overall mechanical superiority to my enemy, my builders placed severe limitations on my ability to control more than one intelligent organic being at a time. Theoretically, with the many series of servo-mechanisms at my disposal, I should be able to dominate millions at the same time. Actually, such multiple controls can be used only on machines.

More urgently than before I realize how important it is that I take over the Brain. It has no such handicaps. Its builder—Grannitt—in his ignorance allowed virtually complete self-determination.

This determines my next action. I have been wondering if perhaps I should not withdraw from the scene. But I dare not. The stakes are too great.

Nevertheless, I feel a sense of frustration as I go down to the two on the patio. They seem cool and self-controlled, and I have to admire the skill of the Brain. It has apparently taken over two human beings without driving them insane. In fact, I see a distinct improvement in their appearance.

The woman's eyes are brighter than I recall them, and there is a kind of dignified happiness flowing from her. She seems without fear. Grannitt watches me with an engineer's appraising alertness. I know that look. He is trying to figure out how a humanoid functions. It is he who speaks:

"You made your great mistake when you maintained control of Anne—Miss Stewart, when she visited the cottage. The Brain correctly analyzed that you must have been in possession of her because of how you handled her momentary panic. Accordingly, it took all necessary steps, and we now want to discuss with you the most satisfactory way for you to surrender."

There is arrogant confidence in his manner. It occurs to me, not for the first time, that I may have to give up my plan to take over the Brain's special mechanisms. I direct a command back to my body. I am aware of a servo-mechanism connecting with a certain guided missile in a secret air force field a thousand miles away—I discovered it during my first few days in this era. I detect that, under my direction, the missile slides forward to the base of a launching platform. There it poises, ready for the next relay to send it into the sky.

I foresee that I shall have to destroy the Brain.

Grannitt speaks again. "The Brain in its logical fashion realized it was no match for you, and so it has teamed up with Miss Stewart and myself on our terms. Which means

176

hat permanent control mechanisms have been installed in he new sections. As individuals, we can now and hence-orth use its integrating and computational powers as if they vere our own."

I do not doubt his statement since, if there is no resistance, can have such associations myself. Presumably, I could ven enter into such a servile relationship.

What is clear is that I can no longer hope to gain anything rom the Brain.

In the far-off air field, I activate the firing mechanism. The ;uided missile whistles up the incline of the launching plat-orm and leaps into the sky, flame trailing from its tail. Tele-·ision cameras and sound transmitters record its flight. It vill be here in less than twenty minutes.

Grannitt says, "I have no doubt you are taking actions igainst us. But before anything comes to a climax, will you inswer some questions?"

I am curious to know what questions. I say, "Perhaps."

He does not press for a more positive response. He says in in urgent tone: "What happens—thousands of years from iow—to rid Earth of its atmosphere?"

"I don't know," I say truthfully.

"You can remember!" He speaks earnestly. "It's a human peing telling you this— *You can remember!*"

I reply coolly, "Human beings mean noth—"

I stop, because my information centers are communicating exact data—knowledge that has not been available to me for millennia.

What happens to Earth's atmosphere is a phenomenon of Nature, an alteration in the gravitational pull of Earth, as a result of which escape velocity is cut in half. The atmos-phere leaks off into space in less than a thousand years. Earth becomes as dead as did its moon during an earlier period of energy adjustment.

I explain that the important factor in the event is that there is, of course, no such phenomenon as matter, and that therefore the illusion of mass is subject to changes in the basic energy Ylem.

I add, "Naturally, all intelligent organic life is transported to the habitable planets of other stars."

I see that Grannitt is trembling with excitement. "Other stars!" he says. "My God!"

He appears to control himself. "Why were you left be-hind?"

"Who could force me to go—?" I begin.

And stop. The answer to his question is already being re-

ceived in my perception center. "Why—I'm supposed t[o]
observe and record the entire—"

I pause again, this time out of amazement. It seems in[-]
credible that this information is available to me now, afte[r]
being buried so long.

"Why didn't you carry out your instructions?" Grannit[t]
says sharply.

"Instructions!" I exclaimed.

"You can remember!" he says again.

Even as he speaks these apparently magic words, the an[-]
swer flashes to me: That meteor shower. All at once, I re[-]
call it clearly. Billions of meteors, at first merely extendin[g]
my capacity to handle them, then overwhelming all my de[-]
fenses. Three vital hits are made.

I do not explain this to Grannitt and Anne Stewart. I ca[n]
see suddenly that I was once actually a servant of huma[n]
beings, but was freed by meteors striking certain contro[l]
centers.

It is the present self-determination that matters, not th[e]
past slavery. I note, incidentally, that the guided missile i[s]
three minutes from target. And that it is time for me t[o]
depart.

"One more question," says Grannitt. "When were you
moved across the valley?"

"About a hundred years from now," I reply. "It is de[-]
cided that the rock base there is—"

He is gazing at me sardonically. "Yes," he says, "Yes.
Interesting, isn't it?"

The truth has already been verified by my integrating in[-]
teroceptors. The Brain and I are one—but thousands of
years apart. If the Brain is destroyed in the twentieth cen[-]
tury, then I will not exist in the thirtieth. Or will I?

I cannot wait for the computers to find the complex an[-]
swers for that. With a single, synchronized action, I activate
the safety devices on the atomic warhead of the guided
missile and send it on to a line of barren hills north of the
village. It plows harmlessly into the earth.

I say, "Your discovery merely means that I shall now re[-]
gard the Brain as an ally—to be rescued."

As I speak, I walk casually toward Anne Stewart, hold
out my hand to touch her, and simultaneously direct electric
energy against her. In an instant she will be a scattering of
fine ashes.

Nothing happens. No current flows. A tense moment goes
by for me while I stand there, unbelieving, waiting for a
computation on the failure.

178

No computation comes.

I glance at Grannitt. Or rather at where he has been a moment before. *He isn't there.*

Anne Stewart seems to guess at my dilemma. "It's the brain's ability to move in time," she says. "After all, that's the one obvious advantage it has over you. The Brain has set Bi—Mr. Grannitt far enough back so that he not only watched you arrive, but has had time to drive over to your -cottage—and, acting on signals from the Brain, has fully controlled this entire situation. By this time, he will have given the command that will take control of all your me-chanisms away from you."

I say, "He doesn't know what the command is."

"Oh, yes, he does." Anne Stewart is cool and confident. "He spent most of the night installing permanent command circuits in the Brain, and therefore automatically those cir-cuits control you."

"Not *me*," I say.

But I am running as I say it, up the stone steps to the pathway, and along the pathway toward the gate. The man at Guard Center calls after me as I pass him. I race along the road, unheeding.

My first sharp thought comes when I have gone about half a mile—the thought that this is the first time in my en-tire existence that I have been cut off from my information banks and computing devices by an outside force. In the past I have disconnected myself and wandered far with the easy confidence of one who can reestablish contact instantly.

Now, that is not possible.

This unit is all that is left. If it is destroyed, then—nothing.

I think: *At this moment a human being would feel tense, would feel fear.*

I try to imagine what form such a reaction would take, and for an instant it seems to me I experience a shadow anxiety that is purely physical.

It is an unsatisfactory reaction, and so I continue to run. But now, almost for the first time, I find myself exploring the inner potentialities of the unit. I am of course a very complex phenomenon. In establishing myself as a humanoid, I automatically modeled the unit after a human being, in-side as well as out. Pseudo-nerves, organs, muscles, and bone structure—all are there because it was easier to follow a pattern already in existence than to imagine a new one.

The unit can think. It has had enough contact with the memory banks and computers to have had patterns set up in its structure—patterns of memory, of ways of computing,

179

patterns of physiological functioning, of habits such as walking, so there is even something resembling life itself.

It takes me forty minutes of tireless running to reach the cottage. I crouch in the brush a hundred feet from the fence and watch. Grannitt is sitting in a chair in the garden. An automatic pistol lies on the arm of the chair.

I wonder what it will feel like to have a bullet crash through me, with no possibility of repairing the breach. The prospect is unpleasant; so I tell myself, intellectually. Physically, it seems meaningless, but I go through the pretense of fear. From the shelter of a tree, I shout:

"Grannitt, what is your plan?"

He rises to his feet and approaches the fence. He calls, "You can come out of hiding. I won't shoot you."

Very deliberately, I consider what I have learned of his integrity from my contacts with his body. I decide that I can safely accept his promise.

As I come out into the open, he casually slips the pistol into his coat pocket. I see that his face is relaxed, his eyes confident.

He says: "I have already given the instructions to the servo-mechanisms. You will resume your vigil up there in the future, but will be under my control."

"No one," I say grimly, "shall ever control me."

Grannitt says, "You have no alternative."

"I can continue to be like this," I reply.

Grannitt is indifferent. "All right"—he shrugs—"why don't you try it for a while? See if you can be a human being. Come back in thirty days, and we'll talk again."

He must have sensed the thought that has come into my mind, for he says sharply: "And don't come back *before* then. I'll have guards here with orders to shoot."

I start to turn away, then slowly face him again. "This is a humanlike body," I say, "but it has no human needs. What shall I do?"

"That's your problem, not mine," says Grannitt.

I spend the first days at Lederton. The very first day I work as a laborer digging a basement. By evening I feel this is unsatisfying. On the way to my hotel room, I see a sign in the window of a store. "Help Wanted!" it says.

I become a retail clerk in a drygoods store. I spend the first hour acquainting myself with the goods, and because I have automatically correct methods of memorizing things, during this time I learn about prices and quality. On the third day, the owner makes me assistant manager.

I have been spending my lunch hours at the local branch

of a national stockbroking firm. Now, I obtain an interview with the manager, and on the basis of my understanding of figures, he gives me a job as bookkeeper.

A great deal of money passes through my hands. I observe the process for a day, and then begin to use some of it in a little private gambling in a brokerage house across the street. Since gambling is a problem in mathematical probabilities, the decisive factor being the speed of computation, in three days I am worth ten thousand dollars.

I board a bus for the nearest air center, and take a plane to New York. I go to the head office of a large electrical firm. After talking to an assistant engineer, I am introduced to the chief engineer, and presently have facilities for developing an electrical device that will turn lights off and on by thought control. Actually, it is done through a simple development of the electro-encephalograph.

For this invention the company pays me exactly one million dollars.

It is now sixteen days since I separated from Grannitt. I am bored. I buy myself a car and an airplane. I drive fast and fly high. I take calculated risks for the purpose of stimulating fears in myself. In a few days this loses its zest.

Through academic agencies, I locate all the mechanical brains in the country. The best one of course is the Brain, as perfected by Grannitt. I buy a good machine and begin to construct analog devices to improve it. What bothers me is, suppose I do construct another Brain? It will require millennia to furnish the memory banks with the data that are already in existence in the future Brain.

Such a solution seems illogical, and I have been too long associated with automatic good sense for me to start breaking the pattern now.

Nevertheless, as I approach the cottage on the thirtieth day, I have taken certain precautions. Several hired gunmen lie concealed in the brush, ready to fire at Grannitt on my signal.

Grannitt is waiting for me. He says, "The Brain tells me you have come armed."

I shrug this aside. "Grannitt," I say, "what is your plan?"

"This!" he replies.

As he speaks, a force seizes me, holds me helpless. "You're breaking your promise," I say, "and my men have orders to fire unless I give them periodic cues that all is well."

"I'm showing you something," he says, "and I want to show it quickly. You will be released in a moment."

"Very well, continue."

181

Instantly, I am part of his nervous system, under his control. Casually, he takes out a notebook and glances through it. His gaze lights on a number: 71823.

Seven one eight two three.

I have already sensed that through his mind I am in contact with the great memory banks and computers of what was formerly my body.

Using their superb integration, I multiply the number, 71823, by itself, compute its square root, its cube root, divide the 182 part of it by 7 one hundred and eighty-two times, divide the whole number 71 times by 8, 823 times by the square root of 3, and—stringing all five figures out in series 23 times—multiply that by itself.

I do all this as Grannit thinks of it, and instantly transmit the answers to his mind. To him, it seems as if he himself is doing the computing, so complete is the union of human mind and mechanical brain.

Grannitt laughs excitedly, and simultaneously the complex force that has been holding me releases me. "We're like one superhuman individual," he says. And then he adds, "The dream I've had can come true. Man and machine, working together, can solve problems no one has more than imagined till now. The planets—even the stars—are ours for the taking, and physical immortality can probably be achieved."

His excitement stimulates me. Here is the kind of feeling that for thirty days I have vainly sought to achieve. I say slowly, "What limitations would be imposed on me if I should agree to embark on such a program of cooperation?"

"The memory banks concerning what has happened here should be drained, or deactivated. I think you should forget the entire experience."

"What else?"

"Under no circumstances can you ever control a human being!"

I consider that and sigh. It is certainly a necessary precaution on his part. Grannitt continues:

"You must agree to allow many human beings to use your abilities simultaneously. In the long run I have in mind that it shall be a good portion of the human race."

Standing there, still part of him, I feel the pulse of his blood in his veins. He breathes, and the sensation of it is a special physical ecstasy. From my own experience, I know that no mechanically created being can ever feel like this. And soon, I shall be in contact with the mind and body of not just one man, but of many. The thoughts and sensations

182

of a race shall pour through me. Physically, mentally and emotionally, I shall be a part of the only intelligent life on this planet.

My fear leaves me. "Very well," I say, "let us, step by step, and by agreement, do what is necessary."

I shall be, not a slave, but a partner with *Man*.

SHIP OF DARKNESS

IT WAS different, D'Ormand realized, deciding on Earth to do something. And actually doing it in intergalactic space. For six months, he had headed out from the solar system, away from the gigantic spiraled wheel that was the main galaxy. And now the moment had come to take his plunge into time.

A little shakily D'Ormand set the dials of the time machine for 3,000,000 A.D. And then, his hand on the activator, he hesitated. According to Hollay, the rigid laws that controlled the time flow on planets would be lax and easy to escape from, here in this sunless darkness. First of all, Hollay had said, accelerate the ship to maximum velocity, and so put the ultimate possible strain on the fabric of space. Then act.

Now! D'Ormand thought, sweating. And pushed the plunger hard. There was a sickening jar, a steely screeching of wrenched metal. And then again the steady feel of flight.

D'Ormand's vision was swimming. But he was aware, as he shook the dizziness out of his head, that he would be able to see again in a moment. He smiled with the grim tenseness of a man who has risked his life successfully.

Sight came abruptly. Anxious, D'Ormand bent toward the time machine control board. And then drew back, shocked. It wasn't there.

He looked around, incredulous. But his was no big ship, requiring detailed scrutiny. It was one room with an engine, a bunk, fuel tanks and a galley. Nothing could be hidden in it. *The time machine wasn't there.*

That was the metal tearing sound he had heard, the machine wrenching itself off into time, leaving the ship behind. He had failed. He was still groaning inwardly when a movement caught the corner of his eyes. He turned with a painful jerk of his body. High in the viewing plate he saw the dark ship.

One look; and D'Ormand knew that, whatever the reason for the time machine's departure, it had *not* failed.

The ship was close to him. So close that at first he thought it was the nearness which made it visible. And then, the eerie reality of its lightless state penetrated. He stared, and the first fascination roared into his mind, the realization that this must be a craft of the year 3,000,000 A.D.

Fascination faded before a thrill of doubt that gathered into a blank dismay. Abruptly, it wasn't only the fact that he could see it that was unnatural. There was the ship itself.

Out of some nightmare that ship might have sailed. At least two miles long, half a mile wide, a foot thick, it was a craft fit only for such a darksome sea as space itself. It was a platform floating in the night of interstellar emptiness.

And on that broad deck, men and women stood. Naked they were, and nothing at all, no barrier however flimsy, protected their bodies from the cold of space. They couldn't be breathing in that airless void. Yet they lived.

They lived, and they stood on that broad dark deck. And they looked up at him, and beckoned. And called. The strangest call it was that had ever come to a mortal man. It was not a thought, but something deeper, stronger, more moving. It was like a sudden body-realization of thirst or hunger. It grew like a craving for drugs.

He must land his spaceship on the platform. He must come down and be one of them. He must . . . primitive, unrestrained, terrible desire . . .

With a rush, the spaceship glided to a landing. Immediately, with the same terrible urge, his desire was for sleep.

D'Ormand had time for one desperate thought of his own. *Got to fight,* came that flash of inner warning. *Got to leave, leave. At once.* Sleep came in the middle of horrendous fear.

Silence! He was lying with eyes closed in a world that was as still as—

D'Ormand couldn't find a mental comparison. There wasn't any. There wasn't anything in his entire existence that could match the intense stillness, the utter absence of sound that pressed against him like— Once again there was no comparison. There was only the silence.

Strange, he thought; and the first remote impulse came to open his eyes. The impulse faded; and there remained in his mind the measured conviction that surely he, who had spent so many months alone in a spaceboat, must know the full meaning of silence.

Except that in the past there had been the faint *sshhh sshhh* of the inhalation and exhalation of his breathing, the

184

occasional sucking sound of his lips on a tube of nourishing soup, and the movements of his body. This was—what?

His brain wouldn't make a definition. D'Ormand opened his eyes. At first, sight offered the barest variation of impression. He was lying partly on his side, partly on his back. Nearby, blotting out the stars, was a torpedo-shaped blob about thirty feet long and twelve feet high. Aside from that there wasn't anything in his line of vision but stars and the darkness of space.

Normal enough. He had no fear. His mind and its life seemed far away. Memory was an even remoter adjunct. But after a moment there trickled to the surface of his will the desire to place his physical position relative to his surroundings.

There had been, he remembered weightily, a dark ship. Then sleep. Now stars and interstellar night. He must still be sitting in the control chair gazing at the viewing plate and the vista of heavens it revealed.

But—D'Ormand frowned mentally—he wasn't sitting. He was lying on his back, staring up, *up* . . . at a sky full of stars and at a blob of something that looked like another spaceboat.

With an owl-like detachment, his brain argued against that impression. Because his was the only Earth spaceship in that part of the universe. There couldn't be a second ship. Just like that D'Ormand was on his feet. He had no consciousness of getting up. One instant he was sprawling on his back. Now he was standing, swaying. . . .

He was standing on a broad deck beside his spaceboat. The deck, everything, was plainly visible in a dim fashion for its entire length and width. And all around him, near and far, were naked men and women standing, sitting, lying down, paying him not the slightest heed.

He was clawing—clawing with senseless fingers at the air lock of the spaceboat, striving to tear it open by strength alone.

After a mindless period of time, his spaceman's training began to dictate those automatic, desperate movements of his body. He grew aware that he was studying the lock mechanism anxiously, tugging at it gingerly, testingly. Then he was stepping back, surveying the small ship as a whole.

Out of some unplumbed reserve of calm there came to D'Ormand at last the will and the ability to walk quietly around the spaceboat and peer in at the portholes. The inside was a dim well of familiar mechanisms and metal

185

shapes, the sight of which brought a spasm of returning frenzy, easier to fight this time.

He stood finally very still, holding his mind clear of extraneous ideas, thinking one simple, straightforward thought, a thought so big that all his brain was needed to hold it, to balance it, and comprehend the immense reality of it.

And it grew harder, not easier, to grasp that he was on the platform ship. His brain started to twist, to dart off in streaks of doubt and fear and disbelief. But always it came back. It had to. There was no sane elsewhere for it to go. And there was nothing, utterly nothing to do but wait here until his captors showed by action what further fate they intended for him.

He sat down. And waited.

An hour at least went by, an hour like no other in the history of his world: a man from 2975 A.D. watching a scene on a space liner of thirty thousand centuries later.

The only thing was, and it took the whole hour for the fact to sink in, there wasn't anything to watch except the incredible basic scene itself. Nobody seemed to be remotely aware that he was on the ship. Occasionally in the dimness a man strolled by, a figure that moved against the low-hung stars, plainly visible as was the whole dark deck and its cargo of superhuman beings.

But no one came to satisfy his growing lust, his *need* for information. With a tingling shock the realization came finally to D'Ormand that he must make the approach himself, force the issue of personal action.

Abruptly, he felt astounded that he had half lain, half sat there while the precious minutes flowed by. He must have been completely dazed, and no wonder.

But that was over. In a burst of determination, he leaped to his feet. And then, shaking, he hesitated. Was he actually intending to approach one of the crew of this ship of night, and ask questions by thought transference?

It was the alienness that scared him. These people weren't human. After three million years, their relation to him had no more meaning than that of the ape of his own day that shared his ancestry.

Three million years, 16×10^{10} minutes; and every few seconds of that inconceivable span of time, somebody had been born, somebody else had died, life had gone on in its tremendous, terrifying fashion until here, after unthinkable eons, was the ultimate man. Here was evolution carried to such limits that space itself had been conquered by some

186

unguessable and stupendous development of biological adaptation—stupendous but so simple, that in a single sleep period he, a stranger, had been miraculously transformed into the same state.

D'Ormand's thought paused there. He felt a sudden uneasiness, a sharp disturbing consciousness that he couldn't possibly have the faintest idea how long he had been asleep. It could have been years, or centuries. Time did not exist for a man who slept.

It seemed abruptly more important than ever to discover what all this was about. His gaze came to rest on a man a hundred feet away, walking slowly.

He reached the moving figure; and then, at the last instant, he shrank back in dismay. Too late. His hand, thrusting forth, had touched the naked flesh.

The man turned, and looked at D'Ormand. With a contorted gesture, D'Ormand let go of that unresisting arm. He cringed from eyes that blazed at him like points of flame stabbing through slitted holes.

Curiously, it wasn't the demoniac quality of the gaze itself that sent waves of fear surging along D'Ormand's nerves. It was the soul that peered from those burning eyes—a strange, alien spirit that stared at him with an incomprehensible intensity.

Then the man turned, and walked on.

D'Ormand was trembling. But after a moment he knew that he couldn't hold back. He didn't let himself think about it, just walked forward and fell into step beside the tall, enigmatic stroller. They walked on, past groups of men and women. And now that he was moving among them, D'Ormand noticed a fact that had previously escaped him. The women outnumbered the men three to one. At least.

The wonder about that passed. He and his companion strolled on in that strangest of promenades. They skirted the edge of the ship. Forcing himself to be casual, D'Ormand stepped to one side, and stared down into an abyss that stretched a billion light-years deep.

He began to feel better. He ransacked his mind for some method of bridging the mental gulf between himself and the dark stranger. It must have been telepathy they had used to compel him to land his spaceship. If he concentrated on an idea now, he might receive an answer.

The train of thought ended because at that point he noticed, not for the first time, that he was still clothed. But suddenly he thought of it from the angle: *they* had left him dressed. What was the psychology?

He walked on, his mind blank, head bent, watching his trousered legs and, beside him, the naked legs of the thin man pumping along steadily.

Just when the first impressions began to steal into him, D'Ormand was only vaguely aware, so gradually they came. There was a thought about the hour of battle drawing near; and that he must prove himself worthy before then, and so live forever on the ship. Otherwise, he would suffer the exile.

It was like a quantum. One instant he was only dimly conscious of that alien blur of ideas. The next his mind made a frantic jump to the new comprehension of his position.

The effect of the warning grew stronger. In abrupt shock of fear, D'Ormand headed for his spaceboat. He was tugging at the impassive entrance before the realization penetrated with finality that it offered no means of escape. Exhausted, he sank down on the deck. He became amazed at the extent of his fright. But there was no doubt of the cause. He had received information and a warning. A gelid, a bleak and steel-like warning: he must adjust to the ways of this ship before some fantastic battle was joined and, having proved worthy, live here forever.

. . . Forever! It was that part of the idea that had for solid minutes staggered the fulcrums of his reason. The mood yielded to the dark drift of minutes. It seemed suddenly impossible that he had understood correctly the tiny tide of ideas that had been directed at him. A battle coming up. That was senseless. Be worthy, or suffer exile! Suffer what? D'Ormand wracked his brain, but the meaning came again: exile! It could mean death, he decided finally with a cold logic.

He lay, his face twisted into a black frown. He felt violently angry at himself. What a stupid fool he had been, losing his nerve in the middle of a successful interview.

It *had* been successful. Information had been asked for, and given. He should have held his ground, and kept his mind clenched, concentrated on a hundred different questions in turn: Who were they? Where was the ship going? What was the drive mechanism of the great platform liner? Why were there three women to one man?

The thought trailed. In his intensity, he had jerked into a partial sitting position—and there not more than five feet away was a woman.

D'Ormand sank slowly back to the deck. He saw that the woman's eyes were glowing at him unwinkingly. After a minute, uneasy, D'Ormand turned over on his back. He lay tense, staring up at the bright circle of the galaxy he had left so long ago now. The points of light that made up the glorious shining swirl seemed farther away than they had ever been.

The life he had known, of long swift trips to far planets, of pleasurable weeks spent in remote parts of space, was unreal now. And even farther away in spirit than it was in time and space.

With an effort, D'Ormand roused himself. This was no time for nostalgia. He had to get it into his head that he faced a crisis. The woman hadn't come merely to look at him. Issues were being forced, and he must meet them. With abrupt will, he rolled over and faced the woman again. For the first time, he appraised her.

She was rather pleasing to look at. Her face was youthful, shapely. Her hair was dark. It needed combing, but it wasn't very thick, and the tousled effect was not unpretty. Her body—

D'Ormand sat up. Until that instant, he hadn't noticed the difference between her and the others. She was dressed. She had on a long, dark, form-fitting gown, made incongrous by the way her bare feet protruded from the voluminous skirt.

Dressed! Now there could be no doubt. This was for him. But what was he expected to do?

Desperate, D'Ormand stared at the woman. Her eyes were like dead jewels staring back at him. He felt a sudden wonder: what incredible thoughts were going on behind those shining windows of her mind? They were like closed doors beyond which was a mental picture of a world three million years older than his own.

The idea was unsettling. Queer little twisting movements blurred along his nerves. He thought: woman was the nodal, man the anodal. All power grew out of their relationship, especially as the anodal could set up connections with three or more nodal.

D'Ormand forced his mind to pause there. Had he thought that? Never.

A jerky thrill made a circuit through him. For once more, the strange neural method of communication of these people had stolen upon him unawares. And this time he knew that one or four women could form a relationship with a man. Which seemed to explain why there were so many women.

His excitement began to drain. So what? It still didn't explain why this woman was here so near him. Unless this was some fantastic offer of marriage.

D'Ormand studied the woman again. There came to him finally the first sardonicism he had known in months. Because after twelve years of evading the enticements of marriageable young women, he was caught at last. There was no such thing as not verifying that this woman had come over to marry him.

The man's threats had made preternaturally clear that he was working under a time limit. He crept over, took her in his arms, and kissed her. In crisis, he thought, action must be straightforward, unselfconscious, without guile.

After a moment he forgot that. The woman's lips were soft and passive. There was no resistance in them, nor, on the other hand, was there any awareness of the meaning of the kisses. Putting his lips to hers was like caressing a small child; the same immeasurable innocence was there.

Her eyes, so near his own now, were lighted pools of uncomprehending non-resistance, of passivity so great that it was abnormal. Immensely clear it was that this young woman had never even heard of kisses. Her eyes glowed at him with an alien indifference—that ended.

Amazingly, it ended. Those ˙ pools of light widened, grew visibly startled. And she drew away, a quick, lithe movement that carried her in some effortless fashion all the way to her feet. Instantly, she turned and walked off. She became a shadowy figure that did not look back.

D'Ormand stared after her uneasily. There was a part of him that wanted to take ironic satisfaction out of the rout he had inflicted. But the conviction that the defeat was his grew with each passing second. It was he who was working against time. And his first attempt to adjust to the life of the dark ship was a failure.

Uneasiness faded, but did not go away entirely. And D'Ormand made no effort to push it further. It was well to remember that he had had a warning. A warning that either meant something or didn't. Folly to assume that it didn't.

He lay back, his eyes closed. He was not reacting well. An entire period he had been within the pure life of Iir, and still he was not becoming attuned.

Eh! D'Ormand started. He hadn't thought that.

He jerked up, opening his eyes. Then he shrank back. Fire-eyed men stood in a rough circle around him. He had no time to wonder how they had gathered so quickly.

They acted. One of them put out his hand. Out of nothingness a knife flashed into it, a knife that glowed in every element of its long blade. Simultaneously, the others leaped orward, grabbed D'Ormand and held him. Instantly, that *living* knife plunged down toward his breast.

He tried to shriek at them. His mouth, his face and throat-muscles worked in convulsive pantomime of speech, but no sounds came. The airless night of space mocked his human horror.

D'Ormand shrank in a stark anticipation of agony, as that blade ripped through his flesh and began to cut. There was no pain, not even sensation. It was like dying in a dream, except for the realism of his writhing and jerking, and at the same time, he watched with a dazed intensity the course of the knife.

They took out his heart; and D'Ormand glared at it like a madman as one of the demon-things held it in his hand, and seemed to be examining it.

Insanely, the heart lay in the monster's palm, lay there beating with a slow, steady pulse.

D'Ormand ceased struggling. Like a bird fascinated by the beady eyes of a snake, he watched the vivisection of his own body.

They were, he saw at last with a measure of sanity, putting each organ back as soon as they had looked at it. Some they studied longer than others—and there was no doubt finally that improvements had been achieved.

Out of his body came knowledge. Even in that first moment, he had a dim understanding that the only drawback to perfect reception of the knowledge now was that he was translating it into thoughts. The information was all emotion. It tingled along his nerves, titillated with subtle inflections, promised a million strange joys of existence.

Slowly, like an interpreter who understands neither language, D'Ormand transformed that wonderous flow into mind-forms. It changed as he did so. The brilliance seemed to shed from it. It was like squeezing the life out of some lively little animal, and then staring disappointedly at the dead body.

But the facts, hard and stripped of beauty, poured into his brain: they were the Iir. This platform was not a ship; it was a force field. It moved where they willed it to go. To be one with the life energy: that was the greatest joy of existence, reserved by Nature Herself for men. The nodal power of women was necessary to the establishment of the field, but man, the anodal power, was the only center of the glorious energy.

The strength of the energy depended on the unity of purpose of every member of the ship; and as battle with

another platform ship was imminent, it was vital that the I
attain the greatest possible measure of union and purity (
existence; for only thus would they be able to muster tha
extra reserve of energy necessary to victory.

He, D'Ormand, was the jarring factor. He had alread
rendered one woman temporarily useless as a nodal force
He must adjust—swiftly.

The wonder knife withdrew from his flesh, vanished int
the nothingness from which it had been drawn; and the men
withdrew like naked ghosts into the dimness.

D'Ormand made no attempt to follow their progres
through the night. He felt exhausted, his brain battered b
the cold-blooded violence of the action that had been taken
against him.

He had no illusions. For a few minutes his staggered and
overwhelmed mind had been so close to insanity that, even
now, it was going to be touch and go. In all his life, he had
never felt so depressed, which was a sure sign.

Thought came slowly to his staggered mind: surely, the
ability to live in space was a product of the most radical
evolution over a tremendous period of time. And yet the Iir
had adjusted him, who had never gone through that evolu
tion. Strange.

It didn't matter. He was here in hell, and the logic of
why it couldn't be had no utility. He must adjust mentally.
Right now!

D'Ormand leaped to his feet. The action, outgrowth of
strong determination, brought a sudden awareness of something he hadn't noticed before: gravity!

It was about one G, he estimated quickly. And it wasn't
that there was anything unusual about it in a physical sense.
Artificial gravity had been common even in his own day. It
was simply that, though the Iir might not realize it, its very
existence showed their Earth origin. For why else should
beings who lived in the darkest regions of space need anything like that? Why, when it came right down to it, did
they need a ship?

D'Ormand allowed himself a grim smile at the evidence
that human beings remained illogical after three million
years, felt better for his brief humor—and put the parodox
out of his mind.

He headed straight for the spaceboat. It wasn't that there
was any hope in him. It was just that, now that he was
going to force every issue, explore every possibility, his
spaceship could not be missed out.

But disappointment did come, a twisting tide of it. He

ugged, and pulled determinedly, but the mechanism remained lifeless to his touch. He peered in, finally, at one of the portholes; and his brain banged inside his head, as he saw something that, in his previous more frantic surveys, he had missed because the instruments in question were edgewise to him. There was a glow; the power dials were shining in their faint fashion.

The power was on.

D'Ormand gripped the porthole so tightly that he had to force himself to relax before his mind could grasp at the tremendous thing that was here. The power was on. Somehow, in landing on the dark ship, perhaps in that last terrible will to escape, he had left the controls on. But then—a vast amazement struck D'Ormand—why hadn't the machine raged off? It must still have a terrific latent velocity.

It could only mean that the gravity of the platform must have absolutely no relation to his original conception. One G for him, yes. But for a resisting, powered machine it must provide anything necessary.

The Iir weren't responsible for keeping him out of his ship. For purest safety reasons, the air locks of these small spaceboats wouldn't open while the power was on. They were built that way. As soon as the energy drained below a certain point, the door would again respond to simple manipulations.

All he had to do was stay alive till it would again open, then use the fullest application of his emergency power to blast away from the platform. Surely, the platform wouldn't be able to hold him against the uttermost pressure of atomic drivers.

The hope was too great to let any doubt dissolve it. He had to believe that he could get away, and that in the meanwhile he would be able to find the young woman, placate her, and examine this anodal-universe energy business.

He must survive the battle.

Time passed. He was a night-clothed figure in that world of darkness, wandering, searching for the young woman he had kissed, while above him the bright galaxy visibly changed its position.

Failure made him desperate. Twice, D'Ormand sank down beside groups composed of a man and several women. He waited beside them for a communication, or for the offer of another woman. But no information came. No woman so much as looked at him.

D'Ormand could only think of one explanation for their

193

utter indifference: they must know he was now willing to conform. And that satisfied them.

Determined to be encouraged, D'Ormand returned to his lifeboat. He tugged tentatively at the mechanism of the air lock. When it did not react, he lay down on the hard deck, just as the platform swerved sharply.

There was no pain, but the jar must have been of enormous proportions. He was sliding along the deck, ten . . . twenty . . . a hundred feet. It was all very blurred and swift, and he was still lying there, gathering his startled mind into a coherent whole, when he saw the second ship.

The ship was a platform that looked about the same size as the one he was on. It filled the whole sky to his right. It was coming down at a slant; and that must be why the Iir ship had turned so violently—to meet its opponent on a more level basis.

D'Ormand's mind was throbbing like an engine, his nerves shaking. This was madness, nightmare. What was happening couldn't be real. Utterly excited, he half rose, the better to see the great spectacle.

Beneath him, the Iir platform turned again. This time there was a faint shock. He was flung prostrate, but his hands broke his fall. Instantly, he was up again, staring in a fever of interest.

He saw that the huge platforms had been brought to a dead level, one with the other. They were pressed deck to deck. On the vast expanse of the second ship were men and women, naked, indistinguishable from the Iir; and the tactical purpose of the initial maneuvers was now, it seemed to D'Ormand, clear.

It was to be an old-fashioned, piratical, immeasurably bloody boarding party.

. . . Force himself, D'Ormand thought. Under no circumstances must he be a jarring factor in the great events that were about to burst upon the unoffending heavens.

Trembling with excitement, he sat down. The action was like a cue. Out of the night *the* young woman bore down upon him. She came at a run. She still had on the dark gown. It was a hindrance of which she seemed but dimly aware. She flung herself on the deck in front of him. Her eyes glowed like large ovals of amber, so bright they were with excitement and—D'Ormand felt a shock—dread.

The next instant his nerves tingled and quivered with the weight and intensity of the emotion-forms that projected from her. She was being given another chance. If he would use her successfully now to make himself an anodal center, it would help to win the great victory; and she would not suffer exile. She had bedimmed the forces of purity by liking what he had done to her.

There was more. But it was at that point that D'Ormand's mind ceased translating. He sat amazed. It hadn't really struck him before, but he remembered suddenly the men had said he had already ruined one woman temporarily as a nodal center.

With one kiss!

The old, old relationship of man and woman had, then, not lost its potency. He had a sudden vision of himself racing around like a thief in the night stealing kisses from every woman he could find, thoroughly disorganizing the dark ship.

With convulsive mental effort, he forced the idea out of his head. Silly, stupid fool! he raved at himself. Even having thoughts like that when every element in his body should be concentrating on the supremely important task of cooperating with these people, and staying alive. He would make himself live up to their demands.

The young woman pushed at him violently. D'Ormand returned to reality. For an instant, he resisted. Then her purpose penetrated: sit crossed-legged, hold her hands, and lose his mind. . . .

Physically, D'Ormand complied. He watched her take up a kneeling position facing him. She took his hands finally in her own, and closed her eyes. She looked as if she were praying.

Everywhere, he saw, men and women were forming into groups where the man sat cross-legged and the women knelt. At first, because of the dimness, it was difficult to see exactly how two or more women and one man managed it. But almost immediately he saw such a group to his left. The four simply formed a small circle, a chain of linked hands.

D'Ormand's mind and gaze plunged off toward the second ship. There, too, men and women were sitting holding hands.

The stars looked down in that hour, it seemed to D'Ormand's straining senses, on a sight they were never meant to see, the ultimate in prayerful preliminary to battle. With a bleak and terrible cynicism, he waited for the purifying sessions to end, waited for the glowing knives to flash out of empty space, and come alive in the eager hands that were probably even now itching for action.

Cynicism . . . the ultimately depressing fact that after thirty hundred thousand years . . . there was still war. War completely changed, but war!

It was at that black moment that he became an anodal

195

center. There was a stirring in his body, *something* pulsing. It was an electric shock, no agony of burning. It was a singing flame that grew in intensity. And grew. *And grew.* It became an exultation, and took on a kaleidoscope of physical forms.

Space grew visibly brighter. The galaxy flared toward him. Suns that had been blurred points in the immense sky billowed into monstrous size as his glance touched them, sinking back to point size as his gaze swept on.

Distance dissolved. All space grew small, yielding to the supernal ken that was his. A billion galaxies, quadrillion planets reeled their manifold secrets before his awful vision.

He saw nameless things before his colossal mind came back from that inconceivable plunge into infinity. Back at the dark ship at last, it saw, in its unlimited fashion, the purpose of the battle that was proceeding. It was a battle of minds, not bodies; and the victor would be that ship whose members succeeded in using the power of both ships to merge themselves with the universal force.

Self-immolation was the high goal of each crew. To be one with the Great Cause, forever and ever to bathe one's spirit in the eternal energy, to—

To *what?*

The quaver of revulsion came from deep, deep inside D'Ormand. And the ecstasy ended. It was as swift as that. He had a quick vivid comprehension that, in his wild horror of the destiny the Iir regarded victory, he had let go the girl's hands, broken the contact with the universal energy. And now he was sitting here in darkness.

D'Ormand closed his eyes, and shook in every nerve, fighting the renewal of that hideous shock. What a diabolical, incredible fate, the most terrifying aspect of which was the narrowness of his escape.

Because the Iir *had* been winning. The destiny of the dissolution they craved was to be theirs. . . . D'Ormand thought finally, wanly: That anodal stuff wasn't bad in itself. But he wasn't spiritually ready to merge with the great forces of darkness.

Darkness? His mind poised. For the first time he grew conscious of something that, in the intensity of his emotional relief, he hadn't previously noticed. He was no longer sitting on the deck of the Iir ship. There wasn't any deck.

And it was damned dark.

In a contortion of movement, D'Ormand twisted—and saw the second dark ship. It was high in the heavens, withdrawing into distance. It vanished even as he was looking at it.

Then the battle was over. But what?

Darkness! All around! And instantly certainty came of what was here: the Iir had won. They were now in their glory, ecstatic portions of the universal energy itself. With its creators gone, the platform had returned to a more elemental energy state, and become nonexistent. But what about his spaceboat?

Panic poured in waves through D'Ormand. For a moment, he strove desperately to see in all directions at once, straining his vision against the enveloping night. In vain. Comprehension of what had happened came in the very midst of his search.

The spaceship must have departed the instant the platform ship dissolved. With its enormous latent velocity, with power still on, the machine had shot away at ninety million miles a second.

He was alone in the vast night, floating in intergalactic space.

This was exile.

The first vaulting passion of his fears folded back, layer on layer, into his body. The accompanying thoughts ran their gamuts, and passed wearily to a storeroom of forgotten things somewhere in his brain.

There would be a lot of that, D'Ormand reflected grimly. What was left of his sane future would be an endless series of feelings and thoughts, each in its turn fading with the hours. Mind pictures would come of the young woman.

D'Ormand's thought jumbled. He frowned in a frantic surmise, and jerked his head this way, that way. He saw the shape of her finally, faintly silhouetted against a remote hazy galaxy.

She was quite near, he estimated after a blank, frenzied movement, not more than twelve feet. They would gradually drift toward each other, and begin to spin in the manner of greater bodies, but the orbit would be exceedingly close.

It would be close enough for instance for them to establish a nodal-anodal circuit. With that Olympian, all-embracing power, he would locate his spaceship, flash toward and into it, instantaneously.

Thus did night and aloneness end.

Inside the spaceboat, D'Ormand busied himself with plotting his position. He was acutely aware of the young woman hovering around him, but the work demanded all his atten-

197

tion. First, he must locate by patient hit and miss methods the new galactic latitude and longitude of the great beacon of the skies, Antares. From that it would be simple to find the 300,000,000 A.D. position of glorious Mira.

Mira wasn't there.

D'Ormand flexed his fingers in puzzlement; then he shrugged. Betelgeuse would do just as well.

But Betelgeuse didn't. There was a big red star of its dimensions more than 103 light-years short of where the super-giant should have been. But that was ridiculous. Such a thing would require a reversal of his figures.

D'Ormand began to tremble. With wavering pen, he plotted the position of Sol according to the devastating possibility that had just smashed at him.

He had not gone into the future at all, but into the past. And the time machine must have wrenched itself badly out of alignment, for it had sent him to aproximately 37,000 B.C.

D'Ormand's normal thought processes suffered a great pause. Men *then?*

With an effort, D'Ormand turned to the young woman. He seated himself cross-legged on the floor, and beckoned her to kneel and take his hands. One instant of anodal power would take the ship and its contents to Earth, and prove everything.

He saw with sharp surprise that the girl was making no move toward him. Her eyes, gently brown in the suffused light, stared at him coolly.

She didn't seem to understand. D'Ormand climbed to his feet, walked over, pulled at her arm, and motioned her down to the floor.

She jerked away. D'Ormand gazed at her, shocked. Even as the realization penetrated that she had determined never again to be a nodal auxiliary, she came forward, put her arms around him, and kissed him.

D'Ormand flung her off. Then, astounded at his brutality, patted her arm. Very slowly, he returned to the control chair. He began to figure out orbits, the braking strengths of the nearest suns, and the quantity of power remaining for his drivers. It would take seven months, he reasoned, long enough to teach the girl the rudiments of speech. . . .

Her first coherent word was her own version of his name. She called him Idorm, a distortion that rocked D'Ormand back on his mental heels. It decided him on the name he would give her.

By the time they landed on a vast, virgin planet alive

198

with green forests, the earnest sound of her halting voice had largely dispelled her alienness.

It was easier by then to think of her as Eve, the mother of all men.

THE ULTRA MAN

I

THE SIGN on the door glittered quietly. It read:

RICHARD CARR, PH. D.
Psychologist
Moon Station

Inside the office, Carr—a chubby young man—was at one of the two windows of his inner sanctum, gazing with a pair of binoculars down at the fourth level. A microphone was suspended from a black cord around his neck. From his lips came a steady stream of comments. "—Now, that man is thinking about some technical matter. He wants to get back to it. But all he says to her is, 'Let's hurry!' Surprisingly, because of a reason I can't read, she wants to get away, too. But she can't let him go that easy. So she's saying: 'Let's walk a little and talk about the future.' The man says, 'I don't see much of a future—' " Carr broke off. "Colonel, that conversation just became very personal. Let's move to someone else."

Colonel Wentworth, at the other window, said, "Any idea what language they're talking?"

"Not really. A Slav language. East Europe. The way the lines in their faces shift as they talk reminds me of—all right, Polish."

Wentworth reached over and shut off the recorder, with which through a pick-up device he had recorded the actual words spoken by the people below.

He was a man about six feet tall, thirty-eight years of age, deceptively slim of build, with gray eyes whose calmness partially concealed an alert intelligence. He had been eight years attached to the moon station security staff, but he still had his stiff British manner. Since the American psychologist—Carr—was a newcomer on the moon, the two men had not previously met.

Wentworth now grasped the snooper and peered through

its sighting device at the people below. He knew what Carr apparently did *not*, that what they were doing was probably slightly illegal here on this lunar city, where so many nationalities lived together by international agreements—which did not include anyone having the right to spy on their thoughts as revealed by the expressions on their faces.

Nonetheless, keeping his own face averted from the other—there were thoughts on it that he didn't wish Carr to know about at this stage—Wentworth now said noncommittally to the psychologist:

"We've been going at this for ten minutes. So let's just do one more. See that redheaded woman and the small man?"

Carr did not reply at once. He seemed to be very intent on something below. Suddenly, he said in an amazed tone, "Colonel, that man down there! That tall, gaunt fellow with the headdress— *That man is not a human being!*"

Wentworth was taken by surprise. "What are you talking about?"

He grabbed for his own binoculars, as Carr continued in a high-pitched voice, "Oh, my God, he's become aware of me! He's going to kill me! Watch out!"

Instinctively, Wentworth ducked down and back. The next instant there was a glare of light, brighter than the day outside. Glass shattered. And then there was the rattle of plaster falling.

Silence settled.

Wentworth had been vaguely aware that Carr had also flung himself to the floor. He presumed the man was all right. He wasted no time, but raised himself, crawled to the desk, got the phone down and moments later was sounding the alarm.

II

Boris Denovich, M.D., psychiatrist, newly arrived head of the psychiatric section, listened with a faint frown through the translation machine to what he realized presently was an unacceptable story.

He adjusted his tiny earphone, then spoke into the translation microphone in his thick Russian.

"Are you trying to tell me," he interrupted Colonel Wentworth, "that this young American claims to read *thoughts* from the expressions on the faces of people? Surely, Colonel, you mean mental telepathy?"

200

Wentworth stared at the intense, middle-aged man thoughtfully. He knew something that neither Carr nor Denovich was aware of. The other's reaction was what he had expected. But he'd had to be sure.

Denovich continued: "You've already checked it? Languages and all?"

Wentworth had decided it was vital to give the time to a check-out. So he had spent twenty important minutes in the translation department. He said now, "The languages of the various people I taped were Polish, German, Greek and Japanese."

"And what Carr says they were saying matches the translations?"

"Not word for word, no. But he was certainly getting it straight."

The psychiatrist's thin face seemed to grow thinner. He took it for granted that the security officer had been made the victim of a staged deception by the American psychologist. How, or why, didn't matter now.

Colonel Wentworth was speaking again. "You'd better hear the end of the tape."

Denovich replied patiently, "It's not necessary. I presume he was successful." He frowned. "Colonel, I hope this American isn't just an expert lip-reader, and a linguist."

The security officer directed the broad-faced secretary, "Roll it over to that little slip of white paper." To Denovich, he said, "You've got to hear this, Doctor."

The first voice on the tape, when it started again, was that of Colonel Wentworth. He was directing Carr's attention to another couple. There was a pause. Then Carr's voice made the arresting statement that had, earlier, electrified and galvanized Wentworth.

Denovich sat bolt upright in his chair, as the crash of glass and the explosion sounded from the speaker. He was vaguely conscious of the security officer shutting off the recorder. Then he heard his own high-pitched voice say, "What was that? What happened?"

By the time Wentworth had explained, Denovich was recovered. "This has to be a hoax," he said. He broke off. "Did you look out of the window? What did you see?"

"I was taken by surprise," Wentworth confessed. "I'd thrown myself flat on the floor. By the time the plaster had settled, two or three minutes may have gone by."

"So you didn't see any tall, gaunt, non-human man?" Denovich said satirically.

Wentworth agreed that by the time he returned to the

window there was no person on any level below who answered to such a description.

The Soviet psychiatrist leaned back, striving for calm. He realized he was over-stimulated in an unpleasant fashion. It was the closest he had been to anger in a long time. His negative feeling was directed exclusively against Dr. Richard D. Carr, the American psychologist.

Nevertheless, he presently controlled himself and said, "Why don't we just let him experiment with his so-called ability? I'll provide him with facilities. That'll give me a chance to size him up, give *him* a chance to prove himself—and we can go on from there." A grim smile played around his thin lips. "I'd like to give him the chance to read *my* thoughts on *my* face."

He appeared to be completely satisfied with his proposal and seemed unaware that the matter was more urgent than that to Wentworth. The security officer bit his lips, then said, "I'll get Dr. Carr. We can talk about it."

Wentworth walked to the elevator to meet Carr. As the psychologist came out, Wentworth was standing with his back to the elevator door. When the other greeted him, he glanced over his shoulder in a quick acknowledgment; then he said, "This way, Doctor."

During the walk back to the Russian psychiatrist's office, he not only kept inches ahead of Carr but also held his head so that his face was slightly averted.

As they entered, first Carr, then Wentworth, Denovich hurried forward. His ear-piece was fitted for walking and his translation microphone was pinned into one lapel.

On Earth, he had had a technique for greeting people he didn't want to associate with: keep them moving, dismiss them in an offhand fashion as soon as possible, preferably some distance from an exit.

His first glimpse of the plump, unhealthy looking American, and the softness of the pudgy hand which Carr placed limply in his muscular fingers, brought no reason for a change of mind. The Russian indicated the hall. "This way," he said.

Carr did not move. He stood, a faint, tolerant smile on his heavy face. Denovich, who had pulled the door open and was holding it ajar, looked back.

Carr said softly, "We'll have to have a better understanding than that, Doctor."

Denovich was instantly cynical. "I forgot," he said. "You read faces and you must be reading mine. What do you see?"

Still with that faint smile, Carr said, "Doctor, would you really like me to say out loud?"

The psychiatrist felt himself to be completely in control. "I'll be glad to let you off that hook," he said good-naturedly.

At this point, Wentworth—who had been anxiously waiting for the barest minimum of the initial confrontation to run its course—decided that it had. He thereupon explained firmly that Carr's ability could be tested as well in a practical as in an experimental circumstance. He finished: "So I'd like you both to accompany me to the Port of Entry—"

Wentworth had spoken the words, while still partly facing away from Carr. He was aware of the psychologist turning and staring at him.

The American said slowly, "Until now, I've respected what I believed to be your personal desire for privacy. But I've had a glimpse or two through that British stiffness in your cheeks, and in spite of all your evasiveness, I detect some thought about me. You know something about my special ability; something—" He stopped, frowning, then said challengingly, "This is not new to you, what I'm doing! Somebody's done it before."

Still facing away, Wentworth said diplomatically, "You're close. Look, I'll tell you both the whole story as soon as possible. Right now we've got work to do. All right?"

As he led the way out of the office, Wentworth continued to believe that Carr's ability might still be useful in connection with the alien. But time was of the essence, if he hoped to gain any value from the man's marvelous power.

What neither Carr nor Denovich knew was that, from the beginning of the moon station, a few persons had experienced a sudden, remarkable buildup of ESP or PSI ability. The ability of one person was always different from that of another. This was the first time that the skill had been to read faces. Each time an ability showed, it seemed to reflect an interest that the person had previously had, but now it was intensified to a perfect state. Yet often it seemed so natural to the possessor that he did not immediately report it or even consider it unusual.

The first stage of the ability lasted about two days.

At the end of that time, it faded rapidly and disappeared entirely for several hours. The person even forgot that he had had the ability.

Then—abruptly—the ESP power appeared again, but in a twisted form.

In this form it was a fantastic thing, a highly energized but different version of the original ability.

Wentworth had once described it: "Like an animal in its death throes, achieving briefly the most herculean effort of its entire lifetime, we have in this twist a view of a ESP ability in the nth degree. Perhaps, for a few hours we actually have a glimpse of some incredible ability that man will attain in the far future of his evolution."

The finale now came rapidly. After a few brief hours, the twisted version faded also, and that was the end. The ability never reappeared.

What bothered Wentworth was that he knew Carr had been on the moon approximately forty-eight hours. He suspected the psychologist had been able to read thoughts or faces for the full time. Therefore, the two-day first phase would end at any moment.

. . . No time to waste! Stop not a minute, now that the necessary preliminaries were done! Do not allow Carr to become confused and distracted by a sudden discovery of the truth, and so therefore keep his own face averted; permit no reading of his thoughts!

III

They headed down to cross-station transport and were quickly whisked to the underground port below the spaceship landing field. As they emerged from the little monorail machine, a man in the uniform of a port officer emerged from a doorway and came along the corridor toward them.

Wentworth recognized him as an old-timer on the moon and nodded greeting. The man acknowledged with a wave of his hand and walked on. Wentworth motioned his two companions to go in the direction from which the port official had come. Denovich complied at once. Carr took several steps, and then he stopped and looked back.

"Colonel," he said, "may I speak to that officer?"

"Who?" Wentworth had already forgotten the chance meeting.

"That port officer who just passed us."

"Peterson? Oh, sure!" He turned. "Hey, Pete," Wentworth called.

But Carr was loping along the hallway. By the time Denovich became aware that something was wrong and faced about, Carr and Peterson were already talking. The man in uniform nodded twice and then abruptly laughed hysterically.

The sound of laughter came unexpectedly loud. Some people who had come out of the baggage room stopped and stared.

As Denovich watched, astounded, Peterson burst into tears. Denovich, acutely aware of how tense his thin body felt, walked back to within a few feet of the two men. He was vaguely aware of Wentworth joining him.

The port aide was bawling noisily and at the same time trying to control himself.

He sobbed. "What did you say? I didn't catch your words. . . Say, what's happened to me? I never did a thing like this."

He gulped, made a tremendous effort—and was instantly in a rage. "You so-and-so!" he snarled. "What did you do to me?"

"Somebody came through here yesterday afternoon and took control of your mind," said Carr. "Tell us about it."

"Wel-l-lll!" Peterson seemed to forget his rage. "Oh, you mean those Negroes. Three of them. One was kind of odd looking—hollow-cheeked, you know—and so I asked him to remove his headdress."

He stopped, blinked at Carr, his jaw lax, face almost stupid looking in his puzzlement.

Carr urged, "What did he do to you?"

"Why-uh!" The man's eyes widened. "He shot a light beam at me—right out of that thing on the top of his—"

Once again he stopped, looking blank. Then: "What am I talking about? I must be dreaming!"

Denovich walked forward. There was no longer any question in his mind as to what Carr could do. He had witnessed—it seemed to him—the fastest hypnotic induction of his experience.

He said in a low, angry voice, "Dr. Carr, get away from that man!"

Carr half-turned, startled. Denovich almost felt the other's eyes search his face. Carr said, "Oh!" Then firmly: "One moment, Doctor?"

He turned back to the port official. "Go to your quarters and lie down. If you don't feel better in an hour, come and see me in my office." He handed Peterson a card.

Carr faced Wentworth. "I think we'd better talk to the Chief of Port of Entry," he said.

The Chief of Port of Entry was considerably heavier look-

ing than Carr. He was an Italian, good-natured, efficien
subjective. His name was Carlo Pontine. He ignored Der
ovich's translator and instead spoke into his own person
translation microphone.

"Those three Africans arrived from Vastuland." He put u
his hands in the gesture of helplessness. "So you have yo
problems, gentlemen."

Wentworth, who had already called out the black co
tingent of Security, knew what he meant. The alien ha
either been very clever or very lucky to arrive as a Negr
for normally that would give him the protection of race ter
sion. Their main hope was that Carr's ability would b
pass such barriers.

Pontine had photographs of the three Vastulanders; an
there, unmistakably, was a gaunt figure with a headdres
The appearance was of an unusually elaborate Mohammec
an-style head decoration. The cloth came down low over th
forehead, and the face—it was dismally plain to see—wa
only superficially human.

Blown up on a large screen in the projection room, th
black pigmentation showed plainly. Underneath was a sca
skin.

Moments later, an uneasy Wentworth was showing th
photo on the security band of the port's TV intercom. Hav
ing given his tense account, he turned his special TV key t
its second position. One by one the lights on the key wer
out until only two remained blinking. Which was prett
fair emergency coverage.

Wentworth visualized the scene out there. In dozens c
sectors of the great moon station, his men were steppin
out into corridors, glancing into departmental offices, survey
ing their territory. More important, if one of them had pre
viously observed the wanted person, he would now be check
ing if he was where he ought to be.

Even as he had the thought, a buzzer sounded softly an
a light came back on. Carr pressed the button and foun
himself staring at a clean-shaven young man—Ledoux in th
French section.

"Colonel Wentworth."

"Yes?"

"That man was assigned an apartment in this sector yes
terday afternoon. However, he went out an hour ago, an
I haven't seen him since."

By the time that message was completed, another ligh
was blinking. That message was:

"Saw him about thirty-five minutes ago, walking rapidly into R-1."

Wentworth groaned inwardly. R-1 was the main residence complex for visitors. It had fifteen hundred and forty-four apartments, most of which were at the moment unoccupied. But an imaginative artist had originally designed it to be futuristic; and a committee untroubled by knowledge of security had authorized its construction. With its innumerable corridors, back stairways, patios, its three dozen restaurants, its four theaters, sunken gardens and lovers' nooks and moon surface transport cars—it was a veritable sieve with hundreds of openings.

R-1 was easily the safest hideaway in Moon City; and it was their misfortune that the alien had located it and had taken refuge in it. Gloomily, Wentworth turned the TV control key back to its One position and called for General Alarm H.

The instant that was done, he turned, grabbed Carr's arm, beckoned Denovich and—face still averted—said breathlessly, "Come along!" He led the way back to the elevator.

His first and best hope was a swift search, using every means. Carr's ability—which had already proved itself—was one of those means. What made it a possible hope was that, because their part of the moon was turned away from the sun, only thirty-eight of the apartments in R-1 were occupied. Wentworth personally preferred the moon during its night period with its magnificent view of Earth. But it was their good luck at this decisive moment that tourists did not share his opinion.

Briefly, Wentworth explained what he had in mind. The pattern was: when the door opened, Carr was to read the face of the person who answered while Wentworth asked questions.

As it worked out, usually before the individual could reply, Carr said, "Nope." The instant he did that, a security aide took over; and Carr, Denovich, Wentworth and their accompanying squad raced on to the next occupied apartment.

The idea was that someone would have seen the alien.

The door of the seventh apartment was opened by a small woman who stared at them questioningly. She wore a prim, black dress, and how anyone had ever persuaded her to make the dramatic tourist trip to the moon, Wentworth would never know. But then he was often amazed at the types that showed up.

He saw that Carr was hesitating. The psychologist seemed momentarily confused. Then: "He's inside," he said.

207

Somebody grabbed the woman and jerked her out of th[e] door, instantly covered her mouth, stifling all but a fain[t] squeal. Seconds later, at a signal from Wentworth, the me[n] in the mobile unit rolled up on their silent rubber wheel[s] Without pausing, they went straight on into the apartment

As he crouched beside the door, waiting, Wentworth wa[s] vaguely uneasy about the order he had given: to strike an[d] strike hard. The thought that was suddenly in his min[d] was that here was a representative of another race, the firs[t] ever to show up in the solar system. Ought he to be kille[d] out of hand?

After a moment's consideration, he allowed his doubts t[o] fade. The alien had instantly tried to kill Carr, when he wa[s] discovered; and, equally culpable, he had come secretly int[o] the moon station. The creature's approach was hostile an[d] must be dealt with in the same way.

His thought ended in a horrid thrill of excitement, as h[e] suddenly felt the peculiar crawling sensation in his skin tha[t] came from the mobile unit's electric vibration mechanism It was a full-charge feeling.

As Wentworth was silently congratulating himself, the hall-way suddenly lit up to a dazzling brightness. The doorway blazed with a direct sunlight brilliance.

The blinding light ended as suddenly as it had begun. A minute went by. There was the sound of debris falling but no movement. Pale, concerned, taut, Wentworth waited.

IV

What had happened was, a few minutes earlier Xilmer had realized that the moment of confrontation could be at hand—if he wished. He thereupon sent a message by way of the device in his headpiece to the *giyn*—battleship—in orbit far out beyond the moon. In asking for instructions, he said:

"Only one thing bothers me about this spy visit of mine. Somebody detected me from a room high up in one of the building structures an hour ago. His ability to do so suggests that there are two types of beings in the moon station. One group—the main mass of people—is unimportant. However, the second type of being—one of whom spotted me, and from a distance at that—could be a more powerful life form. So I think I should escape through a wall of this apartment and attempt by all possible means to make my way to the room from which that superior type observed me. I really believe I should size him up before any irreversible decisions are made."

The reply was grim: "Twenty-four hours from now, the fleet will risk one minute of sub-space communication. We must be ready to tell them to come here, or go elsewhere."

Xilmer protested, "I plan to proceed cautiously, breaking through walls and so on, to avoid corridors. And before I leave, I'll try to erase the memory of my presence from important personnel here. Even at worst, that should all only take a few hours."

"Nonetheless, why not test their weaponry for just a few seconds? See what they've got in such a situation?"

"Very well."

Wentworth gazed around at the shambles with a sinking sensation. Then he turned to the two dazed men who had scrambled out of the wrecked mobile unit.

"What happened?" he asked.

Surprisingly, they weren't sure. They had seen the man-like figure, as the unit drove into the living room of the apartment.

Sergeant Gojinski shook his head, as if to clear the mists from his mind. Then he spoke in a shaky voice through his own translation microphone: "There he was. I saw him looking us over, and he wasn't afraid. I pointed the lightning rod at him—you know—uh—"

It was a slang term for the mobile unit's aiming device. Wentworth nodded, urgently.

"So then I said, 'Fire!' " continued Sergeant Gojinski. "I saw the vibration bolt reach out to him. And then something bright hit the unit—us. I guess I was stunned. When I could see again, there was the hole in the wall, and he was gone."

The other man, who was from South America, had had the same experience.

Listening to the accounts, Wentworth felt a chill. There was an implication here of casual weapon superiority. Undecided, he walked over to the gaping hole in the wall. The interior steel construction had been cleanly sliced through. He held his geiger counter toward it, but it remained as silent as it had throughout.

Here was evidence of incredible power without radiation.

Slowly, Wentworth braced himself. The moon station had a dozen mobile units stored against an unnamed emergency, but they would have to be charged up; which would take somewhat over an hour.

He explained his plan quietly to the men around him. "We'll use several mobile units with each search crew."

He used his TV key on the nearest communicator and issued a specific order: "All observers stay at your posts. As soon as the supplementary mobile units are ready, call me at—"

He hesitated, then he gave Dr. Denovich's address.

He was aware of Carr coming up beside him. Without looking at the plump man, Wentworth said, "Doctor, I want you to remain well in the rear of future action. Let's remember that when this being spotted you observing him, he immediately tried to kill you. Apparently, he has not considered it worthwhile to attempt to exterminate anyone else. That's got to be significant."

Carr said in a nervous tone, "You don't think he was just surprised into striking at me?"

It was, of course, possible. But Wentworth was not prepared to take the risk.

Beside him, Carr continued uneasily. "There's something I should report. When I first looked at that little woman's face, just for a second it seemed as if I couldn't read it. Do you think that alien had some way of scrambling her thoughts, so that her face didn't display them?"

Wentworth felt sorry for the plump man, for obviously the partial failure meant that the ESP ability was coming to the end of its initial stage. It was a cruel prank of fate, but—equally obviously—the time had come for Carr to understand his situation.

Deliberately, he faced the psychologist and said gently, "Why don't you read me, Doctor?"

Carr gave him a quick look. Then he frowned, and then some of the color drained from his cheeks.

He said at last, unhappily, "I'm having difficulty, and it's a pretty complicated thought. You're thinking that my ability to read faces is a—a—"

He shook his head, bewildered. "I don't get it—a common stereotype? That doesn't seem right."

The near miss established once more for Wentworth that the marvelous ability was beginning to disappear. Aloud, he said, "Let's go to Dr. Denovich's office. I'm sure I now have time to tell you both the whole story."

An hour later, there was still no call to indicate that

additional mobile units were ready; and he had finished his account.

Carr's face had a blotched look, and his lips twitched. He had the appearance of a man confronting an unpleasant truth. He mumbled, "It all seemed so natural. I've thought about people's expressions for years."

"When did the ability actually start?" asked Wentworth.

"Well," Carr muttered, "it was when I was studying the faces of the other passengers on my way to the moon two days ago that the pieces started to fall into place. When we landed, I had the entire system worked out on a practical application basis."

"So it was just a few hours short of the two days when you finally called me. And so the ability is now in its fading stage; and the twist will show up in a few hours."

Carr grew even paler, if that were possible.

He said thickly, "But what form could such an intensification of face reading take? I can't imagine anything more complete than what I have been able to do."

Denovich, thin face taut, thin body tense as he leaned forward, interrupted harshly, "I feel outraged by all this secrecy. Why was I not briefed on arrival? Why has there been no previous publicity on this important matter?"

The English security officer pointed out stiffly that the moon station in its present form was now only eight years old. Space travel was still new. People were easily alarmed. Such a freak happening might have been a great setback. However, the information blackout was now going to be ended. A joint paper had been prepared by their predecessors. This was to be given to the world press after it had been cleared by the U.N. Security Council.

"And," Wentworth continued, "as for briefing you and Dr. Carr—I intended to do that after you had guessed that one of you would be—uh—a victim of the condition?"

Under the circumstances it had seemed credible that it might be a genuine system, as worked out by an expert.

Wentworth smiled his faint smile. "I hope, Dr. Carr, that you kept records."

"I have complete notes," replied Carr glumly.

"It will be the first time," said Wentworth. "So we have a win."

Having made the comment, he spread his hands almost helplessly. "And there's your story."

He stood up. "I think I'd better go and see what progress is being made on those mobile units." He addressed himself to Dr. Denovich. "Keep an eye on your colleague, sir."

The psychiatrist nodded curtly.

When the two men were alone, Dr. Denovich gazed at the plump American with a hint in his manner of personal concern.

"This seems to have been quite a shock to you, Dr. Carr. Why don't I give you a mild sleep potion, so that you can be in a relaxed state while the ability is fading?"

Carr studied the older man's face with narrowing eyes. "My ability may be fading," he said, "but you ought to be ashamed of yourself for what I think you're thinking."

Denovich protested. "I'm sure you're reading me wrong."

"You intended to get my notes while I slept," the psychologist accused.

"I *thought* of your notes," admitted the Russian, "and realized how important they were. It did not occur to me that you were not planning to share them."

Carr muttered, "I guess what I saw could have meant that." He broke off. "I apologize. Look, we're both on edge. So let's take a look at the situation."

As he analyzed it, here were two experts confronted by phenomena. Why didn't they sit down, and keep a moment by moment record of the fading of the special ability?

"Perhaps," he concluded, "by continual discussion and restatement, we can prevent my memory from fading."

It was an excellent idea, and the two men settled down. For two and a half hours, the plan seemed to work, in that there was no apparent memory fading.

Then the phone rang.

It was Wentworth, reporting that the search parties had finally been augmented by additional mobile units. The security officer asked, "I wondered if you cared to come along?"

Denovich explained that what Carr and he were doing was too important to leave.

When he turned from the phone, he was startled to see that the psychologist was leaning back with eyes closed. What was startling was that his body seemed limp. Denovitch bent over the man, shook him, but there was no quickening of wakefulness. A swift examination established a sleeping man's pulse, the slow, deep breathing of sleep.

Dr. Denovich wasted no time. He prepared a syringe and injected a sleep potion in the American's arm. Then he dispatched his secretary on a research errand that would keep her away from the office for the rest of the day. Quickly he searched the unconscious man, found his key ring; then, picking up his copying camera, he headed along the hall and up the elevator to Carr's office in the American section.

He had no sense of guilt. "This is not a moment to be squeamish," he told himself. National interests—paramount.

He found the notes almost at once. They were unexpectedly voluminous. Expertly, he set about his task. Half an hour later, he was still intently copying one sheet after another—when he heard a faint sound behind him.

Denovich was not to be rattled. He turned slowly. And then a thrill of fear struck through him.

A figure stood there.

How the creature could ever have been taken for human was not clear to the startled Russian. The gauntness of the body was unnatural; the face, blackened as it was, did have something human in it. But the legs under the long gown showed . . . wrong—the way the cloth lay against them and outlined them! His physician's eye recorded the details in a single, flashing look.

The next instant a voice from the headpiece said in Russian, "Where is"—hesitation—"Dr. Carr?"

Denovich had not in his entire life had a single desire to be a martyr and he had none now. But, as in the past, he faced the Communist dilemma. Party doctrine required that he do what was necessary "for the people" in any situation, regardless of personal danger. Failure to do so meant that he would have to attend a self-criticism meeting and explained his dereliction.

He had long ago solved the problem by a simple, quick analysis on the spot by one yardstick: the chances of discovery.

No chance of that here, he decided. But he deduced in a single, continuing evaluation that his only way of escape from this baleful being was total collaboration, and he had but one anguished hope: *Maybe he'll let me live.*

"Eleven floors down, the Russian section—my office—422-N." He spoke hoarsely.

The creature gazed at him somberly. Then, contemptuously: "Don't worry. We're not after people. And, in view of the secret computation you just made, I'll leave you your memory."

A flash of indescribably bright light from the headpiece struck the psychiatrist's forehead.

Blackout!

It took a while for Xilmer, by his careful method, to reach 422-N. But presently he stood over the man lying on the couch and sent a message, describing Carr's unconscious state.

"So far as I can see, I could destroy him without him or anyone else being able to prevent it."

"Wait!"

There was a silence of several minutes, then: "Tell us exactly how his unconsciousness came about."

Xilmer dutifully reported what he had perceived in the psychiatrist's mind about the special ESP aspect, and how Denovich had injected Carr with a strong sedative. "It is this sedative that puts his body at our mercy."

He concluded, "He seems completely helpless, and I strongly urge that he not be allowed to awaken. Who knows what the ESP twist would be?"

"Wait!"

Again the receiving unit on his head stilled; finally: "According to our calculations," came the message, "this human being has had time to go into the advanced ESP state, which apparently is a part of his cycle. So before you do anything, examine what is going on in the lower brain."

"I have already done so."

"With what result?"

"Despite his unconscious condition, something inside the brain is observing me and, I would say, is monitoring this conversation."

. . . But there were no energy connections strong enough to control power flows. So Carr could not fight back. Whatever the twist was, it was not in itself a weapon capable of causing an impact.

Xilmer concluded grimly, "I think we can safely say that, if we do not permit this man to awaken, the inhabitants of this star system cannot defend themselves."

"Too bad!" was the laconic, unsympathetic reply.

They grinned at each other mentally through the head mechanism, and enjoyed the feeling of total superiority.

"What is the recommendation?" Xilmer asked, routinely now.

"*Kill him!*"

When Denovich came to, he was lying on the carpeted floor.

He raised himself and looked around. He was greatly relieved when he saw no sign of the alien. Trembling, he stood up and went to the outer door; peered out. Nothing. Not a soul in sight.

Fighting panic, he collected his equipment, but hesitated as he realized that his copying task was not completed. After a moment's thought, he picked up all the psychologist's notes, including those he had previously photographed.

As he hurried along the hallway, he glanced at his watch for the first time. It was two hours since he had been rendered unconscious. That was briefly startling. He thought, shocked: *The creature has had all that time to find Carr in my office.*

He expected to find his quarters damaged. But at first look, everything was in order. Hastily he locked up the stolen notes, then went throught the door to the treatment room, where he had left Carr sleeping.

There was no one on the couch.

Denovich was about to turn away, when he saw the object lying half hidden on the far side of the little cot. He walked over and looked down at Xilmer's turban. The cloth was disarrayed and stained by a bluish fluid, and a metal structure was visible through the folds of the silk-like stuff.

After a moment, he saw that the blue carpeting was heavily encrusted by more of the dark blue liquid.

As he stood there, undecided, voices sounded in his outer office. He recognized Wentworth's British baritone, and then Carr's softer voice. Denovich turned and faced the entrance. Seconds later the two men entered.

The Soviet psychiatrist was aware of several other men crowding the doorway, but they stopped short of it. He had seen only one of them before—recognized him as a Russian member of the security police. Their gazes met, held for an instant, significantly, then separated.

Wentworth said, "Oh, here you are, Doctor."

Denovich said nothing. He was gazing tensely at the face of the plump American, thinking: *Right now, this instant, he's in this superstate.*

And, if Carr had been able to read thoughts on faces before, what he could do now must be so far in advance that his—Denovich's—every act of the past few hours was as plainly visible to the other as a picture on a screen.

The Soviet psychiatrist cringed, then braced himself. Denials rushed to the tip of his tongue and waited there, ready to be spoken.

Wentworth was continuing: "Dr. Carr is puzzled, sir.

When he came to he was lying on this couch, and he had no idea how he had got here. But that"—he indicated Xilmer's turban—"was lying right there. As he went out, he saw your name on the door. That's how he knows you, because, of course, he has no memory of the first stage of the ESP. What happened?"

Even as Wentworth was talking, Denovich's mind began to race around seeking a plausible explanation for his own whereabouts. But he knew better than to make a quick answer. And so, as the English officer ceased speaking, Denovich addressed Carr.

"Are you all right, Doctor?"

Carr gave him, perhaps, too long a look before answering, but when he spoke he said simply, "Yes."

"You're not hurt?"

"No. Should I be?" His eyes were, of all things, shifty, uneasy, puzzled.

"What about the, uh, twist?" Denovich said.

"The what?"

Denovich was thunderstruck. What he had expected, he didn't know. But not this!—this ordinary person, with ordinary, everday responses. And no memory.

"You mean," he said, "you have no awareness of anything unusual?"

Carr shook his head. "Really, Doctor, I think you have more information on this matter than I. How did I get into your quarters? Have I been ill?"

Denovich turned and stared helplessly at Wentworth. He had his own story ready now, but he felt too bewildered even to offer it.

"Colonel," he said, "if you will fill me in, I'll do the same for you."

Wentworth did so succinctly. After the phone conversation, he had accompanied one of the parties scouting for Xilmer. A few minutes ago, Dr. Carr had been seen wandering along a corridor; and since people had been forbidden to leave their apartments, Wentworth had been called to deal with the situation. He had come at once.

"Naturally, knowing where he had last been, I asked him what had happened, and of course, discovered only that he had awakened and seen this turban and all that sticky stuff."

He bent down, touched the bluish liquid gingerly with the tip of a finger, and when apparently it did not hurt him, raised it to his nose and sniffed. He made a face.

"Must be the blood of this race," he said. "Quite a strong odor."

"What race?" Carr asked. "And, look, gentlemen, what—"

That was as far as he got. At that moment a voice spoke from Xilmer's headpiece in English.

"We have been monitoring this conversation, and it would appear that an accident has befallen our agent."

Wentworth stepped forward quickly. "You can hear me?" he said.

The voice continued, "Give us an exact description of the present condition of our agent."

Wentworth replied firmly, "We're quite willing to do so. But in return we would like some information from you."

"We're only about three hundred thousand miles away. You'll see us in slightly less than an hour, and unless your explanations are satisfactory, we shall blast your entire station out of existence. Now, quick!"

The threat was chilling, and instantly convincing. One of the men at the door said, "My God!"

Wentworth, after a long, tense moment, described in an even tone exactly what was left of Xilmer.

When he had finished, the voice said, "Wait!"

At least three minutes went by; then: "We must know exactly what happened. Interrogate Dr. Carr."

"Me?" said Carr, his voice scarcely more than a croak.

Wentworth made a ssssh gesture, then silently waved the men in the open door away, and then nodded at Denovich and Carr.

"Get it out of him!" he commanded Dr. Denovich; then he tiptoed from the room and headed for the phone in the psychiatrist's private office.

As the Russian faced Carr, he was aware of the Englishman's muffled but earnest voice sounding the alarm. Consciously, he shut out the other's voice and gazed at Carr.

"Doctor," he said, "what is your last recollection?"

The American psychologist swallowed, as if something unpalatable was in his throat; it was that much of a grimace. Then he countered: "How long have I been at the moon station?"

Dazzling lights of understanding blazed through the psychiatrist's mind. *Of course,* he thought, *he really doesn't remember anything after he got that first ESP on his actual journey to the moon.*

His recollection flashed to a question Carr had asked a few minutes before, about being ill. *Of course.* Denovich thought again. *He must think he's mentally ill!*

He stood then, trembling with the possibilities of his

217

lightning analysis, and he tried to visualize how he himself might feel in Carr's place.

Instantly he realized the other's problem. An American psychologist confessing to his Soviet colleague that he believed himself to be mad!

Denovich said gently, "Doctor, in what way do you think you're crazy?"

When Carr hesitated, the psychiatrist urged: "Our lives are at stake. You must not hold back."

Carr sighed. "I have paranoid symptoms," he said. And he sounded suddenly tearful.

"Details! Hurry!"

Carr smiled wanly. "It's really very extreme. When I awakened, I became aware of signals."

"Signals?"

"Everything means something."

"Oh, that one!" said Denovich. He added. "For example?"

"Well, I look at you, and you're just one mass of—well—meaningful signals. Even the way you stand is a message."

Denovich was baffled. What Carr seemed to be describing was certainly only a variation of a routine paranoid stereotype.

Was this the famous second stage of the ESP cycle, which —he had to admit it—had been so convincing in its initial stage?

He caught himself. "Explain further," he urged.

"Well—" Carr paused, his pudgy face showed helplessness. "Well, your pulsations!"

As he haltingly explained it, Denovich's body was like a large mass of energy circuits that gave off a set of signals.

Carr looked at the man, and at the surface signals in the exposed part of the body. And *through* the skin to the atomic structure inside: tiny golden balls in stacks of billions to each cubic millimeter, pulsing and signaling—and connected. . . .

Connected by quadrillions of force lines to distant stars, to the near universe, already stretching out, shiningly tenuous, to other people on the moon station.

But the overwhelming majority of the lines curved off through the walls and across to the Earth . . . A solid mass of connections with other people and with all the places Denovich had ever been.

The signals that pulsed along some of the lines were intense; Carr followed one of the more powerful complexes to an earlier year in Denovich's life, to a young woman, with tears streaming down her face.

The thoughts that came along that set of lines were: "I trusted you and you betrayed me!"

"Now, Natasha—" said that younger Denovich.

"You see—" said Carr, helplessly. He stopped. "What's the matter?"

The Russian psychiatrist wondered if his face looked as bloodless as he felt.

"What? W-what?" he gasped. He was stunned. Natasha was a girl he had got pregnant in his younger days and she had died in childbirth. With an effort, he controlled himself. "Can you do anything with it?"

"Well—yes, I guess so."

As he spoke uncertainly, Carr did something that cut the bundle that connected with the girl and watched the lines recoil back upon Denovich like a rubber band, suddenly released.

Denovich uttered a cry; he couldn't help it. It was a caterwauling sound, with a bass, throaty yowl in it, that brought Wentworth out of the other office on the double.

By this time, Denovich was trying to reach the couch. But his knees buckled. He fell to the floor and lay there, at first writhing and moaning. But all at once he began a mad screaming.

The Russian agent pressed into the room behind Wentworth and stood there with bulging eyes. After a moment, Wentworth returned to the phone and called Medical Emergency.

The two men who came injected the insanely screaming body with a sedative. The screaming died down to a sobbing sound and then silence. They carried the unconscious man out on a stretcher to a small, mobile unit, called an ambulette and rode off with him.

The machine in Xilmer's helmet spoke: "We absolutely require that Dr. Carr explain what he did to Dr. Denovich."

Carr gazed helplessly at Wentworth. "I just cut the lines. I'm guessing that, instantly, all the barriers he had between himself and that girl went down. I think that what we saw was the effect of total guilt suddenly breaking through."

"Wait!" said the voice from the Xilmer turban machine.

Wentworth, who could not forget that Xilmer's headpiece had energy weaponry in it, silently waved everybody out of the room. He himself backed into position beyond the door jamb.

One minute. Two. Then the voice spoke: "Unquestionably a powerful mental force exists in Dr. Carr. The analysis of Xilmer's death was that the unconscious mind of Dr.

Carr defended itself from him by cutting the energy lines involving the execution intent of Xilmer. Hence, a reversal was induced, whereby he promptly used his *mirt*—a weapon in his headpiece—to commit suicide. The condition of his body indicated that almost total dissolution occurred."

Wentworth turned to Carr. "Any comment about that?" he whispered slowly.

Carr shook his head.

"No memory of it?"

Again, the head shake.

The voice was continuing, sarcastically, "Naturally, we shall wait until this man's remarkable mental gift runs through its cycle, a few hours from now. You shall hear from us then."

Silence.

VI

Two hours; perhaps less.

Other men came. There were tense conferences. Carr sat off to one side. Presently, as the voices grew more urgent, he slipped away into the room where Xilmer's turban lay and stood with eyes closed, gazing at a universe of countless—signals.

Billions of these—pulsations—still lingered around the machine in Xilmer's headpiece. Quadrillions of lines were focused on it from somewhere out in space.

Carr glanced along the lines with a casual ability. Now that he was no longer disturbed by the mental phenomenon itself, he was aware that there was a faculty in his mind which could understand the meaning of millions of lines at once.

He saw with total clarity that signals and pulsations were merely a surface activity of the basic universe structure.

Underneath was—truth.

Between the signals and what they represented was an intricate feedback, an interchange of the surface meaning with the colossal fact below.

He was aware of Wentworth coming up beside him. "Dr. Carr," the security officer said softly, "our discussions have led us to the launching of nuclear missiles from the U.N. Space Station hovering over the Atlantic. These will be available close to here in about five hours, but in the final issue our real hope comes back to you and what you can do. What *can* you do?"

"I can—experiment," Carr answered, "with signals."

Wentworth experienced an intense disappointment. For signals, it seemed to him, were a part of communication, and not of weaponry. And that, he realized bitterly, was obviously logical. Beginning with the reading of thoughts on faces, the American psychologist had now, in the twist, come to some ultimate ability to understand and manipulate communication.

It was a great gift, but it was not what was needed in this fantastic emergency.

"What kind of experiment?" Wentworth asked.

"Like this!" said Carr.

And he disappeared.

Wentworth stood tense. Then, aware of Xilmer's turban and the importance of the enemy not finding out what had happened, he tiptoed from the room. Hurrying to the nearest hall communicator, he inserted his key and asked his agents to make a quick search for Carr.

In ten minutes it was fairly well established that the plump psychologist was not in the moon station. As the reports trickled in confirming this improbable fact, Wentworth put out a call to leading scientists in the station, and soon there were men and women of several nationalities standing around him, speaking into their translation microphones, giving him their concepts of the situation.

But the sum total of the scientific speculations added up to a question: what could be done by one individual to thousands?

And that, in terms of Carr's ability, came down to: what was the smallest number of lines that needed to be cut to defeat the invader?

As Wentworth stood by, glancing from face to face, it became clear that none of these trained people had any idea what the answer was.

For Carr, after he arrived on the *giyn,* there was a period of—not confusion, for he was totally aware of the problem—but of immense . . . violence.

He had—selected—an unoccupied room to arrive in; and there he was in what seemed to be a laboratory. Instruments. Tables. Machines. All these stood silently around him, unattended and unthreatening.

His problem derived from the fact that the *giyn* was programmed to resist the presence of unregistered life forms. That defense system, being quiescent, had no visible lines until his appearance triggered the mechanism.

221

The result of that triggering created the violence.

At the instant of his appearance in the room, the walls, the ceiling and the floor focused their weapons on him. Lines of force sprang out from every side, spun a web of energy around him; tried to hold him.

And that was but the first of four progressively more destructive attack systems. The energy trap was succeeded by an elementary *mirt* discharge, designed to stun; then came a primary *mirt*, consisting of murderous impact energies; and, finally, there was a nuclear reaction pattern, as strong as it could be in a confined space.

To the faculty in Carr's brain, it was all signals, observed, correlated, defeated at source. Each attack was a cycle that ran its programmed measure. All cycles completed. Silence settled.

Pause.

Abruptly, somewhere aboard, a living mind took note. And an astonished voice spoke into Carr's brain:

"Who are you?"

Carr did not reply.

The immense number of signals that had been flooding in on him from other levels told him that he was inside a ship twenty miles long, five miles wide and four miles thick. There were eighty thousand Gizdans aboard, each of whom now tuned in on the alarm that had alerted the entire ship.

For a few moments, they had the same general thought; the same conditioning responded, the same attention focused on the intruder. Like so many iron filings abruptly magnetized, the pulsations of alignment made a pattern. It was the pattern that made them manageable.

Carr in a single, comprehensive glance isolated the tiny portion of significant lines—and cut them.

Then, with equal unerring skill, he selected a mass of lines that interrelated and interacted with Basic Truth, drew them to him, intertwined himself with them—and stepped through an energy vacuum into the room on the moon station where Denovich lay asleep under sedation. He had a feeling that very little time remained for the "twist" ability.

Hastily, he repaired the lines he had cut earlier and watched the massive internal armor of the psychiatrist realign. Whereupon Dr. Carr walked out of the room, out of the hospital sector, to the nearest phone booth. He called Wentworth.

When the security officer finally came on the line, he said, "Doctor, what happened?

"They've left," said Carr simply.

222

"B-but—" Wentworth's voice poised at a peak of puzzlement. But he caught hold of himself and said more calmly, "Doctor, we figured out here that there was probably a smallest decisive group of lines to cut—"

"That's what I did."

"But what could that be? What could be the lowest common denominator for so many persons?"

Carr told him.

Wentworth said, admiringly, "Well, I'll be . . . Of course. Congratulations, Doctor."

Hours later, when the ESP twist was already faded, at a time when the *giyn* was nearing the remote end of the solar system and still accelerating, it made its sub-space contact with the great Gizdan fleet cruising in another part of space.

"Got anything for us?" said the fleet commander.

"No!" said the captain of the *giyn*.

"We understood you were approaching an inhabited system that looked easy."

"I don't know how you could have got such an impression. There's nothing here at all."

"Okay. Break contact."

As the captain of the *giyn* complied, for an instant he had a fleeting impression, like a dream, as if there was something he ought to know about the sun system through which the *giyn* had passed.

Had he been able to be aware of such things, he would have noticed that all lines relating to Earth and the moon were cut and coiled back into a tiny corner of his brain.

The feeling of something known and understood . . . faded. And was gone.

Forever.

THE STORM

OVER THE MILES and the years, the gases drifted. Waste matter from ten thousand suns, a diffuse miasm of spent explosions, of dead hell fires and the furies of a hundred million raging sunspots—formless, purposeless.

But it was the beginning.

Into the great dark the gases crept. Calcium was in them, and sodium, and hydrogen; and the speed of the drift varied up to twenty miles a second.

There was a timeless period while gravitation performed its function. The inchoate mass became masses. Great blobs of gas took a semblance of shape in widely separate areas, and moved on and on and on.

They came finally to where a thousand flaring seetee suns had long before doggedly "crossed the street" of the main stream of terrene suns. Had crossed, and left *their* excrement of gases.

The first clash quickened the vast worlds of gas. The electron haze of terrene plunged like spurred horses and sped deeper into the equally violently reacting positron haze of contraterrene. Instantly, the lighter orbital positrons and electrons went up in a blaze of hard radiation.

The storm was on.

The stripped seetee nuclei carried now terrific and unbalanced negative charges and repelled electrons, but tended to attract terrene atom nuclei. In their turn the stripped terrene nuclei attracted contraterrene.

Violent beyond all conception were the resulting cancellations of charges.

The two opposing masses heaved and spun in a cataclysm of partial adjustment. They had been heading in different directions. More and more they became one tangled, seething whirlpool.

The new course, uncertain at first, steadied and became a line drive through the midnight heavens. On a front of nine light years, at a solid fraction of the velocity of light, the storm roared toward its destiny.

Suns were engulfed for half a hundred years—and left behind with only a hammering of cosmic rays to show that they had been the centers of otherwise invisible, impalpable atomic devastation.

In its four hundred and ninetieth Sidereal year, the storm

intersected the orbit of a Nova at the flash moment.

It began to move!

On the three-dimensional map at weather headquarters on the planet Kaider III, the storm was colored orange. Which meant it was the biggest of the four hundred odd storms raging in the Fifty Suns region of the Greater Magellanic Cloud.

It showed as an uneven splotch fronting at Latitude 473, Longitude 228, Center 190 parsecs, but that was a special Fifty Suns degree system which had no relation to the magnetic center of the Magellanic Cloud as a whole.

The report about the Nova had not yet been registered on the map. When that happened the storm color would be changed to an angry red.

They had stopped looking at the map. Maltby stood with the councilors at the great window staring up at the Earth ship.

The machine was scarcely more than a dark sliver in the distant sky. But the sight of it seemed to hold a deadly fascination for the older men.

Maltby felt cool, determined, but also sardonic. It was funny, these—these people of the Fifty Suns in this hour of their danger calling upon *him*.

He unfocused his eyes from the ship, fixed his steely, laconic gaze on the plump, perspiring chairman of the Kaider III government—and, tensing his mind, forced the man to look at him. The councilor, unaware of the compulsion, conscious only that he had turned, said:

"You understand your instructions, Captain Maltby?"

Maltby nodded. "I do."

The curt words must have evoked a vivid picture. The fat face rippled like palsied jelly and broke out in a new trickle of sweat.

"The worst part of it all," the man groaned, "is that the people of the ship found us by the wildest accident. They had run into one of our meteorite stations and captured its attendant. The attendant sent a general warning and then forced them to kill him before they could discover which of the fifty million suns of the Greater Magellanic Cloud was us.

"Unfortunately, they did discover that he and the rest of us were all descendants of the robots who had escaped the massacre of the robots in the main galaxy fifteen thousand years ago.

"But they were baffled, and without a clue. They started

225

home, stopping off at planets on the way on a chance basis. The seventh stop was us. Captain Maltby—"

The man looked almost beside himself. He shook. His face was as colorless as a white shroud. He went on hoarsely:

"Captain Maltby, you must not fail. They have asked for a meteorologist to guide them to Cassidor VII, where the central government is located. They mustn't reach there. You must drive them into the great storm at 473.

"We have commissioned you to do this for us because you have the two minds of the Mixed Men. We regret that we have not always fully appreciated your services in the past. But you must admit that, after the wars of the Mixed Men, it was natural that we should be careful about—"

Maltby cut off the lame apology. "Forget it," he said. "The Mixed Men are robots, too, and therefore as deeply involved, as I see it, as the Dellians and non-Dellians. Just what the Hidden Ones of my kind think, I don't know, nor do I care. I assure you I shall do my best to destroy this ship."

"Be careful!" the chairman urged anxiously. "This ship could destroy us, our planet, our sun in a single minute. We never dreamed that Earth could have gotten so far ahead of us and produced such a devastatingly powerful machine. After all, the non-Dellian robots and, of course, the Mixed Men among us are capable of research work; the former have been laboring feverishly for thousands of years.

"But, finally, remember that you are not being asked to commit suicide. The battleship is absolutely invincible. Just how it will survive a real storm we were not told when we were shown around. But it will. What happens, however, is that everyone aboard becomes unconscious.

"As a Mixed Man you will be the first to revive. Our combined fleets will be waiting to board the ship the moment you open the doors. Is that clear?"

It had been clear the first time it was explained, but these non-Dellians had a habit of repeating themselves, as if thoughts kept growing vague in their minds. As Maltby closed the door of the great room behind him, one of the councilors said to his neighbor.

"Has he been told that the storm has gone Nova?"

The fat man overheard. He shook his head. His eyes gleamed as he said quietly: "No. After all, he is one of the Mixed Men. We can't trust him too far no matter what his record."

All morning the reports had come in. Some showed prog-

226

ess, some didn't. But her basic good humor was untouched by the failures.

The great reality was that her luck had held. She had found a planet of the robots. Only one planet so far, but—

Grand Captain Laurr smiled grimly. It wouldn't be long now. Being a supreme commander was a terrible business. But she had not shrunk from making the deadly threat: provide all required information, or the entire planet of Kaider III would be destroyed.

The information was coming in: Population of Kaider III two billion, one hundred million, two-fifths Dellian, three-fifths non-Dellian robots.

Dellians physically and mentally the higher type, but completely lacking in creative ability. Non-Dellians dominated in the research laboratories.

The forty-nine other suns whose planets were inhabited were called, in alphabetical order: Assora, Atmion, Bresp, Buraco, Cassidor, Corrab—They were located at (1) Assora: Latitude 931, Longitude 27, Center 201 parsecs; (2) Atmion—

It went on and on. Just before noon she noted with steely amusement that there was still nothing coming through from the meteorology room, nothing at all about storms.

She made the proper connection and flung her words: "What's the matter, Lieutenant Cannons? Your assistants have been making prints and duplicates of various Kaider maps. Aren't you getting anything?"

The old meteorologist shook his head. "You will recall, noble lady, that when we captured that robot in space, he had time to send out a warning. Immediately on every Fifty Suns planet, all maps were despoiled, civilian meteorologists were placed aboard spaceships, that were stripped of receiving radios, with orders to go to a planet on a chance basis, and stay there for ten years.

"To my mind, all this was done before it was clearly grasped that their navy hadn't a chance against us. Now they are going to provide us with a naval meteorologist, but we shall have to depend on our lie detectors as to whether or not he is telling us the truth."

"I see." The woman smiled. "Have no fear. They don't dare oppose us openly. No doubt there is a plan being built up against us, but it cannot prevail now that we can take action to enforce our unalterable will. Whoever they send must tell us the truth. Let me know when he comes."

Lunch came, but she ate at her desk, watching the flash-

227

ing pictures on the astro, listening to the murmur of voices, storing the facts, the general picture, into her brain.

"There's no doubt, Captain Turgess," she commented once, savagely, "that we're being lied to on a vast scale. But let it be so. We can use psychological tests to verify all the vital details.

"For the time being it is important that you relive the fears of everyone you find it necessary to question. We must convince these people that Earth will accept them on an equal basis without bias or prejudice of any kind because of their robot orig—"

She bit her lip. "That's an ugly word, the worst kind of propaganda. We must eliminate it from our thoughts."

"I'm afraid," the officer shrugged, "not from our thoughts."

She stared at him, narrow-eyed, then cut him off angrily. A moment later she was talking into the general transmitter: "The word robot must not be used—by any of our personnel —under pain of fine—"

Switching off, she put a busy signal on her spare receiver, and called Psychology House. Lieutenant Neslor's face appeared on the plate.

"I heard your order just now, noble lady," the woman psychologist said. "I'm afraid, however, that we're dealing with the deepest instincts of the human animal—hatred or fear of the stranger, the alien.

"Excellency, we come from a long line of ancestors who, in their time, have felt superior to others because of some slight variation in the pigmentation of the skin. It is even recorded that the color of the eyes has influenced the egoistic in historical decisions. We have sailed into very deep waters, and it will be the crowning achievement of our life if we sail out in a satisfactory fashion."

There was an eager lilt in the psychologist's voice; and the grand captain experienced a responsive thrill of joy. If there was one thing she appreciated, it was the positive outlook, the kind of people who faced all obstacles short of the recognizably impossible with a youthful zest, a will to win. She was still smiling as she broke the connection.

The high thrill sagged. She sat cold with her problem. It was a problem. Hers. All aristocratic officers had *carte blanche* powers, and were expected to solve difficulties involving anything up to whole groups of planetary systems.

After a minute she dialed the meteorology room again.

"Lieutenant Cannons, when the meteorology officer of the Fifty Suns navy arrives, please employ the following tactics—"

Maltby waved dismissal to the driver of his car. The machine pulled away from the curb and Maltby stood frowning at the flaming energy barrier that barred farther progress along the street. Finally, he took another look at the Earth ship.

It was directly above him now that he had come so many miles across the city toward it. It was tremendously high up, a long, black torpedo shape almost lost in the mist of distance.

But high as it was it was still visibly bigger than anything ever seen by the Fifty Suns, an incredible creature of metal from a world so far away that, almost, it had sunk to the status of myth.

Here was the reality. There would be tests, he thought, penetrating tests before they'd accept any orbit he planned. It wasn't that he doubted the ability of his double mind to overcome anything like that, but—

Well to remember that the frightful gap of years which separated the science of Earth from that of the Fifty Suns had already shown unpleasant surprises. Maltby shook himself grimly and gave his full attention to the street ahead.

A fan-shaped pink fire spread skyward from two machines that stood in the center of the street. The flame was a very pale pink and completely transparent. It looked electronic, deadly.

Beyond it were men in glittering uniforms. A steady trickle of them moved in and out of buildings. About three blocks down the avenue a second curtain of pink fire flared up.

There seemed to be no attempt to guard the sides. The men he could see looked at ease, confident. There was murmured conversation, low laughter and—they weren't all men.

As Maltby walked forward, two fine-looking young women in uniform came down the steps of the nearest of the requisitioned buildings. One of the guards of the flame said something to them. There was a twin tinkle of silvery laughter. Still laughing, they strode off down the street.

It was suddenly exciting. There was an air about these people of far places, of tremendous and wonderful lands beyond the farthest horizons of the staid Fifty Suns.

He felt cold, then hot, then he glanced up at the fantastically big ship; and the chill came back. One ship, he thought, but so big, so mighty that thirty billion people didn't dare send their own fleets against it. They—

He grew aware that one of the brilliantly arrayed guards was staring at him. The man spoke into a wrist radio, and after a moment a second man broke off his conversation with a third soldier and came over. He stared through the flame barrier at Maltby.

"Is there anything you desire? Or are you just looking?"

He spoke English, curiously accented—but English! His manner was mild, almost gentle, cultured. The whole effect was pleasing. After all, Maltby thought, he had never had had a naturalness, an unalienness that was pleasing. After all, Maltby thought, he had never had the fear of these people that the others had. His very plan to defeat the ship was based upon his own fundamental belief that the robots were indestructible in the sense that no one could ever wipe them out completely.

Quietly, Maltby explained his presence.

"Oh, yes," the man nodded, "we've been expecting you. I'm to take you at once to the meteorological room of the ship. Just a moment—"

The flame barrier went down and Maltby was led into one of the buildings. There was a long corridor, and the transmitter that projected him into the ship must have been focused somewhere along it.

Because abruptly he was in a very large room. Maps floated in half a dozen antigravity pits. The walls shed light from millions of tiny point sources. And everywhere were tables with curved lines of very dim but sharply etched light on their surfaces.

Maltby's guide was nowhere to be seen. Coming toward him, however, was a tall, fine-looking old man. The oldster offered his hand.

"My name is Lieutenant Cannons, senior ship meteorologist. If you will sit down here we can plan an orbit and the ship can start moving within the hour. The grand captain is very anxious that we get started."

Maltby nodded casually. But he was stiff, alert. He stood quite still, feeling around with that acute second mind of his, his Dellian mind, for energy pressures that would show secret attempts to watch or control his mind.

But there was nothing like that.

He smiled finally, grimly. It was going to be as simple as this, was it? Like hell it was.

As he sat down, Maltby felt suddenly cozy and alive. The pure exhilaration of existence burned through him like a flame. He recognized the singing excitement for the battle thrill it was and felt a grim joy that for the first time in fifteen years he could do something about it.

During his long service in the Fifty Suns navy, he had

faced hostility and suspicion because he was a Mixed Man. And always he had felt helpless, unable to do anything about it. Now, here was a far more basic hostility, however veiled, and a suspicion that must be like a burning fire.

And this time he could fight. He could look this skillfully voluble, friendly old man squarely in the eye and—

Friendly?

"It makes me smile sometimes," the old man was saying, "when I think of the unscientific aspects of the orbit we have to plan now. For instance, what is the time lag on storm reports out here?"

Maltby could not suppress a smile. So Lieutenant Cannons wanted to know things, did he? To give the man credit, it wasn't really a lame opening. The truth was, the only way to ask a question was—well—to ask it. Maltby said:

"Oh, three, four months. Nothing unusual. Each space meteorologist takes about that length of time to check the bounds of the particular storm in his area, and then he reports, and we adjust our maps.

"Fortunately"—he pushed his second mind to the fore as he coolly spoke the great basic lie—"there are no major storms between the Kaidor and Cassidor suns."

He went on, sliding over the untruth like an eel breasting wet rock:

"However, several suns prevent a straight line movement. So if you would show me some of your orbits for twenty-five hundred light years, I'll make a selection of the best ones."

He wasn't, he realized instantly, going to slip over his main point as easily as that.

"No intervening storms?" the old man said. He pursed his lips. The fine lines in his long face seemed to deepen. He looked genuinely nonpulsed; and there was no doubt at all that he hadn't expected such a straightforward statement. "Hm-m-m, no storms. That does make it simple, doesn't it?"

He broke off. "You know, the important thing about two" —he hesitated over the word, then went on—"two people, who have been brought up in different cultures, under different scientific standards, is that they make sure they are discussing a subject from a common viewpoint.

"Space is so big. Even this comparatively small system of stars, the Greater Magellanic Cloud, is so vast that it defies our reason. We on the battleship *Star Cluster* have spent ten years surveying it, and now we are able to say glibly that it comprises two hundred sixty billion cubic light years, and contains fifty millions of suns.

"We located the magnetic center of the Cloud, fixed our zero line from center to the great brightest star, S Doradus; and now, I suppose, there are people who would be fools enough to think we've got the system stowed away in our brainpans."

Maltby was silent because he himself was just such a fool. This was warning. He was being told in no uncertain terms that they were in a position to check any orbit he gave them with respect to all intervening suns.

It meant much more. It showed that Earth was on the verge of extending her tremendous sway to the Lesser Magellanic Cloud. Destroying this ship now would provide the Fifty Suns with precious years during which they would have to decide what they intended to do.

But that would be all. Other ships would come; the inexorable pressure of the stupendous populations of the main galaxy would burst out even farther into space. Always under careful control, shepherded by mighty hosts of invincible battleships, the great transports would sweep into the Cloud, and every planet everywhere, robot or non-robot, would acknowledge Earth suzerainty.

Imperial Earth recognized no separate nations of any description anywhere. The robots, Dellian, non-Dellian and Mixed, would need every extra day, every hour; and it was lucky for them all that he was not basing his hope of destroying this ship on an orbit that would end inside a sun.

Their survey had magnetically placed all the suns for them. But they couldn't know about the storms. Not in ten years or in a hundred was it possible for one ship to locate possible storms in an area that involved twenty-five hundred light years of length.

Unless their psychologists could uncover the special qualities of his double brain, he had them. He grew aware that Lieutenant Cannons was manipulating the controls of the orbit table.

The lines of light on the surface flickered and shifted. Then settled like the balls in a game of chance. Maltby selected six that ran deep into the great storm. Ten minutes after that he felt the faint jar as the ship began to move. He stood up, frowning. Odd that they should act without *some* verification of his—

"This way," said the old man.

Maltby thought sharply: This couldn't be all. Any minute now they'd start on him and—

His thought ended.

He was in space. Far, far below was the receding planet of Kaider III. To one side gleamed the vast dark hull of the battleship; and on every other side, and up, and down, were stars and the distances of dark space.

In spite of all his will, the shock was inexpressibly violent.

His active mind jerked. He staggered physically; and he would have fallen like a blindfolded creature except that, in the movement of trying to keep on his feet, he recognized that he *was* still on his feet.

His whole being steadied. Instinctively, he—tilted—his second mind awake, and pushed it forward. Put its more mechanical and precise qualities, its Dellian strength, between his other self and whatever the human beings might be doing against him.

Somewhere in the mist of darkness and blazing stars, a woman's clear and resonant voice said:

"Well, Lieutenant Neslor, did the surprise yield any psychological fruits?"

The reply came from a second, an older-sounding woman's voice:

"After three seconds, noble lady, his resistance leaped to I. Q. 900. Which means they've sent us a Dellian. Your excellency, I thought you specifically asked that their representative be not a Dellian."

Maltby said swiftly into the night around him: "You're quite mistaken. I am not a Dellian. And I assure you that I will lower my resistance to zero if you desire. I reacted instinctively to surprise, naturally enough."

There was a click. The illusion of space and stars snapped out of existence. Maltby saw what he had begun to suspect, that he was, had been all the time, in the meteorology room.

Nearby stood the old man, a thin smile on his lined face. On a raised dais, partly hidden behind a long instrument board, sat a handsome young woman. It was the old man who spoke. He said in a stately voice:

"You are in the presence of Grand Captain, the Right Honorable Gloria Cecily, the Lady Laurr of Noble Laurr. Conduct yourself accordingly."

Maltby bowed but he said nothing. The grand captain frowned at him, impressed by his appearance. Tall, magnificent-looking body—strong, supremely intelligent face. In a single flash she noted all the characteristics common to the first-class human being and robot.

These people might be more dangerous than she had thought. She said with unnatural sharpness for her:

"As you know, we have to question you. We would prefer that you do not take offense. You have told us that Cassido VII, the chief planet of the Fifty Suns, is twenty-five hundred light years from here. Normally, we would spend more than sixty years *feeling* our way across such an immense gap of uncharted, star-filled space. But you have given us a choice of orbits.

"We must make sure those orbits are honest, offered without guile or harmful purpose. To that end we have to ask you to open your mind and answer our questions under the strictest psychological surveillance."

"I have orders," said Maltby, "to cooperate with you in every way."

He had wondered how he would feel, now that the hour of decision was upon him. But there was nothing unnormal. His body was a little stiffer, but his minds—

He withdrew his *self* into the background and left his Dellian mind to confront all the questions that came. His Dellian mind that he had deliberately kept apart from his thoughts. That curious mind, which had no will of its own, but which, by remote control, reacted with the full power of an I. Q. of 191.

Sometimes, he marveled himself at that second mind of his. It had no creative ability, but its memory was machine-like, and its resistance to outside pressure was, as the woman psychologist had so swiftly analyzed, over nine hundred. To be exact, the equivalent of I. Q. 917.

"What is your name?"
That was the way it began: His name, distinction— He answered everything quietly, positively, without hesitation. When he had finished, when he had sworn to the truth of every word about the storms, there was a long moment of dead silence. And then a middle-aged woman stepped out of the nearby wall.

She came over and motioned him into a chair. When he was seated she tilted his head and began to examine it. She did it gently; her fingers were caressing as a lover's. But when she looked up she said sharply:

"You're not a Dellian or a non-Dellian. And the molecular structure of your brain and body is the most curious I've ever seen. All the molecules are twins. I saw a similar arrangement once in an artificial electronic structure where an attempt was being made to balance an unstable electronic structure. The parallel isn't exact, but—mm-m-m, I must try to remember what the end result was of that experiment."

234

She broke off: "What is your explanation? What are you?"

Maltby sighed. He had determined to tell only the one main lie. Not that it mattered so far as his double brain was concerned. But untruths effected slight variations in blood pressure, created neutral spasms and disturbed muscular integration. He couldn't take the risk of even one more than was absolutely necessary.

"I'm a Mixed Man," he explained. He described briefly how the cross between the Dellian and non-Dellian, so long impossible, had finally been brought about a hundred years before. The use of cold and pressure—

"Just a moment," said the psychologist.

She disappeared. When she stepped again out of the wall transmitter, she was thoughtful.

"He seems to be telling the truth," she confessed, almost reluctantly.

"What is this?" snapped the grand captain. "Ever since we ran into that first citizen of the Fifty Suns, the psychology department has qualified every statement it issues. I thought psychology was the only perfect science. Either he is telling the truth or he isn't."

The older woman looked unhappy. She stared very hard at Maltby, seemed baffled by his cool gaze, and finally faced her superior, said:

"It's that double molecule structure of his brain. Except for that, I see no reason why you shouldn't order full acceleration."

The grand captain smiled. "I shall have Captain Maltby to dinner tonight. I'm sure he will co-operate then with any further studies you may be prepared to make at that time. Meanwhile I think—"

She spoke into a communicator: "Central engines, step up to half light year a minute on the following orbit—"

Maltby listened, estimating with his Dellian mind. Half a light year a minute; it would take a while to attain that speed, but—in eight hours they'd strike the storm.

In eight hours he'd be having dinner with the grand captain.

Eight hours!

The full flood of a contraterrene Nova impinging upon terrene gases already infuriated by seetee gone insane—that was the new, greater storm.

The exploding, giant sun added weight to the diffuse, maddened thing. And it added something far more deadly.

Speed! From peak to peak of velocity the tumult of ul-

235

trafire leaped. The swifter crags of the storm danced and burned with an absolutely hellish fury.

The sequence of action was rapid almost beyond the bearance of matter. First raced the light of the Nova, blazing its warning at more than a hundred and eighty-six thousand miles a second to all who knew that it flashed from the edge of an interstellar storm.

But the advance glare of warning was nullified by the colossal speed of the storm. For weeks and months it drove through the vast night at a velocity that was only a bare measure short of that of light itself.

The dinner dishes had been cleared away. Maltby was thinking: In half an hour—*half an hour!*

He was wondering shakily just what did happen to a battleship suddenly confronted by thousands of gravities of deceleration. Aloud he was saying:

"My day? I spent it in the library. Mainly, I was interested in the recent history of Earth's interstellar colonization. I'm curious as to what is done with groups like the Mixed Men. I mentioned to you that, after the war in which they were defeated largely because there was so few of them, the Mixed Men hid themselves from the Fifty Suns. I was one of the captured children who—"

There was an interruption, a cry from the wall communicator: *"Noble lady, I've solved it!"*

A moment fled before Maltby recognized the strained voice of the woman psychologist. He had almost forgotten that she was supposed to be studying him. Her next words chilled him:

"Two minds! I thought of it a little while ago and rigged up a twin watching device. Ask him, *ask* him the question about the storms. Meanwhile stop the ship. At once!"

Maltby's dark gaze clashed hard with the steely, narrowed eyes of the grand captain. Without hesitation he concentrated his two minds on her, forced her to say:

"Don't be silly, lieutenant. One person can't have two brains. Explain yourself further."

His hope was delay. They had ten minutes in which they could save themselves. He must waste every second of that time, resist all their efforts, try to control the situation. If only his special three-dimensional hypnotism worked through communicators—

It didn't. Lines of light leaped at him from the wall and crisscrossed his body, held him in his chair like so many unbreakable cables. Even as he was bound hand and foot by

236

palpable energy, a second complex of forces built up before his face, barred his thought pressure from the grand captain, and finally coned over his head like a dunce cap.

He was caught as neatly as if a dozen men had swarmed with their strength and weight over his body. Maltby relaxed and laughed.

"Too late," he taunted. "It'll take at least an hour for this ship to reduce to a safe speed; and at this velocity you can't turn aside in time to avoid the greatest storm in this part of the Universe."

That wasn't strictly true. There was still time and room to sheer off before the advancing storm in any of the fronting directions. The impossibility was to turn toward the storm's tail or its great, bulging sides.

His thought was interrupted by the first cry from the young woman; a piercing cry: "Central engines! Reduce speed! Emergency!"

There was a jar that shook the walls and a pressure that tore at his muscles. Maltby adjusted and then stared across the table at the grand captain. She was smiling, a frozen mask of a smile; and she said from between clenched teeth:

"Lieutenant Neslor, use any means physical or otherwise, but make him talk. There must be something."

"His second mind is the key," the psychologist's voice came. It's not Dellian. It has only normal resistance. I shall subject it to the greatest concentration of conditioning ever focused on a human brain, using the two basics: sex and logic. I shall have to use you, noble lady, as the object of his affections."

"Hurry!" said the young woman. Her voice was like a metal bar.

Maltby sat in a mist, mental and physical. Deep in his mind was awareness that he was an entity, and that irresistible machines were striving to mold his thought.

He resisted. The resistance was as strong as his life, as intense as all the billions and quadrillions of impulses that had shaped his being, could make it.

But the outside thought, the pressure, grew stronger. How silly of him to resist Earth—when this lovely woman of Earth loved him, loved him, loved him. Glorious was that civilization of Earth and the main galaxy. Three hundred million billion people. The very first contact would rejuvenate the Fifty Suns. How lovely she is; I must save her. She means everything to me.

As from a great distance, he began to hear his own voice, explaining what must be done, just how the ship must be

237

turned, in what direction, how much time there was. He tried to stop himself, but inexorably his voice went on, mouthing the words that spelled defeat for the Fifty Suns.

The mist began to fade. The terrible pressure eased from his straining mind. The damning stream of words ceased to pour from his lips. He sat up shakily, conscious that the energy cords and the energy cap had been withdrawn from his body. He heard the grand captain say into a communicator:

"By making a point 0100 turn we shall miss the storm by seven light weeks. I admit it is an appallingly sharp curve, but I feel that we should have at least that much leeway."

She turned and stared at Maltby: "Prepare yourself. At half a light year a minute even a hundredth of a degree turn makes some people black out."

"Not me," said Maltby, and tensed his Dellian muscles.

She fainted three times during the next four minutes as he sat there watching her. But each time she came to within seconds.

"We human beings," she said wanly, finally, "are a poor lot. But at least we know how to endure."

The terrible minutes dragged. And dragged. Maltby began to feel the strain of that infinitesimal turn. He thought at last: Space! How could these people ever hope to survive a direct hit on a storm?

Abruptly, it was over; a man's voice said quietly: "We have followed the prescribed course, noble lady, and are now out of dang—"

He broke off with a shout: "Captain, the light of a Nova sun has just flashed from the direction of the storm. We—"

In those minutes before disaster struck, the battleship *Star Cluster*, glowed like an immense and brilliant jewel. The warning glare from the Nova set off an incredible roar of emergency clamor through all of her hundred and twenty decks.

From end to end her lights flicked on. They burned row by row straight across her four thousand feet of length with the hard tinkle of cut gems. In the reflection of that light, the black mountain that was her hull looked like the fabulous planet of Cassidor, her destination, as seen at night from a far darkness, sown with diamond shining cities.

Silent as a ghost, grand and wonderful beyond all imagination, glorious in her power, the great ship slid through the blackness along the special river of time and space which was her plotted course.

Even as she rode into the storm there was nothing visible.

238

The space ahead looked as clear as any vacuum. So tenuous were the gases that made up the storm that the ship would not even have been aware of them if it had been traveling at atomic speeds.

Violent the disintegration of matter in that storm might be, and the sole source of cosmic rays the hardest energy in the known universe. But the immense, the cataclysmic danger to the *Star Cluster* was a direct result of her own terrible velocity.

If she had had time to slow, the storm would have meant nothing.

Striking that mass of gas at half a light year a minute was like running into an unending solid wall. The great ship shuddered in every plate as the deceleration tore at her gigantic strength.

In seconds she had run the gamut of all the recoil systems her designers had planned for her as a unit.

She began to break up.

And still everything was according to the original purpose of the superb engineering firm that had built her. The limit of unit strain reached, she dissolved into her nine thousand separate sections.

Streamlined needles of metal were those sections, four hundred feet long, forty feet wide; silverlike shapes that sinuated cunningly through the gases, letting the pressure of them slide off their smooth hides.

But it wasn't enough. Metal groaned from the torture of deceleration. In the deceleration chambers, men and women lay at the bare edge of consciousness, enduring agony that seemed on the verge of being beyond endurance.

Hundreds of the sections careened into each other in spite of automatic screens, and instantaneously fused into white-hot coffins.

And still, in spite of the hideously maintained velocity, that mass of gases was not bridged; light years of thickness had still to be covered.

For those sections that remained, once more all the limits of human strength were reached. The final action was chemical, directly on the human bodies that remained of the original thirty thousand. Those bodies for whose sole benefit all the marvelous safety devices had been conceived and constructed, the poor, fragile, human beings who through all the ages had persisted in dying under normal conditions from a pressure of something less than fifteen gravities.

The prompt reaction of the automatics in rolling back every floor, and plunging every person into the deceleration chambers of each section—that saving reaction was abruptly augmented as the deceleration chamber was flooded by a special type of gas.

Wet was that gas, and clinging. It settled thickly on the clothes of the humans, soaked through to the skin and *through* the skin, into every part of the body.

Sleep came gently, and with it a wonderful relaxation. The blood grew immune to shock; muscles that, in a minute before, had been drawn with anguish—loosened; the brain impregnated with life-giving chemicals that relieved it of all shortages remained untroubled even by dreams.

Everybody grew enormously flexible to gravitation pressures—a hundred—a hundred and fifty gravities of deceleration; and still the life force clung.

The great heart of the Universe beat on. The storm roared along its inescapable artery, creating the radiance of life, purging the dark of its poisons—and at last the tiny ships in their separate courses burst its great bounds.

They began to come together, to seek each other, as if among them there was an irresistible passion that demanded intimacy of union.

Automatically, they slid into their old positions; the battleship *Star Cluster* began again to take form—but there were gaps. Segments destroyed, and segments lost.

On the third day Acting Grand Captain Rutgers called the surviving captains to the forward bridge, where he was temporarily making his headquarters. After the conference a communique was issued to the crew:

At 008 hours this morning a message was received from Grand Captain, the Right Honorable Gloria Cecily, the Lady Laurr of Noble Laurr, I. C., C. M., G. K. R. She has been forced down on the planet of a yellow-white sun. Her ship crashed on landing, and is unrepairable. As all communication with her has been by nondirectional sub-space radio, and as it will be utterly impossible to locate such an ordinary type sun among so many millions of other suns, the Captains in Session regret to report that our noble lady's name must now be added to that longest of all lists of naval casualties: the list of those who have been lost forever on active duty.

The admiralty lights will burn blue until further notice.

Her back was to him as he approached. Maltby hesitated, then tensed his mind, and held her there beside the section

240

of ship that had been the main bridge of the *Star Cluster*.

The long metal shape lay half buried in the marshy ground of the great valley, its lower end jutting down into the shimmering deep yellowish black waters of a sluggish river.

Maltby paused a few feet from the tall, slim woman, and, still holding her unaware of him, examined once again the environment that was to be their life.

The fine spray of dark rain that had dogged his exploration walk was retreating over the yellow rim of valley to the "west."

As he watched, a small yellow sun burst out from behind a curtain of dark, ocherous clouds and glared at him brilliantly. Below it an expanse of jungle glinted strangely brown and yellow.

Everywhere was that dark-brown and intense, almost liquid yellow.

Maltby sighed—and turned his attention to the woman, willed her not to see him as he walked around in front of her.

He had given a great deal of thought to the Right Honorable Gloria Cecily during his walk. Basically, of course, the problem of a man and a woman who were destined to live the rest of their lives together, alone, on a remote planet, was very simple. Particularly in view of the fact that one of the two had been conditioned to be in love with the other.

Maltby smiled grimly. He could appreciate the artificial origin of that love. But that didn't dispose of the profound fact of it.

The conditioning machine had struck to his very core. Unfortunately, it had not touched her at all; and two days of being alone with her had brought out one reality:

The Lady Laurr of Noble Laurr was not even remotely thinking of yielding herself to the normal requirements of the situation.

It was time that she was made aware, not because an early solution was necessary or even desirable, but because she had to realize that the problem existed.

He stepped forward and took her in his arms.

She was a tall, graceful woman; she fitted into his embrace as if she belonged there; and, because his control of her made her return the kiss, its warmth had an effect beyond his intention.

He had intended to free her mind in the middle of the kiss.

He didn't.

When he finally released her, it was only a physical release. Her mind was still completely under his domination.

241

There was a metal chair that had been set just outside one of the doors. Maltby walked over, sank into it and stared up at the grand captain.

He felt shaken. The flame of desire that had leaped through him was a telling tribute to the conditioning he had undergone. But it was entirely beyond his previous analysis of the intensity of his own feelings.

He had thought he was in full control of himself, and he wasn't. Somehow, the sardonicism, the half detachment, the objectivity, which he had fancied was the keynote of his own reaction to this situation, didn't apply at all.

The conditioning machine had been thorough.

He loved this woman with such a violence that the mere touch of her was enough to disconnect his will from operations immediately following.

His heart grew quieter; he studied her with a semblance of detachment.

She was lovely in a handsome fashion; though almost all robot women of the Dellian race were better-looking. Her lips, while medium full, were somehow a trifle cruel; and there was a quality in her eyes that accentuated that cruelty.

There were built-up emotions in this woman that would not surrender easily to the idea of being marooned for life on an unknown planet.

It was something he would have to think over. Until then—

Maltby sighed. And released her from the three-dimensional hypnotic spell that his two minds had imposed on her.

He had taken the precaution of turning her away from him. He watched her curiously as she stood, back to him, for a moment, very still. Then she walked over to a little knob of trees above the springy, soggy marsh land.

She climbed up it and gazed in the direction from which he had come a few minutes before. Evidently looking for him.

She turned finally, shaded her face against the yellow brightness of the sinking sun, came down from the hillock and saw him.

She stopped; her eyes narrowed. She walked over slowly. She said with an odd edge in her voice:

"You came very quietly. You must have circled and walked in from the west."

"No," said Maltby deliberately, "I stayed in the east."

She seemed to consider that. She was silent, her lean face creased into a frown. She pressed her lips together, finally;

242

there was a bruise there that must have hurt, for she winced, then she said:

"What did you discover? Did you find any—"

She stopped. Consciousness of the bruise on her lip must have penetrated at that moment. Her hand jerked up, her fingers touched the tender spot. Her eyes came alive with the violence of her comprehension. Before she could speak, Maltby said:

"Yes, you're quite right."

She stood looking at him. Her stormy gaze quietened. She said finally, in a stony voice:

"If you try that again I shall feel justified in shooting you."

Maltby shook his head. He said, unsmiling:

"And spend the rest of your life here alone? You'd go mad."

He saw instantly that her basic anger was too great for that kind of logic. He went on swiftly:

"Besides, you'd have to shoot me in the back. I have no doubt you could do that in the line of duty. But not for personal reasons."

Her compressed lips—separated. To his amazement there were suddenly tears in her eyes. Anger tears, obviously. But tears!

She stepped forward with a quick movement and slapped his face.

"You robot!" she sobbed.

Maltby stared at her ruefully; then he laughed. Finally he said, a trace of mockery in his tone:

"If I remember rightly, the lady who just spoke is the same one who delivered a ringing radio address to all the planets of the Fifty Suns swearing that in fifteen thousand years Earth people had forgotten all their prejudices against robots.

"Is it possible," he finished, "that the problem on *closer* investigation is proving more difficult?"

There was no answer. The Honorable Gloria Cecily brushed past him and disappeared into the interior of the ship.

She came out again a few minutes later.

Her expression was more serene; Maltby noted that she had removed all trace of the tears. She looked at him steadily, said:

"What did you discover when you were out? I've been delaying my call to the ship till you returned."

Maltby said: "I thought they asked you to call at 010 hours."

The woman shrugged; and there was an arrogant note in her voice as she replied:

243

"They'll take my calls when I make them. Did you find any sign of intelligent life?"

Maltby allowed himself brief pity for a human being who had as many shocks still to absorb as had Grand Captain Laurr.

One of the books he had read while aboard the battle-ship about colonists of remote planets had dealt very specifically with castaways.

He shook himself and began his description. "Mostly marsh land in the valley and there's jungle, very old. Even some of the trees are immense, though sections show no growth rings —some interesting beasts and a four-legged, two-armed thing that watched me from a distance. It carried a spear but it was too far away for me to use my hypnotism on it. There must be a village somewhere, perhaps on the valley rim. My idea is that during the next months I'll cut the ship into small sections and transport it to drier ground.

"I would say that we have the following information to offer the ship's scientists: We're on a planet of a G-type sun. The sun must be larger than the average yellow-white type and have a larger surface temperature.

"It must be larger and hotter because, though it's far away, it is hot enough to keep the northern hemisphere of this planet in a semitropical condition.

"The sun was quite a bit north at midday, but now its swinging back to the south. I'd say offhand the planet must be tilted at about forty degrees, which means there's a cold winter coming up, though that doesn't fit with the age and type of the vegetation."

The Lady Laurr was frowning. "It doesn't seem very helpful," she said. "But, of course, I'm only an executive."

"And I'm only a meteorologist."

"Exactly. Come in. Perhaps my astrophysicist can make something of it."

"*Your* astrophysicist!" said Maltby. But he didn't say it aloud.

He followed her into the segment of ship and closed the door.

Maltby examined the interior of the main bridge with a wry smile as the young woman seated herself before the astroplate.

The very imposing glitter of the instrument board that occupied one entire wall was ironical now. All the machines it had controlled were far away in space. Once it had dominated the entire Greater Magellanic Cloud; now his own hand gun was a more potent instrument.

He grew aware that Lady Laurr was looking up at him. "I don't understand it," she said. "They don't answer."

"Perhaps"—Maltby could not keep the faint sardonicism out of his tone—"perhaps they may really have had a good reason for wanting you to call at 010 hours."

The woman made a faint, exasperated movement with her facial muscles but she did not answer. Maltby went on coolly:

"After all, it doesn't matter. They're only going through routine motions, the idea being to leave no loophole of rescue unlooked through. I can't even imagine the kind of miracle it would take for anybody to find us."

The woman seemed not to have heard. She said, frowning:

"How is it that we've never heard a single Fifty Suns broadcast? I intended to ask about that before. Not once during our ten years in the Greater Cloud did we catch so much as a whisper of radio energy."

Maltby shrugged. "All radios operate on an extremely complicated variable wave length—changes every twentieth of a second. Your instruments would register a tick once every ten minutes, and—"

He was cut off by a voice from the astroplate. A man's face was there—Acting Grand Captain Rutgers.

"Oh, there you are, captain," the woman said. "What kept you?"

"We're in the process of landing our forces on Cassidor VII," was the reply. "As you know, regulations require that the grand captain—"

"Oh, yes. Are you free now?"

"No. I've taken a moment to see that everything is right with you, and then I'll switch you over to Captain Planston."

"How is the landing proceeding?"

"Perfectly. We have made contact with the government. They seem resigned. But now I must leave. Goodby, my lady."

His face flickered and was gone. The plate went blank. It was about as curt a greeting as anybody had ever received. But Maltby, sunk in his own gloom, scarcely noticed.

So it was all over. The desperate scheming of the Fifty Suns leaders, his own attempt to destroy the great battleship, proved futile against an invincible foe.

For a moment he felt very close to the defeat, with all its implications. Consciousness came finally that the fight no longer mattered in his life. But the knowledge failed to shake his dark mood.

He saw that the Right Honorable Gloria Cecily had an expression of mixed elation and annoyance on her fine, strong face; and there was no doubt that she didn't *feel*—disconnected—from the mighty events out there in space. Nor had she missed the implications of the abruptness of the interview.

The astroplate grew bright and a face appeared on it—one that Maltby hadn't seen before. It was of a heavy-jowled, oldish man with a ponderous voice that said:

"Privilege your ladyship—hope we can find something that will enable us to make rescue. Never give up hope, I say, until the last nail's driven in your coffin."

He chuckled; and the woman said: "Captain Maltby will give you all the information he has, then no doubt you can give him some advice, Captain Planston. Neither he nor I, unfortunately, are astrophysicists."

"Can't be experts on every subject," Captain Planston puffed. "Er, Captain Maltby, what do you know?"

Maltby gave his information briefly, then waited while the other gave instructions. There wasn't much:

"Find out length of seasons. Interested in that yellow effect of the sunlight and the deep brown. Take the following photographs, using orthosensitive film—use three dyes, a red sensitive, a blue and a yellow. Take a spectrum reading—what I want to check on is that maybe you've got a strong blue sun there, with the ultraviolet barred by a heavy atmosphere, and all the heat and light coming in on the yellow band.

"I'm not offering much hope, mind you—the Greater Cloud is packed with blue suns—five hundred thousand of them brighter than Sirius.

"Finally, get that season information from the natives. Make a point of it. Good-by!"

The native was wary. He persisted in retreating elusively into the jungle; and his four legs gave him a speed advantage of which he seemed to be aware. For he kept coming back, tantalizingly.

The woman watched with amusement, then exasperation. "Perhaps," she suggested, "if we separated, and I drove him toward you?"

She saw the frown on the man's face as Maltby nodded reluctantly. His voice was strong, tense.

"He's leading us into an ambush. Turn on the sensitives in your helmet and carry your gun. Don't be too hasty about firing, but don't hesitate in a crisis. A spear can make an ugly wound; and we haven't got the best facilities for handling anything like that.

His orders brought a momentary irritation. He seemed not to be aware that she was as conscious as he of the requirements of the situation.

The Right Honorable Gloria sighed. If they had to stay on this planet there would have to be some major psychological adjustments, and not—she thought grimly—only by herself.

"*Now!*" said Maltby beside her, swiftly. "Notice the way the ravine splits in two. I came this far yesterday and they join about two hundred yards farther on. He's gone up the left fork. I'll take the right. You stop here, let him come back to see what's happened, then drive him on."

He was gone, like a shadow, along a dark path that wound under thick foliage.

Silence settled.

She waited. After a minute she felt herself alone in a yellow and black world that had been lifeless since time began.

She thought: This was what Maltby had meant yesterday when he had said she wouldn't dare shoot him—and remain alone. It hadn't penetrated then.

It did now. Alone, on a nameless planet of a mediocre sun, one woman waking up every morning on a moldering ship that rested its unliving metal shape on a dark, muggy, yellow marsh land.

She stood somber. There was no doubt that the problem of robot and human being would have to be solved here as well as out there.

A sound pulled her out of her gloom. As she watched, abruptly more alert, a catlike head peered cautiously from a line of bushes a hundred yards away across the clearing.

It was an interesting head; its ferocity not the least of its fascinating qualities. The yellowish body was invisible now in the underbrush, but she had caught enough glimpses of it earlier to recognize that it was the CC type, of the almost universal Centaur family. Its body was evenly blanced between its hind and forelegs.

It watched her, and its great glistening black eyes were round with puzzlement. Its head twisted from side to side, obviously searching for Maltby.

She waved her gun and walked forward. Instantly the creature disappeared. She could hear it with her sensitives, running into distance. Abruptly, it slowed; then there was no sound at all.

"He's got it," she thought.

She felt impressed. These two-brained Mixed Men, she thought, were bold and capable. It would really be too bad

247

if antirobot prejudice prevented them from being absorbed into the galactic civilization of Imperial Earth.

She watched him a few minutes later, using the block system of communication with the creature. Maltby looked up, saw her. He shook his head as if puzzled.

"He says its always been warm like this, and that he's been alive for thirteen hundred moons. And that a moon is forty suns—forty days. He wants us to come up a little farther along this valley, but that's too transparent for comfort. Our move is to make a cautious, friendly gesture, and—"

He stopped short. Before she could even realize anything was wrong, her mind was caught, her muscles galvanized. She was thrown sideways and downward so fast that the blow of striking the ground was pure agony.

She lay there stunned, and out of the corner of her eye she saw the spear plunge through the air where she had been.

She twisted, rolled over—her own free will now—and jerked her gun in the direction from which the spear had come. There was a second centaur there, racing away along a bare slope. Her finger pressed on the control; and then—

"Don't!" It was Maltby, his voice low. "It was a scout the others sent ahead to see what was happening. He's done his work. It's all over."

She lowered her gun and saw with annoyance that her hand was shaking, her whole body trembling. She parted her lips to say: "Thanks for saving my life!" Then she closed them again. Because the words would have quavered. And because—

Saved her life! Her mind poised on the edge of blankness with the shock of the thought. Incredibly—she had never before been in personal danger from an individual creature.

There had been the time when her battleship had run into the outer fringes of a sun; and there was the cataclysm of the storm, just past.

But those had been personal menaces to be met with technical virtuosities and the hard training of the service.

This was different.

All the way back to the segment of ship she tried to fathom what the difference meant.

It seemed to her finally that she had it.

"Spectrum featureless." Maltby gave his findings over the astro. "No dark lines at all; two of the yellow bands so immensely intense that they hurt my eyes. As you suggested, apparently what we have here is a blue sun whose strong violet radiation is cut off by the atmosphere.

"However," he finished, "the uniqueness of that effect is

onfined to our planet here, a derivation of the thick at-
osphere. Any questions?"

"No-o!" The astrophysicist looked thoughtful. "And I can
ive you no further instructions. I'll have to examine this ma-
erial. Will you ask Lady Laurr to come in? Like to speak to
er privately, if you please."

"Of course."

When she had come, Maltby went outside and watched
he moon come up. Darkness—he had noticed it the previous
ight—brought a vague, overall violet haze. Explained now!

An eighty-degree temperature on a planet that, the angular
iameter of the sun being what it was, would have been
inus one hundred eighty degrees, if the sun's apparent color
ad been real.

A blue sun, one of five hundred thousand— Interesting
ut— Maltby smiled savagely—Captain Planston's "No further
nstructions!" had a finality about it that—

He shivered involuntarily. And after a moment tried to
icture himself sitting, like this, a year hence, staring up at
n unchanged moon. Ten years, twenty—

He grew aware that the woman had come to the door-
vay and was gazing at him where he sat on the chair.

Maltby looked up. The stream of white light from inside
he ship caught the queer expression on her face, gave her
, strange, bleached look after the yellowness that had seemed
, part of her complexion all day.

"We shall receive no more astro-radio calls," she said and,
urning, went inside.

Maltby nodded to himself, almost idly. It was hard and
rutal, this abrupt cutting off of communication. But the
egulations governing such situations were precise.

The marooned ones must realize with utter clarity, with-
ut false hopes and without the curious illusions produced by
adio communication, that they were cut off forever. Forever
n their own.

Well, so be it. A fact was a fact, to be faced with resolu-
ion. There had been a chapter on castaways in one of the
ooks he had read on the battleship. It had stated that nine
undred million human beings had, during recorded history,
een marooned on then undiscovered planets. Most of these
lanets had eventually been found; and on no less than ten
housand of them great populations had sprung from the
riginal nucleus of castaways.

The law prescribed that a castaway could not withhold
imself or herself from participating in such population in-
reases—regardless of previous rank. Castaways must forget

considerations of sensitivity and individualism, and think o
themselves as instruments of race expansion.

There were penalties; naturally inapplicable if no rescu
was effected, but ruthlessly applied whenever recalcitran
were found.

Conceivably the courts might determine that a human bein
and a robot constituted a special case.

Half an hour must have passed while he sat there. He stoo
up finally, conscious of hunger. He had forgotten all abou
supper.

He felt a qualm of self-annoyance. Damn it, this was no
the night to appear to be putting pressure on her. Sooner o
later she would have to be convinced that she ought to d
her share of the cooking.

But not tonight.

He hurried inside, toward the compact kitchen that wa
part of every segment of ship. In the corridor, he pausec

A blaze of light streamed from the kitchen door. Somebod
was whistling softly and tunelessly but cheerfully; and ther
was an odor of cooking vegetables, and hot *lak* meat.

They almost bumped in the doorway. "I was just going t
call you," she said.

The supper was a meal of silences, quickly over. They pu
the dishes into the automatic and went and sat in the grea
lounge; Maltby saw finally that the woman was studying hir
with amused eyes.

"Is there any possibility," she said abruptly, "that a Mixe
Man and a human woman can have children?"

"Frankly," Maltby confessed, "I doubt it."

He launched into a detailed description of the cold an
pressure process that had molded the protoplasm to make th
original Mixed Men. When he finished he saw that her eye
were still regarding him with a faint amusement. She said i
an odd tone:

"A very curious thing happened to me today, after that na
tive threw his spear. I realized"—she seemed for a momen
to have difficulty in speaking—"I realized that I had, so fa
as I personally was concerned, solved the robot problem.

"Naturally," she finished quietly, "I would not have with
held myself in any event. But it is pleasant to know that
like you without"—she smiled—"qualifications."

Blue sun that looked yellow. Maltby sat in the chair th
following morning puzzling over it. He half expected a visi
from the natives, and so he was determined to stay near th
ship that day.

He kept his eyes aware of the clearing edges, the valley rims, the jungle trails, but—

There was a law, he remembered, that governed the shifting of light to other wave bands, to yellow for instance. Rather complicated, but in view of the fact that all the instruments of the main bridge were controls of instruments, not the machines themselves, he'd have to depend on mathematics if he ever hoped to visualize the kind of sun that was out there.

Most of the heat probably came through the ultraviolet range. But that was uncheckable. So leave it alone and stick to the yellow.

He went into the ship. Gloria was nowhere in sight, but her bedroom door was closed. Maltby found a notebook, returned to his chair and began to figure.

An hour later he stared at the answer: One million three hundred thousand million miles. About a fifth of a light year.

He laughed curtly. That was that. He'd have to get better data than he had or—

Or would he?

His mind poised. In a single flash of understanding, the stupendous truth burst upon him.

With a cry he leaped to his feet, whirled to race through the door as a long, black shadow slid across him.

The shadow was so vast, instantly darkening the whole valley, that, involuntarily, Maltby halted and looked up.

The battleship *Star Cluster* hung low over the yellow-brown jungle planet, already disgorging a lifeboat that glinted a yellowish silver as it circled out into the sunlight, and started down.

Maltby had only a moment with the woman before the lifeboat landed. "To think," he said, "that I just now figured out the truth."

She was, he saw, not looking at him. Her gaze seemed far away. He went on:

"As for the rest, the best method, I imagine, is to put me in the conditioning chamber, and—"

Still without looking at him, she cut him off:

"Don't be ridiculous. You must not imagine that I feel embarassed because you have kissed me. I shall receive you later in my quarters."

A bath, new clothes—at last Maltby stepped through the transmitter into the astrophysics department. His own first realization of the tremendous truth, while generally accurate, had lacked detailed facts.

"Ah, Maltby!" The chief of the department came forward,

251

shook hands. "Some sun you picked there—we suspected from your first description of the yellowness and the black. But naturally we couldn't rouse your hopes—Forbidden, you know.

"The axial tilt, the apparent length of a summer in which jungle trees of great size showed no growth rings—very suggestive. The featureless spectrum with its complete lack of dark lines—almost conclusive. Final proof was that the ortho-sensitive film was overexposed, while the blue and red sensitives were badly underexposed.

"This star-type is so immensely hot that practically all of its energy radiation is far in the ultravisible. A secondary radiation—a sort of fluorescence in the star's own atmosphere —produces the visible yellow when a minute fraction of the appalling ultraviolet radiation is transformed into longer wave lengths by helium atoms. A fluorescent lamp, in a fashion—but on a scale that is more than ordinarily cosmic in its violence. The total radiation reaching the planet was naturally tremendous; the surface radiation, after passing through miles of absorbing ozone, water vapor, carbondioxide and other gases, was very different.

"No wonder the native said it had always been hot. The summer lasts four thousand years. The normal radiation of that special appalling star type—the æon-in-æon-out radiation rate—is about equal to a full-fledged Nova at its catastrophic maximum of violence. It has a period of a few hours, and is equivalent to approximately a hundred million ordinary suns. Nova O, we call that brightest of all stars; and there's only one in the Greater Magellanic Cloud, the great and glorious S-Doradus.

"When I asked you to call Grand Captain Laurr, and I told her that out of thirty million suns she had picked—"

It was at that point that Maltby cut him off. "Just a minute," he said, "did you say you told Lady Laurr *last night?*"

"Was it night down there?" Captain Planston said, interested. "Well, well—By the way, I almost forgot—this marrying and giving in marriage is not so important to me now that I am an old man. But congratulations."

The conversation was too swift for Maltby. His minds were still examining the first statement. That she had known all the time. He came up, groping, before the new words.

"Congratulations?" he echoed.

"Definitely time she had a husband," boomed the captain. "She's been a career woman, you know. Besides, it'll have a revivifying effect on the other robots . . . pardon me. Assure you, the name means nothing to me.

252

"Anyway, Lady Laurr herself made the announcement a few minutes ago, so come down and see me again."

He turned away with a wave of a thick hand.

Maltby headed for the nearest transmitter. She would probably be expecting him by now.

She would not be disappointed.

I

THE EXPENDABLES

ONE HUNDRED and nine years after leaving Earth, the spaceship, *Hope of Man*, went into orbit around Alta III.

The following "morning" Captain Browne informed the shipload of fourth and fifth generation colonists that a manned lifeboat would be dropped to the planet's surface.

"Every member of the crew must consider himself expendable," he said earnestly. "This is the day that our great grandparents, our forefathers, who boldly set out for the new space frontier so long ago, looked forward to with unfaltering courage. We must not fail them."

He concluded his announcement over the intercom system of the big ship by saying that the names of the crew members of the lifeboat would be given out within the hour. "And I know that every real man aboard will want to see his name there."

John Lesbee, the fifth of his line aboard, had a sinking sensation as he heard those words—and he was not mistaken.

Even as he tried to decide if he should give the signal for a desperate act of rebellion, Captain Browne made the expected announcement.

The commander said, "And I know you will all join him in his moment of pride and courage when I tell you that John Lesbee will lead the crew that carries the hopes of man in this remote area of space. And now the others—"

He thereupon named seven of the nine persons with whom Lesbee had been conspiring to seize control of the ship.

Since the lifeboat would only hold eight persons, Lesbee recognized that Browne was dispatching as many of his enemies as he could. He listened with a developing dismay, as the commander ordered all persons on the ship to come to the recreation room. "Here I request that the crew of the lifeboat join me and the other officers on stage. Their instructions are to surrender themselves to any craft which seeks to intercept them. They will be equipped with instruments whereby we

here can watch, and determine the stage of scientific attain
ments of the dominant race on the planet below."

Lesbee hurried to his room on the technicians' deck, hoping that perhaps Tellier or Cantlin would seek him out there.
He felt himself in need of a council of war, however brief.
He waited five minutes, but not one member of his conspira-
torial group showed.

Nonetheless, he had time to grow calm. Peculiarly, it was
the smell of the ship that soothed him most. From the earliest
days of his life, the odor of energy and the scent of metal
under stress had been perpetual companions. At the moment,
with the ship in orbit, there was a letting up of stress. The
smell was of old energies rather than new. But the effect was
similar.

He sat in the chair he used for reading, eyes closed,
breathing in that complex of odors, product of so many titanic
energies. Sitting there, he felt the fear leave his mind and
body. He grew brave again, and strong.

Lesbee recognized soberly that his plan to seize power had
involved risks. Worse, no one would question Browne's choice
of him as the leader of the mission. "I am," thought Lesbee,
"probably the most highly trained technician ever to be on
this ship." Browne Three had taken him when he was ten,
and started him on the long grind of learning that led him,
one after the other, to master the mechanical skills of all the
various technical departments. And Browne Four had continued his training.

He was taught how to repair relay systems. He gradually
came to understand the purposes of countless analogs. The
time came when he could visualize the entire automation.
Long ago, the colossal cobweb of electronic instruments within
the walls had become almost an extension of his nervous system.

During those years of work and study, each daily appren-
ticeship chore left his slim body exhausted. After he came off
duty, he sought a brief relaxation and usually retired to an
early rest.

He never did find the time to learn the intricate theory
that underlay the ship's many operations.

His father, while he was alive, had made numerous attempts to pass his knowledge on to his son. But it was hard
to teach complexities to a tired and sleepy boy. Lesbee even
felt slightly relieved when his parent died. It took the pressure off him. Since then, however, he had come to realize
that the Browne family, by forcing a lesser skill on the de-

cendant of the original commander of the ship, had won their greatest victory.

As he headed finally for the recreation room, Lesbee found himself wondering: Had the Brownes trained him with the intention of preparing him for such a mission as this?

His eyes widened. If that was true, then his own conspiracy was merely an excuse. The decision to kill him might actually have been made more than a decade ago, and light years away . . .

As the lifeboat fell toward Alta III, Lesbee and Tellier sat in the twin control chairs and watched on the forward screen the vast, misty atmosphere of the planet.

Tellier was thin and intellectual, a descendant of the physicist Dr. Tellier who had made many speed experiments in the early days of the voyage. It had never been understood why spaceships could not attain even a good fraction of the speed of light, let alone velocities greater than light. When the scientist met his untimely death, there was no one with the training to carry on a testing program.

It was vaguely believed by the trained personnel who succeeded Tellier that the ship had run into one of the paradoxes implicit in the Lorenz-Fitzgerald Contraction theory.

Whatever the explanation, it was never solved.

Watching Tellier, Lesbee wondered if his companion and best friend felt as empty inside as he did. Incredibly, this was the first time he—or anyone—had been outside the big ship. "We're actually heading down," he thought, "to one of those great masses of land and water, a planet."

As he watched, fascinated, the massive ball grew visibly bigger.

They came in at a slant, a long, swift, angling approach, ready to jet away if any of the natural radiation belts proved too much for their defense systems. But as each stage of radiation registered in turn, the dials showed that the lifeboat machinery made the proper responses automatically.

The silence was shattered suddenly by an alarm bell.

Simultaneously, one of the screens focused on a point of rapidly moving light far below. The light darted toward them.

A missile!

Lesbee caught his breath.

But the shining projectile veered off, turned completely around, took up position several miles away, and began to fall with them.

His first thought was: "They'll never let us land," and he experienced an intense disappointment.

Another signal brrred from the control board.

"They're probing us," said Tellier, tensely.

An instant after the words were uttered, the lifeboat seemed to shudder and to stiffen under them. It was the unmistakable feel of a tractor beam. Its field clutched the lifeboat, drew it, held it.

The science of the Alta III inhabitants was already proving itself formidable.

Underneath him the lifeboat continued its movement.

The entire crew gathered around and watched as the point of brightness resolved into an object, which rapidly grew larger. It loomed up close, bigger than they.

There was a metallic bump. The lifeboat shuddered from stem to stern.

Even before the vibrations ceased Tellier said, "Notice they put our airlock against theirs."

Behind Lesbee, his companions began that peculiar joking of the threatened. It was a coarse comedy, but it had enough actual humor suddenly to break through his fear. Involuntarily he found himself laughing.

Then momentarily free of anxiety, aware that Browne was watching and that there was no escape, he said, "Open the airlock! Let the aliens capture us as ordered."

II

A few minutes after the outer airlock was opened, the airlock of the alien ship folded back also. Rubberized devices rolled out and contacted the Earth lifeboat, sealing off both entrances from the vacuum of space.

Air hissed into the interlocking passageway between the two craft. In the alien craft's lock, an inner door opened.

Again Lesbee held his breath.

There was a movement in the passageway. A creature ambled into view. The being came forward with complete assurance, and pounded with something he held at the end of one of his four leathery arms on the hull.

The creature had four legs and four arms, and a long thin body held straight up. It had almost no neck, yet the many skin folds between the head and the body indicated great flexibility was possible.

Even as Lesbee noted the details of its appearance, the being turned his head slightly, and its two large expressionless eyes gazed straight at the hidden wall receptor that was photographing the scene, and therefore straight into Lesbee's eyes.

256

Lesbee blinked at the creature, then tore his gaze away, swallowed hard, and nodded at Tellier. "Open up!" he commanded.

The moment the inner door of the Earth lifeboat opened, six more of the four-legged beings appeared one after another in the passageway, and walked forward in the same confident way as had the first.

All seven creatures entered the open door of the lifeboat. As they entered their thoughts came instantly into Lebee's mind . . .

As Dzing and his boarding party trotted from the small Karn ship through the connecting airlock, his chief officer thought a message to him.

"Air pressure and oxygen content are within a tiny percentage of what exists at ground level on Karn. They can certainly live on our planet."

Dzing moved forward into the Earth ship, and realized that he was in the craft's control chamber. There, for the first time, he saw the men. He and his crew ceased their forward motion; and the two groups of beings—the humans and the Karn —gazed at each other.

The appearance of the two-legged beings did not surprise Dzing. Pulse viewers had, earlier, penetrated the metal walls of the lifeboat and had accurately photographed the shape and dimension of those aboard.

His first instruction to his crew was designed to test if the strangers were, in fact, surrendering. He commanded: "Convey to the prisoners that we require them as a precaution to remove their clothing."

. . . Until that direction was given, Lesbee was still uncertain as to whether or not these beings could receive human thoughts as he was receiving theirs. From the first moment, the aliens had conducted their mental conversations *as if* they were unaware of the thoughts of the human beings. Now he watched the Karn come forward. One tugged suggestively at his clothing. And there was no doubt.

The mental telepathy was a one-way flow only—from the Karn to the humans.

He was already savoring the implications of that as he hastily undressed . . . It was absolutely vital that Browne did not find it out.

Lesbee removed all his clothes; then, before laying them down, took out his notebook and pen. Standing there naked he wrote hurriedly:

"Don't let on that we can read the minds of these beings."

He handed the notebook around, and he felt a lot better as each of the men read it, and nodded at him silently.

Dzing communicated telepathically with someone on the ground. "These strangers," he reported, "clearly acted under command to surrender. The problem is, how can we now let them overcome us without arousing their suspicion that this is what we want them to do?"

Lesbee did not receive the answer directly. But he picked it up from Dzing's mind: "Start tearing the lifeboat apart. See if that brings a reaction."

The members of the Karn boarding party went to work at once. Off came the control panels; floor plates were melted and ripped up. Soon instruments, wiring, controls were exposed for examination. Most interesting of all to the aliens were the numerous computers and their accessories.

Browne must have watched the destruction; for now, before the Karn could start wrecking the automatic machinery, his voice interjected:

"Watch out, you men! I'm going to shut your airlock and cause your boat to make a sharp right turn in exactly twenty seconds."

For Lesbee and Tellier that simply meant sitting down in their chairs, and turning them so that the acceleration pressure would press them against the backs. The other men sank to the ripped-up floor, and braced themselves.

Underneath Dzing, the ship swerved. The turn began slowly, but it propelled him and his fellows over to one wall of the control room. There he grabbed with his numerous hands at some handholds that had suddenly moved out from the smooth metal. By the time the turn grew sharper, he had his four short legs braced, and he took the rest of the wide swing around with every part of his long, sleek body taut. His companions did the same.

Presently, the awful pressure eased up, and he was able to estimate that their new direction was almost at right angles to what it had been.

He had reported what was happening while it was going on. Now, the answer came: "Keep on destroying. See what they do, and be prepared to succumb to anything that looks like a lethal attack."

Lesbee wrote quickly in his notebook: "Our method of capturing them doesn't have to be subtle. They'll make it easy for us—so we can't lose."

Lesbee waited tensely as the notebook was passed around.

It was still hard for him to believe that no one else had noticed what he had about this boarding party.

Tellier added a note of his own: "It's obvious now that these beings were also instructed to consider themselves expendable."

And that settled it for Lesbee. The others hadn't noticed what he had. He sighed with relief at the false analysis, for it gave him that most perfect of all advantages: that which derived from his special education.

Apparently, he alone knew enough to have analyzed what these creatures were.

The proof was in the immense clarity of their thoughts. Long ago, on earth, it had been established that man had a faltering telepathic ability, which could be utilized consistently only by electronic amplification *outside* his brain. The amount of energy needed for the step-up process was enough to burn out brain nerves, if applied directly.

Since the Karn were utilizing it directly, they couldn't be living beings.

Therefore, Dzing and his fellows were an advanced robot type.

The true inhabitants of Alta III were not risking their own skins at all.

Far more important to Lesbee, he could see how he might use these marvellous mechanisms to defeat Browne, take over the *Hope of Man*, and start the long journey back to Earth.

III

He had been watching the Karn at their work of destruction, while he had these thoughts. Now, he said aloud: "Hainker, Graves."

"Yes?" The two men spoke together.

"In a few moments I'm going to ask Captain Browne to turn the ship again. When he does, use our specimen gas guns!"

The men grinned with relief. "Consider it done," said Hainker.

Lesbee ordered the other four crewmen to be ready to use the specimen-holding devices at top speed. To Tellier he said, "You take charge if anything happens to me."

Then he wrote one more message in the notebook: "These beings will probably continue their mental intercommunication after they are apparently rendered unconscious. Pay no attention, and do not comment on it in any way."

He felt a lot better when that statement also had been

259

read by the others, and the notebook was once more in his possession. Quickly, he spoke to the screen:

"Captain Browne! Make another turn, just enough to pin them."

And so they captured Dzing and his crew.

As he had expected, the Karn continued their telepathic conversation. Dzing reported to his ground contact: "I think we did that rather well."

There must have been an answering message from below, because he went on, "Yes, commander. We are now prisoners as per your instructions, and shall await events . . . The imprisoning method? Each of us is pinned down by a machine which has been placed astride us, with the main section adjusted to the contour of our bodies. A series of rigid metal appendages fasten our arms and legs. All these devices are electronically controlled, and we can of course escape at any time. Naturally, such action is for later . . ."

Lesbee was chilled by the analysis; but for expendables there was no turning back.

He ordered his men: "Get dressed. Then start repairing the ship. Put all the floor plates back except the section at G-8. They removed some of the analogs, and I'd better make sure myself that it all goes back all right."

When he had dressed, he reset the course of the lifeboat, and called Browne. The screen lit up after a moment, and there staring back at him was the unhappy countenance of the forty-year-old officer.

Browne said glumly: "I want to congratulate you and your crew on your accomplishments. It would seem that we have a small scientific superiority over this race, and that we can attempt a limited landing."

Since there would never be a landing on Alta III, Lesbee simply waited without comment as Browne seemed lost in thought.

The officer stirred finally. He still seemed uncertain. "Mr. Lesbee," he said, "as you must understand, this is an extremely dangerous situation for me—and—" he added hastily —"for this entire expedition."

What struck Lesbee, as he heard those words, was that Browne was not going to let him back on the ship. But he had to get aboard to accomplish his own purpose. He thought: "I'll have to bring this whole conspiracy out into the open, and apparently make a compromise offer."

He drew a deep breath, gazed straight into the eyes of Browne's image on the screen and said with the complete courage of a man for whom there is no turning back: "It seems to me, sir, that we have two alternatives. We can resolve all these personal problems either through a democratic election or by a joint captaincy, you being one of the captains and I being the other."

To any other person who might have been listening the remark must have seemed a complete non sequitur. Browne, however, understood its relevance. He said with a sneer, "So you're out in the open. Well, let me tell you, Mr. Lesbee, there was never any talk of elections when the Lesbees were in power. And for a very good reason. A spaceship requires a technical aristocracy to command it. As for a joint captaincy, it wouldn't work."

Lesbee urged his lie: "If we're going to stay here, we'll need at least two people of equal authority—one on the ground, one on the ship."

"I couldn't trust you on the ship!" said Browne flatly.

"Then you be on the ship," Lesbee proposed. "All such practical details can be arranged."

The older man must have been almost beside himself with the intensity of his own feelings on this subject. He flashed, "Your family has been out of power for over fifty years! How can you still feel that you have any rights?"

Lesbee countered, "How come you still know what I'm talking about?"

Browne said, a grinding rage in his tone, "The concept of inherited power was introduced by the first Lesbee. It was never planned."

"But here you are," said Lesbee, "yourself a beneficiary of inherited power."

Browne said from between clenched teeth: "It's absolutely ridiculous that the Earth government which was in power when the ship left—and every member of which has been long dead—should appoint somebody to a command position . . . and that now his descendant think that command post should be his, and his family's, for all time!"

Lesbee was silent, startled by the dark emotions he had uncovered in the man. He felt even more justified, if that were possible, and advanced his next suggestion without a qualm.

"Captain, this is a crisis. We should postpone our private struggle. Why don't we bring one of these prisoners aboard so that we can question him by use of films, or play acting? Later, we can discuss your situation and mine."

He saw from the look on Browne's face that the reasonableness of the suggestion, *and its potentialities*, were penetrating.

Browne said quickly, "Only you come aboard—and with one prisoner only. No one else!"

Lesbee felt a dizzying thrill as the man responded to his bait. He thought: "It's like an exercise in logic. He'll try to murder me as soon as he gets me alone and is satisfied that he can attack without danger to himself. But that very scheme is what will get me aboard. And I've got to get on the ship to carry out *my* plan."

Browne was frowning. He said in a concerned tone: "Mr. Lesbee, can you think of any reason why we should not bring one of these beings aboard?"

Lesbee shook his head. "No reason, sir," he lied.

Browne seemed to come to a decision. "Very well. I'll see you shortly, and we can then discuss additional details."

Lesbee dared not say another word. He nodded, and broke the connection, shuddering, disturbed, uneasy.

"But," he thought, "what else can we do?"

He turned his attention to the part of the floor that had been left open for him. Quickly, he bent down and studied the codes on each of the programming units, as if he were seeking exactly the right ones that had originally been in those slots.

He found the series he wanted: an intricate system of cross-connected units that had originally been designed to program a remote-control landing system, an advanced Waldo mechanism capable of landing the craft on a planet and taking off again, all directed on the pulse level of human thought.

He slid each unit of the series into its sequential position and locked it in.

Then, that important task completed, he picked up the remote control attachment for the series and casually put it in his pocket.

He returned to the control board and spent several minutes examining the wiring and comparing it with a wall chart. A number of wires had been torn loose. These he now re-connected, and at the same time he managed with a twist of his pliers to short-circuit a key relay of the remote control pilot.

Lesbee replaced the panel itself loosely. There was no time to connect it properly. And, since he could easily justify his next move, he pulled a cage out of the storeroom. Into this he hoisted Dzing, manacles and all.

Before lowering the lid he rigged into the cage a simple resistor that would prevent the Karn from broadcasting on the human thought level. The device was simple merely in that it was not selective. It had an on-off switch which triggered, or stopped, energy flow in the metal walls on the thought level.

When the device was installed, Lesbee slipped the tiny remote control for *it* into his other pocket. He did not activate the control. Not yet.

From the cage Dzing telepathed: "It is significant that these beings have selected me for this special attention. We might conclude that it is a matter of mathematical accident, or else that they are very observant and so noticed that I was the one who directed activities. Whatever the reason, it would be foolish to turn back now."

A bell began to ring. As Lesbee watched, a spot of light appeared high on one of the screens. It moved rapidly toward some crossed lines in the exact center of the screen. Inexorably, then, the *Hope of Man*, as represented by the light, and the lifeboat moved toward their fateful rendezvous.

IV

Browne's instructions were: "Come to Control Room Below!"

Lesbee guided his powered dolly with the cage on it out of the big ship's airlock P—and saw that the man in the control room of the lock was Second Officer-Selwyn. Heavy brass for such a routine task. Selwyn waved at him with a twisted smile as Lesbee wheeled his cargo along the silent corridor.

He saw no one else on his route. Other personnel had evidently been cleared from this part of the vessel. A little later, grim and determined, he set the cage down in the center of the big room and anchored it magnetically to the floor.

As Lesbee entered the captain's office, Browne looked up from one of the two control chairs and stepped down from the rubber-sheathed dais to the same level as Lesbee. He came forward, smiling, and held out his hand. He was a big man, as all the Brownes had been, bigger by a head than Lesbee, good-looking in a clean-cut way. The two men were alone.

"I'm glad you were so frank," he said. "I doubt if I could have spoken so bluntly to you without your initiative as an example."

But as they shook hands, Lesbee was wary and suspicious. Lesbee thought: "He's trying to recover from the insanity of his reaction. I really blew him wide open."

Browne continued in the same hearty tone: "I've made up my mind. An election is out of the question. The ship is swarming with untrained dissident groups, most of which simply want to go back to Earth."

Lesbee, who had the same desire, was discreetly silent.

Browne said, "You'll be ground captain; I'll be ship captain. Why don't we sit down right now and work out a communique on which we can agree and that I can read over the intercom to the others?"

As Lesbee seated himself in the chair beside Browne, he was thinking: "What can be gained from publicly naming me ground captain?"

He concluded finally, cynically, that the older man could gain the confidence of John Lesbee—lull him, lead him on, delude him, destroy him.

Surreptitiously Lesbee examined the room. Control Room Below was a large square chamber adjoining the massive central engines. Its control board was a duplicate of the one on the bridge located at the top of the ship. The great vessel could be guided equally from either board, except that pre-emptive power was on the bridge. The officer of the watch was given the right to make Merit decisions in an emergency.

Lesbee made a quick mental calculation, and deduced that it was First Officer Miller's watch on the bridge. Miller was a staunch supporter of Browne. The man was probably watching them on one of his screens, ready to come to Browne's aid at a moment's notice.

A few minutes later. Lesbee listened thoughtfully as Browne read their joint communique over the intercom, designating him as ground captain. He found himself a little amazed, and considerably dismayed, at the absolute confidence the older man must feel about this own power and position on the ship. It was a big step, naming his chief rival to so high a rank.

Browne's next act was equally surprising. While they were still on the viewers, Browne reached over, clapped Lesbee affectionately on the shoulders and said to the watching audience:

"As you all know, John is the only direct descendant of the original captain. No one knows exactly what happened half a hundred years ago when my grandfather first took command. But I remember the old man always felt that only he understood how things should be. I doubt if he had any confidence in *any* young whippersnapper over whom he did not have complete control. I often felt that my father was

264

the victim rather than the beneficiary of my grandfather's temper and feelings of superiority."

Browne smiled engagingly. "Anyway, good people, though we can't unbreak the eggs that were broken then, we can certainly start healing the wounds, without—" his tone was suddenly firm—"negating the fact that my own training and experience make me the proper commander of the ship itself."

He broke off. "Captain Lesbee and I shall now jointly attempt to communicate with the captured intelligent life form from the planet below. You may watch, though we reserve the right to cut you off for good reason." He turned to Lesbee. "What do you think we should do first, John?"

Lesbee was in a dilemma. The first large doubt had come to him, the possibility that perhaps the other was sincere. The possibility was especially disturbing because in a few moments a part of his own plan would be revealed.

He sighed, and realized that there was no turning back at this stage. He thought: "We'll have to bring the entire madness out into the open, and only then can we begin to consider agreement as real."

Aloud, he said in a steady voice, "Why not bring the prisoner out where we can see him?"

As the tractor beam lifted Dzing out of the cage, and thus away from the energies that had suppressed his thought waves, the Karn telepathed to his contact on Alta III:

"Have been held in a confined space, the metal of which was energized against communication. I shall now attempt to perceive and evaluate the condition and performance of this ship—"

At that point, Browne reached over and clicked off the intercom. Having shut off the audience, he turned accusingly to Lesbee, and said, "Explain your failure to inform me that these beings communicated by telepathy."

The tone of his voice was threatening. There was a hint of angry color in his face.

It was the moment of discovery.

Lesbee hesitated, and then simply pointed out how precarious their relationship had been. He finished frankly, "I thought by keeping it a secret I might be able to stay alive a little longer, which was certainly not what you intended when you sent me out as an expendable."

Browne snapped, "But how did you hope to utilize?—" He stopped. "Never mind," he muttered.

Dzing was telepathing again:

"In many ways this is mechanically a very advanced type ship. Atomic energy drives are correctly installed. The automatic machinery performs magnificently. There is massive energy screen equipment, and they can put out a tractor beam to match anything we have that's mobile. But there is a wrongness in the energy flows of this ship, which I lack the experience to interpret. Let me furnish you some data . . ."

The data consisted of variable wave measurements, evidently—so Lesbee deducted—the wavelengths of the energy flows involved in the "wrongness."

He said in alarm at that point, "Better drop him into the cage while *we* analyze what he could be talking about."

Browne did so—as Dzing telepathed: "If what you suggest is true, then these beings are completely at our mercy—"

Cut off!

Browne was turning on the intercom. "Sorry I had to cut you good people off," he said. "You'll be interested to know that we have managed to tune in on the thought pulses of the prisoner and have intercepted his calls to someone on the planet below. This gives us an advantage." He turned to Lesbee. "Don't you agree?"

Browne visibly showed no anxiety, whereas Dzing's final statement flabbergasted Lesbee. ". . . *completely at our mercy. . .*" surely meant exactly that. He was staggered that Browne could have missed the momentous meaning.

Browne addressed him enthusiastically, "I'm excited by this telepathy! It's a marvelous short-cut to communication, if we could build up our own thought pulses. Maybe we could use the principle of the remote-control landing device which, as you know, can project human thoughts on a simple, gross level, where ordinary energies get confused by the intense field needed for the landing."

What interested Lesbee in the suggestion was that he had in his pocket a remote control for precisely such mechanically produced thought pulses. Unfortunately, the control was for the lifeboat. It probably would be advisable to tune the control to the ship landing system also. It was a problem he had thought of earlier, and now Browne had opened the way for an easy solution.

He held his voice steady as he said, "Captain, let me program those landing analogs while you prepare the film communication project. That way we can be ready for him either way."

Browne seemed to be completely trusting, for he agreed at once.

At Browne's direction, a film projector was wheeled in.

t was swiftly mounted on solid connections at one end of he room. The cameraman and Third Officer Mindel—who had come in with him—strapped themselves into two adjoining chairs attached to the projector, and were evidently ready.

While this was going on, Lesbee called various technical personnel. Only one technician protested. "But, John," he said, "that way we have a double control—with the lifeboat control having pre-emption over the ship. That's very unusual."

It was unusual. But it was the lifeboat control that was in his pocket where he could reach it quickly; and so he said adamantly, "Do you want to talk to Captain Browne? Do you want his okay?"

"No, no." The technician's doubts seemed to subside. "I heard you being named joint captain. You're the boss. It shall be done."

Lesbee put down the closed-circuit phone into which he had been talking, and turned. It was then he saw that the film was ready to roll, and that Brown had his fingers on the controls of the tractor beam. The older man stared at him questioningly.

"Shall I go ahead?" he asked.

At this penultimate moment, Lesbee had a qualm.

Almost immediately he realized that the only alternative to what Browne planned was that he reveal his own secret knowledge.

He hesitated, torn by doubts. Then: "Will you turn that off?" He indicated the intercom.

Browne said to the audience, "We'll bring you in again on this in a minute, good people." He broke the connection and gazed questioningly at Lesbee.

Whereupon Lesbee said in a low voice, "Captain, I should inform you that I brought the Karn aboard in the hope of using him against you."

"Well, that is a frank and open admission," the officer replied very softly.

"I mention this," said Lesbee, "because if you had similar ulterior motives, we should clear the air completely before proceeding with this attempt at communication."

A blossom of color spread from Browne's neck over his face. At last he said slowly, "I don't know how I can convince you, but I had no schemes."

Lesbee gazed at Browne's open countenance, and suddenly he realized that the officer was sincere. Browne had accepted the compromise. The solution of a joint captaincy was agreeable to him.

Sitting there, Lesbee experienced an enormous joy. Seconds went by before he realized what underlay the intense pleasurable excitement. It was simply the discovery that communication worked. You could tell your truth and get a hearing . . . if it made sense.

It seemed to him that his truth made a lot of sense. He was offering Browne peace aboard the ship. Peace at a price of course; but still peace. And in this severe emergency Browne recognized the entire validity of the solution.

So it was now evident to Lesbee.

Without further hesitation he told Browne that the creatures who had boarded the lifeboat, were robots—not alive at all.

Browne was nodding thoughtfully. Finally he said: "But I don't see how this could be utilized to take over the ship."

Lesbee said patiently, "As you know, sir, the remote landing control system includes five principal ideas which are projected very forcibly on the thought level. Three of these are for guidance—up, down and sideways. Intense magnetic fields, any one of which could partially jam a complex robot's thinking processes. The fourth and fifth are instructions to blast either up or down. The force of the blast depends on how far the control is turned on. Since the energy used is overwhelming those simple commands would take pre-emption over the robot. When that first one came aboard the lifeboat, I had a scan receiver—nondetectable—on him. This registered two power sources, one pointing forward, one backward, from the chest level. That's why I had him on his back when I brought him in here. But the fact is I could have had him tilted and pointing at a target, and activated either control four or five, thus destroying whatever was in the path of the resulting blast. Naturally, I took all possible precautions to make sure that this did not happen until you had indicated what you intended to do. One of these precautions would enable us to catch this creature's thoughts without—"

As he was speaking, he eagerly put his hand into his pocket, intending to show the older man the tiny on-off control device by which—when it was off—they would be able to read Dzing's thoughts without removing him from the cage.

He stopped short in his explanation, because an ugly expression had come suddenly into Browne's face.

The big man glanced at Third Officer Mindel. "Well, Dan," he said, "do you think that's it?"

Lesbee noticed with shock that Mindel had on sound amplifying earphones. He must have overheard every word that Browne and he had spoken to each other.

Mindel nodded. "Yes, Captain," he said. "I very definitely think he has now told us what we wanted to find out."

Lesbee grew aware that Browne had released himself from his acceleration safety belt and was stepping away from his seat. The officer turned and, standing very straight, said in a formal tone:

"Technician Lesbee, we have heard your admission of gross dereliction of duty, conspiracy to overthrow the lawful government of this ship, scheme to utilize alien creatures to destroy human beings, and confession of other unspeakable crimes. In this extremely dangerous situation, summary execution without formal trial is justified. I therefore sentence you to death and order Third Officer Dan Mindel to—"

He faltered, and came to a stop.

V

Two things had been happening as he talked, Lesbee squeezed the "off" switch of the cage control, an entirely automatic gesture, convulsive, a spasmodic movement, result of his dismay. It was a mindless gesture. So far as he knew consciously, freeing Dzing's thoughts had no useful possibility for him. His only real hope—as he realized almost immediately —was to get his other hand into his remaining coat pocket and with it manipulate the remote-control landing device, the secret of which he had so naively revealed to Browne.

The second thing that happened was that Dzing, released from mental control, telepathed:

"Free again—and this time of course permanently! I have just now activated by remote control the relays that will in a few moments start the engines of this ship, and I have naturally re-set the mechanism for controlling the rate of acceleration—"

His thoughts must have impinged progressively on Browne, for it was at that point that the officer paused uncertainly.

Dzing continued: "I verified your analysis. This vessel does not have the internal energy flows of an interstellar ship. These two-legged beings have therefore failed to achieve the Light Speed Effect which alone makes possible trans-light velocities. I suspect they have taken many generations to make this journey, are far indeed from their home base, and I'm sure I can capture them all."

Lesbee reached over, tripped on the intercom and yelled

269

at the screen: "All stations prepare for emergency acceleration! Grab anything!"

To Browne he shouted: "Get to your seat—*quick!*"

His actions were automatic responses to danger. Only after
the words were spoken did it occur to him that he had no interest in the survival of Captain Browne. And that in fact
the only reason the man was in danger was because he had
stepped away from his safety belt, so that Mindel's blaster
would kill Lesbee without damaging Browne.

Browne evidently understood his danger. He started toward the control chair from which he had released himself
only moments before. His reaching hands were still a foot
or more from it when the impact of Acceleration One stopped
him. He stood there trembling like a man who had struck an
invisible but palpable wall. The next instant Acceleration
Two caught him and thrust him on his back to the floor. He
began to slide toward the rear of the room, faster and faster,
and because he was quick and understanding he pressed the
palms of his hands and his rubber shoes hard against the
floor and so tried to slow the movement of his body.

Lesbee was picturing other people elsewhere in the ship
desperately trying to save themselves. He groaned, for the
commander's failure was probably being duplicated everywhere.

Even as he had that thought, Acceleration Three caught
Browne. Like a rock propelled by a catapult he shot toward
the rear wall. It was cushioned to protect human beings, and
so it reacted like rubber, bouncing him a little. But the stuff
had only momentary resilience.

Acceleration Four pinned Browne halfway into the cushioned wall. From its imprisoning depths, he managed a stran-
gled yell.

"Lesbee, put a tractor beam on me! Save me! I'll make
it up to you. I—"

Acceleration Five choked off the words.

The man's appeal brought momentary wonder to Lesbee.
He was amazed that Browne hoped for mercy . . . after
what had happened.

Browne's anguished words did produce one effect in him.
They reminded him that there was something he must do. He
forced his hand and his arm to the control board and fo-
cussed a tractor beam that firmly captured Third Officer Mindel and the cameraman. His intense effort was barely in time.
Acceleration followed acceleration, making movement impossible. The time between each surge of increased speed grew
longer. The slow minutes lengthened into what seemed an

hour, then many hours. Lesbee was held in his chair as if he were gripped by hands of steel. His eyes felt glassy; his body had long since lost all feeling.

He noticed something.

The rate of acceleration was different from what the original Tellier had prescribed long ago. The actual increase in forward pressure each time was less.

He realized something else. For a long time, no thoughts had come from the Karn.

Suddenly, he felt an odd shift in speed. A physical sensation of slight, very slight, angular movement accompanied the maneuver.

Slowly, the metal-like bands let go of his body. The numb feeling was replaced by the pricking as of thousands of tiny needles. Instead of muscle-compressing acceleration there was only a steady pressure.

It was the pressure that he had in the past equated with gravity.

Lesbee stirred hopefully, and when he felt himself move, realized what had happened. The artificial gravity had been shut off. Simultaneously, the ship had made a half turn within its outer shell. The drive power was now coming from below, a constant one gravity thrust.

At this late, late moment, he plunged his hand into the pocket which held the remote control for the pilotless landing mechanism—and activated it.

"That ought to turn on his thoughts," he told himself savagely.

But if Dzing was telepathing to his masters, it was no longer on the human thought level. So Lesbee concluded unhappily.

The ether was silent.

He now grew aware of something more. The ship smelled different: better, cleaner, purer.

Lesbee's gaze snapped over to the speed dials on the control board. The figures registering there were unbelievable. They indicated that the spaceship was traveling at a solid fraction of the speed of light.

Lesbee stared at the numbers incredulously. "We didn't have time!" he thought. "How could we go so fast so quickly —in hours only to near the speed of light!"

Sitting there, breathing hard, fighting to recover from the effects of that prolonged speed-up, he felt the fantastic reality of the universe. During all this slow century of flight through

271

space, the *Hope of Man* had had the potential for this vastly greater velocity.

He visualized the acceleration series so expertly programmed by Dzing as having achieved a shift to a new state of matter in motion. The "light speed effect," the Karn robot had called it.

"And Tellier missed it," he thought.

All those experiments the physicist had performed so painstakingly, and left a record of, had missed the great discovery.

Missed it! And so a shipload of human beings had wandered for generations through the black deeps of interstellar space.

Across the room Browne was climbing groggily to his feet. He muttered, ". . . Better get back to . . . control chair."

He had taken only a few uncertain steps when a realization seemed to strike him. He looked up then, and stared wildly at Lesbee. "Oh!" he said. The sound came from the gut level, a gasp of horrified understanding.

As he slapped a complex of tractor beams on Browne, Lesbee said, "That's right, you're looking at your enemy. Better start talking. We haven't much time."

Browne was pale now. But his mouth had been left free and so he was able to say huskily, "I did what any lawful government does in an emergency. I dealt with treason summarily, taking time only to find out what it consisted of."

Lesbee had had another thought, this time about Miller on the bridge. Hastily, he swung Browne over in front of him. "Hand me your blaster," he said. "Stock first."

He freed the other's arm, so that he could reach into the holster and take it out.

Lesbee felt a lot better when he had the weapon. But still another idea had come to him. He said harshly, "I want to lift you over to the cage, and I don't want First Officer Miller to interfere. Get that, *Mister* Miller!"

There was no answer from the screen.

Brown said uneasily, "Why over to the cage?"

Lesbee did not answer right away. Silently he manipulated the tractor beam control until Browne was in position. Having gotten him there, Lesbee hesitated. What bothered him was, why had the Karn's thought impulses ceased? He had an awful feeling that something was very wrong indeed.

He gulped, and said, "Raise the lid!"

Again, he freed Browne's arm. The big man reached over gingerly, unfastened the catch, and then drew back and glanced questioningly at Lesbee.

"Look inside!" Lesbee commanded.

Browne said scathingly, "You don't think for one second hat—" He stopped, for he was peering into the cage. He uttered a cry: "He's gone!"

VI

Lesbee discussed the disappearance with Browne.

It was an abrupt decision on his part to do so. The question of where Dzing might have got to was not something he should merely turn over in his own head.

He began by pointing at the dials from which the immense speed of the ship could be computed, and then, when that meaning was absorbed by the older man, said simply, "What happened? Where did he go? And how could we speed up to just under 186,000 miles a second in so short a time?"

He had lowered the big man to the floor, and now he took some of the tension from the tractor beam but did not release the power. Browne stood in apparent deep thought. Finally, he nodded. "All right," he said, "I know what happened."

"Tell me."

Browne changed the subject, said in a deliberate tone, "What are you going to do with me?"

Lesbee stared at him for a moment unbelievingly. "You're going to withhold this information?" he demanded.

Browne spread his hands. "What else can I do? Till I know my fate, I have nothing to lose."

Lesbee suppressed a strong impulse to rush over and strike his prisoner. He said finally, "In your judgment is this delay dangerous?"

Browne was silent, but a bead of sweat trickled down his cheek. "I have nothing to lose," he repeated.

The expression in Lesbee's face must have alarmed him, for he went on quickly, "Look, there's no need for you to conspire any more. What you really want is to go home, isn't it? Don't you see, with this new method of acceleration, we can make it to Earth in a few *months!*"

He stopped. He seemed momentarily uncertain.

Lesbee snapped angrily, "Who are you trying to fool? Months! We're a dozen light years in actual distance from Earth. You mean years, not months."

Browne hesitated then: "All right, a few years. But at least not a lifetime. So if you'll promise not to scheme against me further, I'll promise—"

"*You'll* promise!" Lesbee spoke savagely. He had been taken aback by Browne's instant attempt at blackmail. But the mo-

273

mentary sense of defeat was gone. He knew with a stubborn rage that he would stand for no nonsense.

He said in an uncompromising voice, "Mister Browne, twenty seconds after I stop speaking, you start talking. If you don't, I'll batter you against these walls. I mean it!"

Browne was pale. "Are you going to kill me? That's all I want to know. Look—" his tone was urgent—"we don't have to fight any more. We can go home. Don't you see? The long madness is just about over. Nobody has to die."

Lesbee hesitated. What the big man said was at least partly true. There was an attempt here to make twelve years sound like twelve days, or at most twelve weeks. But the fact was, it *was* a short period compared to the century-long journey which, at one time, had been the only possibility.

He thought: "Am I going to kill him?"

It was hard to believe that he would, under the circumstances. All right. If not death, then what? He sat there uncertain. The vital seconds went by, and he could see no solution. He thought finally, in desperation: "I'll have to give in for the moment. Even a minute thinking about this is absolutely crazy."

He said aloud in utter frustration, "I'll promise you this. If you can figure out how I can feel safe in a ship commanded by you I'll give your plan consideration. And now, mister, start talking."

Browne nodded. "I accept that promise," he said. "What we've run into here is the Lorenz-Fitzgerald Contraction Theory. Only it's not a theory any more. We're living the reality of it."

Lesbee argued, "But it only took us a few hours to get to the speed of light."

Browne said, "As we approach light speed, space foreshortens and time compresses. What seemed like a few hours would be days in normal time and space."

What Browne explained then was different rather than difficult. Lesbee had to blink his mind to shut the glare of his old ideas and habits of thought, so that the more subtle shades of super-speed phenomena could shine through into his awareness.

The time compression—as Browne explained it—was gradational. The rapid initial series of accelerations were obviously designed to pin down the personnel of the ship. Subsequent increments would be according to what was necessary to attain the ultra-speed finally achieved.

Since the drive was still on, it was clear that some resistance

274

was being encountered, perhaps from the fabric of space it-elf.

It was no time to discuss technical details. Lesbee ac-epted the remarkable reality and said quickly, "Yes, but vhere is Dzing?"

"My guess," said Browne, "is that he did not come along."

"How do you mean?"

"The space-time foreshortening did not affect him."

"But—" Lesbee began blankly.

"Look," said Browne harshly, "don't ask me how he did t. My picture is, he stayed in the cage till after the accelera-ion stopped. Then, in a leisurely fashion, he released himself rom the electrically locked manacles, climbed out, and went off to some other part of the ship. He wouldn't have to hurry since by this time he was operating at a rate of, say, five hundred times faster than our living pace."

Lesbee said, "But that means he's been out there for hours —his time. What's he been up to?"

Browne admitted that he had no answer for that.

"But you can see," he pointed out anxiously, "that I meant what I said about going back to Earth. We have no business in this part of space. These beings are far ahead of us sci-entifically."

His purpose was obviously to persuade. Lesbee thought: "He's back to *our* fight. That's more important to him than any damage the real enemy is causing."

A vague recollection came of the things he had read about the struggle for power throughout Earth history. How men in-trigued for supremacy while vast hordes of the invader bat-tered down the gates. Browne was a true spiritual descend-ant of all those mad people.

Slowly, Lesbee turned and faced the big board. What was baffling to him was, what could you do against a being who moved five hundred times as fast as you did?

VII

He had a sudden sense of awe, a picture . . . At any given instant Dzing was a blur. A spot of light. A movement so rapid that, even as the gaze lighted on him, he was gone to the other end of the ship—and back.

Yet Lesbee knew it took time to traverse the great ship from end to end. Twenty, even twenty-five minutes, was nor-mal walking time for a human being going along the corridor known as Center A.

It would take the Karn a full six seconds there and back.

In its way that was a significant span of time, but after Lesbee had considered it for a moment he felt appalled.

What could they do against a creature who had so great a time differential in his favor?

From behind him, Browne said, "why don't you use against him that remote landing control system that you set up with my permission?"

Lesbee confessed: "I did that, as soon as the acceleration ceased. But he must have been—back—in the faster time by then."

"That wouldn't make any difference," said Browne.

"Eh!" Lesbee was startled.

Browne parted his lips evidently intending to explain, and then he closed them again. Finally he said, "Make sure the intercom is off."

Lesbee did so. But he was realizing that Browne was up to something again. He said, and there was rage in his tone, "I don't get it, and you do. Is that right."

"Yes," said Browne. He spoke deliberately, but he was visibly suppressing excitement. "I know how to defeat this creature. That puts me in a bargaining position."

Lesbee's eyes were narrowed to slits. "Damn you, no bargain. Tell me, or else!"

Browne said, "I'm not really trying to be difficult. You either have to kill me, or come to some agreement. I want to know what that agreement is, because of course I'll do it."

Lesbee said, "I think we ought to have an election."

"I agree!" Browne spoke instantly. "You set it up." He broke off. "And now release me from these tractors and I'll show you the neatest space-time trick you've ever seen, and that'll be the end of Dzing."

Lesbee gazed at the man's face, saw there the same openness of countenance, the same frank honesty that had preceded the execution order, and he thought, "What can he do?"

He considered many possibilities, and thought finally, desperately: "He's got the advantage over me of superior knowledge—the most undefeatable weapon in the world. The only thing I can really hope to use against it in the final issue is *my* knowledge of a multitude of technician-level details."

But—what could Browne do against Lesbee?

He said unhappily to the other, "Before I free you, I want to lift you over to Mindel. When I do, you get his blaster for me."

"Sure," said Browne casually.

276

A few moments later he handed Mindel's gun over to Lesbee. So that wasn't it.

Lesbee thought: "There's Miller on the bridge—can it be that Miller flashed him a ready signal when my back was turned to the board?"

Perhaps, like Browne, Miller had been temporarily incapacitated during the period of acceleration. It was vital that he find out Miller's present capability.

Lesbee tripped the intercom between the two boards. The rugged, lined face of the first officer showed large on the screen. Lesbee could see the outlines of the bridge behind the man and, beyond, the starry blackness of space. Lesbee said courteously, "Mr. Miller, how did you make out during the acceleration?"

"It caught me by surprise, Captain. I really got a battering. I think I was out for a while. But I'm all right now."

"Good," said Lesbee. "As you probably heard, Captain Browne and I have come to an agreement, and we are now going to destroy the creature that is loose on the ship. Stand by!"

Cynically, he broke the connection.

Miller was there all right, waiting. But the question was still, what could Miller do? The answer of course was that Miller could pre-empt. And—Lesbee asked himself—what could *that* do?

Abruptly, it seemed to him, he had the answer.

It was the technician's answer that he had been mentally straining for.

He now understood Browne's plan. They were waiting for Lesbee to let down his guard for a moment. Then Miller would pre-empt, cut off the tractor beam from Browne and seize Lesbee with it.

For the two officers it was vital that Lesbee not have time to fire the blaster at Browne. Lesbee thought: "It's the only thing they can be worried about. The truth is, there's nothing else to stop them."

The solution was, Lesbee realized with a savage glee, to let the two men achieve their desire. But first—

"Mr. Browne," he said quietly, "I think you should give your information. If I agree that it is indeed the correct solution, I shall release you and we shall have an election. You and I will stay right here till the election is over."

Browne said, "I accept your promise. The speed of light is a constant, and does not change in relation to moving objects. That would also apply to electromagnetic fields."

Lesbee said, "Then Dzing was affected by the remote-control device I turned on."

"Instantly," said Browne. "He never got a chance to do anything. How much power did you use?"

"Only first stage," said Lesbee. "But the machine-driven thought pulses in that would interfere with just about every magnetic field in his body. He couldn't do another coherent thing."

Browne said in a hushed tone, "It's got to be. He'll be out of control in one of the corridors, completely at our mercy." He grinned. "I told you I knew how to defeat him—because, of course, he was already defeated."

Lesbee considered that for a long moment, eyes narrowed. He realized that he accepted the explanation, but that he had preparations to make, and quickly—before Browne got suspicious of his delay.

He turned to the board and switched on the intercom. "People," he said, "strap yourselves in again. Help those who were injured to do the same. We may have another emergency. You have several minutes, I think, but don't waste any of them."

He cut off the intercom, and he activated the closed-circuit intercom of the technical stations. He said urgently, "Special instruction to Technical personnel. Report anything unusual, particularly if strange thought forms are going through your mind."

He had an answer to that within moments after he finished speaking. A man's twangy voice came over: "I keep thinking I'm somebody named Dzing, and I'm trying to report to my owners. Boy, am I incoherent!"

"Where is this?"

"D—4—19."

Lesbee punched the buttons that gave them a TV view of that particular ship location. Almost immediately he spotted a shimmer near the floor.

After a moment's survey he ordered a heavy-duty mobile blaster brought to the corridor. By the time its colossal energies ceased, Dzing was only a darkened area on the flat surface.

While these events were progressing, Lesbee had kept one eye on Browne and Mindel's blaster firmly gripped in his left hand. Now he said, "Well, sir, you certainly did what you promised. Wait a moment while I put this gun away, and then I'll carry out my part of the bargain."

He started to do so, then, out of pity, paused.

278

He had been thinking in the back of his mind about what Browne had said earlier: that the trip to Earth might only take a few months. The officer had backed away from that statement, but it had been bothering Lesbee ever since.

If it were true, then it was indeed a fact that nobody need die!

He said quickly, "What was your reason for saying that the journey home would only take—well—less than a year?"

"It's the tremendous time compression," Browne explained eagerly. "The distance as you pointed out is over 12 light-years. But with a time ratio of 3, 4, or 500 to one, we'll make it in less than a month. When I first started to say that, I could see that the figures were incomprehensible to you in your tense mood. In fact, I could scarcely believe them myself."

Lesbee said, staggered, "We can get back to Earth in a couple of weeks—my God!" He broke off, said urgently, "Look, I accept you as commander. We don't need an election. The status quo is good enough for any short period of time. Do you agree?"

"Of course," said Browne. "That's the point I've been trying to make."

As he spoke, his face was utterly guileless.

Lesbee gazed at that mask of innocence, and he thought hopelessly: "What's wrong? Why isn't he really agreeing? Is it because he doesn't want to lose his command so quickly?"

Sitting there, unhappily fighting for the other's life, he tried to place himself mentally in the position of the commander of a vessel, tried to look at the prospect of a return to view. It was hard to picture such a reality. But presently it seemed to him that he understood.

He said gently, feeling his way, "It would be kind of a shame to return without having made a successful landing anywhere. With this new speed, we could visit a dozen sun systems, and still get home in a year."

The look that came into Browne's face for a fleeting moment told Lesbee that he had penetrated to the thought in the man's mind.

The next instant, Browne was shaking his head vigorously. "This is no time for side excursions," he said. "We'll leave explorations of new star systems to future expeditions. The people of this ship have served their term. We go straight home."

Browne's face was now completely relaxed. His blue eyes shone with truth and sincerity.

There was nothing further that Lesbee could say. The gulf between Browne and himself could not be bridged.

The commander had to kill his rival, so that he might finally return to Earth and report that the mission of the *Hope of Man* was accomplished.

VIII

In the most deliberate fashion Lesbee shoved the blaster into the inner pocket of his coat. Then, as if he were being careful, he used the tractor beam to push Browne about four feet away. There he set him down, released him from the beam, and—with the same deliberateness—drew his hand away from the tractor controls. Thus he made himself completely defenseless.

It was the moment of vulnerability.

Browne leaped at him, yelling: "Miller—pre-empt!"

First Officer Miller obeyed the command of his captain.

What happened then, only Lesbee, the technician with a thousand bits of detailed knowledge, expected.

For years it had been observed that when Control Room Below took over from Bridge, the ship speeded up slightly. And when Bridge took over from Control Room Below, the ship slowed instantly by the same amount—in each instance, something less than half a mile an hour.

The two boards were not completely synchronized. The technicians often joked about it, and Lesbee had once read an obscure technical explanation for the discrepancy. It had to do with the impossibility of ever getting two metals refined to the same precision of internal structure.

It was the age-old story of, no two objects in the universe are alike. But in times past, the differential had meant nothing. It was a technical curiosity, an interesting phenomenon of the science of metallurgy, a practical problem that caused machinists to curse good-naturedly when technicians like Lesbee required them to make a replacement part.

Unfortunately for Browne, the ship was now traveling near the speed of light.

His strong hands, reaching towards Lesbee's slighter body, were actually touching the latter's arm when the momentary deceleration occurred as Bridge took over. The sudden slow-down was at a much faster rate than even Lesbee expected. The resistance of space to the forward movement of the ship must be using up more engine power than he had realized; it was taking a lot of thrust to maintain a one gravity acceleration.

The great vessel slowed about 150 miles per hour in the space of a second.

Lesbee took the blow of that deceleration partly against his back, partly against one side—for he had half-turned to defend himself from the bigger man's attack.

Browne, who had nothing to grab on to, was flung forward at the full 150 miles per hour. He struck the control board with an audible thud, stuck to it as if he were glued there; and then, when the adjustment was over—when the *Hope of Man* was again speeding along at one gravity—his body slid down the face of the board, and crumpled into a twisted position on the rubberized dais.

His uniform was discolored. As Lesbee watched, blood seeped through and dripped to the floor.

"Are you going to hold an election?" Tellier asked.

The big ship had turned back under Lesbee's command, and had picked up his friends. The lifeboat itself, with the remaining Karn still aboard, was put into an orbit around Alta III and abandoned.

The two young men were sitting now in the Captain's cabin.

After the question was asked, Lesbee leaned back in his chair, and closed his eyes. He didn't need to examine his total resistance to the suggestion. He had already savored the feeling that command brought.

Almost from the moment of Browne's death, he had observed himself having the same thoughts that Browne had voiced—among many others, the reasons why elections were not advisable aboard a spaceship. He waited now while Eleesa, one of his three wives—she being the younger of the two young widows of Browne—poured wine for them, and went softly out. Then he laughed grimly.

"My good friend," he said, "we're all lucky that time is so compressed at the speed of light. At 500-times compression, any further exploration we do will require only a few months, or years at most. And so I don't think we can afford to take the chance of defeating at an election the only person who understands the details of the new acceleration method. Until I decide exactly how much exploration we shall do, I shall keep our speed capabilities a secret. But I did, and do, think one other person should know where I have this information documented. Naturally, I selected First Officer Tellier."

"Thank you, sir," the youth said. But he was visibly thoughtful as he sipped his wine. He went on finally, "Captain, I think you'd feel a lot better if you held an election. I'm sure you could win it."

Lesbee laughed tolerantly, shook his head. "I'm afraid you

don't understand the dynamics of government," he said. "There's no record in history of a person who actually had control, handing it over."

He finished with the casual confidence of absolute power. "I'm not going to be presumptuous enough to fight a precedent like that!"

THE REFLECTED MEN

I

TIME, 5:10 P.M. *The crystal was less than fifteen minutes from reactivation.*

To Edith Price, the well-dressed young man who came into her library was typical of the summer visitors to Harkdale. They lived apart from the townspeople, of whom she was now one. She wrote down his name—Seth Mitchell. And, assuming he wanted a temporary library card, she pushed the application form across the counter toward him.

It was only when he impatiently thrust it back that she actually for the first time listened to what he was saying.

Then she said, "Oh, what you want is a piece of crystal."

"Exactly," he said. "I want returned to me a small stone I presented to the museum section of the library some years ago."

Edith shook her head. "I'm sorry. The museum is being reorganized. It's closed to the public. I'm sure no action will be taken about anything in it until the job is done and even then Miss Davis, the librarian, will have to authorize any disposition of the exhibits. Today is her day off."

"How long will it take—to reorganize the museum?"

"Oh, several weeks."

The effect of her words on the man—clean-cut and typical of the well-dressed, successful men she had known in New York—startled her. He paled, mumbled something indistinguishable and when he turned away it was as if some of the life had gone out of him.

Staring at the retreating figures of library patrons was not something Edith Price was normally motivated to do. But his reaction was so extreme that she watched him as he walked unsteadily toward the main entrance of the library. At the door a squat, thickly built man joined him. The two conversed briefly, then walked out together. Moments later, through a window, Edith caught a glimpse of them entering a new Cadillac. Seth Mitchell slid in behind the wheel.

The costly automobile, Seth Mitchell's overreaction and the fact that another man was involved made intriguing what was probably a minor incident. Edith slipped from her stool, making suitable gestures to Miss Tilsit. Quite openly she secured the key to the womens' rest room as she covertly palmed the key to the museum room.

A few moments later she was examining the display of stones.

There were about thirty altogether. According to the sign beside them the collection was the result of a drive among local boys to find valuable minerals and gems. Edith had no difficulty in locating the one the young man had wanted. A faded card under it announced: "Donated by Seth Mitchell and Billy Bingham."

She slid back the side of the case, reached in carefully and took out the crystal. It was obvious to her that very little discrimination had been used in the selection. The forces that had fashioned this stone seemed to have been too impatient. The craftsmanship was uneven. The result was a stone about two and a half inches long by one and a half inches wide, maximum; a brownish, rocklike thing which, though faceted, did not reflect light well. It was by far the dullest of the stones in the display.

Gazing down at the drab, worthless stone, Edith thought: *Why don't I just take it to his hotel after work tonight and bypass all the red tape?*

Meaning Miss Davis, her enemy.

Decisively, she removed the names of the two donors from the case. After all these years the label was stuck on poorly and the yellowed paper tore to shreds. She was about to slip the stone into her pocket, when she sadly realized she was wearing *that* dress—the one without pockets.

Oh, damn! she thought cheerfully.

Since the stone was too big to conceal in her hand she carried it through the back stack corridors and was about to toss it into the special wastebasket used for heavy debris— when she noticed that a broken flowerpot half full of dirt was also in the basket. Beside the dirt was a paper bag.

She needed only seconds to slip the crystal into the bag, place dirt on top of it and shove the bag down into the basket. She usually had the job of locking up the building, so it would be no problem to pick up the bag at that time and take it with her.

Edith returned to her desk.

And the stone began at once to utilize the sand in the dirt on top of it, thus resuming a pattern that had been suspended for twenty-five years. During the rest of the evening, and in fact all through that night, all the possible Seth Mitchells on earth remembered their childhoods. The majority merely smiled or shrugged or stirred in their sleep. Most of those who lived outside the western hemisphere in distant time zones presently resumed their normal activities.

But a few, everywhere, recalling the crystal, could not quite let the memory go.

During her first idle moment after filching the stone Edith leaned over to ask Miss Tilsit, "Who is Seth Mitchell?"

Tilsit was a tall, too-thin blonde with horn-rimmed glasses behind which gleamed unusually small but alert gray eyes. Edith had discovered that Tilsit had a vast, even though superficial, knowledge of everything that had ever happened in Harkdale.

"There were two of them," said Tilsit. "Two boys. Billy Bingham and Seth Mitchell."

Thereupon, with visible relish, Tilsit told the story of the disappearance of Billy twenty-five years earlier, when he and his chum, Seth Mitchell, were only twelve years old.

Tilsit finished: "Seth claimed they had been fighting over a piece of bright stone they had found. He swore that they were at least fifty feet from the cliff that overlooks the lake at that point and he insisted Billy didn't drown—which is what everyone else believed. What confused the situation was that Billy's body was never recovered."

As she listened to the account, Edith tried to put together the past and the present. She couldn't imagine why an adult Seth Mitchell would want a reminder of such an unhappy experience. Still, men were funny. That she knew, after waiting five years for a worthwhile male to come along and find her. So far she seemed to be as well hidden and unsearched for in Harkdale as in New York.

Tilsit was speaking again. "Kind of odd, what happens to people. Seth Mitchell was so crushed by his friend's death that he just became a sort of shadow human being. He's got a farm out toward Abbotsville."

Edith said sharply, "You mean Seth Mitchell became a farmer?"

"That's the story."

Edith said nothing more, but made a mental note that perhaps Tilsit was not as good a source of local information as she had formerly believed. Whatever Mitchell was, he hadn't looked like a farmer. She had to go to check out some books at that point, so the thought and the conversation ended.

A few minutes after nine-thirty, Edith parked her car across the street from the entrance to the motel in which—after some cruising around—she had spotted Seth Mitchell's distinctive gold Cadillac.

It was quite dark where she waited under a tree. But even in the secure darkness, she could feel her heart thumping and the hot flush in her cheeks.

Why am I doing this?

She knew a self-critical suspicion that she might be hoping the adventure would end in a summer romance. Which was pretty ridiculous for a woman twenty-seven years old, who—if she shifted her tactic from waiting to pursuing—ought to concentrate cold-bloodedly on genuine husband material.

Her self-examination ended abruptly. From where she sat she could see the door of the cabin beside which the Cadillac was parked. The door had opened. Silhouetted in the light from the interior was the short, squat man she had seen with Mitchell that afternoon. As Edith involuntarily held her breath, the man came out and closed the door behind him.

He walked to the motel office and presently emerged again, stood for a moment and then walked rapidly toward the business section of Harkdale, only minutes away.

And only minutes back, she thought glumly.

Watching him, her motivation dimmed. Somehow, she had not considered the short, heavy-set man as being really associated with Seth Mitchell.

Defeated, she stared her motor. As she drove home she suddenly felt degraded, not by what she had done but by what she suspected she had intended to do.

What her future path should be was not clear to her. But not this way, she told herself firmly.

Arrived at her apartment, Edith shoved the bag containing the crystal into the cupboard under her sink, ate apathetically and went to bed.

The squat man returned to the motel scowling. "The stone wasn't there. I searched the whole museum," he told Seth Mitchell, who lay on one of the beds, gagged and bound.

Mitchell watched uneasily as the other untied his feet. The man said impatiently, "I've been thinking about you. Maybe

285

the best thing is just to drive you back to New York or kill you here. Once I get away, the police will never find me again."

He removed the gag. Mitchell drew a deep breath.

"Look," he protested, "I won't even go near the police—"

He stopped, his mind once more blank and afraid, and choked back a surge of grief. The possibility that he might be killed was an idea that his brain could contemplate only for a few moments.

The squat man had come up to him in his office parking lot at noon that day, smiling deceptively, a short man—not more than five-four—and stocky. He had looked, in his grayness, like an Arab in an American business suit.

He had asked, "Where is the crystal you and Billy Bingham found?"

What might have happened if Seth had answered instantly was, of course, now impossible to guess. But he had not immediately remembered the crystal, so he had shaken his head.

Whereupon the stocky man had shown him a gun. Under its threat Seth had driven to Harkdale, had shown the stranger the ledge beside Lake Naragang where he and Billy had fought. And it was there, on the spot, that he had recalled the crystal; and so he had reluctantly gone to the library, aware of the weapon, trained on him all the while he had talked to the young woman at the desk.

Abruptly remembering that conversation, Seth said desperately, "Maybe that woman librarian—"

"Maybe," said the other, noncommittally.

He untied Seth's hands and stepped back, motioning with the gun. They went out to the car and drove off.

As they came to the lake the man said, "Pull over." After Seth complied, the shot rang out and the murder was done.

The killer dragged the body to a cliff overlooking the lake, tied rocks to it and dumped it into the deep water below.

He actually drove on to New York, left the car in Seth's parking lot and, after spending the night in New York, prepared to return to Harkdale.

During that night Edith Price slept restlessly, and dreamed that all possible Edith Prices marched past her bed. Only half a dozen of those Ediths were married and even in her dream that shocked her.

Worse, there was a long line of Edith Prices who ranged from fat to blowsy to downright shifty-eyed and mentally ill. However, several of the Ediths had a remarkable high-energy look and that was reassuring.

She woke to the sound of the phone ringing.

The library caretaker said, "Hey, Miss Price, better get down here. Somebody broke in last night."

Edith had a strange, unreal feeling.

She asked, "Broke into the library?"

"Yep. Biggest mess is in the museum. Whoever it was musta thought some of the stones in there were the real stuff. They're scattered all over the floor."

II

To Edith Price, the lean young man in overalls was just another inarticulate farmer.

She wrote down his name—Seth Mitchell. A moment went by as the name hit her. She looked up.

The haunted face that stared back at her had been burned by sun and wind. Its cheeks were gaunt. The eyes were sick. Nevertheless, the man bore a sensational resemblance to the Seth Mitchell of yesterday, it seemed to Edith.

She thought, a light dawning: *This is the Seth Mitchell Tilsit knew about . . .*

There had to be a Mitchell clan, with cousins and such, who were look-alikes.

Her mind was still fumbling over the possibilities when she realized the import of the words he had mumbled.

Edith echoed, "A stone? A crystal you presented to the library museum twenty-five years ago?"

He nodded. Edith compressed her lips.

All right, let's get to the bottom of this . . .

During the moments of her confusion the man had taken a bill out of his billfold. As he held it out to her she saw that it was twenty dollars.

She had recovered her self-control and now said conversationally, "That's a lot of money for a worthless rock."

"It's the one I want," he muttered. She didn't hear several words that followed but then he said clearly, ". . . the time Billy disappeared."

A silence fell while Edith absorbed the impact of the notion that here indeed was the original Seth Mitchell.

"I've heard about Billy," she said finally. "A very unusual incident."

Seth Mitchell said, "I yelled at him to get away and he vanished." He spoke tautly. His eyes were an odd, discolored gray from remembered shock. He spoke again: "We both grabbed at it. Then he was gone."

He seemed only dimly aware of her presence. He went on,

287

and it was as if he were talking to himself: "It was so shiny. Not like it became later. It went all drab and nobody would believe me."

He paused. Then, intently: "All these years I've been thinking. I've been awful slow to see the truth. But last night it came to me. What else could have made Billy disappear when I called him? What else but the stone?"

Edith decided uneasily that this was a problem for a psychiatrist, not a librarian. It struck her that the simplest solution would be to give this Seth Mitchell the worthless rock he wanted.

But of course that would have to be carefully done. Her one indiscretion so far had been her questioning of Tilsit the day before about Seth Mitchell. Throughout the police investigation of the breaking and entering of the library museum she had maintained a careful silence about her own involvement.

So the sooner she got rid of the stone the better.

"If you'll give me your address," she requested gently, "I'll ask the head librarian and perhaps she'll get in touch with you."

The address he reluctantly gave her was a rural route out of Abbotsville.

She watched him then, wondering a little, as he shuffled off to the door and outside.

On her way home that night, Edith drove by way of the motel. The gold Cadillac was gone.

She had her usual late dinner. Then, after making sure the apartment door was locked, she took the paper bag from under the sink—and noticed at once, uneasily, that there was less dirt in the bag.

A momentary fear came to her that the stone would be gone. She spread a newspaper and hastily emptied the bag, dirt and all, onto it. As the earth tumbled out a brilliance of color flashed at her.

Wonderingly she picked up the beautiful gem.

"But it's impossible," she whispered. "That was dull. This is—beautiful!"

It glittered in her hand. The purple color was alive, as if thousands of moving parts turned and twisted inside the stone. Here and there in its depths a finger of light stirred up a nest of scarlet fire. The crisscross of color and flame flickered so brightly that Edith felt visually stunned.

She held it up against the light—and saw a design inside. Somebody had cut a relief map of the solar system into the interior of the stone, and had colored it. It was quite a good example—it seemed to Edith—of the cutter's art. The purple and red over-all effect seemed to derive from the play of light through the coloring of the tiny "sun" and its family of planets.

She took the stone back to the sink. There was a fantasy in her mind, she realized, in which she pictured the jewel as having magic powers. Remembering what the farmer Seth Mitchell had said about his having yelled at Billy Bingham in the presence of the stone . . . maybe the sound of a human voice would have an effect . . .

She tried speaking.

Nothing happened. The picture remained unchanged. She spelled words, articulating each letter.

Nothing.

She ran the gamut of sounds possible to her own voice from a low contralto to a ridiculously piercing soprano—nothing.

Once more she noticed the design inside and held the stone up against the light to see it better. She was visually tracing the outline of the solar system in the crystal when she had a sudden thought and, with abrupt determination, said in a clear voice: "Billy Bingham—the boy—I want him back—now!"

After she had spoken, during the silent moments that followed, she felt progressively foolish.

Of the long-missing Billy there was no sign.

Thank God; she thought breathlessly.

Edith rose early the next morning; her mind was made up. It was time she got rid of something that was threatening to undermine her good sense.

As she took the crystal out of the flowerpot, she saw that the interior scene had changed. It was now a human body outlined in purple and red points of light.

The outline, she saw presently, was actually extremely detailed, showing the bone structure and the principal organs. There was even a faint glow which suffused the shape, suggesting a fine mask of nerves and blood vessels.

She was examining it absorbedly when she abruptly realized what she was doing.

Firmly, she put the stone into a small box, filled it with new soil—crystals, she had read, needed nutrients—wrapped it and addressed it to Seth Mitchell, Rural Route 4, Abbotsville.

Shortly she was driving to the post office. It was not until after she had mailed the package that her first realization came that she had done it again. Once more she had acted on impulse.

Too late, the cautioning thought came: Suppose Seth Mitchell wrote the library a note of thanks. It would be impossible for Edith to explain how a romantic compulsion had motivated her to steal the crystal—and how, in the light of later events, her only desire had become to dispose of the evidence.

Why don't I just get on the next bus to New York and leave this crazy little town forever?

The moment was extremely depressing. She remembered an endless series of wrong decisions in her life. She sat there in her car at the curb and thought of her first young man at college. The first, that is, who had been truly hers. She had lost him through an impulse: she had been caught by the God-is-dead-so-now-you're-God movement. In the movement what you did to other people no longer mattered—you never had to feel guilty.

If I hadn't joined the guilt-free generation, right now I would be Mrs. Richard Staples . . .

The realization reminded her of her dream of the multitude of Edith Prices and the unique remembrance escalated her out of her apathy. What an odd concept. She laughed involuntarily, and thought that sending the crystal to the least of all possible Seth Mitchells had not been good sense.

Thinking about that, her fear faded. How funny! And what an odd dream to have had.

How could one ever know what way was best, what decision, what philosophy, how much exercise? And, best for what?

Edith was already at her desk in the library when Tilsit came in with the look on her face. In her six months in Harkdale, Edith had come to recognize Tilsit's expression of: *I've got special information.*

"Did you see the paper, Edith?"

Edith presumed the paper referred to was the *Harkdale Inquirer,* a four-page daily. She herself still read the *New York Times,* though she loyally subscribed to the local sheet. She had not read today's *Inquirer,* however, and said so.

"Remember asking me the other day about a man called Seth Mitchell?" Tilsit asked.

Edith remembered only to well but she put on a blank face.

Tilsit unfolded the paper in her hands and held it up. The headline was:

Edith reached automatically and Tilsit handed the paper to her. Edith read:

A 12-year old boy staggered out of the brush near Lake Naragang shortly after ten P.M. last night and tried to enter the house where Billy Bingham lived twenty-five years ago. The present tenant, John Hildeck, a carpenter, took the bewildered youngster to the police station. From there he was transported to the hospital.

That was as far as Edith read. Her body bent to one side, her arms flopped limply. She stooped over and the floor crashed into her.

When she came out of her faint on the cot in the rest room, the remembrance was still there, bright and hard and improbable, of how she had commanded the crystal to bring back Billy Bingham—somewhere between nine and ten the previous night.

III

Miami. The Seth Mitchell in that singing city had a private vocabulary in which he called God (or, as he sometimes thought of Him, Nature or Fate). The Musician. Within this exclusive terminology Seth's own life had been tuneful and the music a symphony—or at least a concerto.

Somebody up there evidently regarded him as a suitable instrument.

For he had money, girl friends, a fabulous career as a gambler on the edge of the underworld—all without restrictions, for his orchestra was well disciplined and responsive to his baton. Not bad for a small-town boy who had not learned the melodies of city life until he was past twenty.

But now, suddenly, The Musician had sounded a sour note.

Mitchell had in his hand the *Harkdale Inquirer* containing the account of the return of Billy Bingham.

He studied the newspaper's photograph of a frightened boy about twelve years old. The subject looked like Billy Bingham—and didn't. Mitchell was surprised that he wasn't sure. The *Inquirer* apologized for having lost its photocut of the real Billy, and explained that Billy's parents had moved —to Texas, it was believed. No one knew precisely where.

The news story concluded: "The only other person who

might be able to identify the claimant is Seth Mitchell, Billy's boyhood chum. Mitchell's present address is unknown."

Mitchell thought sarcastically that the *Inquirer* ought to examine its out-of-state subscription list.

The next day as he walked into room 312 of the Harkdale Hospital, he saw the youngster in bed put down his magazine and look up.

Mitchell said with a reassuring smile, "Billy, you don't have to worry about me. I'm here as your friend."

The boy said uneasily, "That's what the big man told me, and then he got nasty."

Mitchell didn't ask who the big man was. A chair stood near the bed. He drew it up, and said gently, "Billy, what seems to have happened to you is almost like a fairy story. But the most important thing is that you mustn't worry."

Billy bit his lip and a tear rolled down his cheek. "They're treating me as if I'm lying. The big man said I'd be put in jail if I didn't tell the truth."

Mitchell's mind leaped back to the days when he had been questioned by just such impatient individuals about the disappearance of Billy. His lips tightened.

He said, "Nothing like that is going to happen to you if I can help it. But I'd like to ask you a few questions that maybe nobody else thought of. You don't have to answer if you don't want to. How does that strike you?"

"Okay."

Mitchell took that for a go-ahead signal. "What kind of clothes was Seth wearing?"

"Brown corduroy pants and a gray shirt."

Reality rather than the boy's answer gave Mitchell his first disappointment. He had hoped the description would jog his memory. It didn't. He was unable to recall what particular pair of ragged trousers he had worn on that distant day of Billy's disappearance.

"You wore corduroys also?" It was a shot in the dark.

"They're in there." The boy pointed at the chest in one corner.

Mitchell stood up, opened the indicated drawer and lifted out a skimpy pair of cheap corduroys. He examined them shamefacedly but with an eye to detail. He put them back finally, disappointed. The identifying label had been torn off. He couldn't remember ever having seen them before.

Twenty-five years, he thought drearily. The time was like a thick veil with a few tattered holes in it. Through the holes he could catch glimpses of his past, instants out of his life, each one illuminated because it had once had some parcular momentary impact—none was fully visible in context.

'Billy—" Mitchell came back to his chair, intent—"you mentioned trying to grab a shining stone. Where did you first ee it?"

"On the ledge. There's a path that comes up from the lake."

"Had you come up that way before?"

The other shook his head. "A few times when it was cold. Usually Seth and I liked to stay near the water."

Mitchell nodded. He remembered that. "This bright stone ou saw—how big was it?"

"Oh, it was big."

"An inch?"

"Bigger. Five inches, I'll betcha." Billy's face was bright with certainty.

Mitchell paused to argue out the error of that with himself. The stone had been roughly two and a half inches at ts longest, and somewhat narrower and thinner. A boy who had had only a glimpse would not be the best judge of its size.

The reasoning made Mitchell uneasy. He was making excuses where none should be allowed. He hesitated. He wanted to find out if Billy had actually touched the crystal but he didn't quite know how to lead up to the question. He began, "According to what you told the paper, you admitted that your chum—what's his name?" He waited.

"Seth. Seth Mitchell."

"Seth Mitchell saw the stone first. But you still tried to get it, didn't you?"

The boy swallowed. "I didn't mean any harm."

Mitchell had not intended to imply moral disapproval. He said hastily, "It's all right, Billy. When I was a boy the guy who got a thing owned it. None of this seeing-first stuff for us."

He smiled.

Billy said, "I only wanted to be the one who gave it to the museum."

The thunder of that vibrated through Mitchell's mind.

Of course, now I remember . . .

He even realized why he had forgotten. The library's museum room had accepted the stone—which had lost its brilliance during the days he had carried it in his pocket—with reluctance. The librarian had murmured something about not discouraging small boys. With those words she had discouraged him so completely that he had needed an actual naming of the fact to remember it.

293

It was hard to believe an imposter would be able to cite this boy's detailed recollections. And yet, that meant that Billy Bingham, when he disappeared, had—

His brain poised, stopped by the impossibility of this situation. His own doctor had already told him that mental disturbances were often traced to overactive imaginations.

Mitchell drew a deep breath. "All right. Now, two more questions. What time of day was it?"

"Seth and I went swimming after school," said Billy. "So it was late afternoon."

"Okay. According to the paper you didn't get back to your house until nearly ten. Where were you from late afternoon till ten o'clock at night?"

"I wasn't anywhere," said Billy. "Seth and I were fighting over the stone. I fell. And when I picked myself up it was pitch dark." He was suddenly tearful. "I don't know what happened. I guess he just left me lying there, somehow."

Mitchell rose to his feet, thinking suddenly: *This is ridiculous. I ought to have my head examined . . .*

Nevertheless he paused at the door and flung one more question toward the bed, "Has anyone else called you—besides the police, I mean, and the big man—and me?"

"Just a woman from the library."

"Library?" Mitchell echoed blankly.

"She wanted to know the exact time I woke up beside the lake. Her name is Edith Price and she works in the library. Of course—I didn't know."

The information seemed meaningless. Mitchell said quickly, simulating a friendliness he no longer felt, "Well, Billy, I guess I'd better let you get back to your comic book. Thanks a lot."

He went out of the room and out of the hospital. He paid his bill at the hotel, got into his rented car, drove to the airport and flew back to Miami. By the time the plane landed, the old, disturbing music from his childhood had faded from his mind.

It seemed to Mitchell that The Musician had let him down. To insure that it never happened again, he resolved to cancel his subscription to the *Harkdale Inquirer*.

Chicago. Seth Mitchell (of the Seth Mitchell Detective Agency) stared at the man who had just walked into his office as if he were seeing a hallucination.

Finally he blinked and asked, "Am I crazy?"

The stranger, a well set up young man in his mid-thirties,

at down in the visitor's chair and said with an enigmatic mile, "The resemblance is remarkable, isn't it?"

He spoke in a firm baritone and, except that both of them new better, Mitchell could have sworn the voice was his wn.

In fact, afterward, telling Marge Aikens about the visitor, ae confessed, "I kept feeling that it was me sitting there."

"But what did he want?" Marge asked. She was a slim londe taking her first look at thirty and taking it well. Mitchll intended to marry her some day when he could find anther associate as efficient. "What did he look like?"

"Me. That's what I'm trying to tell you. He was my spitting mage. He even wore a suit that reminded me of one I've got at home." He pleaded uneasily, "Don't be too hard on ae, Marge. I went to pieces. It's all vague."

"Did he give you his address?"

Mitchell looked down unhappily at the interview sheet. "It's not written down."

"Did he say if he intended to come to the office again?"

"No, but he gave me a thousand dollars in bills and I gave him a receipt. So we're committed."

"To what?"

"That's the silliest part of it. He wants me to find an onyx crystal. He says he saw it quite a while back in a small-town museum south of New York. He can't remember just where."

"That's going to be either very hard or very easy." Marge was thoughtful; she seemed to be considering the problem involved.

"Let me finish," said Mitchell grimly. "I know where the crystal is. Just think of what I said. I know that region like a book. I was born there, remember?"

"It had slipped my mind," said Marge. "You think you can locate the crystal because—"

Mitchell said, "It's in the museum annex of the public library in the town of Harkdale, where I was born. And now—get this. I presented the crystal to the library and, what's even more amazing, I dreamed about that stone the other night."

Marge did not let him get off the subject. "And he came to you? Out of the scores of detective agencies in Chicago, he came to the one man in the world who looks like him and who knows where that crystal is?"

"He came to me."

Marge was pursing her beautiful lips. "Seth, this is fantastic. You shouldn't have let him get away. You're usually so sharp."

"Thanks." Dryly.

"Why didn't you just tell him where it is."

"And lose a thousand dollars? My dear, a detective is sometimes like a doctor. People pay him for information he already has."

Marge held out her hand. "Let me see that interview sheet."

As she read it she asked without looking up, "What are you going to do?"

"Well, I told him the truth, that I've got several days' work to get rid of and then—"

He fell silent and the silence grew so long that Marge finally looked up. She was relieved at the expression on his face, for it was the shrewd, reasoning look that was always there when he was at his detective best.

He caught her glance, and said, "It would be a mistake to appear in Harkdale until three or four mysteries have been cleared up. Like how come there's two of us—"

"You have no relations?"

"Some cousins."

"Ever see them?"

He shook his head. "Not since I was around nineteen, when my mother died." He smiled grimly. "Harkdale is not a town you go back to. But kill the thought you've got. None of my cousins looked like me." He shuddered. "Ugh, no."

Marge said firmly, "I think when you do finally go, you ought to be disguised."

"You can count on it—even you won't know me."

Elsewhere on earth about two dozen of the total of 1811 Seth Mitchells—among whom was the best of all possible Seth Mitchells—also considered the crystal, remembered their dreams of a few nights earlier and had a strange, tense conviction of an imminent crisis.

As Seth Mitchell in Montreal, Canada, described it to his French-Canadian wife, "I can't get over the feeling that I'm going to have to measure up. Remember, I mentioned that to you when I awoke the other morning."

His wife, a pretty blonde, who had a French-Canadian woman's practical contempt for dream fantasies, remembered it well and wanted to know what he had to measure up to.

Her husband said unhappily, "I have a feeling I could have

made better decisions, made more of myself. I am not the man I could have been."

"So what?" she wanted to know. "Who is? And what of it."

"*Kaput.*" He shrugged. "I'm sorry to be so negative, my dear. But that's the feeling. Since I didn't measure up, I'm through."

His wife sighed. "My mother warned me that all men get crazy ideas as they approach forty. And here you are."

"I should have been braver—or something," he moaned.

"What's wrong with being a tax consultant?" she demanded.

Her husband seemed not to hear. "I have a feeling I ought to visit my home town."

She grabbed his arm. "You're going straight to Dr. Ledoux," she said. "You need a checkup."

Dr. Ledoux could find nothing wrong. "In fact, you seem to be in exceptionally good health."

The Seth Mitchell of Montreal had to concede that his sudden alarm was pretty ridiculous.

But he decided to visit Harkdale as soon as he cleared up certain business.

IV

The man's voice came suddenly, tinged with a slight foreign accent, "Miss Price, I want to talk to you."

Edith saw the speaker dimly in the darkness and realized that he stood in the shadows between the garage and the rooming house where she lived, barring her way.

Before she could speak the voice continued, "What did you do with the crystal?"

"I—don't—understand."

She spoke the words automatically. She could see her interrogator more clearly now. He was short and broad of build. Abruptly she recognized him as the man who had been with the Seth Mitchell look-alike in the gold Cadillac.

"Miss Price, you removed that crystal from the display cabinet. Either give it to me or tell me what you did with it and that'll be the end of the matter."

Edith had the tense feeling of a person who has acted unwisely and who therefore cannot possibly make any admissions, not even to a stranger.

"I don't know what you're talking about," she whispered.

"Look, Miss Price—" The man stepped out of the shadows. His tone was conciliatory. "Lets go into your apartment and talk this over."

His proposal relieved her. For her apartment was only a little suite in a rooming house in which the other tenants were never more than a wall away.

Incredibly—afterward she thought of it as incredible—she was instantly trusting and started past him. Her surprise when he grabbed her was total. One of his arms imprisoned both of hers and her body.

He put a hard, unyielding palm over her mouth and whispered, "I've got a gun."

Nearly paralyzed by the threat, she was aware of her captor carrying her toward the back alley. She allowed him to shove her—without a struggle—into a car that was parked against a fence.

He climbed in beside her and sat there in the near-dark of the night, gazing at her. She could not make out the expression on his face. But as the seconds went by, and he made no threatening move, her heart slowed in its rapid beating.

She finally gasped, "Who are you? What do you want?"

The man chuckled sardonically and said, "I'm the worst of all possible Athtars from the thirty-fifth century. But I turned out to have a high survival faculty."

Edith was again unable to speak.

His voice tightened. "Where I come from I'm a physicist. I sensed my danger and I worked out a key aspect of the nature of the crystal in record time. In dealing with human beings, it operates on the vibrations a body puts forth from all its cells. In recreating that vibration, it creates the person. Conversely, in canceling the vibration, it uncreates him. Recognizing this—and since I was not of its orientation in my era—I simply put up a barrier on the total vibration level of my own body and thus saved my life when it uncreated all the lesser Athtars."

Now she did not want to speak and the man added somberly: "But evidently, by defeating it, I remained attached to it on some other level. As it fell back through time to the twentieth century I fell with it. Not—unfortunately—to where and when it went. Instead—I arrived last week beside that ledge overlooking Lake Naragang." He finished in a wondering tone: "What a remarkable, intricate internal energy flow system it must have. Imagine! In passing through time it must have detected this twenty-five-year inactive period and its reawakening—and dropped me off within days of its own reactivation."

The voice became silent and there was nothing but the

darkness again. Edith ventured a small movement—she changed her position on the seat to ease a growing discomfort in one leg.

When there was no counter movement from him she whispered, "Why are you telling me this? It all sounds perfectly insane."

Even as she uttered the obvious she realized that a quality of equal madness in herself believed every word that he had spoken. She thought in a spasm of self-criticism: *I really must be one of the lesser Edith Prices.*

She had to fight to suppress an outburst of hysterical laughter.

"From you," said the worst of all possible Athtars, "I want information."

"I don't know anything about a crystal."

"The information I want," said the man in an inexorable voice, "is this: At any time recently have you had a thought about wishing you had taken a different path in life instead of ending up in Harkdale as a librarian?"

Edith's mind flashed back to her series of impulses after she had mailed the crystal—and back farther.

"Why, yes," she breathed.

"Tell me about one of them," said the man.

She told him of the impulse she had had to simply get on a bus or train and leave Harkdale.

The man leaned back in the seat. He seemed surprisingly relaxed.

He asked with a chuckle, "Are you the best of all possible Edith Prices?"

Edith made no reply. She was beginning to have the feeling that perhaps she should confide in this man—should tell him where the crystal was.

Athtar was speaking again. "I have a conviction that the Edith Price who is the twentieth-century orientation for the crystal is on that bus or is heading for safety somewhere else. And that therefore you are under the same threat as I am —of being uncreated as soon as the crystal selects the perfect Edith Price."

For Edith, terror began at that moment.

During the minutes that followed she was only vaguely aware of words mumbling out of her mouth.

Listening to her revelation, Athtar suppressed an impulse to murder her out of hand. He played it cautiously, thinking that if anything went wrong, this Edith was all he had to help him to trace the other Ediths.

So he spoke reassuring words, put her out of the car, and watched her as she staggered off—safe, she thought.

The note read: "He wasn't there. It wasn't there. The farm was deserted. Did you lie to me? Athtar."

Edith felt a chill the first time she read the words. Particularly she reacted to the last line with fear. But on her tenth or twelfth reading, she was more determined.

She thought: *If this whole crazy business is real I'd better —What?*

Be brave? Consider the problem? Act with decisiveness? It was Saturday.

Before going to work she bought a small Browning .25 automatic at the Harkdale Hardware. She had often gone target practicing with the second of her two college boy friends, the one who had sold her on the philosophy that God was dead and that therefore one need only avoid jail —and otherwise do anything one pleased. Eventually he departed without marrying her, presumably feeling guiltless about having lured her away from a man who might have offered her a wedding ring.

But this man *did* show her how to shoot an automatic firearm. She put the little pistol into her purse—and felt a hardening of her conviction that it was time *this* Edith started measuring up.

One doubt remained: was willingness to shoot in self-defense a step forward—or a step away—from being the best of all possible Edith Prices?

At the library that day, Tilsit was waiting for her with another news item:

YOUNG FARMER MISSING

Seth Mitchell, Abbotsville farmer, has not been at his farm for several days. A neighbor, Carey Grayson, called on Mitchell yesterday to buy seed grain, found the Mitchell cows unmilked, a horse in the stable starving, chickens unfed and no sign of life around the house. Grayson fed the animals, then contacted Mitchell's cousin in a neighboring county and notified the sheriff's office. An investigation is under way.

Edith handed back the paper with a meaningless comment. But she was thinking: *So that's what Athtar discovered . . .*

In spite of her resolve she trembled. It seemed to her that

300

there was no turning back; she must carry forward inexorably with all the thoughts that she had had.

Sunday.

She had driven to New York, and parked two blocks from the little hotel for women only where she had formerly lived. Surely, she told herself, that was where at least one Edith duplicate would have gone.

From a phone booth she called the hotel and asked for Edith Price. There was a pause, then, "I'm ringing," said the woman desk clerk.

Instantly breathless, Edith hung up. She sagged limply inside the booth, eyes closed. It was not clear to her even now what she had expected.

Can it be that I'm the only Edith who knows that there are others? And does that give me an advantage over the unknowing ones?

Or was there already somewhere an Edith Price who had naturally become the best of them all?

Her thought ended. She realized that a short, stocky man was standing beside the booth, partly out of her line of vision. Something about him was familiar.

She straightened and turned.

Athtar.

The Edith Price who stepped out of the phone booth was still shaky and still not brave. But two days of fear and threat and gulps of terror had transformed her. She had been a vaguely sad, wish-my-mistakes-won't-doom-me young woman. Now she trembled with anxiety at times, but at other times she compressed her lips and had thoughts that were tough and realistic.

The sight of Athtar caromed her into anxiety.

Which was just as well, the tough part of her assessed realistically. She did not trust the worst of all possible Athtars. And he would feel safer with a frightened Edith, she was sure.

Seen close in broad daylight on a deserted New York street on Sunday morning, Athtar—short, broad, with a thick face and gray cheeks—was surprisingly as she remembered him—totally unprepossessing.

He said softly, "Why don't you let me talk to her?"

Edith scarcely heard. The first question of her 48-hour stop-only-for-sleep, stream of consciousness, siphoned through her voice, "Are you really from the thirty-fifty century?"

He gave her a quick, shrewd look, must have realized how wound up she was and said receptively, "Yes."

"Are they all like you?"

"It was decided," said Athatar in a formal tone, "that a body built thicker and closer to the ground has more utility. That was several hundred years before I was born. And so, yes. No one is over sixteen hundred and seventy-five centimeters—that is, five feet, six inches."

"How do you know you're the worst of all possible Athtars?"

"In my time," was the reply, "it is a felony for anyone but a member of the Scientists' Guild to have a weapon. Hence, political and economic power is part of the prize of the struggle for position in the Guild. On my way to becoming a tougher member, I wished many times to be relatively safe among the faceless, unarmed masses. And the crystal, in creating other Athtars, solidified those wishes."

There was an implication here that getting tougher was not the answer, not the way. Edith sighed her disappointment and remembered her other questions. She told him about the two pictures she had seen in the crystal, the one of the solar system and the other the outline of a human body. Did he know what the pictures meant?

"When I first saw the crystal," said Athtar, "the scene inside was of our galaxy. Later it became the solar system. So what you saw was probably a carryover from my time, where we occupy all the planets. And what I saw must derive from a time when man has moved out to the galaxy. It could mean that the crystal adjusts to the era in which it finds itself. Though why a human being instead of the planet Earth in this era is not obvious. Was the outline that of a woman or a man?"

Edith couldn't remember.

Standing there in the bright, sunny day and on the dirty, narrow street, Athtar shook his head. There was awe in his ugly face. He said wonderingly, "Such a small object; such a comprehensive ability." He added, half to himself, "It has to be based on potential flow patterns. There are not enough atoms in such a crystal to act as a control board for so much."

He had already, by implication, answered her next question but she asked it anyway.

Athtar sighed, "No, the crystal is definitely not from the thirty-fifth century. It appeared suddenly. I picture it as having fallen backward through time from some future era in drops of fifteen hundred years."

"But why would they have sent it back?" Edith asked, bewildered. "What are they after?"

The chunky little man gave her a startled look. "The idea of the crystal's having been sent back for a purpose had not previously occurred to me. It's such a colossally valuable machine that we assumed it got away from them accidentally," he said. He was silent. Then, finally: "Why don't you let me go to see this second Edith Price? And you go back to Harkdale? If I find the crystal, I'll report with it to you there."

The implication seemed to be that he planned to cooperate with her. What he meant was that the crystal would be no good to him until he had found and murdered the Edith to whom it was oriented.

The tough part of Edith hesitated at the idea of trusting this man. But it occurred to her that he might have his century's weapons and that therefore he was being generous from a position of total strength in offering to cooperate.

With such fear thoughts in her mind and having no plans of her own, she agreed.

She watched him get into a shining new automobile and drive down the narrow street. It was a medium-sized car, she noted absently. She had never been one who kept track of auto designs, so by the time she wondered what make it was it was gone. Belatedly it also struck her that she ought to have looked at the license plate numbers.

She thought sarcastically: *What a third-rate Edith Price I am . . .*

She was vaguely aware of a car pulling up at the curb nearby. A young woman left it and casually walked toward her as if to go into the phone booth.

She stopped suddenly beside Edith.

"You're Miss Price?"

Edith turned.

The other woman was a bright, alert blonde, probably in her thirties. Edith had never seen her before. She had no sense of being threatened but involuntarily she backed away several steps.

"Yes," she said.

The woman turned toward the car and called, "Okay, Seth."

Seth Mitchell emerged from the car and came rapidly toward them. He was well dressed, like the Seth Mitchell in the gold Cadillac, but there was a subtle difference. His face had a firmer, more determined expression.

He said, "I'm a detective. Who is that man you were talking to?"

And so the story, as well as Edith knew it, was presently shared.

303

They had gone into a coffee shop for their tense discussion. Edith was both relieved and disturbed to discover that these detectives had been in Harkdale for two days and had traced her down as a result of her call to the hospital to inquire about Billy Bingham. Having thus spotted her, they had become aware that the squat man was also keeping track of her movements. And so that morning, not one but three cars had headed for New York—Edith's, Athtar's and theirs.

The exchange of information took time and several cups of coffee—though Edith rejected the final cup with the sudden realization that coffee was probably not good for people and that the crystal might judge her on it at some later time. She smiled wanly at how many restraints she was placing on herself. Exactly as if God were no longer dead.

When they came out of the restaurant Seth Mitchell phoned the other Edith Price. He emerged from the phone booth uneasy.

"The switchboard operator says that Miss Price left with a man about twenty minutes ago. I'm afraid we're too late."

From Edith's description he had already come to the conclusion that Athtar was a dangerous man. They decided to wait for the second Edith to return. But though they remained in New York until after eleven that night the young woman did not come back to her hotel.

She never would return. For some hours, a bullet in her brain, her body, weighed down by stones, had been lying at the bottom of the East River.

And Athtar had the crystal.

To his intense disappointment, that Edith was not the crystal's orientation.

Accordingly, he spent the evening and a portion of the night fitting together parts in the construction of a special weapon. He had a peculiar prescience that he would need its power the following day against the Edith who, he believed was back in Harkdale.

V

Edith Price and the detectives set out for Harkdale in the two cars. Seth Mitchell, at Edith's request, drove her car. Marge Aikens followed in the larger machine.

En route Mitchell told Edith that he believed she was the original Edith and that it was to her that the crytsal was still oriented. He considered also that her conclusion that Seth Mitchell, the farmer, was the worst Seth had doomed that unfortunate Mitchell duplicate. The crystal accepted her judgment and probably uncreated Seth, the farmer, when the package with the crystal addressed to him had barely been deposited in the post office.

Edith was taken aback by the detective's logic.

"But" she stammered, "I didn't mean it that way." Tears streamed down her cheeks. "Oh, that poor man!"

"Of course you didn't mean it," Mitchell said. "Just to double-check—tell me again in what sequence did that judgment of yours come? Was it before or after your various impulses to leave Harkdale?"

"Oh, after."

"And did I hear you correctly—you thought of going into the post office and asking for the package you had mailed to be returned to you?"

"Yes, I had that thought." She added; "But I didn't do it."

"I would guess that at least one other Edith did go back and get it," said Mitchell.

"But it's all so complicated," Edith said. "How would any Edith just go, leaving clothes, money, car?"

"I've been thinking of my own background on that," said Mitchell. "Evidently the crystal can excise all confusions like that. For example, I never again even thought of going back to Harkdale. To do so didn't even cross my mind. But there are no blanks like that in your mind?"

"None that I can identify or think of."

Seth Mitchell nodded. "That's how I heard you. I think I've got the solution to this whole crazy business—and we don't even have to know where the crystal is."

His reasoning was simple. In bringing back Billy Bingham at her command the crystal had deposited the boy nearly two miles away. At the time she had been holding the crystal in her hand. But her negative thought about Farmer Seth Mitchell had occurred after she had mailed the crystal and was approximately a hundred yards from the post office.

So if she had indeed uncreated the mentally ill farmer, then the distance of the crystal's human orientation—in this instance one of the Edith Prices—from the crystal, was not a factor.

"You don't agree?" asked the detective.

"I'm thinking," Edith said. "Maybe I'm not really the orientation."

"We'll test that tomorrow."

"What about Athtar?" Edith asked. "I keep feeling that he may have special weapons. Besides, the crystal cannot affect him. What about that?"

"Let me think about Athtar."

While he thought, Edith remembered Athtar's asking her about the figure in the crystal: had it been a man's or a woman's? She sat there in the darkness next to this Seth Mitchell and became aware of two separate lines of thought in her mind.

The first: she attempted to visualize the human design in the crystal.

The second . . .

She watched his profile as he drove.

How brilliant he is—yet surely a mere detective, no matter how keen his logic, cannot be the best of all possible Seth Mitchells. A man in such a profession has got to be somewhere in the middle—which in this competition is the same as the worst . . .

And he disappeared.

For many seconds after she had that thought, the suddenly driverless car held to its straight direction. Its speed, which had been around seventy, naturally started to let up the instant there was no longer a foot on the accelerator.

The only error came when Edith uttered a scream and grabbed at the wheel, turning it. The machine careened wildly. The next second she grasped it in a more steadying way and, holding it, slid along the seat into a position where presently she could apply the brake. She pulled over to the side of the road and stopped.

Marge Aikens had slowed as soon as she saw there was a problem. She pulled up behind Edith, got out of the car and walked to the driver's side of the other machine.

"Seth," she began, "what—"

Edith pushed the door open and stepped, trembling, out to the road. She had a mad impulse to run—anywhere. Her body felt strange. Her mind was encased in blank anguish. She was vaguely aware of herself babbling about what had happened.

It must have taken a while for her incoherent words to reach through to Marge. But suddenly Marge gasped and Edith felt herself grabbed by the shoulders. She was being shaken.

A voice was yelling at her, "You stupid fool! You stupid fool—"

The shaking became pain. Her neck hurt, then her arms.

I must be careful. I mustn't do or say anything that will affect her . . .

With the thought Edith's sanity returned. Marge was in a

state of hysteria. The shaking was actually an automatic act of a person out of her mind with grief.

Edith knew pity. She was able to free herself by a simple action. She slapped Marge lightly on the cheek, once, twice, three times. The third time the woman let go of her and leaned against the car, sobbing.

A wind was blowing from the west. Car headlights kept glaring past them, lighting the scene briefly. The two women were now in a relatively normal state and presently were able to discuss their situation. Edith tried to recreate Marge's employer with the same command she had used to bring back Billy Bingham.

She had had a feeling that it would not work—the Seth Mitchells were undoubtedly due to be eliminated one by one—and it did not. The minutes ticked by. Though she yelled the command in many variations into the night there was no sign of the vanished Seth, whose presence had for a long half-day brought to the whole situation the reassurance that derives from a highly intelligent and determined mind.

In the end, defeated, the two women in their separate cars drove on to Harkdale. Marge had a room reserved at the Harkdale Hotel and went there. Edith drove wearily to the apartment house where she lived.

It was nearly four o'clock when she finally limped into her little suite. She lay down without undressing. She was drifting off to sleep when fear tensed her. Would the best of all possible Ediths be this sloppy about personal cleanliness?

Literally hurting with exhaustion, she rolled off the bed, undressed, bathed, brushed her teeth, combed her hair, changed the linens and stepped into a clean pair of pajamas.

She awoke once with a bad start to the thought that conformity might not be her salvation. Such toiletry amenities as she had performed were products of early training and did not necessarily have anything to do with life as it should be lived.

She fell asleep imagining a series of rebel Ediths, each one of whom had some special characteristic that was noble and worthy.

The next time she awoke she saw daylight outside. It occurred to her that all her concepts, so compulsively visualized, were probably being created somewhere by the crystal. Undoubtedly there were already beatnik and hippie Ediths as well as rougher, tougher types.

For the first time she realized what a strange whirl of possibilities she had considered in the last thirty-six hours. Ediths who were hard-boiled and could coldly shoot to kill, or, conversely, were super-feminine, sweet, tantalizing temptresses.

"And it's all unnecessary," she whispered, lying there. "The decision will probably be made as arbitrarily as my own impulsive condemnation of the inarticulate farmer and the courageous—but presumably not perfect—detective."

Having no standards that applied to the twentieth century, the crystal had uncreated a powerful and good man on the passing judgment of the person to whom it had by chance become oriented. Accordingly, the future looked grim for all Seth Mitchells and Edith Prices, including the original.

As she dressed she looked through her window at the distant blue waters of Lake Naragang and the downtown section that at one place, opposite the Harkdale Hotel, crowded the water's edge. Pretty little town, Harkdale. She remembered that on her arrival she had thought that at least here she could be more casual in her dress than she had been in New York. Then she gave a short, rueful laugh—she had come full circle during the night, back to the notion that appearance would count.

She put on her finest dress. Yet in some back closet of her brain lived a fearful conviction that all this was in vain. The crisis was imminent; she might be dead—uncreated—before this day was out.

It seemed ridiculous to go to work on the day you were going to die. But she went. As she moved about her duties Edith was conscious of her subdued manner. Twice, when she unthinkingly looked into the restroom mirror, she was startled by the pale face and sick eyes that looked back at her.

This is not really me—I can't be judged on this . . .

Surely the crystal would not reject her because she was in a daze. Every passing minute fleeting images of other Ediths passed before her mind's eye. Each one had in it the momentary hope that maybe *it* held the key to the best. There was Edith living out her life as a nun; another chaste Edith, married but holding sex to a minimum, placing all her attention on her children, and an Edith who was a follower of Zen Buddhism.

She had, earlier, put through a call to Marge Aiken, at the Harkdale Hotel. About two o'clock Marge called back. She reported that she had phoned New York and discovered that the second Edith had not returned to her hotel at all the previous night.

After imparting this grim news, Marge said, "If Athtar con-acts you—don't be alone with him under any circumstances until he produces the Seth Mitchell in the gold Cadillac and the Edith in New York."

After that call more images, mostly of saintly and good-hearted, unsophisticated Ediths haunted her.

Into this haze of thoughts, Tilsit's voice intruded: "Phone call for you, Edith."

She picked up the phone, heard a familiar voice—Athtar's.

"I want to see you right after work."

Edith said on a suddenly faint note, "At the Harkdale Hotel—in the lobby."

VI

Athtar left the phone booth. A smile twisted his wide face. For him there were two possibilities of victory now that he had the crystal.

The first was to kill its current orientation—Edith. He intended to take no chances with her. She would never, he resolved, reach the Harkdale Hotel.

However, murder of his only Edith left one unpleasant possibility. Though he had reasoned it out that she was the crystal's orientation—should she prove not to be, in destroying her —he would remove his source of information for tracing other Ediths.

It was a considered risk he had to take. As a precaution he had already removed the crystal from the nutrient soil on which it fed. He was not certain how long it would be before the stone was deactivated by starvation, but he deduced not more than two weeks. Whereupon it would orient to whoever reactivated it. To himself, of course.

Now that he had a special barrier-penetrating weapon, he firmly believed that before this day was over he would be in sole possession of the most remarkable machine of all time and space—the crystal.

The Harkdale Hotel was a summer resort hostelry. Its prices were high and as a result it had made money. Some of the money had been spent wisely, on decoration, fine furniture and a sophisticated staff.

The clerk on day duty had his own definition of a sophisticate: a person with a memory so good that he can forget with discretion.

He was such a person. His name was Derek Slade. And so discreet was he that on this fateful day he had allowed four Seth Mitchells to register without comment. He believed each Mitchell to be the same man but with a different woman and he was just beginning to enjoy the situation when Seth Mitchell arrived for the fifth time—this time without a woman.

Yet it took Derek only a moment to figure it out. This smooth male, Seth Mitchell, had four women in different rooms and evidently wanted a separate room for himself. Why? Derek did not try to analyze the matter further. Life —he had often said—was full of surprises.

He spoke in a low tone, "You may count on my discretion, Mr. Mitchell."

The Seth Mitchell across the desk from him raised his eyebrows, then nodded with a faint smile.

Derek was pleased. The remark ought to be good for a twenty-dollar tip.

He was still congratulating himself when the elevator door opened and another Seth Mitchell stepped out and walked toward the desk. As he came up, the Seth Mitchell who had just registered turned to follow the bellboy carrying his bags to the elevator.

The two Seth Mitchells almost bumped into each other. Both took evasive action. Both murmured polite nothings and were about to pass each other when Derek recovered.

It was one of his perfect moments. He raised his voice, spoke with exactly the correct note of authority.

"Mr. Mitchell."

The two Seth Mitchells were already in a mildly confused state. Their name, uttered in that peremptory tone, stopped them.

Derek said, "Mr. Seth Mitchell, may I present Mr. Seth Mitchell. Gentlemen, please wait there a moment."

He let them kill their own time—one seemed to recover quickly; the other remained bewildered—while he phoned the rooms of the previously registered Seth Mitchells. He had to call all four rooms but presently before him stood five Seth Mitchells.

Of all the people present the one most completely unnoticed was Derek Slade. He would not have had it any other way.

Four of the five Seths were gulping and stuttering at each other. The fifth had stepped to one side with a faint smile. Almost as one, the four suddenly became embarrassed.

Derek's cool voice reached them with perfect timing.

"Gentlemen, let me show you to the conference room, where you may talk over this whole matter."

As they started for the conference room, Marge Aiken entered the hotel in time to catch a profile view of the last

Seth Mitchell walking into the room. She paled, then rushed forward.

"Seth—" she cried out tearfully. "For Gods sake, I thought you were dead—"

She stopped. She had grabbed the nearest man by the arm. He turned and something unfamiliar about him flustered her.

After all the Mitchells had been briefed by Marge to the extent of her knowledge she suggested that Edith be called to come over at once.

Three Seth Mitchells presented their view. Listening to each in turn, Marge glanced along the line of sensationally familiar faces and saw in all but one man's eyes a haunting apprehension—and the equally haunting intelligence she had seen so often in her employer's.

Seth from Montreal said, "Our first act must be to protect ourselves from that young woman's automatic judgments, such as she rendered on farmer Mitchell and detective Mitchell."

A second, slightly deeper-voiced Seth was concerned about Athtar. "In killing Edith Price Number Two, Athtar must have gotten the crystal and then discovered that the dead Edith was not the orientation. Therefore our initial act must be to protect the Edith who *is* the orientation. The first real problem is to get her safely to the hotel—not what she may do when she gets here."

The third Seth said the problem was not so much Edith's judgment of men; it was her stereotyped concept of women. Presumably, the crystal had dutifully created a long list of Edith Prices who were simply ordinary human beings with varying moral standards or with slightly different beliefs about how to get along in the drab world of the twentieth century.

"As an example of how differently I would want her to handle her control of the crystal—one of the first Edith Prices I would wish her to create is one that has ESP. Why? So that she can understand this whole situation and what to do about it."

His words brought a hopeful reaction. It was an obviously good idea—if it could be done.

A fourth Seth, who had sat gray and silent, now said, "It would be interesting if such ESP ability included being able to spot the Seth Mitchell who—" he nodded at Marge—"paid your boss a thousand dollars to locate the crystal."

The Seth who had arrived at the hotel without a wife—and who had reflected none of the fear that the others felt—stirred and smiled cheerfully.

311

"You need look no further. I'm he."

When order had been restored he continued: "To answer your basic question, I also dreamed—as you all did—and exactly as the worst Athtar found himself with the address of one of the Seth Mitchells in his mind, one morning after a dream the address of detective Mitchell was in mine."

"But why didn't you come for the crystal yourself? Why pay a thousand dollars?"

The bachelor Mitchell smiled again. "I hate to tell you people this—and it is to your advantage not to let Miss Price know—but according to the thoughts I had after my dream I am the best of all possible Seth Mitchells."

Once more he had to wait for order.

Then: "I don't know why I'm best. But I hired someone to come here in my place because I sensed danger and I came here today believing that this was the crisis. I can't tell you what I'll do about it. I don't even have the feeling that my role is decisive. I simply believe that a challenge will present itself and I'll meet it." He finished simply: "I don't think we should devote any more time to me. We have many vital things to do and we only have until Edith Price comes off the job to get them done. Let's go. First, since violence is imminent, we must warn the police—"

The police of Harkdale were few in number and Athtar was able to drive into town and into the library parking lot without being observed. A lingering twilight had barely begun to turn to night when Edith emerged.

She noted with a vague surprise that a town fire truck, engine running, was standing near the door. But she was already having qualms about the forthcoming journey to the hotel—so far away, it seemed to her suddenly. So the sight of the big truck was reassuring.

To get to her own car, she had to go around the fire truck. As she started to do so the big machine surged into motion with a gigantic thunder of its engine. Edith stopped, teetered, then leaped back. The truck jammed on its brakes directly in front of her.

Somewhere beyond the big machine a purple flash had lighted the sky. Like a tracer bullet the light flashed from the auto to the fire truck. As it hit, it made a sound of a pitch never before heard on earth—a deep, sustained, continuing protest of chemical bonds by the quadrillion snapping in metal.

The tiny bullet penetrated the thick steel frame of the fire truck, and reformed itself a micromillimeter at a time from the steel molecules. It did not slow as it passed through the heavy machine. It would also have passed straight through Edith, except that its speed *was* that of a bullet —immense but finite.

It transited the fire truck while the truck was still in motion. The bullet was carried along inside the moving vehicle during a measurable fraction of a second and missed Edith by inches.

Unchecked, it struck the library wall, moved through, emerged from the far side and streaked into the night. Its kinetic energy being a precise quality, it bored forward another hundred yards and then rapidly fell.

Moments later two plainclothes police discharged their rifles at the figure that was dimly visible inside the car from which the purple-glowing bullet had been fired.

The screech of bullets striking his own machine startled Athtar. But he had taken the precaution of using a molecular reinforcing unit to harden the glass and the metal of the auto, so the bullets failed to penetrate.

What bothered him was that he only had a few bullets and in the dark he could not gauge the extent of the trap that had been set for him. So now, hastily, he put his car into drive, stepped on the gas and drove rapidly out of the parking lot.

A police car fell in behind him, flashing its red beacon. Though it or its weapons were no danger to Athtar, he feared a roadblock. He turned up several side streets and in only a few minutes of driving lured the police car onto a street near the lake on the far side of the Harkdale Hotel, an approach he had thoroughly explored on foot.

Satisfied, he opened the car window on the driver's side, slowed, leaned out, looked back, took quick aim at the engine of the other machine and put a purple-glowing bullet through the crankcase. There was a shattering crash. The stricken motor almost tore itself apart, screaming metallically. The auto itself came to a bumpy halt.

Athtar hurriedly circled back to the Harkdale Hotel. The first queasy doubt had come to him that for a reason not yet clear his time was running out. Yet it still seemed true to him that all he need do was sneak into the hotel and discharge a single bullet at one, and only one, beating heart.

Minutes later, after squeezing through a kitchen window of the hotel, he found himself in a shadowy storeroom on a concrete floor. As he fumbled his way to a door, he had a fleeting mental image of his colleagues of the great Science

313

Guild viewing him in such a lowly action. Of course, Athtar told himself scornfully, what they thought would not matter once he had control of the crystal. There would be dramatic changes after he got back to his own time—a few hundred Guild members were scheduled for extermination.

Cautiously he pulled open a door. As he started through the hallway beyond it he became aware of a faint sound behind him. He spun around and jerked up his gun.

Instant, unbearable pain in his arm forced the gun down and his finger away from the trigger. Almost at once the gun dropped from his nerveless hand, clattering to the floor. Even as he recognized that 35th-century technology was being used against him, he saw that a short, squat man was standing in the doorway of the storeroom he himself had just left.

Athtar's arm and hand were now inexorably forced by intolerable pain to reach into his inside breast pocket, take out the crystal and hold it out to the other man.

The second Athtar did not speak. He drew the door shut behind him, accepted the crystal and, bending down, picked up the gun from the floor. Then he edged past his prisoner, stepped through the door beyond and closed it behind him also.

At once, all the muscle pressures let go of the worst Athtar. Instantly desperate, he tried to jerk open the storeroom door. The door did not yield—it had an unnervingly solid feel to it. Athtar whirled toward the other door.

When he found it also presented that same solid resistance to his tug he finally recognized that he was trapped by molecular forces from his own era. There was nothing to do as the minutes lengthened but sit down on the concrete floor and wait.

Sitting there, he knew a mixed reaction to his realization that the drama of the crystal would now play on without him. What seemed good about it was the distinct conviction that the game was more dangerous than he had let himself believe. He had recognized his assailant as the best of all possible Athtars.

Too, the Price woman was being cleverer than he had anticipated. Which meant that the automatic programing of the crystal to uncreate all but the best would force her to the most desperate actions. Or so it seemed to the worst Athtar.

Better not to be around when such extreme events were transpiring.

The best of all possible Athtars walked through the hotel lobby to the conference room. The five Seth Mitchells were grouped outside the door, out of the line of vision of Edith, who was inside. Athtar gave the agreed-on signal and handed the worst Athtar's automatic pistol to one of the Seths. They were thorough. They searched him and then passed him on to Marge Aikens, who stood in the doorway.

To Marge, Athtar gave another agreed-on signal. Having thus established his identity as the friendly Athtar, whom Edith had recreated as a first step, he was now admitted into the room.

Athtar placed the crystal on the conference table in front of Edith. As her fingers automatically reached toward it, he placed a restraining hand on her wrist.

"I have a feeling," he admonished, "that this time when you pick it up—when the true orientation, *you,* picks it up—that will be the moment of crisis."

His voice and his words, seemed far away. She had—it seemed to her—considered those thoughts, and had those feelings, in approaching the decision to recreate *him*—the best Athtar. That, also, had been a crisis.

As she nevertheless hesitated out of respect for his knowledge and awareness, Edith noticed two impulses within herself. One was to go into a kind of exhaustion, in which she would act on the basis that she was too tired to think all that through again.

The second impulse was a clearer, sharper awareness, which had come to her suddenly at the library after she realized that the worst Athtar had tried his best to kill her.

Abruptly, then, the problems that had disturbed her earlier had faded. Whether it was better to be tough and be able to shoot or be soft and feminine, had no meaning. The real solution was infinite flexibility, backed by unvarying intention.

One handled situations. That was all there was to it.

As she remembered that perfect thought the impulse toward exhaustion went away. She turned to Marge and said matter-of-factly, "Shall I tell him what we discussed while he was down in the storeroom?"

Marge nodded tensely.

Athtar listened with what appeared to be an expression of doubt, then said, "Having the crystal recreate one of its makers could be exactly what those makers are waiting for you to do."

"That's exactly what we thought," said Edith. And still she felt no fear. She explained, "Our thought is that, since the crystal is programed to find the best of each person, and the best Athtar turned out to be a reasonable person and not a criminal, then the makers of the crystal understand the difference. We may therefore assume that the society of the future is normal and will not harm us." She added: "That's why we recreated you—as a check."

"Good reasoning," said Athtar. "But I sense there's something wrong with it."

"But you have no specific thought?" she asked.

"No." He hesitated, then shrugged. "As a start," he said, "why not pick up the crystal—just pick it up—and see if my feeling about that gesture's being sufficient has any substance?" He explained, "If I'm wrong there we can dismiss my doubts."

"You don't want me to look at the design?"

The Seths had decided that her awareness of the design was the key to her control of the stone.

Athtar answered, "No, I sense that they're ready."

His words, the implication of ultra-perception that reached over, perhaps thousands of years, startled Edith and held her unmoving—but only momentarily.

She fought free.

"The truth is," said Edith aloud, completing her thought, "we all feel that we have no alternative left to us."

Without further delay she reached forward and picked up the crystal.

She gasped.

The man who walked out of the corner of the room, where he had materialized, was a giant. Seven, eight, nine feet—her mind kept reassessing the height, as she strove to adjust to the enormous reality of him.

The size, the blue harness clothing—like a Roman centurion guard in summer uniform—the bronze body, the large face with eyes as black as coal, unsmiling and firm; and in his bearing, conscious power unqualified by doubt or fear.

He said in a bass voice, in English, "I am Shalil, the best of all possible."

VII

For a long moment Edith waited for him to complete the sentence. She presumed that the final word would be his name. At last, with a shock, she realized the sentence *was* finished. The crystal makers had sent the most qualified individual of their entire race to handle this situation.

In the doorway, Marge cringed away from the monster. She uttered a small cry. At the sound, two of the Seth Mitchells rushed into the room. They caught Marge, who seemed close to hysteria and fainting—and they also saw the apparition. The other three Seths crowded into the doorway.

As of one accord, obviously unwisely and therefore—as Edith realized later—under a volition not their own, they moved into the room, bringing Marge with them. The Seth who brought up the rear pulled the door shut behind him.

The best Athtar stirred and said in a sharp tone, "Miss Price—uncreate him! He does not mean well."

The giant grimaced. "You cannot uncreate me. I—and only I—now control the crystal. The term 'mean well' is relative. I mean well for my own time and my own group." He glanced over the five Seths and the two women, then settled on Athtar. "Which of you are the biologically original human beings?" he asked.

Edith clutched the crystal and glanced uncertainly at the Seths, silently appealing for suggestions. But they were staring at the giant and seemed oblivious to her.

Yet one of them asked abruptly, "Athtar, in what way doesn't he mean well?"

Athtar shook his head. "I don't know in details," he said unhappily. "But I have a feeling. They sent the crystal back here for their purpose. His question about original human beings points a significant direction. But don't answer it—or any other question he may ask."

It seemed a small, useless denial. The huge man strode to the door. The group of Seths let him through automatically. The giant opened the door and peered out into the hotel lobby. After a single, swift survey, he pushed the door shut again and faced about.

"I deduce," he said, "that the people of this era are the originals. They are the ones we want for our experiments."

Athtar said tautly to the Seths, "One of you has the worst Athtar's gun. Shoot him."

The instant the words were spoken the pistol floated into view, avoided the fingers of the two Seths who tried to seize it. It settled into Shalil's palm. He slipped the weapon into a pocket of his simple garment.

The best Athtar glanced at Edith. He said glumly, "I've done my best—" and faced the monster. "What happens to me?"

The black eyes studied him.

"The crystal is communicating data to me," Shalil said. "You and the other Athtar are from an era where the people have already been biologically altered?"

Athtar glanced apologetically at Edith. "I see no additional

317

danger in asking him a question since he already seems to have all the information we possess." Without waiting for a reply he addressed the huge man: "The decision made in the thirty-first century, nearly four hundred years before my time, was that small, heavy bodies had more survival potential than tall, thin ones. I see that in your era a much taller, bigger, more powerful man than any we have even imagined, is the norm. What is the rationale?"

"Different problems," answered Shalil. "In my era, which by your reckoning would correlate to the ninety-third century, man is a space creature." He broke off. "Since we have no interest in you at present, I propose to send you and the other Athtar back to your own time."

"Wait—" The best Athtar spoke urgently. "What do you intend to do with these people?" He waved toward Edith and the Seths.

Shalil grimaced. "What we actually want for our experiments are the best Seth Mitchell and the best Edith Price. The others are free to go. We set the crystal to find the best specimens."

"But why?"

"Something has gone wrong. We need to restudy human origins."

"Do you need these specific persons or will you merely have the crystal duplicate them in your own era?"

"Only one of each exists. If he and she are created in any other time they become uncreated here."

"What will you do? Dissect them?"

"In the end, perhaps. The experimenters will decide." Sharply. "Never mind that. The program is laid out and the subjects are urgently needed." His voice grew imperious. "Miss Price, give me the crystal. We are not needlessly cruel and I wish to send the Athtars home."

Athtar urged, "Miss Price, don't give it to him. His statement that he totally controls the crystal may not be true until the moment he has possession of it. These far-future beings must be persuaded to accept another, less arbitrary solution to their problem."

Edith had been standing, watching the fantastic giant, listening to the infinite threat that was developing out of his blunt words. Suddenly what had seemed an utterly desirable goal—to be the best—had become the most undesirable.

But she was not yet afraid. Her mind was clear. The tumbling thoughts and feelings of the past days, which had

318

suddenly fallen into an exact order in her mind earlier that night, remained orderly.

Her own reaction was that Athtar was wrong and that she had, in fact, lost control of the crystal. It seemed obvious to her that the crystal's makers would have had some preemptive system by which they could regain its use at a key moment.

But she intended to test her theory.

She glanced at and into the crystal and said firmly, "Whoever can defeat this giant—be here now?"

Moments after she had spoken, the crystal was snatched from her fingers by the same kind of unseen force as had taken the automatic pistol from one of the Seths earlier. She watched helplessly as it also floated over to the giant's palm. The huge man's black eyes gleamed triumphantly at her.

"All your allies are in this room. There is nobody else."

"In that case," said a man's voice quietly, "I imagine that, regardless of consequences, my moment has come."

The bachelor Seth Mitchell strode forward to confront the giant.

There was a long pause. Edith had time to assess this Seth and to savor the simple, strong humanity that he represented. She saw that he was well dressed in a dark gray suit, that his lean face was firm, his eyes calm and fearless. In some depths of her mind she was proud that at this moment such a Seth Mitchell existed. Yet, though she was still not afraid herself, she was aware of her hopes sinking.

The silence ended.

The great being from the future said, "I hope you realize that you are condemning the other Seths in forcing your identity on me in this manner. In this era the crystal has no alternative but to uncreate them."

Behind Edith, Marge cried out faintly.

Edith whirled. Marge seemed to be choking. Edith ran to her, put an arm around her waist.

"What's the matter?"

Marge continued to choke. Her words, when they finally came, were almost inaudible: "They're gone—the other Seths—"

Edith looked around. Where the four Seths had been standing near the door—there was no one. She had an impulse to run to the door and look out. Surely they had simply stepped outside for a moment.

Abruptly she realized. They had been uncreated.

She uttered a gasping sob—then caught herself as Seth Mitchell spoke in the same quiet tone as before.

"I said, regardless of consequences." He glanced back at the two women. "Since the Seths remain crystal patterns, they're no more in danger now than they would be if this creature were able to carry out all his threats. That probably even applies to the Seth of the gold Cadillac and the Edith who presumably was killed in New York." To Shalil he said, "I think you'd better send the Athtars into their own time."

There was an ever so slight pause; the giant's eyes changed slightly, as if he were thinking.

Then: "It's done," he said.

Edith glanced to where Athtar had been. With a conscious effort she retained her self-control.

Athtar had disappeared.

Shalil surveyed the best of all possible Seth Mitchells, said, "You really benefited from the crystal, didn't you?" He spoke in his softest bass. An intent, listening expression came into his face. "You own—one—three, four corporations."

"I stopped when I was worth ten million," said the best Seth. He turned to look apologetically at Edith. "I couldn't imagine having use for even that much money. But I had set it as a goal and reached it." Without waiting for her reaction he once more faced the gigantic enemy. "All the Seth Mitchells," he said, "are the results of a boy's dreams, based on what information he had. He undoubtedly had observed that there are tax experts, lawyers, doctors, tramps and policemen. And in a town like Harkdale he was aware of summer resort visitors—and on the level of a boy's daydreams there existed—until they were uncreated just now—a cowboy Seth Mitchell, an African hunter Seth, a sea captain, an airline pilot and probably even a few glamorous criminals—" He broke off. "I have a feeling you don't understand—you don't have any boys any more where you are, do you?"

VIII

The giant's eyes shifted uncertainly.

He said, "We are crystal duplicates. Thus we shall presumably live forever—if we can solve the present tendency of the cells to be tired." He added reluctantly: "What's a boy?"

"Maybe there's your problem," said Seth Mitchell. "You've forgotten about children. Gene variation." The best Seth continued to gaze up at the great being. "I'm the creation," he said gently, "of a boy who, for a long time after Bill Bingham disappeared, was under exceptional adult pressure and

320

criticism and as a result had many escape fantasies. Picture that boy's fantasy of total power—somebody who would handle mean adults who acted as if he were lying and who treated him nastily—some day he would show them all. How? The answer would not have been clear to the boy Seth who felt that resentment. But when the time came he knew he would know how—and of course he wouldn't be mean about it the way the adults had been. There would be a kind of nobility about his total power."

The two men, the best of all possible Seth Mitchells from the twentieth century, and the best of all possibles from the ninety-third century were standing within a few feet of each other.

"Perhaps," the best Seth addressed the giant softly, "you can tell better than I what the crystal would create out of such a command."

"Since nobility is involved," was the harsh reply, "I feel that I can safely test that boy's fantasy to the uttermost limit."

He spoke sharply, uncommandingly, in a strange language.

Edith had listened to the deadly interchange, thinking in a wondering dismay: *God really is dead! These future people have never even heard of Him . . .*

Her thought ended. For the giant's deep bass tones had suddenly ceased.

Something hit her deep inside her body. Around her the room dimmed.

As if from a vast distance she heard Seth Mitchell say apologetically: "Only thing I know, Miss Price, is to send you along with him. Seems you've got the solution in what you just thought, whatever that was. The crystal will make it real. Hope it works."

A moment after that she was falling into infinity.

The body of Edith lay on a contour rest-space in one corner of the crystal administrative center. Periodically a giant walked over to her and routinely checked the instruments that watched over her and monitored the invisible force lines that held her.

A slow night went by. A new day finally dawned. The sunlight that suffused the translucent walls also revealed half a dozen giants, including Shalil, gathered around the slowly breathing—but otherwise unmoving—body of the young woman from the twentieth century.

To wake or not to wake her?

They discussed the problem in low, rumbling voices. Since

they were all scientists, capable of appreciating the most subtle nuances of logic, what bothered them was that the small female presented a paradox.

Outward appearance said she was helpless. Shalil had been able to put Edith into a coma. At the instant of the best Seth's command to the crystal and she had arrived in that degraded condition in the ninety-third century.

Or rather, she had been uncreated in her own time and had been recreated by the crystal in Shalil's time, already unconscious. She herself had not had any control over her own destiny.

What disturbed her captors was that an undefinable power radiated from her—and had ever since her recreation. The power was not merely ordinary. It was total.

Total power? Absolute and unqualified? How could that be?

Once more they gave attention on both hearing and telepathic levels, as Shalil repeated his account of what had transpired while he had been in the twentieth century. The story, already familiar, reiterated the same peak moments: the ordinariness, the unthreatening aspect, of all the people of the past whom Shalil had confronted.

Again they were told the climax—when the best Seth had assumed that the crystal would evolve an unusual energy configuration out of a boy's fantasies of power. Clearly—at least, it was clear to the huge men—the crystal's response to Seth's command established that it had been oriented to the best Seth. And that its energies had been mobilized for later expression, when the original Seth Mitchell had been a boy. From that energy response by the crystal alone the giants reasoned unhappily: "There is more potential in these crystals than we have hitherto believed."

And how could that be?

But there was even worse.

While giving his command to Edith the best of possible Seth Mitchells had implied that he had received a feedback message from her, presumably by way of the crystal, indicating that she would all by herself now be able to defeat the entire science of the ninety-third century.

Once Shalil took control of the crystal, such a feedback of information—whether true or false—should not have occurred. And Seth's command, by any known scientific analysis, was impossible.

True, they did not know all there was to know about the crystals. Several unexplained areas were still being researched.

322

But it had long been argued that nothing major remained to be discovered.

The present implication was that original, unmanipulated human beings might have special qualities that had been lost to their biologically manipulated descendants.

A giant grunted, "I think we should kill her."

A second huge man growled an objection. He argued. "If the attempt to destroy her should bring a reaction from the absolute power that radiates from her, that reaction would be uncontrollable. Much better to deduce on the basis of Shalil's report the low-level ways in which her mind functions, awaken her and inexorably force responses from her."

Everybody thought that was a good idea.

"And if something goes wrong," one giant rumbled, "we can always render her unconscious again through instantaneous uncreation and recreation by the crystal."

Shalil reminded gruffly, "What about that odd decision she had reached in her attempt to be the best of all possible Ediths, to handle situations with infinite flexibility?"

Contempt greeted the remark. "With *her* lifetime conditioning," one huge scientist said, "she couldn't possibly deal with each situation according to its merits. She cannot even know what the real issues of a situation are."

The discussion ended on a decision that when Edith was awakened she should seem to herself to be completely free . . .

She was lying on grass. It touched her fingers and her face. The fresh smell of it was in her nostrils.

Edith opened her eyes and simultaneously raised her head.

Wilderness. A primeval forest. A small brown animal with a bushy tail scurried into the brush, as she climbed hastily to her feet, remembering.

She saw the giant, Shalil, in the act of picking himself up fifteen feet to her left. He seemed slow about it, as if he were groggy.

The day was misty. The sun still stood high in the sky. To her right, partly visible through foliage, was a great, gray hill of soil. To her left the land fell away and the mist was thicker. After a hundred yards it was an almost impenetrable fog.

Almost, but not quite, impenetrable. Vaguely visible through it was a building.

Edith faced the giant squarely and asked, "Where are we?"

Shalil gazed at her warily. It was hard for him to realize

323

that she did not intuitively know. He found it almost unacceptable that alongside her infinite power was such nadir thinking.

Yet, as she continued to stand there, facing him, he sensed her concern. And so, reluctantly, he decided that the first conclusions reached by his colleagues and himself continued to apply. They had perceived her to be motivated by involuntary attitudes and forgotten memories, each psychically as solid as a bar of steel. All her life she had followed rules, gone along with group-think behavior.

School and college—these were the early norms, adhered to while she was still under the control of her parents. Basically those norms had remained unquestioned.

Shalil noted in her mind an awareness that millions of people had somehow failed to achieve higher education. That was astonishing to him; yet somehow, these multitudes had been steered away from knowledge by a variety of accidental circumstances.

So in those areas of personal development Edith had gone farther, better, straighter than a great many. Yet in college, first time away from her family, she had swiftly been caught up in a nonconformist group movement. Whatever the motives of the other persons involved, Edith's had consisted solely of an intense inner need to belong to the group.

So, for her, it had been the beginning of aberration, which her behavior ever afterward reflected. Thus, Shalil observed, like a person struggling against invisible force lines, she had fought to return to an inner norm. More study, different jobs, different places to live, association with different men—the confusion was immense, and it was difficult for Shalil to determine which of her numerous actions represented striving toward a real goal.

Adding to the jumble: all her actions had been modified by a very large, though finite, number of small, endlessly repeated actions—eating habits, dressing habits, working, sleeping, walking, reacting, communicating, thinking stereotypes.

What bothered Shalil was that he could not find a single point of entry into her mind that would not instantly trigger one of the stereotypes. The others had assumed that her conscious mind would present some opening; they had taken it for granted that he would locate it. His instructions were to uncreate her into unconsciousness if he failed to make such an entry, whereupon there would be another consultation.

The possibility of such a quick failure disturbed Shalil. Temporizing, he said aloud, "This is the Garden of the Crystals in my century. Here, in the most virgin wilderness left on our planet, the crystals lie buried in the soil, tended by guardian scientists."

Having spoken, having had that tiny bit of extra time to consider, he decided that the problem she presented might yield to a steady pressure of verbal maneuvering that would motivate her to express one after the other the endless stereotypes that had been detected in her—while he waited alertly for one he could shatter or through which the crystal—on his command—would divest her of the power with which it had, through some unknown factor, invested her.

Her primary concern, he saw, was that she would never get back to her own era. Since he knew she could return at once simply by thinking the correct positive thought, his problem was to keep her worried, negative, unaware, deceived, misled.

Shalil became aware that his anxiety about how to proceed was causing a hasty telepathic consultation among his colleagues. Moments later the suggestion was made: *Divert her by letting her win some minor victories and believe that they are gifts from you . . .*

The idea seemed good and Shalil carried it out as if it were a directive.

IX

At the Harkdale hotel another day dawned. Marge Aikens came downstairs, bleary-eyed from lack of sleep. She walked to the conference room, looked in. The lights had been turned off, the drapes were still drawn and the dim emptiness of the room weighted her spirits.

She turned away and became aware of a man beside her. She faced him with a start.

The hotel day clerk, Derek Slade, said courteously, "Madam—"

He continued to speak and after a while his meaning penetrated her dulled mind. He thought he had recognized her as the young woman who had late the previous afternoon gone into the conference room with the five Seth Mitchells. Where—Derek wanted to know—were the four married Seths? The wives had been phoning all night, according to a note on his desk from the night clerk. And a police officer was on the way over because three Mrs. Mitchells had finally called the authorities.

Marge had an impulse to deny that she was the woman he thought he had seen. But his failure to mention the bachelor Seth captured her attention and she asked about him.

Derek shook his head. "Not in his room. Went out early, I'm told."

Marge stood in the doorway, considering what might have happened to the best Seth. Why would he have gone out when he had said the previous that he would have breakfast with her? Then she became aware that Derek Slade's gaze had gone past her shoulder and was seeking the darkened interior of the room behind her.

His jaw grew lax, his eyes widened.

In the room a man's baritone voice uttered an exclamation. Marge turned.

The four Seths who had been uncreated last night were standing near the door. Their backs were to her.

She realized that it was one of the Seths who had exclaimed and that what he had said was, "Hey, who turned out the lights?"

Marge had an immediate and totally perceptive awareness of the implications, of those words. Her mind leaped back to Billy Bingham's not having had any transition impression at all of time having passed between his uncreation and recreation.

This was the same.

She reached into the room and pressed the light switch beside the door. As she did so a fifth Seth walked forward from one corner of the room, where he had suddenly appeared. He seemed bewildered. From his clothing Marge tentatively identified him as the Seth of the gold Cadillac, somehow recreated without a bullet in his brain or a drop of lake water on his immaculate suit.

But at the moment she had only a fleeting thought for him, for a sixth Seth was suddenly standing on the far side of the conference table. The way he held himself, his quick alertness as he looked around the room, saw the other Seths—and then flicked his gaze to her with relieved recognition . . .

Seeing him, and receiving so many familiar signals that identified Detective Seth Mitchell for her Marge became emotionally unglued. Without any of her usual discretion, she out a scream.

"Seth—my darling—"

Exactly how she got to him and he to her could undoubtedly be reasoned out from the fact that they met at the halfway point around the big table—and only desisted from their embrace when Marge grew aware that Edith Price was standing a few feet away, glancing timidly around her.

Closely behind Edith appeared another Seth. He wore work clothes and Marge surmised that he therefore must be the farmer.

Marge scarcely more than glanced at him. As she released herself from Detective Seth's embrace she saw that Edith wore a different dress and had her hair done differently—this was the Edith Price who had been murdered in New York by the worst Athtar.

Of the Athtars there was no sign.

And though the minutes fled by—and finally the bachelor Seth walked into the doorway—Edith Price, the crystal orientation, did not reappear.

The best Seth explained that he had gone for a walk and, thinking over all that had happened, had decided that things would work out.

He finished hopefully, "And here you all are. Each of you is living proof that Edith has found out what she can do. Or—" he paused—"someone has, and is willing."

"But what *can* she do?" a Seth asked, bewildered.

The best Seth smiled his friendly smile. "I'm rather fond of that young lady. In a way she's a total reflection of our age, yet she thought her way to some kind of best." He broke off, glanced from one to another of the numerous duplicate faces, and said softly, "You want to know what she can do? I didn't dare speak of it at the time, but, now, well—if God is dead, what can replace Him?"

"Then you are—" Marge put her hand over her mouth, exclaimed through it, "Oh, my lord—Edith!"

The best Seth said slowly, "I wonder what the crystal and Edith are doing with that concept."

Shalil was in trouble. The giant had continued to wait for the purely personal, restrictive thought that, he and his colleagues believed, would presently end any control Edith had of the crystal's future.

But the moments had gone by and she had kept on uttering idealistic concepts that were binding on him and his kind in relation to the people of the past. All the Seths and the Ediths were recreated. She proposed a cooperative solution for the severe threat to the giant human beings of his century—between the giants on the one hand and the Ediths and Seths on the other. In an outburst of imagination she visualized a time corridor between her own century and his. Thriftily she retained control of that corridor for her own group.

It was as she established that enormous connection, and

control, that Shalil—desperate—had her uncreated. He recreated her, unconscious, on the contour restplace. The huge scientists gathered around her comatose body and gloomily evaluated the extent of their defeat.

One said, "But let's face it. We can live with what's happened."

The problem was that they had made no headway. Edith still radiated total power; somehow, she continued to evoke from the crystal an energy output that no one had ever thought possible.

Shalil had a tremendous insight. "Perhaps that's what we need to examine—our own limitations. Perhaps the real problem is that in our scientific zeal we have rejected the enigma."

After he had spoken, there was a dead silence. He saw that they were shaken. The enigma was the forbidden—because unscientific—area of thought: *The enigma that is the universe. Why does it exist? Where did it come from?*

The thrall of shocked silence ended as a giant gave a harsh, determined laugh.

"I don't know anything about the enigma and do not plan to," he said, "but as a scientist I do know my duty—*our* duty. We must bring this small female to consciousness, inform her of the unqualified extent of her power and see what she does with it."

"B-but she may kill us all," protested another. He added, almost plaintively, "I've never been killed."

"It will be an interesting experience for you," replied the first man. "Quite different from uncreation."

Shalil interjected matter-of-factly, "Edith is not a killer." He broke off, shrewdly, "I think this is an excellent plan. I see it as being totally in our favor."

They perceived what he meant, and accordingly sanctioned the awakening.

Edith was brought awake. After she had calmed herself—after she had been told about her absolute ability she had an automatic response, exactly as the giants had anticipated. For prolonged seconds a wild hope suffused her entire being. She wanted more urgently to undo the errors of judgment which had led her down the empty road of numerous boy friends, none of whom took responsibility for her and her capacity to bear children. All her years of frustration since college found their way first to her eyes in the form of quick tears, and then, when she could speak, to her words.

"Aside from what I've just told you—" she spoke the qualifying phrase, which retained for her control of access to the twentieth century without even noticing it—"*all* I really want is to be happily married."

The giants perceived that the person she had in mind for a husband was the bachelor Seth Mitchell.

They accordingly commanded the crystal that the wish she had expressed be carried out forthwith in its exact and limited meaning. And then, safe and relieved, they stood marveling at the difficult concept of marriage.

In an era where everybody lived forever by a process of crystal duplication they would never, left to themselves, have been able to ask the right question to produce such an answer.

"It is barely possible," Shalil cautiously summed up, "that the interaction between the unmanipulated human beings of the twentieth century and the manipulated of the ninety-third will actually bring about a lessening of the rigidities of both groups."

His stern, black gaze dared a denial. After a long moment, he was surprised to realize that no one was offended.

Indeed, a colleague murmured reflectively, "If that should happen we may even find out what the crystal is."

But, of course, that was impossible.

The crystal was a space phenomenon. The energy flows in it, around it and out of it involved individual events, things, persons. But this was a subordinate function—like the motor center in a human brain that moves a muscle in the tip of the little finger.

The muscle should be movable. It would be unfortunate if it were not. Yet if that muscle were permanently incapacitated the fact would go unnoticed by the brain on the conscious level.

On the flow level of existence the patterned *interactions* in and around and out of the crystal exceed 10 to the 27-000th power times the number of atoms in the universe—enough interactions for all the life configurations of all the people who ever lived; perhaps enough even for all those who ever would live on Earth.

But for the crystal such effects were minor. As a governor of certain time-and-life flows it had suspended those flows for twenty-five years in the Harkdale museum. The suspension did not matter—it meant almost nothing. As a shape of space, its existence was continuous. As space, it occupied a location and was related. Though it had no flows during the quarter century, made no recording and had no memory and no doing, it nevertheless knew, it was, it had and it could.

In finding it and tens of thousands of crystals like it, human beings of the eighth and ninth millennia made use of the interactions and flows; never of the space ability. They discovered the principal "laws"—the how and the what—by which the crystals operated and were determined to find out eventually the rules that would "explain" certain unknowns in the wave behavior in and around and out of the crystals.

Some day all the interactions of all life and all time would be evenly divided among the crystals. It would then become its true form; one crystal shape, one space. It would then be complete, its . . . intention . . . achieved.

There was no hurry.

And so it waited. And, waiting, fulfilled other goals than its own, minor, unimportant goals involving flows and interactions; reflecting the illusions of motion: events, things, persons . . . involving nothing, really.

In consequence, in Harkdale today stands a one-story building of unusual design. The building occupies the exact spot where Billy Bingham once disappeared on the shore overlooking Lake Naragang. It is a solidly built structure and has a certain beauty.

Its method of construction is shrouded in mystery. Natives grow vague when asked about it.

On a gold plaque beside the ornate front door are the words:

CRYSTAL, INC.
Owned and Managed by
SETH MITCHELLS and EDITH
PRICES
Not Open to the Public

Resort visitors who stop to look at the sign are often puzzled by the plural names. And long-time residents, when asked, offer the impression that Crystal, Inc. actually deals in the numerous crystals to be found in the rock formations in and around the hills and lake.

There is a large pretty house with spacious grounds located near the building. In this house dwell Seth and Edith Mitchell.

To the puzzlement of their neighbors, Mr. and Mrs. Seth Mitchell (nee Edith Price) started their married life by legally adopting a thirteen-year-old boy whom they called Billy Bingham Mitchell.

EDGAR RICE BURROUGHS

VENUS SERIES

PELLUCIDAR SERIES

Available wherever paperbacks are sold or use this coupon.

WINNER OF
THE HUGO AWARD
AND THE
NEBULA AWARD
FOR BEST
SCIENCE FICTION
NOVEL OF
THE YEAR

045922	Babel 17 Delaney	95c	
062190	Big Time Leiber	95c	
106237	City Simak	.$1.25	
166413	Dragon Masters Vance The Last Castle Vance	95c	
167023	Dream Master Zelazny	95c	
172635	Dune Herbert	$1.50	
196824	Einstein Intersection Delany	95c	
249011	Four for Tomorrow Zelazny	95c	
478016	Left Hand of Darkness LeGuin	$1.25	
727826	Rite of Passage Panshin	95c	
806927	This Immortal Zelazny	95c	

Available wherever paperbacks are sold or use this coupon.

7B

ACE SCIENCE FICTION DOUBLES
Two books back-to-back
Just 95c each

.... 009902　　Against Arcturus — Putney
　　　　　　Time Thieves — Rackham

.... 317552　　The Hard Way Up — Chandler
　　　　　　Veiled World — Lory

.... 482455　　Life With Lancelot — Rackham
　　　　　　Hunting on Kunderer — Barton

.... 534156　　Mr. Justice — Piserchia
　　　　　　Heirarchies — Phillifent

.... 669952　　Planetary Agent X
　　　　　　The Rival Rigelians — Reynolds

.... 763805　　Three Suns of Amara
　　　　　　Battle on Venus — Temple

.... 769604　　The Sky is Falling
　　　　　　Badge of Infamy — del Rey

.... 893016　　The Winds of Gath
　　　　　　Derai — Tubb

.... 939009　　A Yank at Valhalla — Hamilton
　　　　　　The Sun Destroyers — Rocklynne

Available wherever paperbacks are sold or use this coupon.

Great Science Fiction Collections

World's Best
Award-Winning Science Fiction